W9-BVQ-860

# STATE OF THE UNION

Also by David Callahan

*Dangerous Capabilities*
*Between Two Worlds*

# STATE OF THE UNION

A Novel

by

## David Callahan

LITTLE, BROWN AND COMPANY

*Boston   New York   Toronto   London*

First Edition

The characters and events in this book are fictitious.
Any similarity to real persons, living or dead, is coincidental
and not intended by the author.

Library of Congress Cataloging-in-Publication Data

Callahan, David.
    State of the union : a novel / by David Callahan. — 1st ed.
      p.  cm.
    ISBN 0-316-12490-7
    I. Title.
      PS3553.A42164S7   1997
      813'.54 — dc21          96-47114

10 9 8 7 6 5 4 3 2 1

Designed by Bruce Taylor Hamilton
MV-NY

Published simultaneously in Canada
by
Little, Brown & Company (Canada) Limited

Printed in the United States of America

*If there is one basic element of our Constitution,*
*it is civilian control of the military.*

**— Harry S. Truman**

# ★ STATE OF THE UNION ★

Lieutenant Zachary Turzin stood stiffly in the White House Rose Garden under a powerful sun. He was sweltering in his dress uniform. The chairman of the Joint Chiefs of Staff, standing next to him, plump and pale, looked even hotter. Beads of sweat rolled down the side of the chairman's face and neck, gathering between folds of flesh. It wasn't supposed to be this hot in late October, even in Washington.

Only the President looked cool. He had, apparently, learned to control his sweat glands along with so much else.

"Testing, testing." A junior aide fiddled with the microphone on the podium.

Zach glanced at his parents, seated in the small audience on white folding chairs a few feet in front of the podium. His father was flushed. His mother fanned herself languidly. They looked awkward together. Zach wondered how long the ceremony would take.

The secretary of defense approached the podium. "Ladies and gentlemen, ladies and gentlemen." The rustling and talking in the crowd died down. The secretary fumbled with his reading glasses and unfolded a piece of paper he had taken from his jacket pocket.

"Mr. President, Chairman Reynolds, Lieutenant Turzin, friends. It is my greatest pleasure to be here today. As many of you know, the United States armed forces has awarded very few Congressional Medals of Honor since the Vietnam War. It is, of course, the highest citation that any U.S. serviceperson can win. It is reserved for gallantry above and beyond the call of duty — bravery of the most exceptional nature. It gives me enormous pride to serve in office at a time when this medal is bestowed on one of our finest fighting men."

Zach's attention wandered as the secretary launched into a homily on troop readiness and defense spending. Nothing is apolitical in this town, he thought. Especially when the national press corps was present. Zach looked at the sea of cameras. He wondered how he would look on the night's news.

"... and Lieutenant Zachary Turzin reflects the culmination of these trends."

Zach's attention snapped back to the secretary.

"He is, to put it mildly, one of our very best," declared the secretary. "He is a graduate of a top university and is fluent in Arabic, Farsi, and Kurdish. Lieutenant Turzin knows as much about the Middle East as an academic specialist. But he is also a warrior through and through, a warrior of uniquely wide breadth." The defense secretary gestured grandly toward Zach. He was clearly departing from his prepared remarks. "This is a man who can fly a Blackhawk helicopter, kill a T-72 with a TOW, bring down a MiG with a shoulder-held SAM, and yet also has a black belt in tae kwon do. He is a man who can take out bridges with high explosives and crack coded signals with sophisticated computer programs, but can also travel twenty-five miles a day on foot in the harshest of desert terrain."

Zach could see his mother whisper to his father, looking puzzled. His father shrugged. Zach hated Washington types who spouted technomilitary jargon yet had never actually worn a uniform or smelled the stench of decomposing bodies after a battle.

"Lieutenant Turzin is a true American hero," the secretary concluded. "Chairman Reynolds will read the citation. Mr. Chairman."

The JCS chairman mopped his brow and stepped to the podium as the secretary returned to the President's side.

Chairman Reynolds was new in his post, appointed by the

President just six months earlier. Loyalty to the White House had secured him the job, it was said. Zach had heard the derisive talk, but he had never seen the man in person. Now that he had, he was unimpressed. Reynolds looked like an Army bureaucrat of the worst kind, a waddling creature of headquarters who had let his waist widen while his mind narrowed.

The JCS chairman went through the perfunctory opening remarks and then came to the text of the citation. Most of the citation was classified and would remain so for years or even decades. Zach was well aware that the entire citation should have been classified, as his superiors had urged. The White House had ruled otherwise. They wanted a hero.

Chairman Reynolds read from a sanitized version contained in a fancy leather binder. Some of the information had already appeared in the newspapers.

"On July 17 of this year, Lieutenant Zachary Turzin led a six-man team of U.S. Army special forces on a mission into northern Iraq. The objective was to disable the Haisa munitions plant. This heavily defended facility, located two hundred feet underground, had survived repeated aircraft sorties and cruise-missile attacks launched last year after U.S. intelligence discovered the site and after UN inspectors were denied access to its interior. Our information indicated that the facility included state-of-the-art western machine tools that the Baghdad government was using to produce miniaturized chemical and biological warheads that would be mounted on improved Al-Hussein Scud missiles, an advance that Iraq had previously been unable to achieve. This development would have put nearly every major city in the Middle East at risk. Lieutenant Turzin's mission was our only hope for destroying the facility. It was of the highest possible priority."

Zach could feel himself tensing up as Chairman Reynolds began to describe the mission team and the elaborate planning behind the assault. He looked at the President and the secretary of defense and then into the crowd. These people thought they were at a celebration. None of them could imagine the horror in a black desert three months earlier.

Jared Canver had been his best friend in the special forces. His death at Haisa had changed Zach permanently. In the audience, two rows behind his own parents, were Mr. and Mrs. Canver. She wore all black. He, a working man, Zach knew, shifted uncomfortably in a pinstripe charcoal suit. Both looked as if they were attending a memorial.

The chairman described the events of the night of July 17: how the mission team had been captured by an Iraqi patrol and taken to a detention area at the underground facility; how Zach had escaped and killed three Iraqis inside the facility; how he had then freed the other five members of the team; and how the team had managed to complete their objective of blowing up the facility before fleeing.

Canver was killed in a fierce firefight outside the Haisa perimeter. Zach had badly injured his back trying to carry Canver's bloody body before abandoning it to move faster. Baghdad had hinted that they might relinquish the body if the U.S. made certain concessions, and negotiations on this matter had stumbled forward for several weeks in September. Nothing had come of the talks.

The chairman referred in passing to "the regrettable death of Sergeant Canver." Zach shot a glance at the Canvers. Mrs. Canver was crying quietly.

Finally it was over. Zach stepped awkwardly forward and stood near the podium. The President came forward as well and turned to a smartly dressed Army officer who held an open case with the medal laid out in it.

"You have so much to be proud of, Lieutenant Turzin," the President said as he pinned on the medal. "God bless you, son."

Zach found himself nervous and adrift at the reception in the Blue Room that followed the ceremony. The White

House air-conditioning felt good, as did the effects of the champagne. Waiters in tuxedos circulated through the crowd with silver trays of food and drink. Sunshine cascaded through the tall windows and bounced off chandeliers and champagne glasses. There was a splendor here, a sense that history was made in rooms such as this. But so much else felt wrong to Zach.

The praise and the laughter around the Canvers jabbed at him in sharp bursts. The champagne, he realized, was terribly inappropriate.

"So how does it feel to be a hero, Lieutenant?"

Zach turned to find himself facing a Navy admiral. The man was impressive, with silver hair, a powerful build, and a chiseled face that Zach had seen in photos many times before. Several rows of medals covered the admiral's left breast.

"Jeff Forsten," the admiral said, thrusting his hand forward.

Zach shook it in awe, suddenly proud to be wearing the Medal of Honor and standing in the Blue Room. He groped for words. "Admiral Forsten, what a great pleasure to meet you." What was one supposed to say to a man such as this?

Forsten was a legend in the world of special forces. He had gone early to Vietnam and stayed nearly to the end. He had been a pioneer of river-launched special operations, and had left Southeast Asia as one of the most decorated SEAL officers in the U.S. Navy. Now, as vice chairman of the Joint Chiefs of Staff, he was widely considered to be the most powerful man in the Pentagon.

"I can't tell how proud of you we all were," Forsten said. He spoke with a half smile, his blue eyes flashing and alive. "We thought we'd never get Haisa. I bet Saddam went berserk when that place blew. It was the last goddamn jewel he had. Thought he could gas Tel Aviv with one of those warheads. Hell, he doesn't have anything left now."

Zach nodded. "Yes, sir. That's the way it should be."

"You know, I was involved in the planning for your

mission. I followed the whole thing from the War Room. We actually cheered when the place went up. Made me remember the good old days. Shame you lost Canver; a good man from what I understand. But hell, it could have been worse. A lot worse. You're lucky those Mukhabarat bastards didn't slice off your balls when they had you in that dungeon. They love stuff like that. Any Kurd will you tell you."

Forsten laughed heartily, and Zach smiled even as he grimaced inwardly. He had visited some of the Mukhabarat torture chambers in Kurdistan when his unit was there after the Gulf War and he had heard the horrible stories.

"So what's next, Lieutenant?" Forsten asked. "A little R and R, maybe? Flash your medal at the babes for a while?"

"Truthfully, sir, I don't have a clue," Zach replied. The aftermath of the mission had left him in a directionless void of depression. He felt passive and detached, drained of vitality. Nothing in his life seemed to have meaning anymore. The Army had granted him a leave and rented him a furnished apartment in Crystal City, a gleaming complex of apartment buildings, hotels, and underground shops across the Potomac from Washington, just a few miles north of the Pentagon. The whole place reminded him of some futuristic metropolis from a sci-fi movie. After two months the sterility of the complex was beginning to wear him down. He felt his identity being slowly chopped up and vacuumed away. A large color television set dominated the living room. It had come to dominate Zach as well.

"After today there's a lot of covert work you won't be able to do overseas," Forsten continued. "I heard all about your little stay in Tripoli last year. You can forget about that kind of mission now. Frankly, this thing should have been classified. Every Arab intelligence agency in the world will have you on video. But I guess you've thought about that."

"Yes, sir. I suspect my future might be a little less eventful than the past few years. I'll have to brush up on my paper-pushing skills."

"Hell, that's what I do all day. Miss the field, I'll tell you that. The higher you get, the more paper you push. It's an iron law of power."

Zach was surprised at how at ease he felt with Forsten. "Word has it, sir, that you knock heads all day."

Forsten grinned. "Well, there's some of that too. Another iron rule of power." The admiral slapped Zach on the back, getting ready to move on. "Congratulations again. And when you come up for air, give me a buzz if you want to talk about your future. A man like you is a priceless asset in this country, especially the way things have been going lately. See you around, Lieutenant."

By ten in the evening, Zach was back in his apartment. After the reception there had been a long meal at a fancy Washington restaurant with his parents and several high Pentagon officials, including the assistant secretary of defense for special operations. The pain in Zach's back had begun near the end of the White House reception from so much standing and grown during the exhausting dinner, gnawing at his lumbar muscles with each breath he took. The drinks numbed the pain, but they made him feel heavy headed and sluggish. Still, he had stayed on his toes, carefully guiding the conversation away from politics. Zach's father was a liberal, and a belligerent one at that. Alcohol and proximity to the former Mrs. Turzin brought out his worst side. The last thing Zach wanted was an argument about U.S. interventionist policy or military spending levels between his father and his superiors.

That nightmare scenario never came to pass. Zach's father had remained cheerful and noncombative as one glass of white wine followed another. His mother had barely said a word. Later, both had told Zach again how proud they were before grabbing separate cabs to Union Station.

There were almost fifteen messages on Zach's answering machine. He took a painkiller and stood in his darkened kitchen, massaging his lower back and wondering how so many people could have gotten his unlisted number. Most were from the press. They had found it through the Pentagon, no doubt. And indeed, the Army PR people had called a few times to comment on the various people who would be calling, urging Zach to be cooperative. Duty had taken on a new meaning these last weeks.

The eighth message was delivered by a melodic male voice.

"Greetings and congratulations, Lieutenant Turzin. My name is Ron Varant. I'm an assistant to Douglas Sherman. Please call me; tonight, if you can. My number is 703-445-3245. Thank you."

Zach fumbled in the dark for a pen and wrote down the number on the back of a napkin. Strange message.

Zach had been out of the country during Sherman's skyrocketing rise to political stardom three years earlier. But he knew all about the wealthy ex-governor of Virginia who had won 22 percent of the vote in the last presidential election as an independent candidate running against big government. Political observers considered him a wild man who didn't play by the rules. Now, cultivating an aura of shadow president and vowing to be the next occupant of the Oval Office, Sherman thrived amid the ugliness of a new recession. Zach had cast an absentee ballot for Sherman from Morocco. He liked the guy's gusto in taking on the system. He liked his disdain for Washington.

Zach punched in Varant's number on the illuminated keys of the wall phone. He assumed that Sherman wanted to congratulate him about his medal. Sherman had a long history of hanging around military types, many of whom he had met while doing the defense work that had made him much of his fortune. It was another plus in Zach's eyes: The guy knew the armed services.

"Ron Varant."

"Hello, Mr. Varant, this is Zach Turzin returning your call."

"Yes, Lieutenant Turzin, thank you for getting back to me. I'm sure this has been a busy day. Congratulations once again."

"Thank you. Busy would be an understatement. I'm surprised I'm still standing."

"Well, again, I appreciate you getting back to me. The reason I'm calling, Lieutenant, is that, as you may know, Governor Sherman is a big supporter of our men in uniform. And he's been very excited by your medal, very excited. He read all about the mission and thinks you're one of the greatest heroes America has produced in quite some time. He would have liked to have been at that ceremony today, but of course that wasn't quite possible." Varent gave a chuckle. His voice was smooth, accentless, anxious to please. Zach imagined gelled hair and a suit with sheen.

"In any case, let me get straight to the point: The governor insists that you join him out at his home on Saturday night. He's had a black-tie party on the calendar for weeks, and it struck him after seeing the ceremony on the news tonight that he would very much like to have you as his guest of honor. He's just filled with admiration, Lieutenant. I know it's late notice. What do you say?"

Zach hesitated. He worried about crossing the line into politics. Military personnel were supposed to be apolitical. Of course, this was only a social occasion, and it would be interesting to meet Sherman.

"Sure, I think I could do that," Zach said.

"Wonderful, Lieutenant, wonderful."

"You know, I voted for him."

"Oh, I'm sure he'll be delighted to hear that, Lieutenant, just delighted. Saturday then."

"Yes, Saturday."

"Great, Lieutenant. We'll send a car for you at seven."

The next few days passed in a blur. The weather cooled as crisp autumn air arrived from the north, and with it came a momentary refreshing of beleaguered Washington. Cheers rose when a modest farm bill scraped through the gridlocked houses of Congress.

Zach was feted on Tuesday night by the American Security Alliance, then on Wednesday by the Army Officers Club. On Thursday night he was honored by the National Association of Defense Manufacturers. He had never eaten so much chicken breast in his life. Or heard so many platitudes. During the days, Zach spent the bulk of his time with fresh-faced Army PR officers in a comfortable suite at the Crystal City Sheraton. They would greet him each morning with an abundance of cheer and hundreds of fan letters he had received at the Pentagon. The cheer struck him as plastic, but the letters were indisputably real, and Zach was touched by many of them.

The PR people would offer a briefing on the day's interviews, and then the stream of reporters and television crews would begin. After not many sessions Zach decided that journalists, at least these, were a complacent and mediocre lot. No Woodwards here. They wanted pat quotes and not much more. They all asked the same questions about his training, his experiences, his views on the Middle East. They probed for more details about the Haisa mission, incurring frequent admonitions from the PR officers. And always, they ended up dwelling on his education at Cornell and Harvard. It was the easy peg for a story, and Zach had already seen some blurbs about the "Ivy League Warrior" and his journey from "the Groves of Academe to the Deserts of Iraq." Some of the reporters had gone to the same universities and shook their heads in wonder at where Zach had ended up.

Zach was relieved that none of the reporters asked him about Canver. But it also seemed strange. After a few interviews, he wondered whether the PR people had ruled questions about his friend Canver out of bounds when setting the ground rules for the interviews. He didn't ask.

## 2

"I can see that you're getting impatient with this again, Zach."

"It's hard not to be."

"Would you like to talk about it?"

"We already have, but sure, let's talk about it again. You know it's been difficult for me to do this, to be here. I've always felt that I could handle everything thrown my way, and believe me, a lot of shit has been thrown my way. But never have I needed anything like this. Or anyone like you, with all due respect. You know, I just feel so, so —"

"Powerless?"

"Yeah. Powerless, helpless, not in control. All of those things. And when I come here it all seems so much more serious and permanent. Like I'm a goddamn cripple."

"In a way you are. At least for the moment. But remember, Zach, some of our best people have been through this process. It works. And there's no stigma around this, not anymore."

"It's not stigma I'm worried about. That's not where I'm at. It's more that it just seems pointless. I feel like I have to see results if I'm going to come here. I need to feel like things are getting better, progress is being made. That's not happening."

"It takes time, Zach. We've only begun."

"It's been a month. Eight sessions."

"I had a case from Desert Storm that took three years. And I think you're in a much better situation than he was. An Air Force flier, that one. He put a Maverick missile into one of our tanks. Killed four men."

"I killed one of ours. He killed four. I really don't see a big difference, morally."

"Well, now let's talk about that."

"We already have; we do every time. I don't see the point. That's what I'm saying; none of this gets me anywhere."

"We need to keep coming back to this, Zach. Let's talk about why you blame yourself for Canver's death."

"There's nobody else to blame. That's what command is all about. You weren't there, Dr. Klein."

"I've read the file."

"Files don't say shit, if you'll excuse my language. The videotape in my brain tells a very different story. And I play it every day, all day, again and again, over and over. It plays when I eat and when I sleep. It plays when I'm on the can or taking a shower. I know what happened outside that perimeter fence. Believe me, I know."

"What about the medal committees, Zach? And all the mission team members who gave depositions. What do they know? If you screwed up so badly, why would the Army give you anything besides a court-martial?"

"These things just get pushed through. It's all political. Nobody's really interested in the truth."

"Do you really believe that?"

"Jared is dead because of my mistakes. I wasn't ready for Haisa. I screwed up from the word go. They shouldn't have sent me. I should never have won that medal. That's what I believe."

"And what I believe, Zach, is that you'll come to view these events in a different light as time goes on. I know this is frustrating. We'll be coming back to this again and again. We're in a process here. It takes time."

On Saturday, after his therapy session, Zach took a long run through the suburbs of Arlington and then pumped iron in the small gym in his building. He had been there every day, keeping himself hard, pushing a little more each time, fighting the softness and dissipation that seemed to be closing in on him with each passing week in Washington. He was also fighting the injury that had returned to his back at Haisa after a decade-long absence. A private orthopedist Zach had visited in Arlington told him to avoid running and take it easy. Zach did the opposite. He tried to force the frailty out of his body by building strength around it, by denying its severity. He never told the Army about the injury and never would. He had made that mistake before. His one nod to reality was to keep codeine on hand for when the pain flared to blinding levels. He had filled a prescription three times since Haisa.

In the late afternoon Zach rented a tuxedo from a shop in the sprawling underground Crystal City Mall. He put it on as darkness fell and stood before the full-length mirror on the back of his bedroom door. Not bad. On the outside, at least, he looked fully intact. The starched white tux shirt contrasted nicely with his closely cropped black hair and the olive skin that reflected his father's Lebanese blood.

Zach could see a long limousine waiting in front of his building as he stepped out of the elevator into the lobby. It was gray and sleek, and a driver in uniform stood near the passenger-side door.

As the car got under way, the driver's voice came over the intercom. "Please help yourself to a drink, Lieutenant Turzin. Our drive is about twenty minutes."

He slid over to the bar and found a Heineken. He sipped the beer and looked out the window into the early evening light as the limo headed north along the Potomac. The Lincoln Memorial came into view, and Zach could see the Washington Monument beyond it. Signs on the highway announced the exit for the Arlington National Cemetery, and he thought about Canver. He should be in there, not preserved in some Baghdad freezer as a macabre bargaining chip.

He had a general sense of where he was being taken. The

huge Sherman estate, Eldridge, was located about ten miles north of Arlington along the Potomac. Zach had read newspaper accounts that played up the grandeur of Sherman's home and political headquarters. The press occasionally called it "the shadow White House," and Sherman sought to drive home the idea by making sure the media were around when he staged helicopter arrivals and departures on his spacious lawn.

Eldridge was a vast neo-Edwardian monolith set atop a hill. It was bathed by lights and surrounded by manicured grounds. After passing through a security check at the gates, the limo headed up a long tree-lined drive and stopped in front of a columned entryway. Zach was ushered into a huge foyer, where a chandelier glittered overhead and a wide curving staircase wound upward. The floor was marble, set in black and white squares like a giant chessboard. Off to the left, in a richly appointed two-story library, a crowd of people stood milling about, drinking and talking loudly. Off to the right was a large and empty living room. As Zach stepped forward, he saw that Sherman had emerged from the crowd and was coming toward him. With his shock of white hair and angular nose, Sherman looked exactly like he did on television, only thinner.

"Lieutenant Turzin, what a great pleasure this is." Sherman clasped Zach's right hand with both of his, pumping it energetically. "I'm so glad we could get you out to Eldridge on such short notice. I just can't tell you how proud of you I am, son. Damn, I wanted to be at that ceremony."

"Thank you, sir. But you didn't miss anything besides a hot sun and some long speeches."

"Hot air and more hot air, sounds like."

"Precisely, sir. It was hardly worth the medal."

Sherman shook his head and took a step away from Zach, looking him over. He was a good five inches shorter than Zach's six-one. "The Congressional Medal of Honor. Boy, that's something. You even look the part, I'll tell you that. A genuine American hero. Bet your parents are the toast of the block, proud as can be. Is the Army treating you all right?"

"Yes, sir. No problems there. Just lots of press interviews and —"

Sherman sped ahead. "Here, let me introduce you around." Sherman put his arm around Zach and ushered him into the library, where the conversation died away.

"Everybody, I'd like you to meet our guest of honor, Lieutenant Zachary Turzin. The lieutenant, as you all know, was awarded the Congressional Medal of Honor at the White House this week. This man is a genuine hero, folks."

Zach looked over the crowd. The guests were mostly men in their late forties or fifties. They were a fit and hard-jawed group, not the average conglomeration of Washington types with bodies of mush. Still, there was little question as to the city in which these people worked. After ten minutes Zach found himself with a half dozen business cards in his tuxedo jacket pocket, four or five invitations for lunch, and more advice on making money and acquiring power than he could possibly digest.

"This town loves a hero, son," one defense executive told him, offering a cigar. Zach turned it down but listened patiently to a two-minute lecture on the lucrative opportunities that awaited him in the private sector. "You've served your country," the executive said, waving his cigar in the air. "Served it damn well. Why not serve yourself for a while? That's what this city is all about." Six-figure incomes, the executive hinted, were not uncommon for lobbyists at the very company for which he worked.

Zach nodded and continued mingling. Other offers of this kind, implied or explicit, had been coming at him every night for the past week, along with the entreaties from publishers and agents.

"So, Lieutenant, how are you holding up?"

Zach turned around, already knowing who the owner of the low voice was.

"Admiral Forsten, pleasure to see you, sir."

They shook hands, and Forsten gestured him to step over to the bar. "You look like you need a refill." The admiral summoned the bartender, who took Zach's order for a beer.

"Remember one rule about parties around these parts," Forsten said as they clinked their glasses together. "Try to drink as much as you can to thicken your skin but never so much that you dull your edge. This town is a snake pit." Forsten laughed and took a sip of his beer. "I've suffered some near fatal bites myself."

"That may be, sir, but you're also known as something of a snake charmer."

"Hell, I'm lucky to even have a job in Washington. If George Herbert Walker Bush had had his way, my career would have ended in the early 1990s. I would have been out on my ass as chief of naval operations. That whole inner circle despised me. Cheney, Scowcroft, Baker, Powell, all those guys. Said I wasn't a team player. Cheney would have fired me in a second if he could have. That bastard loved firing people to prove he had balls. But I never gave him a chance."

"You're a survivor, sir. That's another thing everybody says about you."

"So far, Lieutenant, so far." Forsten gestured at the tuxe-doed bartenders and the long table of caviar and other hors d'oeuvres. "Not a bad little party Doug has here, wouldn't you say?"

"Mr. Sherman is a very impressive host, sir," Zach answered. "Although I must say, sir, that I'm somewhat surprised to see you here." Zach had had his own reservations about accepting Sherman's invitation. But the second-highest-ranking military man in the Pentagon was surely out of his mind to be attending a party given by a politician who had vowed to bring down the President in the next election.

"Doug and I go way back," Forsten said. "Way back. I knew him long before he got into politics. I figure that the unwritten rule on politics can bend a bit in my case. Anyway, what's Chairman Reynolds going to do, fire me?" Forsten let out a derisive laugh. "The man couldn't operate the Pentagon for five seconds without me. My office does all the damn work at the JCS. Reynolds just schmoozes Congress and does the President's bidding. He pisses when the White House tells him to piss. Problem is, he's pissing all over the services right now."

Zach was jolted by Forsten's bluntness. Damn, this guy had zing.

"By the way, Lieutenant, have you thought any more about your future?" Forsten asked.

"No, sir, not much. The National Defense University has said that they might want me to teach a classified seminar next semester on special operations tactics in the Middle East. But after that, sir, I don't know."

"Well, I've thought a bit about your future, Lieutenant."

Forsten paused and scooped up a chicken wing from a passing tray. He exchanged greetings with someone at the bar. Zach waited.

Forsten turned back. "I think you should come and work for me."

Zach broke eye contact with the admiral and scrambled for a response. He downed a large swallow of beer, flattered and nervous.

"I'm not sure what to say, Admiral. I've never done a tour in the Pentagon."

"I would suggest that you say yes. Let me tell you what I'm thinking here." Forsten put his drink down on the bar. He began ticking off points with the fingers of his left hand.

"One, I've done some checking up on you, Lieutenant. And you're even more impressive than you look with that medal on your chest. I knew that you had some academic training, but I had no idea that you came within an inch of getting your Ph.D. at Harvard. I also didn't know that you had done a stint in Army intelligence's Cairo office and that you have special training in counterterrorism."

"I did some regional liaison with Delta Force, sir. Even thought of joining."

"Good thing you didn't. Those guys just sit on their asses. But the point I'm driving at is that you probably know twice as much about the region than any yahoo on the Joint Staff's Middle East division. I need a man like you. Hell, and on top of everything else, you're even chopper certified."

"Yes, sir. I spent some time training with the 160th Aviation Regiment," Zach said. "Three members of my A-Detachment rotated through with them."

"The Night Stalkers."

"Yes, sir. That's what the 160th call themselves."

"They do some hairy stunts."

"I'd agree with you there, sir. Flying a Blackhawk twelve meters above the desert at night is hairy, all right. Frankly, I never felt comfortable below thirty."

"In any case, Lieutenant, you're the kind of man I can appreciate. Your combination of knowledge, skills, and experience is not easy to come by. Hell, no."

"Thank you, Admiral."

"But let me finish. The second point is that you'll be happy in my shop. It's where the action is, just ask anybody in town. The new vice chairman post is nothing like the old one. You probably know the dope. Last year's reforms chopped off the service chiefs at the knees in the name of ending interagency rivalry and vastly strengthened both the chairman and the vice chairman's position."

"Yes, sir, I've heard about that."

Forsten lowered his voice. "But Reynolds doesn't know shit, as I said. He can't even wipe his ass by himself. He has no vision, no balls. And he has no support whatsoever in the building. The only reason he's in there is to push through the President's agenda — what I call the A and D plan — appeasement and disarmament."

Forsten was a wild man. But Zach agreed with him about the President's policies. Whatever the polls said about his rebound, he was dragging down the nation's security. Zach had been amazed that the President had even struck at Haisa.

"And so, guess who is really running the show at JCS?" Forsten continued, beaming at Zach. He pointed his finger in close to Zach's chest, almost touching it. "I guarantee that if you work for me you'll get a piece of the action. I want you as one of my special assistants; intelligence, mainly, but lots else. My shop is fighting a war in there, and nobody's taking prisoners these days, Lieutenant. I need a man like you. You're one of our best."

Dinner was announced at that moment. Zach put his empty glass on the bar and managed to tell Forsten that he was flattered and would consider the offer. His mind was racing.

## 3

"You know, Lieutenant, Governor Sherman oversaw every detail of Eldridge's construction himself," Ron Varant said, sidling up to Zach as the crowd was herded into a vast dining room where a dinner table stretched for some fifteen feet. Varant was not the unctuous Cadillac salesman Zach had expected. Instead, he was a slight and awkward man with spectacles — a coat holder.

Zach scanned the dining room. A fire burned in the largest fireplace he had ever seen. Two chandeliers hung from the ceiling, glittering dimly. Below, spread along the table in silver holders, a dozen candles flickered. Waiters in white jackets floated about in silent efficiency. Zach wasn't surprised to hear of Sherman's role in the building of the house. The heavy-handed look of the place mirrored perfectly Sherman's public personality — excessive, hyperbolic, unabashed about wealth. Zach himself preferred sparse accommodations. Luxury led to softness, softness to weakness, and weakness equaled death. For the first month in Crystal City he had slept on the floor, resisting the spongy complacency of the queen-size bed.

"Will Mrs. Sherman be joining us tonight?" Zach asked Varant.

"Mrs. Sherman is traveling in Europe," the assistant answered tersely. Zach suddenly remembered reading something about Sherman's alleged marital problems. He was sorry he had asked.

Sherman appeared at Zach's side and guided him toward the head of the table. "You're up here with me, my friend."

Zach sat on Sherman's right. On Sherman's immediate left

sat Admiral Forsten, and next to Forsten was an empty seat. Zach was wondering who would occupy it when he noticed a woman come through a door on the far end of the room. In a moment she was at the table. She was dressed in a business outfit and seemed flustered. Clearly she had just returned from some sort of meeting or trip. Zach couldn't help staring; she was beautiful.

Sherman spoke: "Lieutenant Zach Turzin, I'm pleased to introduce you to Ms. Justine Arledge." Zach and the woman locked eyes and both smiled, nodding a hello. Their eye contact lingered. Zach looked away first, uncomfortable.

"Justine is our communications director. A real high-technology-whiz, I'll tell you, but she also has that soft touch with the press. Snatched her away from the Democratic National Committee three years ago. Her talents were unappreciated there."

Justine smiled at Zach again. Her lips were full and sensuous. Her skin was pale but slightly tanned; her hair fell just to her shoulders and was a light shade of brown that glimmered in the light.

"Justine agrees with me that you're quite the hero, Zach," Sherman said. "But I should warn you that she doesn't think much of the military profession as a whole. Just ask Jeff."

"Doug, you're such a provocateur," Justine protested.

"It's true," Admiral Forsten said. " 'Mongoloid' is a term I've heard her use."

"And I suppose that —"

"But one wonders," continued a grinning Forsten, "what the result would be if you polled most Americans about who they thought was a lower form of life: a professional military officer who risks his neck in the field or a campaign spin doctor. Lieutenant, you might have a view on that."

"I suppose it's nice to have both around," Zach said. "Can't win elections without one, can't win wars without the other."

Justine smiled at Zach once more and tilted her head to

the side, inviting his eyes to meet hers. "Well, maybe there's not that much difference in our work after all. Men like you, Lieutenant, destroy enemy installations in far-off countries. Monsters like myself destroy political reputations right here at home."

Forsten nudged Justine with his elbow. "Monster. Now I'd say that's about the most accurate assessment you've ever given of yourself."

"Now Jeff, you know I've never tried to deny my vices, just to capitalize on them."

Zach found himself transfixed by Justine as the dueling among her, Forsten, and Sherman continued. There was a charged air around her, a magnetism that was at once sexual and intellectual. She slung barbs with pursed lips and responded to attacks with either slashing wit or feminine pouting. Everything about her was inviting.

"My friends, could I have a moment of your attention, a moment of your attention." Sherman was on his feet, tapping a wine glass with his salad fork.

"We have tonight a guest of unusual distinction. Lieutenant Zach Turzin has been to hell and come back a hero. And we should all be damn proud of him, damn proud. Many of you have served in our armed forces. You know how it is."

There were murmurs of assent in the crowd, and Sherman poured it on: "You know what it means to risk life and limb for your country. You know that the Medal of Honor is not something that comes easily, no siree. It's one soldier in a million who gets one of those babies. I can tell you off the record that Lieutenant Turzin also won a classified Silver Star hunting Scuds in Desert Storm. Lieutenant Turzin is a rare fighting man indeed."

The crowd applauded. Zach acknowledged the clapping with a nod down the table.

"And I'd just like to say something else while I'm up here," Sherman continued. "Now I don't want to get political, because we have among us here tonight a loyal member of our military high command. A man, I dare say, who would never, ever countenance the slightest hint of criticism directed at his brave commander in chief."

Sherman gestured to Forsten, and laughter erupted at the table. "But thank god, thank god that that man in the White House finally took some action in the Middle East. Now all we need is more of the same. I've said it before, I'll say it again: Unless we move more decisively against terrorist states abroad and work harder to smash terrorist networks here at home, we are all sitting ducks, I can tell you that. Again, hats off to the lieutenant for showing how to get things done."

There was more applause at the table and a smattering of "hear, hear" as Sherman sat down. Zach was familiar with Sherman's passionately held views on Islamic fundamentalism and the threat of terrorism. It was his main foreign policy issue. Sherman liked to warn that "the next bomb at the World Trade Center could be a nuclear one." And he made the idea seem plausible, talking endlessly of stolen Russian warheads, black-market plutonium sales, and mercenary scientists. He also pointed to evidence that Iran's attempt to build a bomb was nearing fruition. And in an addendum that played nicely into his anti-immigration and antidrug positions, Sherman railed that "our borders are like a sieve. Anybody carrying anything can get in anywhere."

The dinner was all-American fare. There were slabs of steak and mashed potatoes and corn on the cob. Opened bottles of Budweiser and Coors stood next to glasses of the finest crystal. For a different crowd Sherman might have flown in a guest chef from Paris or procured the flesh of an exotic mammal. Perhaps an assistant would have been sent to scour Bordeaux for a case of some legendary rare wine. But Sherman knew these men better than that. These were not Georgetown snobs who disdained Sherman as a barbarian yet accepted his hospitality. Nor were they old-money

Virginia aristocrats from nearby estates who could tell whether the pheasant had been shot on the grounds or bought at a store. The men here had the simple tastes of the heartland. And for many, the most basic of home-cooked meals tasted forever extraordinary after years of military mess.

When the dinner broke up, the crowd drifted into the living room. Cigars came out, and brandy was poured. The talk turned to shop — weapons systems in development, Pentagon contracts lost or gained, politics and policy. No conversation got far without a swipe at the current administration.

Sherman pummeled the President for his softness on Libya and then excused himself to make some phone calls. Various of the men, their restraint washed away by a river of drink, approached Zach and offered effusive praise. Some tried to pry more details about the mission. As usual, Zach didn't yield. The military classification status of the mission was and would remain extremely sensitive. Years down the road, when Saddam was gone, the whole story might be made public. Until then, Zach was prepared to always just smile and say, "Well, you know, I really can't get into that part."

Zach saw Justine standing near the fireplace, her eyes glazing over as two men talked loudly about the logistics end of the Balkans operation. He approached her from the left.

"Fascinating stuff, the issue of the C-17's reliability, wouldn't you say?" Zach said softly.

"Can't get enough of it," Justine said, smiling and stepping away from the men.

"I'm a sea-lift man myself," Zach said. "Why talk about C-17s and C-5s when you can talk about FSSs and RRFs? Now those are some impressive ships."

"My feeling exactly, Lieutenant. My parents were sea-lift people, which I guess explains why I'm a sea-lift person too."

"Really? Now that's interesting. Most kids I knew tried to be the opposite of what their parents were. If Mom and Dad were sea-lift people, they'd be into airlift for sure."

"I guess I'm not much of a rebel," Justine said, breaking into a laugh.

"Quite the contrary. I'd say working for Douglas Sherman gives you rebel credentials in this town."

"True enough," Justine said with a sigh. "I'll probably never find work again after the election."

"Well, it's never too late for a second career in the armed forces, Justine. Mongoloids like me need leaders like you."

"I'm glad you understand how the natural order works."

"I know my place." Zach broke eye contact with Justine, sneaking a glance downward and appreciating her curves. Christ, she was hot.

"Military men always do. They can't forget it with those little stripes on their shoulders." Justine tilted her head and looked Zach over in his tux. She reached out to his chest and brushed off some lint, letting her fingers linger on the fabric. "Speaking of which, it's a shame you didn't wear your uniform tonight. I like the hero look I saw on television. A tux makes you seem so, well, ordinary. Cute, yes, but not heroic."

"One out of two is better than nothing," Zach said with a smile. He wondered whether what he thought was happening really was happening.

"I'm a two-out-of-two woman, myself."

"I can relate to that. You know, Justine, it's not like I've burned the uniform or anything."

"I should hope not. Aren't there laws against that?"

"You're thinking of flags. Tell you what, I'll wear the uniform next time we see each other."

Sherman had materialized across the room and was heading toward them through the crowd. Justine glanced at him quickly and then back at Zach with a coy smile. "And when will that be, Lieutenant?"

Zach stumbled for a response, surprised. "Uh, sooner rather than later, I would hope."

"So would I."

Sherman emerged from the crowd and took Justine by the arm. "I need you." He turned to Zach. "It's been a great honor having you here tonight. But I'm afraid we're going to have be off. Something's come up. You know politics. Never ends. Hope to see you again real soon." Zach shook hands with both of them and watched as they threaded their way through the crowd. At the door, Justine kept going, but Sherman stopped to talk with a well-built blond-haired man who hadn't been at the party earlier. He wore a suit rather than a tux. He looked maybe thirty-five or forty, with weathered features. Zach was sure he knew him from somewhere, definitely from the service. The man nodded as Sherman talked, and then they both exited the room.

Zach felt drunk as the limo headed down the long driveway through the night. The switch to ginger ale had come too late. He opened a Diet Coke from the limo fridge, as if somehow more soda would burn up the alcohol in his bloodstream.

"Glad to see you again, Lieutenant," Forsten had said as Zach left. "Now remember, you think about my offer."

"Yes, sir. I certainly will."

"I need an answer soon — within a couple of days," Forsten said.

"And you'll have one, sir."

Zach used the remote control to turn on one of the limo's televisions. He flipped through the channels, settling as usual on CNN. Footage on the screen showed large crowds of ethnic Albanian refugees at some relief center. This Balkan thing will never end, Zach thought. Permanent war. He poured a refill of the Coke. The next morning was not going to be pleasant.

The limo had already passed under the Key Bridge and

was nearing Crystal City when the blond-haired man's identity abruptly came into focus. Zach wondered how it could ever have been hazy. His name was Riley, Colonel Riley. Zach remembered meeting him shortly after joining up, at a two-week desert training exercise at a base in California in late 1989. Riley came from the squalor of South Carolina's Appalachia and he represented the sociopathic side of the special forces: the men who were there because they liked killing people and sometimes doing worse. His eyes showed it; they were the black beads of a Charlie Manson or a Ted Bundy. They alternated between a blazing intensity and a frozen deadness. Rumor had it that Riley had fought alongside the Contras inside Nicaragua during the 1980s, and it was said that he had shared the rebels' sadistic approach to war.

Riley's career had come to an end after the Panama invasion, when he was accused of killing captured members of the Panamanian Defense Forces in a special forces mission that took place just hours before the main invasion. Zach didn't know any more details than that.

So what would Riley be doing at Eldridge? It was hard to believe that Justine and Riley could work for the same man. Zach wondered whether Justine had any idea about Riley's past. Surely Sherman must.

After the limo had dropped him off and he had taken off the tux, Zach lay in bed thinking about Justine. He imagined her there next to him, her body soft and warm, one of his hands on her hip, the other behind her neck, pulling her toward him.

The guests were long gone from Eldridge. The servants had turned in for the night. Far off on the edge of the great estate, two guards, German shepherds at their sides, walked the narrow gravel path that followed along a razor-wire-tipped chain-link fence for no fewer than four miles.

Sherman poured himself a second whiskey and returned to a deep leather chair. Smoke from his cigar curled toward the study's ceiling far above. He flipped once more through the contents of a green folder and tossed it onto the coffee table.

"We still don't know enough about him."

Forsten shifted uneasily in his chair. "I know his type."

"Oh, and what's that, exactly?"

"He's hungry for more. He wants to keep the high going. I've been there, believe me. But he's smart too. He knows the ride is over after that show-and-tell session in the Rose Garden. He knows they'll never send him into the field again, not for a real mission, at least. He's going to want something else, something just as intense."

"But can he be trusted? And do we really need him? Those are the issues here, Jeff."

"There's no question in my mind about the issue of need. That medal goes a long way with the rank and file. We either need him or somebody very much like him. As for his trustworthiness, we'll see about that over time."

"We don't have much time."

"I think we'll know soon after he comes on board with me."

"So you think he'll take it?"

"He'll take it. He'd be a fool not to."

"And where will you put him?"

Forsten paused to relight his cigar. He exhaled upward. "Intelligence, no question. With Hansen gone I'm understaffed in that department."

Sherman rose to pace the room, swirling the ice about in his glass. He gazed for a long moment through the French doors to a rolling lawn well lit by security lights.

"Are you sure the Hansen thing was clean?"

Forsten nodded. "It doesn't get any cleaner. Our people aren't amateurs."

"Nobody's come to the office asking questions?"

"Of course not. For christ's sake, Doug, the case is closed.

Alexandria police stirred things up at the projects but came up with zilch. End of story."

"Fine. But let me just say this. If Turzin comes on board, I want you to find out more about him and keep a goddamn eye on him. What happened last time shouldn't have happened."

"I agree. Riley can handle that project."

Sherman seemed to relax, but he kept pacing. "What's the latest?" he asked finally.

"On which front?" Forsten asked.

"Anderson first."

"Our team is now in place. Anderson's itinerary is unchanged. I predict no problems."

"There are always problems."

"Not this time. Believe me, Doug, Oman is the best place for this. We have more friends there than we need. This will be just as easy as doing Neuwirth."

"Are you sure we need to do both? It just seems like too much. Too many risks, too much attention."

"Jesus, Doug. How many times do we have to go over this? I know what I need. You worry about what you need. Besides, they won't appear to be connected. I guarantee it."

Sherman nodded his head reluctantly. He had stopped next to a large antique globe and was absentmindedly spinning it. "What about everything else? What's the status of Chen's contact with Sheik Tabrata?"

Forsten looked at his watch. "Actually, the two should be meeting right about now. Donny sent a message earlier in the day. I'll have a full briefing by the morning."

"Tell me this: What if Tabrata isn't interested?" The anxiety was back in Sherman's voice.

"He'll be interested. When you're in business, you want business."

"And the other matter. Where do things stand there?"

"Our friend at the Bureau says the investigation remains

at a dead end. They're far from anything that will hold up."

"As of now."

"As of now. But I'd say we're doing okay. The President's running scared on this. He's not going to turn up the heat on us, believe me." Forsten stretched his legs and rose.

Sherman fished the admiral's coat from a massive closet off the foyer and escorted him to the door. "Let me know how it goes with our boy," he said as Forsten left.

## 4

He was in a gray and endless wasteland of scree and dust. It was neither day nor night. The ground underfoot, a shifting gravel, grasped at his boots. Each step forward was a giant labor. His lower back was ablaze with pain that shot into his hips and up his spine. A fine silt, salty and bitter, gathered in his mouth and throat, and he struggled to breathe. His eyes stung as he scanned a horizon dominated by plumes of black smoke that bent in the wind. He was tired, lost, losing strength. He sank to his hands and knees and began to crawl. The sharp rock bit into his flesh.

He found Canver in a shallow ditch, bloodied but alive. He gave him water. The wounds, he saw, were minor. He heard the thump of helicopter blades, faint but growing. Soon they would leave this place. The noise turned deafening. The machine was above them now, but it could not be seen. A powerful wind rose to feed the swirl of the stinging stand. For a moment he couldn't see anything. He groped downward to hold Canver. His hand sank into a mass of pulverized flesh.

And then the chaos began, a furious onslaught of tracer bullets and rockets. Explosions, blossoming in bright gray, rose all around them. The shriek of a man dying nearby was heard through the clatter and lingered in the air. Zach pulled Canver and tried to rise, but his legs were wobbly and pulsated with pain. He felt leaden, helpless. The sound of the helicopter shut off suddenly. It was gone. A babble of strange and foreign voices was now heard. The enemy was close and coming closer. He fumbled for a new clip to his M16. It slipped from his grasp and was swallowed by the sand. He looked to Canver. The blood had gone. His face was chalky, his eyes closed. A horn sounded, and Zach heard the sound of tramping feet and clanking weapons. The distinctive rumble of a tank's treads murmured in the background. The horn blared loudly again and then once more.

Zach lurched up in his bed, breathing hard. His face and neck were damp with sweat. His hands trembled as he shut off the alarm and gazed around the room, trying to calm himself. A dull ache throbbed at the base of his spine. The dreams had started a month after the Haisa mission and came often. Always Zach was helpless. Always Canver was there, sometimes dead, sometimes alive. Black and gray were the only colors, desert the only background.

Zach took a shower and went for a run. He fell to the shag carpeting upon returning and pumped his body up and down in set after set of push-ups, even as the pain in his lower back turned sharp. Soon the residue of nocturnal horror had receded, and his mind turned to other matters. Forsten, Justine, Sherman. Christ, what a night. He read the Sunday paper and sipped coffee, pondering the job offer from Forsten. He had his doubts. Two months in Washington had been enough for him, too much. He had known before coming, from a thousand stories heard and read, that Washington was a city of dissipation. It was a place where even the strongest were sucked dry of their vitality by a thicket of bureaucratic obstructions. Zach had known many officers who had left for a rotation at the Pentagon talking of strategies and missions and policy changes, and had emerged from their stint weary and changed, talking of procedure and clarification and oversight. He feared a similar fate. He imagined himself forgetting why he had come and not knowing where to go next. He worried about staying too long and learning to lie too well. In a city where soldiers were ground into clerks, he would live the life of a bureaucrat and lose the edge that made the difference between life and death in combat. He thought of his father in the make-believe world of Princeton, placid and satisfied, numbed by his evening wine. It was an image of complacency that loomed as a fate to be avoided at almost any cost.

But the pull of Admiral Jeffrey Forsten was strong. It was hard to envision a path of decline in the presence of such strength. And it was difficult to see how the habits of hesitation and the language of half-truths could be learned at that man's side. Zach imagined the opposite: He felt there was an energy in Forsten that he could tap into. During his years in the special forces he had been inspired by many superiors but actually mentored by none. Nobody had generated in him that level of respect. Always he had found flaws. It was a devotion to truth that mattered most to Zach and this, it turned out, was a hard thing to find among those with power.

He wanted more information about Forsten. The admiral had checked up on him; there was no reason he couldn't do the same. Zach pulled out his address book and began working the phone.

"You'd be where the action is, no doubt about it," said one former SOF buddy, who now worked as a military aide at the NSC. "It's true what everybody says — that Forsten is the one who really runs the Pentagon. Last year's reorganization gave the JCS chairman vast new powers, but Reynolds either doesn't want the power or doesn't know how to use it and has abdicated to Forsten on a lot of matters."

Forsten had been down as many times as he'd been up, Zach was told by others. He came out of Vietnam highly decorated and well respected, but he soon made a name for himself by shaking things up and getting into trouble. There was talk of him getting the Seventh Fleet in the late 1970s, which would have made him the youngest commander ever in that post, but he had botched it by pushing too hard on the MIA issue. Forsten angered enough brass that instead of getting the Seventh he was banished in 1979 to the job of running the Foreign Military Sales and Assistance program, a post that everybody in town saw as a dead end. But Forsten always came back, leaning on a vast following in the services that made him something of a cult leader. The so-called Forstenites were devoted to him because he was the antithesis of the fat-assed four-star generals who usually ran the show. By 1989 Forsten had gotten his career back on track and become Chief of Naval Operations right before Saddam went into Kuwait. He was a major figure during Operation Desert Storm. After a few years in that post, he had moved up again.

"Forsten is one caustic son of a bitch, famous for his mouth, and Reynolds is his whipping boy of choice," Zach was told by a former superior officer who now taught at the Defense University. "It's like a duoumverate over there, with Forsten as the stronger emperor. Basically Reynolds handles relations with Congress and the White House and works with the defense secretary on delicate political issues. Things like the new round of base closing and weapons cancellations. Forsten is left with almost everything else. In terms of the actual working of the Pentagon, Forsten is definitely the one in control. Reynolds has a few allies in the regional commands, but he doesn't have many of his own people in Washington. He really hasn't yet learned how this town works."

Nearly everybody urged Zach to take the job. It was an offer he couldn't refuse, a chance to move into the epicenter of national security policy, a shot at being part of history. But nearly everybody also noted Forsten's liabilities and referred to the rumors that surrounded the man. Forsten could blow a fuse at any time, many said. He shot from the hip too often. He hated the President with a visceral intensity and let too many people know about it. His open relationship with Sherman didn't help matters. Everybody agreed: Today Forsten was vice chairman, his power near its zenith; tomorrow he could be sipping martinis on the terrace of a cheap condo in Florida.

A few of the people Zach talked to mentioned rumors about his service in Vietnam that lingered over Forsten's head. In the military Forsten was viewed as a hero. Some of his operations were the stuff of textbooks. But the 1979 publication of the book *Battle for the Mekong* by investigative reporter Donald Leffler had raised questions about Forsten's conduct in Vietnam, charging that he and his teams of "River Rats" had committed widespread atrocities. A few newspapers had picked up on Leffler's charges, but the story had never gone anywhere.

Zach found the book in the Defense University library on Monday afternoon and read through it in a few hours. The book claimed that the remote nature of Forsten's Brown Water operations in the Rung Sat Special Zone had prevented much of the information on the atrocities from being previously told. Forsten, it said, had taken special pleasure in enforcing the dusk-to-dawn curfew on all boat traffic in the delta, and his men had killed hundreds of innocent fishermen and traders. More seriously, Leffler charged that the River Rats may have been responsible for a major massacre at a remote village called Chisir on a Mekong tributary that ran within a few miles of the Cambodian border. Finally, Leffler wrote that in the last few years of the war, when all was clearly lost, Forsten and his River Rats had turned to personal enrichment. They had started off with small change, taking bribes from the drug smugglers who plied the Mekong. But soon, according to Leffler, greed had gotten the best of them, and they had become smugglers themselves, transporting heroin from sellers in the interior out to waiting merchant ships in the South China Sea that were operated by a Hong Kong drug syndicate.

Zach skimmed *Battle for the Mekong* with skepticism. Most of the charges appeared to be based on interviews with unnamed sources. The book had no footnotes or bibliography. It was laced with left-wing polemics. The whole thing looked sloppy and uncredible. The blurb about the author said that he was at work on a more comprehensive investigation of unreported war crimes in Vietnam. Zach checked standard bibliographic references and found that no such book had ever been published. He wouldn't worry about the fantasies of Donald Leffler.

On Monday night he sat at the glass dining table and made a list of the pros and cons of taking the job with Forsten. The pro list filled half a page. The con list contained only one item: "Staying in Washington."

He decided to take the job.

## ★ 5 ★

General Carl Anderson stepped into the sweltering cargo bay of the C-141 and took the first empty seat he saw. Like the other metal seats that lined each side of the plane's cavernous interior, it looked akin to a storage rack, with only the faintest hint of cushioning. Anderson buckled himself in and acknowledged the salutes of the Air Force personnel already in the plane. They were mechanics and ground crew mainly, and they were impressed with Anderson. As usual. A four-star Air Force general was not a common sight in the cargo area of a C-141. But Anderson fancied himself as a populist, and ever since taking over as head of Central Command he had made this mode of transport his trademark. It was good for morale, he told his aides. And it helped him get to know the people he commanded.

It was not until the C-141 was at thirty-thousand feet over the Indian Ocean that the temperature in the cargo area dipped down under ninety degrees. It hovered in the eighties and then the seventies before plunging quickly lower, finally settling at around forty-five degrees. Anderson shoved his hands deep into his pockets and shot questions at the men to his immediate right and left, talking loudly to be heard. He had just seen for himself living conditions on Diego Garcia and judged them to be adequate given the desolation of the island base. But he wanted to hear the views of everybody he could. Anderson cared about his men. Indeed, if he was known for anything, it was his obsession with quality-of-life issues. His old friend JCS Chairman Reynolds had put him in the CENTCOM post for exactly this reason, and while there was grumbling that Anderson was a puppet in the President's tireless crusade to win over the military, he was immensely popular with enlisted men and officers alike. The talk was that Reynolds planned to push Anderson even higher because he was one of the few real allies the JCS chairman had.

Shortly before the plane began its descent toward Oman, Anderson used the lavatory to change into civilian clothes. No sultanate in the Persian Gulf had been more receptive to the U.S. military than that of Oman. But while the U.S. bases in the country were common knowledge to all in the region, the Omanis officially denied any U.S. military presence. Civvies were standard wear for visiting U.S. officers, especially when they had meetings with top Omanis in Muscat, as Anderson did today.

The Nazwa U.S. air base sat alone in a low desert valley seventy miles to the west of Muscat. Beyond the perimeter fences, bleak mountains of gray and brown rose to meet a deep blue sky. There wasn't a village for ten miles in any direction, or much other sign of life. The ninety-five Americans who worked on the base for three-month stints were not permitted to leave and mingle with the natives. Their lives consisted of twelve-hour days and videos at night. Nazwa was a hardship post of the first order.

Stepping off the plane, Anderson exchanged salutes in the blazing sun with the base commander and his top officers. A short tour of the base was followed by a briefing on recent U.S. training activities in Oman. Then Anderson and his hosts had an early lunch in the main mess used by enlisted men. "Always like to see how the other half eats," Anderson had insisted. A lavish buffet in the officers' dining room went untouched.

At one P.M. three blue Chevrolet Suburbans with tinted windows of bulletproof glass set out for Muscat. Exactly on schedule. Anderson and his two aides were in the middle car with an American driver, four Omani special service men were in the lead, and four American Air Force security officers brought up the rear. Anderson pulled out a briefing book and began reading, asking an occasional question of his aides. Traffic on the two-lane road was light. The temperature had edged past one hundred degrees well before noon.

Twenty miles from the base, not far past the tiny town of Izki, the road passed through scorched hills of red stone. It curved and climbed next through low, jagged cliffs with holes visible from dynamite drilling. Anderson didn't notice that the convoy was slowing until it was almost stopped. He looked up from his briefing book.

The lead Chevrolet was stopped behind a dilapidated truck parked diagonally across the road. Behind it, bags of grain were spilled on the road. Not a person was in sight. "What's up?" Anderson asked the driver.

As the driver began to answer, the figure of a man was seen rising from the back of the truck. There was a flash, and the lead car exploded into flames. Burning debris rained down on the windshield of the middle vehicle. "Out, out," Anderson screamed. He pulled open the door and hurled himself to the ground, tumbling forward. The next missile hit the middle vehicle from above and sideways. A burst of fire swept over Anderson, and he thrashed to throw off something on his back that was burning through his shirt into his flesh. The rear vehicle surged forward, plunging off the road and almost crushing Anderson. A missile from above swooshed by the Suburban, exploding into the ground behind it and throwing up a hail of dirt and rocks. Machine-gun fire from a heavy-caliber weapon began as the American security men clambored from their vehicle. The two on the right side fired wildly upward before being cut down, their bright polo shirts exploding into blood and tatters of cloth. The two others crouched with their M16s behind the Suburban as it was raked by bullets. Air hissed loudly from punctured tires.

There was silence for a moment, and then a loud ping followed by another as two grenades landed on the vehicle's hood and bounced to the ground next to the men. They exploded at the same time in a blast fed by a nearly full tank of gasoline. Anderson felt a wave of intense heat and a sudden searing pain as a piece of metal gashed across the backs of his thighs, ripping away clothing and flesh. There was a wetness in his hair, and a trickle of warm blood found its way into his mouth. Another grenade went off in the remains of the middle vehicle, rocking the ground beneath him.

Anderson slithered into a drainage ditch and lay pressed against the ground in a blur of pain, his ears ringing. The shooting had stopped now, but he could see nothing from the ditch. Nearby he heard the sound of gravel under feet and then the murmur of voices. There was a brief burst of gunfire and then another. The crackling of shifting gravel moved closer, and Anderson looked about for something to use as a weapon. He heard the voices again, closer, and felt a surge of euphoria as he made out English words and a distinct accent from the American South. "Over here!" he yelled. He was in too much pain to rise.

A moment later a grenade landed by his feet.

## 6

"Your gatekeeper is really something," Zach said when Justine finally came on the line. Her assistant had grilled him for forty-five seconds and then put him on hold for nearly two minutes, allowing plenty of time for his doubts about calling to multiply.

"I get a lot of nutcases calling," Justine said. "Nuts and pests."

"If I'm talking to you I guess that means I'm in neither category."

"As far as we know, anyway. But really, Lieutenant, it's nice to hear from you."

"Just thought I'd call to tell you how nice it was to meet you at the party."

"You were a hit. Doug thinks you're really something."

"It's not often I dine in a room larger than my whole apartment. What a place."

"Yes, Eldridge is something."

Zach paused and cleared his throat. He had never been good at the next part.

"So, Justine, I had an absolutely brilliant idea today. I thought —"

"Do you get those often?"

"Not often enough to get me into Mensa, but yeah, I have my share. Military intelligence is not really a contradiction in terms, you know."

Justine laughed. "Well, I guess I'll have to peel that bumper sticker off my car, then. So let's hear this brilliant idea of yours."

"Dinner. You and I."

"Dinner?"

"Yes. You know, the meal, usually of a substantial nature, that is shared during evening hours in western cultures."

Justine chuckled. "I do think I've heard of that tradition."

Zach imagined her smile over the phone. He smiled himself. He wanted to get back the connection they had had at Eldridge.

"I realize that pols like you usually eat overcooked chicken breast served at a round eight-person table with an hour of boring oratory for dessert, but I assure you that there are other ways to enjoy the tradition."

"Are you going to offer me some Army rations, Lieutenant? What are they called again? Meals — "

"Meals Ready to Eat, or MREs," Zach said. "Delicious stuff. Everybody jokes that the initials stand for Meals Rejected by Ethiopians."

Justine laughed. Zach loved the way she laughed. "So I guess those aren't on the menu," she said. "But really, what did you have in mind?"

"Middle Eastern food, but of course," he said.

"I guess there is a certain logic in that choice. I've had it a few times."

Zach stayed on the offensive. He felt Justine could float out of reach at any moment. "How about tonight? I know a great place near Dupont Circle."

"Tonight?" Justine sounded incredulous, as if she hadn't done anything spontaneous in a decade.

"Yes. The point of time, following the afternoon, at which darkness has fallen and —"

"Okay, okay." Justine laughed and paused for a long moment. "As a matter of fact, there's nothing on my schedule for tonight."

"Really. How lucky for me."

"It is unusual, actually."

"Uh huh." Zach waited.

"Doug's out of town, so things are pretty quiet."

"Good."

"So, yeah," Justine said. "Let's do dinner."

Zach arrived at the restaurant one minute early. Punctuality was a way of life in the military, but there were no rewards for it in the rest of the world, he was learning. After twenty minutes of waiting, gulping a beer down nervously, he began to worry that he had been stood up.

Her entrance, when it finally came, was much as it had been at Sherman's. She looked rushed and scattered as she sat down, apologizing profusely. There had been a last-minute call, some problem in Chicago. She had on a tight-fitting black dress that was cut low at the top and ended just above her knees. Her hair was pushed back in a headband, highlighting a high brow and distinct but soft cheekbones. Zach felt his intense attraction to her come rushing back as she settled in across from him.

"This place is great," Justine said looking around. The ceiling was low, with exposed beams. The walls were adobe and covered with Persian rugs. The lighting was dim, provided by antique lamps hanging overhead. Some of the tables were more like cubbyholes carved in the walls. Zach had insisted on one of the darkest available, slipping the waiter a five.

"I'm glad you're here," he said.

She smiled, her lips parting just slightly. "Me too. I don't often get an opportunity to dine with war heroes, you know."

"Remember, Justine. War heroes are just average grunts who did something really stupid once and happened to survive."

"I'd consider you neither average nor a grunt, and from what I heard you did something extraordinary."

Zach shook his head. "Congressional Medal of Honor. CMH. The saying in the military is that those initials stand for Casket Metal Handles, because anybody who wins the medal should really be dead."

"That doesn't mean that what they did was stupid."

"Actually, Justine, staying alive is considered an important career goal in today's Army."

The waiter came and took their order for drinks. Zach ordered a second beer. Justine got a white wine.

"I myself don't get to dine with many political operatives," Zach said. "In fact, you're the first, and you don't exactly fit my stereotype. You're not bald, for one thing."

"I should hope not."

"And you don't radiate nastiness, exactly. I'll be spoiled from now on."

Zach guided Justine through the menu, explaining the different dishes. She giggled as she tried to pronounce the names. Zach feigned horror, teasing her in Arabic.

"So how'd you get into the politics business?" he asked after they had ordered.

"Oh, it's a long story. But I'll give you the short version. After college — I went to Duke — I came to Washington to join the legions of bright-eyed young people who want to make a difference in the world. I worked on the Hill in some hell job, I slogged away with a nonprofit for peanuts, the usual stuff. Finally I ended up with the DNC in a pretty good position. It seemed I was finally going places, helping to rebuild the Democratic party, actually getting a decent paycheck for once. Also, I was living with a guy who's really plugged in around here. He's a big deal now in the administration, actually. I thought I was in love."

"So what happened?"

"Well, again, the short version. In a nutshsell, it turned out that my boyfriend was sleeping with his assistant and that my party was sleeping with whatever corporate donors wrote the biggest checks. Neither was interested in changing, so I left both."

"Ouch."

"Yeah, it was a tough period, lots of turmoil. I really got hurt."

"I know the feeling — hitting a brick wall in both your personal and professional life at the same time," Zach said. "It's like getting hit by those tornadoes that travel in pairs. Sister twisters, or whatever they're called."

"Exactly. Fortunately, when I emerged from my shelter, Doug's organization was looking for somebody."

"So what do you think Sherman's chances are next time around?" Zach asked.

Justine sighed and sipped her wine. "Frankly, not good. More than seventy percent of the electorate still identify themselves as either Republicans or Democrats. The mood in the country is ugly, very ugly. And people are cynical about the two parties. But as long as those numbers don't change, we face an uphill battle. We need to get really, really lucky."

"And Sherman realizes all this?"

"Basically he does, and it kills him. He's deeply convinced that he should be running the government. He senses, and I couldn't agree more, that things are really falling apart — I mean falling apart to the degree that this country may lose its chance to ever get back to where it was. He also thinks we may be in real danger soon because of this sick marriage of nuclear proliferation and growing terrorism. I gather you agree with him on this?"

Zach nodded. "A hundred percent."

"Anyway, Doug knows he would make a great president. And it's tragic, really, because it's probably never going to happen."

"Christ, you really aren't the prototypical spin doctor. I thought you guys were always supposed to predict victory, no matter what the odds."

"We guys only have to do that in public. In private we're allowed to speak the truth."

"So if Sherman's going to lose, what keeps you in the game?" Zach asked.

"I'm a believer, I really am. I think protest politics can make a difference."

"Ever thought of just getting out of the game altogether?" Zach was still perplexed as to why anyone would choose Washington as a permanent base.

Justine shook her head. "No way. In truth, I can't imagine doing anything else. I love the action. I love being at the center of things that really matter. I can't tell you what it's like to hold a late-afternoon press briefing after a day of turbulent developments in a campaign. The cameras and lights. Reporters firing questions at you, trying to trip you up and make you say things you don't want to say. It's like a ferocious match-point volley in tennis, where you're just hanging on. Except the stakes are infinitely higher, and millions of people are watching. There's nothing like it in the world. It's an incredible high."

"They say politics is show business for ugly people," Zach said, "but obviously that maxim doesn't apply to you. Adrenaline junkie might be a better description."

"There is some of that, I'll admit. You know, I grew up in a house where there were constant explosions. Lots of airborne dishes. I guess I just feel at home in crises and combat."

"You'd do well in my business."

The waiter arrived with their order. As they ate, Justine turned the conversation to Zach. He dodged the job of telling his all-too-complicated life story by using his entrée to segue into a description of the Middle East. He couldn't tell Justine what he had actually done there, but he could describe what the place was like. He talked of the crowded city streets filled with pungent smells and endless commotion; the beauty of the desert, hushed and empty; the villages that looked untouched by the twentieth century. He described the women of Saudi Arabia, veiled and alone in the back of luxury sedans they were not permitted to drive; the men in the marketplaces of Amman who scraped by on the tiniest of incomes, their voices never resting for a moment; the children roaming Cairo in shoeless packs, their future doomed by the forces of demography and poverty.

It had grown late, and they were almost alone now in the restaurant. Quiet sitar music mixed with the rustle of silverware and dishes as tables were cleared. Justine seemed soft and relaxed. Her eyes were warm, beaming at him and reflecting the flame of the candle. He held her gaze. It had been a long time since he had felt this comfortable with a woman. At moments in the conversation she would touch his arm, and after the coffee had come he took her hand and held it while they talked. Gently, almost impercetibly, her fingertips caressed the inside of his palm.

They split the check at her insistence and stepped into the cool night air. They walked along N Street, looking at the townhouses. She took his arm, and he felt a tremor of excitement from having her so close.

"I'd love to live in one of these," he said wistfully of the homes they saw. "You wouldn't believe this Crystal City place that I'm living in now."

"Brave New World."

"Yeah, something like that. Where do you live?"

"Georgetown."

"Kind of expensive there. You got much space?"

"Oh, yeah, lots. A whole townhouse, actually. More than I need."

He slipped his arm around her waist, stopping and looking at her. "I'm really happy to be here with you tonight," he said. "I haven't had such a good time since coming to Washington."

"Even when you got your medal?" Justine teased.

"Especially when I got my medal."

Justine smiled at Zach and then looked down and away, shyly. He reached out and gently tilted her chin up so he could see her eyes again.

"They're incredible," he said softly.

"What are?"

"Your eyes. They glow."

He put his hand up to her neck, brushing back a few strands of hair that had come loose from her headband. He caressed the back of her neck as he pulled her toward him, finding her lips with his. It had been so long for him, this feeling. It was awkward in a delicious way. He put both arms around her and felt more grounded.

She came in closer to him. Her whole body pressed against his. He kissed her neck and ran his hand down her back, and then just a bit farther. For a long moment he held her tightly, closing his eyes and taking in her smell. It was fresh and sweet, familiar. He found her lips again, and they kissed more deeply.

"Zach." She sounded serious. She had turned her face away and looked downward.

"What?" He tilted his head down to follow her lips. She kissed him quickly and then turned away again.

"I'm not sure this is such a good idea," she said slowly. She looked up and away, troubled.

"I think it's a good idea."

"It's really not."

Zach let her go, and she stepped back. She gave him a pitying look and rubbed his chin, running her fingers along the side of his face.

"I'm sorry, it's just that . . . I really want to be here, but I shouldn't be, I . . ." She was struggling. "I loved tonight. It's just that — "

"It's just what?"

She sighed. "There's somebody else."

"Really?" There was an edge of bitterness in his voice. Why the hell had she flirted with him from the second they met? Why had she come out with him?

"I'm sorry," she said. She took his hand and gently caressed it.

"How serious is it?"

"Serious."

"Are you married?"

"No."

"Going to get married?"

"Maybe."

She looked away, and they both were silent. The wind had picked up, and it was suddenly much colder on the street. Zach fumbled with the zipper on his jacket.

"I'm sorry," she said again.

He managed a smile. "Hey, I understand. Bad timing for us." They drew together in a sad embrace. Strangely, this moment didn't feel awkward. He still felt close to her, relaxed. They would be friends, at least. "It's Murphy's Law of gender relations," he joked. "The degree to which I like someone is directly proportionate to the likelihood of them being involved with somebody else. If I'd found you boring tonight, believe me, you'd be single."

Justine laughed, and he kissed her on the cheek. Then she turned her lips to him for one more kiss. It was lingering and uncertain. "God, Zach, I just wish —"

He cut her off. "Come on, let's find you a cab."

They walked toward Dupont Circle. It was bright and busy with the Saturday night barhopping crowd. They moved farther apart. Zach saw his and Justine's reflection in a store window. They looked great together — doomed but great.

He hailed her a cab, and she was gone.

His dream unfolded in a muted light of black and gray. He was searching in the desert night, going forward at a trot even as a crushing load weighed upon his back and fueled a bonfire of pain. He moved over hills and across plains, scouring the terrain ahead, peering into the shadows of ravines. The smell of burning oil hung heavy in the air. It was putrid and nauseating. In the distance there came the flickering gray light from a vast inferno over the horizon. The wind was not strong, but it moaned and whined, sounding lonely in the sky. He tried to call but could not. He continued on, traveling for what seemed to be hours, exhausted and lost. He stopped finally and grappled with the load that burdened him. It was unwieldy and strange, slippery yet clinging. Jabs of intense, twisting pain exploded through his lower back as he wriggled free, dropping the load to the sand behind him. He turned to find the bloodied form of Canver. He was still alive but slipping away, a gurgle coming from his mouth. Zach unbuttoned Canver's shirt as an air-raid siren began to wail. His fist came down on a chest slathered with blood. A streak of light rose from the ground in the distance, and flashes erupted high in the sky. He beat harder with his fist, splattering blood, until the thumping on the chest drowned out the siren. The thumping shifted to a whirring noise, grating and loud.

Zach awoke to the phone ringing. He reached for it, half asleep, and barely recognized Justine's greeting.

"I'm right in your neighborhood and I just wanted to apologize for last night. Can I drop by?"

A few minutes later, still disoriented, Zach opened the door to let Justine in.

Her cheeks were red from the cold air outside, and she wore a skirt and a button-down sweater. She stepped inside without saying a word and put her arms around Zach, kissing him hungrily. She pushed him gently against the wall next to the door, exploring his body with her hands.

"I thought this wasn't such a good idea," Zach said as her lips moved down his neck. He was wide awake now.

She looked at him intensely, placing her forefinger to her lips in the command for silence. She took his hand, leading him toward the bedroom. They stood next to the bed and kissed in the dim light. He kept his eyes open, taking in her beauty, amazed that she was in his arms. He moved a hand down to her stockinged thigh and then slowly upward, beneath the skirt. She moaned softly, and he pulled her closer, feeling her excitement. His free hand found the buttons of her sweater and then the softness of her skin.

In the late afternoon, as twilight arrived, they were still in bed. They talked, made love, and talked some more. He foraged in the kitchen and concocted a passable dinner to bring to her. She laughed when he filled the wineglasses with Budweiser. Later, he drifted in and out of sleep, curled around her body. His dreams that night were of his family, of life in the suburbs as a boy. He woke as the sun was coming up to find himself alone.

## 7

Admiral Forsten sounded harried when Zach called with his acceptance on Wednesday afternoon. "You're making the right choice, Lieutenant. This place is a hot seat, but you're going to love it here."

The next day Zach went to the Pentagon to begin the process of upgrading his clearance status to the level required for work at the JCS. The polished corridors in the building were charged with excitement as speculation swirled that the President would order a military strike of some kind in response to the killing of General Carl Anderson and seven other Americans by a shadowy group called Islamic Vengeance. Two aircraft carriers were said to be moving into position in the Arabian Sea and the Mediterranean. For the first time, Zach was sure of his decision.

Zach's classification status at the Fifth Special Forces Group, or SOF Mid-East, had cleared him to see any regional intelligence that was required for planning on a particular mission. During the Gulf War, when Zach had been part of a team sent into the deserts of western Iraq to reconnoiter on the ground for Scud missiles, he had been briefed on all sorts of sensitive matters relating to local intelligence sources in Iraq and Jordan. In his new job at the JCS, Zach needed clearance to receive a much wider array of classified information. He would be entering a world of intensive secrecy, seeing much of what Forsten saw, and this meant ascending to one of the highest clearance levels in the U.S. government.

He had been through the clearance routine several times before, but it was never as intensive as this time around. Following elaborately prescribed procedures, special DOD investigators began traveling to almost every town and city and military base where Zach had ever lived to find information on his background. The Army had done this when he had received his initial clearances in the Fifth, and Zach had hated the thought then of old friends being interviewed by the intense young investigators. Now DOD was casting a wider net and doing a more thorough job.

During his evenings, pacing in his Crystal City apartment with a cordless phone, Zach called the few old friends he was still in contact with to chat and warn them about the impending visit from Pentagon investigators. Most of them had received similar calls years earlier. They knew the routine. He gently suggested to them, as he had before, that they didn't have to tell the investigators everything, "only the good stuff." His clear hint was that a retelling of stories about his drug experimentation in college would not be helpful. Zach had admitted having used drugs in his past when he joined the Green Berets, but he had never revealed the full extent of it. Not nearly. Of all that lurked in his unconventional past, it was the drugs that embarrassed him most — and the lies he had told about them, his one great compromise with the truth.

Beyond the drugs, Zach didn't have anything to hide. The only real mystery for the investigators would be why he had joined the special forces in the first place. During Zach's second clearance interview, in a windowless gray room in the Pentagon, the two security officials in charge of his case had finally asked about this. Zach sensed a skepticism in their question, a skepticism he had often heard before. The implication seemed to be that only some massive personal failure or breakdown would propel a Harvard Ph.D. student into one of the most dangerous branches of the U.S. military.

"That was a fairly drastic move for you, I'd say," one of the investigators commented, raising a Styrofoam coffee cup to his lips.

"Highly unusual," added the other.

"There's no doubt about that," Zach agreed.

By now his story was well rehearsed. He had told it hundreds if not thousands of times to quizzical friends, to people he met in the military, to the press. Only the most personal parts he left out.

It had all begun in high school. Like his two older sisters, Zach was very much a child of his parents, at least on the surface. He had been prepped for high achievement in a manner that suggested that no other outcome could be imagined, much less accepted. Zach was a straight-A student through high school, and this achievement was so taken for granted that it had rarely won him praise at home. Indeed, there were few things that won him praise at home. Zach's father believed that children needed discipline and exhortation, not approval. He had immigrated to the United States from Lebanon as a young boy and harbored the belief that life wasn't supposed to be either easy or pleasant, especially for the young. His relentless striving had made him a nationally prominent professor of history at Princeton, and he was at the pinnacle of a highly self-absorbed existence around the time Zach entered high school. When he was home, he liked to unwind with a few drinks and some bullying of whomever was in sight, usually his wife. Zach's mother worked as a high-level administrator at the university. She was a strong woman — too strong, it turned out, for a husband with deep cultural roots in the Middle East. The fights between Zach's parents had raged for as long as he could remember. Zach was fifteen when his father took his first two-week vacation from the marriage, moving into a friend's house across town. It was around this time that Zach first heard his sisters using the word *divorce* in their anxious conversations.

By the time he was sixteen, Zach was in his own war with his father. The typical matters that divide teenagers from their parents were not at issue. Zach thought his father was a hard-ass, but that wasn't the main issue between them, as he saw it. Zach's alienation was more philosophical. He came to see his father as a creature of comfort and contradiction. For all his talk of sacrifice and hard work, the man didn't do anything real. He lectured around the country, spouting his liberal views about colonialism, cultural hegemony, and such crap, but he did nothing, besides writing checks for the cause of the month, to change anything. He never once acknowledged that there was anything wrong in the way he lived. He had taught Zach as a child to be honest, but he himself was afraid of the truth.

Zach's parents' marriage had more or less disintegrated by the time he entered his senior year. His father rented an apartment in town and spent most of his time there, living at the house only during truces with Mrs. Turzin that could last anywhere from two days to two weeks. Meanwhile, Zach's own transformation was continuing. A framed photo of Ronald Reagan went up above the desk in his room. *Soldier of Fortune* began arriving once a month. The *National Review* followed. During their visits home, first one older sister and then the other told him he had become a jerk.

The college application process started up in the fall of senior year and steamed forward with little thought on Zach's part. It was one of the rare matters that his parents could work on together, and they took charge. They fumed at Zach for allowing his grades to plummet just as he was entering the final dash in high school. They had to prod him to visit colleges and take the process seriously. Zach sensed a giant cage taking shape around him; ivy covered the bars. His doubts about the whole enterprise had more or less crystallized by the time Cornell emerged as the winner in April. Still, forms were signed, a deposit was sent. To his parents, the deal seemed sealed; to Zach, the noose was tightening. It was around this same time that his parents began divorce proceedings. The house was put up for sale. There were new screaming matches between his parents as the divorce got ugly. Questions were raised about the financing of Zach's education.

The Marines were the sharpest contrast to all Zach sought to escape and so they had been a natural choice. He enlisted secretly two weeks after graduation and slipped away before dawn on a July morning. He left a note on the refrigerator that explained little. It gave the address at Parris Island.

"How'd you take to the Corps?" one of the investigators asked. Copies of Zach's performance reports were no doubt in the thick folder that the men passed back and forth. He refreshed their memories anyway.

The first few weeks had been hell. The heat itself was nearly fatal, and some of the long runs in combat boots had constituted literal torture. But Zach had been in better shape than many of the recruits, and soon his body could take any abuse the drill instructors threw at it. Pain turned to invigoration. His parents had gone ballistic, predictably. Zach wasn't fazed. He never doubted that he had made the right choice. The guns, the uniforms, the exercises in southern woods so dense they were almost like jungle — it all was so real and intense. There was something appealingly primitive about stalking other men in the bush. And even though it was only training, just the abstract idea of death in combat made him feel a thousand times more alive than he had ever been before. He took well, also, to hierarchy. The chain of command appealed to his intense respect for the truth. People didn't need to spew bullshit to get things done. They gave orders. Princeton seemed a million miles away.

A year tumbled past. Zach mastered heavy machine guns, mortars, and antitank weapons. He learned how to lay mines and how to clear them. He took an intensive course in demolition and another in sniping as he searched for his natural strength. His superiors, recognizing his high intelligence, pushed him toward computers and the electronic end of war. These things bored him, but languages and special operations did not, and soon he was immersed in the study of Arabic, which he had often heard his father speaking to relatives when he was younger. He saw no action during this time, but there was the promise of action in the future. Of all the services, it was the Marines who saw combat the most.

His back injury had been a huge shock, a startling introduction to disability of any kind. The injury happened during a routine exercise, and he was in the grip of intense pain for weeks. Corps doctors couldn't do anything for him. There was no point in going on, he was told. Too many limitations, too much of a liability in the field, even if the injury did heal. Zach felt humiliated. There was no question in his mind that he was a failure. The day of his honorable discharge was the saddest in his life.

"So you went to Cornell after all?" one of the investigators asked.

"Yes, sir, that's correct." Was there really confusion on this point?

He had ended up at Cornell because it was easy, the language programs were good, and other choices were scarce. He would forge a career in the analytical side of the national security business, he told himself. The Middle East fascinated him. He may have disliked his father, but he was drawn to that side of his ethnic heritage. He would focus here and master Arabic and other languages. He would then secure a higher degree and work at the Pentagon or in the intelligence world. His parents were overjoyed at developments, and this reaction recharged a bitterness that had begun to fade in the Marines.

College had been a strange and disorienting experience. He was out of sync with the other freshmen, who struck him as a decade younger and a thousand times more naive. Things just never clicked at Cornell. It was Zach's disconnection and loneliness that led him, if only for a short time, into the pot and coke crowd. This part of the story he left out for the investigators, as he had during his first round of clearances. His drug friends weren't hippies or punks or anything like that. Most were returning students, a bit older like himself, contemptuous of starry-eyed kids and Mickey Mouse introductory courses. He met them through intramural softball. They drank hard, and then, later, the other stuff would come out. Zach went along — at first, anyway. Pot made him paranoid; the coke was okay but too expensive. There was also a nagging sense that he was doing the wrong thing. He thought of the cartels and the mayhem they spread. He came clean after just a few months.

The recovery of his back was another factor that moved him away from drugs. When he got his body back he wanted to treat it well. The injury disappeared in the middle of his first year at Cornell, leaving as mysteriously as it had come. He began cross-country skiing, tentatively at first and then with powerful intensity. He returned to martial arts, advancing steadily in tae kwon do. He became a regular at the weight room, and soon his muscles returned, rippling and hard. In time there was nothing he couldn't do. He called one of his former superiors in the Marines with the good news. He was fixed. They could have him back.

No, that wouldn't work, he was told. It turned out that elaborate regulations governed this area. It was rare that someone returned after discharge with a disability. He could try: certainly he could do that. But more time needed to pass, and then there would be lengthy exams. Zach should stay at school in any case, he was told. He had been a great Marine; outstanding, in fact. But he could make a greater contribution as a language specialist.

"They wouldn't take you back, huh?"

"No way," Zach answered. His disappointment had been bitter then. But his superior had been right, he saw later. And so he plowed through courses in languages, the Middle East, and national security policy. He mastered Arabic and began Farsi and Kurdish. He traveled to the region twice and did a summer internship at the Center for International and Strategic Studies in Washington. He worked like a demon and finished Cornell in three years. Harvard's Ph.D.

program in Near East Studies seemed like a logical next step, and he took no time off after college.

"So what went wrong at Harvard?" one of the investigators asked. Zach knew that they knew the answer to that question already; he had told the story in earlier clearance interviews, and they had probably talked with people from his program.

"It was a combination of things," he explained for the thousandth time in the last six years.

Harvard was famous as a training ground for policy experts, but it was also a world of elaborate hoops that nonpersons known as graduate students had to pass through. Zach's impatience had begun as soon as he arrived. Partly it came from him; he was losing momentum after too many years in school. Partly it was the absurdity of advanced scholarship. Academia was the home of those who sought a refuge from reality, he decided. The example of his father bothered him. Zach worried that he too could become affected with the smug superiority of someone who had never set foot in the real world but purported to understand its most complex aspects. On his rare trips home during holidays, his father would try to bond with him. They were practically in the same line of work now. Wasn't that something? The idea sickened Zach. After nearly two years he couldn't stand Harvard any longer. The workload was so great that he didn't even have time to work out or practice martial arts. He was drowning.

Zach would almost always be interrupted around this time in his tale to be asked, often in the sarcastic manner that the Pentagon investigators now used, whether joining the special forces was perhaps a bit of an overreaction to his unhappiness in academia.

It was at this point that he would have to mention Jill. She was a big part of why he had left. They had met at a language program in Vermont during the summer between Zach's second and third years in graduate school. Zach was studying Kurdish, and Jill was doing Arabic. Both, it turned out, were grad students at Harvard, although Jill was in the comparative literature department. The big rule in the summer program was that nobody could speak English during the entire six-week stay. What the rule neglected to cover, however, was speaking in another language that one had previously mastered. Using this loophole, Zach had begun conversing with Jill in Arabic, which he had learned at Cornell. Somehow the game had washed away his usual shyness. By the end of the program they were lovers.

Jill was wild and irreverent, provocative in her conversation and a firestorm in bed. She was drawn to Zach because he came from another world and she was intrigued. He found her the most exciting woman he had ever met, not that there had been many. They remained lovers when they returned to Cambridge, moving in together in the fall. A life at Harvard that had been unbearably lonely during Zach's second year became enrapturing during his third.

"Why did she leave you?" one of the investigators asked.

Zach was annoyed by the question. If the man knew that she had left him, rather than vice versa, he probably already knew what the reason was. And Zach wasn't sure that that was any of the Pentagon's business. But he wanted to be cooperative, so he told the story again. What was the difference? Everybody at Harvard knew. All his friends knew. DOD had probably even gotten the story from Jill herself.

"She fell in love with a junior prof in the English department," Zach said tersely. And there was really not much more to tell. There had been a horrible scene when he first found out about the affair, and another scene when he had confronted the guy. Within months she and the English professor had announced their engagement. Cambridge became intolerable.

The timing of the special forces recruiters could not have been better. A Major Garrety had called Zach out of the blue in the spring of 1989 and asked to set up a meeting in

Cambridge. Zach remembered the call distinctly. It came early in the morning as he lay in bed half asleep, half awake, and totally depressed. He thought he would let the machine get it, but after a few rings he remembered that Jill had taken the machine with her. So he took the call, standing in his underwear on the cold living-room floor.

Garrety's voice had been gravelly, his accent Southern. He was calling from Bragg — Fort Bragg, that was. He wanted to meet with Zach, although he was vague about his agenda. Zach had heard that the Pentagon and various intelligence agencies kept databases that listed all American college and graduate students with special language skills. He knew a few people at Cornell who had parlayed their Arabic or Russian into jobs at the CIA and National Security Agency. He suspected that Garrety was going to tempt him with an intelligence job or maybe even a teaching job. Before going into the meeting, Zach told himself that he would definitely reject any kind of intelligence job. He didn't want to sit in a dark room all day with earphones on, translating phone calls by Syrian or Iranian officials that the NSA had picked up. But he might consider teaching, if the offer was lucrative. It would be one way to get out of Cambridge.

The meeting with Garrety was Zach's favorite part of the story. The major had showed up at a Harvard Square restaurant in his uniform and beret. He was tall and thin with a craggy face; the other patrons stared. In this town Garrety might as well have been a visitor from another planet.

Zach had honed this story for years, but always he felt incapable of communicating his degree of amazement when Garrety had asked him to consider joining the Army special forces. And he was no better at it this time, sitting in the drab room at the Pentagon.

"I'm surprised they ever approached you in the first place, Lieutenant," said one of the investigators. Zach was used to that reaction among military people. Many resented him as an interloper.

One of the first things Garrety had explained was that it was almost unheard of for the special forces to recruit from outside the active armed services. "Our people usually have three to five years of active duty before we will even consider them," Garrety had said. "But frankly we're desperate these days." Garrety went on to explain that the Army was expanding the number of its SOF Middle East teams. At the same time, it was under congressional pressures to upgrade language skills in all of the special forces. Each team, or A-Detachment, consisted of twelve men with various specialties. In theory, at least one member of the team was supposed to be fluent in the language or languages of its theater of operations, and others were supposed to have a working knowledge. Ideally, members could also physically pass as natives of the region. SOF teams were supposed to be able to blend in with local populations, thereby enhancing their ability to mount missions in enemy territory.

"Expanding the SouthCom teams in the eighties was a snap," Garrety had said, referring to the U.S. Southern Command, which was responsible for Latin America. "Fifteen percent of our troops are Latino to begin with, barrio kids some of them, and many speak Spanish pretty well. But expanding the Fifth Special Forces Group — they handle the Mideast — now that has been a real challenge."

Garrety had explained that the number of U.S. servicemen who spoke Arabic was minuscule, as was the number who spoke Farsi or Kurdish. In any case, most of these people had been inappropriate for the special forces for one reason or another. The decision was made to reach outside the active service military. Zach's name had come up during a computer search that matched language skills with previous military training. The shortness of his stay in the Marines was not encouraging, but the reviews he had received there were outstanding, Garrety noted. The major had checked into Zach's back problems and heard about the recovery. With Arabic and Farsi under his belt, Zach was a hot property.

"We think you're our man," Garrety had concluded.

Zach had been astounded by the overture. This was the sort of idiocy that resulted when bureaucracies relied on computers to reach conclusions for them, he thought. Didn't Garrety realize that he was talking to an out-of-shape graduate student whose last combat training was now more than six years in the past? Couldn't he see that Zach had become a sack of flab from years in seminars and the library? He would die in the special forces.

The whole idea was far-fetched, Zach had argued, even as he privately began to grow excited. Garrety must have sensed that Zach was biting, for he pulled out all the stops. Zach, of course, would have to go through the seventeen-week training program at Bragg, but he wouldn't have to be put through the standard qualification, or Q course. His entry was assured. And Garrety had sought to whet Zach's appetite with geopolitical observations. Things were heating up in the world as the Cold War waned, he said. They were entering an era of brushfire wars and local aggression. Resource competition was growing, arms were proliferating, ethnic conflict was on the rise. The gradual exhaustion of non–Persian Gulf oil reserves meant that the Middle East would continue to increase in importance during the 1990s. Zach would see action, he could count on it.

Zach had been noncommittal with Garrety. He said he would think about the offer. He said he was flattered. Later, alone in his apartment with memories of Jill scattered everywhere, the idea grew on him. He couldn't sleep the night after Garrety's visit.

"What made you take the plunge?" one of the investigators asked.

Zach pondered the question. Even though he had heard it so many times before, he was not sure that he really knew the answer. "I desperately wanted something real," he finally said.

"Well, the Green Berets are about as real as it gets." Both investigators laughed.

"But it was also impulsive," Zach added. Like joining the Marines had been. He remembered how the idea had rapidly taken over his mind. He began running again for the first time in months. Over the next few days, after dinner, he would head out into the cool evening and run along the Charles River. He imagined the fat coming off and his body turning hard and lean. He dreamed of escape.

He hadn't discussed the idea with anybody. He had mellowed toward his parents, and right before he left he sent each of them a letter explaining his move back into the military. Two weeks after Garrety's visit, his belongings sold, he was in North Carolina.

"That must have been quite a shock," one of the investigators said.

"They put people through hell at Bragg," said the other.

This was true. But Zach had been through hell before and now, after the atrophy of recent years, he welcomed another trip. The training course took place at Camp Mackall, an outpost within Fort Bragg's complex of two hundred square miles. The first thing Zach saw when he clambored out of a Humvee at Mackall in late May was a twenty-foot sign on a corrugated building. It said SURVIVAL. Next to each giant letter was a maxim: Size up the situation; Undue haste makes waste; Remember where you are; Vanquish fear and panic; Improvise; Value living; Act like natives; Learn basic skills.

The training course began on June 14, 1989, and Zach would remember this date as the most important of his life. The Green Berets, Zach quickly saw, made the Marines look like the raw recruits of a peasant army. These were sophisticated soldiers, masters of blending the art and science of war. Each A-Detachment had an expert in heavy and light arms who was able to fire and strip eighty foreign weapons, an engineer and assistant trained in the construction of sabotage devices, a medical expert with the skills to set up a small field hospital, a communications expert who could handle a variety of secure devices, and a sniper trained to kill from up to a kilometer away. When Zach began his course, special forces was just beginning a program to teach several members of each A-Detachment how to fly helicopters. Zach made a note to volunteer for this training. He had always wanted to fly.

Zach met Jared Canver on the first day of training. Eventually they would be placed in the same A-Detachment, remaining together virtually without interruption until the night at Haisa. Canver was from a lower-middle-class family in Cleveland. He had joined the military after high school because there were not many other options. But it hadn't beaten him down. He was a quiet man, intense and cerebral. He worked hard on his Arabic and was the only other member of Zach's A-Detachment who could speak it in full sentences. They became fast friends. Canver shared with Zach an impatience with anything but the truth, and they ridiculed the petty deceits of military life in their common foreign tongue.

The seventeen weeks of training passed rapidly. Zach learned every means of descent imaginable, from parachuting night or day to rappelling from buildings, helicopters, and cliffs. He learned to navigate through tractless woods and how to survive off the land in desert, jungle, and Arctic terrain. He learned how to handle the Israeli Uzi and the French Mat-49, the British LAW and the Russian RPM-7, the TOW and the Stinger. He learned about mines designed to stop tanks and mines made to maim but not kill. He learned the subtleties of the lightning raid and the midnight ambush. He learned the weak points of bridges and the potential of plastic explosives. He was taught how to kidnap and how to assassinate, and the art of "coercive questioning" was covered in an oblique manner. He learned how to kill a man in silence, not one way but many.

In the tenth week he was dropped alone by parachute into the middle of North Carolina's Uwharrie National Forest and traveled over seventeen miles while being hunted by dogs and aggressor teams from the Eighty-second Airborne Division. They didn't catch him. By the twelfth week the course was focusing heavily on SERE — Survival, Evasion, Resistance, and Escape. This covered more than emerging alive from deep in enemy territory or from the cages of a prison camp. It also tested the ability to resist interrogation, an ordeal effectively simulated through intense mental abuse.

Zach thrived at every stage of the course. Mackall was the scene of his resurrection. He could hear the wood splinter as the casket in which he had lain was pried open. At the end of seventeen weeks he was stronger than he had ever been. Four months of specialized desert training in the Mojave Desert followed his stay at Bragg. His first mission to the Middle East, a foray into Libyan-held northern Chad, came not long afterward.

He was alive again.

★ **8** ★

Riley flicked on the lights and looked around the office. So this was where Forsten's hero boy was getting shrunk. He had expected a couch. Didn't pussies lie on couches when they babbled on about how much they wanted to screw their mothers? Riley saw only a desk and several comfortable chairs. He examined the degrees arrayed in black frames on the wall. Dr. Jessica Klein. What a scam, he thought. You knew things were going downhill when some bitch could get on the Army payroll to do hand-holding sessions with guys whose friends got wasted. People got wasted; that's the way it was and always would be. Discharge the crybabies, fire the shrinks. That would be Riley's policy.

The lock on the filing cabinet was a cinch, easier than the door. Riley browsed through Turzin's file before taking a hand-held scanner out of his knapsack and scanning all its contents. He noted the regular times of Zach's appointments. Once the bug was in, he didn't want to be listening to a minute more of this crap than was necessary.

Riley put away the scanner and pulled out a small box. He removed some tweezers and a small tube of epoxy glue. With the tweezers he picked a tiny transmitter out of a ziplock bag and carefully applied some epoxy to it. Lying on his back, he placed the transmitter on the underside of the desk and held it in place while the glue dried. Riley had already found an unused storage closet one floor up in which to place a small receiver powerful enough to relay the signals from the transmitter back to a larger receiver in his house outside McLean. If Turzin had something important to say, he'd be sharing it with the class.

When Zach started the clearance process, he had been told to expect a two- to four-week wait. It turned out to be only four days. "I've never seen something this high go through so fast," an officer in the security clearance division told him on the phone, delivering the news of his approval.

Two days before his first full workday, Zach went to the Pentagon for an exhaustive briefing with another Forsten special assistant, Lieutenant Stan Duncan. Intense and muscular, Duncan was the most extreme Forstenite that Zach had yet met. He had a maxim for everything and a philosophy of discipline and loyalty that tied them all together. Zach noticed immediately that Duncan talked like his boss, with tough, punchy sentences.

"Twelve-hour working days are the norm, longer during a crisis," Duncan said. "And don't be in the office later than 0630." Forsten's shop tried to get the upper hand each and every day, Duncan said. Reynolds was almost never in the office until 0730. "The chairman needs his beauty sleep to keep that double chin at bay. We're happy to let him have it."

Forsten was particularly vigilant about starting off the day well informed, Duncan stressed. He expected his aides to do the same. "The admiral thinks — or rather knows — that superior knowledge is the key to success in this town. So whatever you do, make sure you've read both the intelligence and the Early Bird before you see him." Duncan explained that the Early Bird was a compilation from newspapers across the country of all the day's articles on national security policy.

"Believe me, the Early Bird is as important as coffee in this business. You can't function without it."

Duncan also explained the Joint Staff. "There are sixteen hundred members of the Joint Staff. It handles everything under the sun. Originally it was created to serve the analytical needs of all four chiefs, but under the 1986 Goldwater-Nichols Reforms the Joint Staff was made to report only to the chairman of the JCS. The idea was to create more firepower at the top to fight interservice rivalry. Now, after the latest round of reforms, the Joint Staff is answerable to the vice chairman too." Duncan shoved an organizational chart at Zach and kept talking. "Of course, it's Admiral Forsten who really runs the Joint Staff. Our people are all over the place in the different directorates. Reynolds barely knows what the directorates do. We try to keep it that way." Duncan let out a derisive laugh. "You've joined the winning team, Lieutenant."

Zach asked about the civilian policymakers at the Pentagon and Duncan waved his hands dismissively. "Takes those guys six months just to find the men's room. Takes them another six months to find their dicks. By the time they've learned how to piss they're back at Harvard. It's the uniforms who run the show here, Lieutenant."

Duncan interrogated Zach about his personal life. "Got a woman in the picture?"

Zach thought for a moment about Justine. They had seen each other a second time, devouring each other at his apartment. He lied, saying that there wasn't much to tell. Duncan nodded with approval. "Good. The admiral likes his aides to be single. If you screw less you'll work more. Do you drink?"

"A couple beers after work sometimes."

"Cut down; it dulls your edge. You work out?"

"Pretty hard."

"Keep it up. The admiral doesn't like flab in his shop." Duncan gestured in the direction of Reynolds's office with a sneer. "There's too much elsewhere in the building. Where are you living?"

"Crystal City."

"Good choice. Safest place in the area. Crime is a fact of life in this city, Lieutenant. Highest murder rate in the nation. We lost one of our own a few weeks back. A Gulf War veteran, no less."

"Christ, what happened?" Zach asked.

"A captain by the name of Craig Hansen. He worked for the admiral on intelligence and lived in Alexandria. Not a bad neighborhood, even. Went out for a run one night and never came back. They found him with two bullets in his head. Left a widow and a kid. Sad story, but not an uncommon one these days. Watch your ass."

As they had finished up the briefing, Duncan's tone softened. "By the way, Lieutenant, I know from reading your file about your friendship with Sergeant Canver and that you had a rough time after Haisa. I understand you've been seeing Dr. Klein over at the VA Annex in McLean."

"That's correct," Zach said, tensing up. Who else got to read that goddamn file?

"I just want you to know that the admiral is aware that you're in that process and he supports this kind of thing. We all know guys who did counseling after Desert Storm. It's common these days, and usually it produces some good results."

The alarm in Zach's bedroom began beeping at 5:20 A.M. He woke up in the shower and was in his uniform by 5:50. By 6:15 he was waiting in the nearly deserted Crystal City metro stop. The Pentagon was only two stops away. At 6:22 he flipped his new ID at an armed guard at the entrance to the building from the metro. At 6:24 he passed another checkpoint and flashed his ID plus a special plastic yellow badge to enter the JCS area on the second floor of the E Ring. At 6:25 Zach walked into Forsten's suite. The secretaries were not there yet, but he could see that the door to Forsten's spacious office was partly open and that the lights were on. He peeked inside and saw the admiral on the phone, nodding his head. Forsten looked up and put his hand over the receiver. "Welcome aboard, Lieutenant. I'll be with you in a moment."

Zach stood outside Forsten's office, looking around the suite. Aides and secretaries had begun to arrive at exactly 6:30. After a few minutes, Forsten came out and pumped his hand. "It's great to have you here, Lieutenant. Let me take a few minutes to show you around. You'll be spending more time around here than you do at home. You'll come to love it, believe me."

The first stop was the JCS's famed meeting room, "the Tank." This bug-proof chamber was the place where the JCS held their collective deliberations. The name suggested a sealed vault lodged deep underground. In fact it was just a medium-size conference room on the second floor near the river entrance, and Zach was surprised by its simple decor. A large table sat in the center of the room, and chairs lined the walls. "I've seen some real bloodbaths in this room, believe me," Forsten said, sitting in the seat at the head of the table that was reserved for Chairman Reynolds. "If Powell had had his way he would have barred me from this place." Forsten laughed. "He and I never saw eye-to-eye on the use-of-force issue, not at all. Powell's basic position was don't intervene unless the goddamn operation is handed to you on a silver platter. Reynolds is the same way. Guys like that want our satellites to pick up a white flag ready to be run up before they'll move their asses. They want guarantees: KIAs under twenty-five, no POWs, minimal collateral damage, and the whole thing wrapped up in forty-eight hours. Ridiculous, impossible stuff. Jerkoffs like Powell and Reynolds come down hard on me because I tell them that war doesn't work that way. There aren't any guarantees. People get hurt, more than you want or can predict. Hell, they knew that might happen when they volunteered. I certainly did; so did you. Soldiering is a dangerous business. End of story. The brass in this building have forgotten how to fight real wars. My job here is to remind them how it's done. And your job, Lieutenant, is help me remind them."

"Yes, sir," Zach said, transfixed by the monologue. Damn, he was glad he worked for someone who believed in action.

"Presidents are even worse," Forsten continued, slapping the table. "Half the time they can't get it up, the other half they don't know whether it's okay to screw. They'll listen to their pollsters, they'll listen to their wives — hell, they'll listen to their goddamn teenage daughters before they'll listen to a military officer with any guts. Before they pull the trigger they want to know whether the people will love them more, whether their numbers will go up and by how many points. Or maybe they want to know whether it jibes with the freaking Bible. Christ. And when they're done listening, they're ready for second-guessing — noodling with Congress, lining up the UN, tangling with the allies, floating trial balloons in the press. You name it. We need to hold one hand and shape the other into a fist to help them do the right thing when we're getting crapped on overseas. But if the people in this building can't do that — if flacks like Reynolds are pissing in their pants all the time — who will? Tell me that, Lieutenant."

"I agree with you, sir," Zach said, not sure whether he was giving the right answer or whether one was expected in the first place.

Forsten was on his feet. "Let me show you the War Room." He led Zach out of the Tank and down a hall. They came to a security checkpoint manned by an armed officer. Forsten nodded and flashed a laminated badge. He passed it over to Zach.

"You'll need one of these to get into this place when you're not with me."

Zach looked at the purple badge and grinned as he passed

it back. He needed one ID to get into the Pentagon, another one to get into the JCS area, and now a third to get into the War Room. Was there one for the men's room too?

Forsten led the way through a set of doors into a large, dimly lit room where military personnel sat at various computer clusters. At the front of the room were six large screens on the walls, all blank. Below them was a long lacquered conference table with fourteen swivel chairs and a multiline phone at each seat. A podium with the DOD seal and an American flag stood off to the left of the table. The floor was a polished gray tile that glistened in the low light. An armed security guard stood next to the inside entrance to the room.

Zach looked around. There was a sleekness and efficiency to the place that could be confused for barrenness. The aroma of sheer power was not as pungent here as he had expected. However, Zach could see nervous deference in the salutes of the men and women on duty. The room may not have oozed power, but its master did.

Forsten's eyes swept the room, and he gestured broadly. "This can be an exhilarating place to be, but it can also be damn depressing. We had a crisis team assembled in here within one hour of receiving news of the Anderson assassination. We had a wing of F-117s in Great Britain in twelve hours. We put Delta Force and SEAL teams at bases in Sicily in fourteen hours. We moved two carrier battle groups into the CENTCOM theater in eighteen hours. If the President had given the order, we would have been ready to strike within twenty-four hours." Forsten's lips curled into a sneer. "Problem is, no order ever came."

Zach began to ask Forsten about the incident, but the admiral waved his hand. "Later. Let's finish the walk-through." He led Zach over to a cluster of terminals. "Over here is where we get information on the status and readiness of our forces around the world. It's updated constantly, giving the exact positions of every single unit in every command. If you want to know what the status is with a fighter wing in Japan or a carrier battle group in the Med, you don't have to talk to fifteen different action officers at the commands, you just come here."

Forsten pointed upward. "During a crisis the screens on the wall are mostly used to display material from these terminals, so everybody in the room knows where everything is and can track the movement of our forces without having to pester the terminal operators."

The admiral stepped over to a last set of terminals. "This cluster used to be a lot more important, but we downsized this part of the War Room during a recent redesign. This is where the readiness and positions of our nuclear forces and strategic defenses are displayed. Of course, most of the heavy stuff is out at NORAD. But we got everything we need here, don't we Captain Williams?" Forsten nodded to the one serviceman who sat at the cluster.

"Yes, sir. Almost as good as being at NORAD itself. But things are definitely slow these days. Frankly, the most action around these machines lately has been from the Capitol Defense System alerts."

"I've never heard of a Capitol Defense System," Zach said.

"Most people haven't," replied Williams. "It's nothing elaborate. The CDS includes three separate SAM sites in the Washington area. There is also at least one fighter overhead in the vicinity at any given time. The system gets put on alert once in a while, which is why it generates more action than a lot of other stuff."

Zach walked with Forsten back to his office. "That Capitol Defense System is fascinating stuff, sir."

"Welcome to the Pentagon, Lieutenant," Forsten said. "You'll learn something new here every day."

## ★ 10 ★

"Are you ready to talk about your parents again, Zach?"

"If you want. But I still don't see what they have to do with anything."

"You had some major issues with them. Those are worth exploring as we try to understand why you blame yourself for what happened outside Haisa."

"I blame myself because I screwed up. It's pretty simple, really."

"Not necessarily. When we discussed how you blamed yourself for your back injury in the Marines, you agreed that it hadn't been your fault, that you had been too harsh on yourself."

"That was different."

"Is it really? That's the question we need to explore. There could be a pattern here related to your issues with your parents."

"Everybody has issues with their parents. It's part of growing up. I don't see my issues as anything particularly special. We were different, especially my father and I. We had different political views, and I could never take seriously what he did, however many honorary degrees he got. Also, I just never liked him as a person. He's not very likeable. Kind of an asshole, actually. We didn't get along."

"Did you stop getting along before or after the divorce?"

"It was around that time. I can't remember."

"Try."

"It's hazy, you know. Things were getting bad before the divorce; they got worse once it was in full swing. Whatever. The point is that I needed to find my own way, become my own person. I didn't reject them exactly, not my mother, anyway. I rejected their world and what they stood for. They were armchair liberals. I wanted to do something real."

"Has it ever occurred to you that you were punishing them?"

"Punishing them? What do you mean by that?"

"That you were angry at them for divorcing and you wanted to get back at them."

"How would I punish them? By doing what?"

"By joining the Marines. By taking a step that you knew was about the worst thing they could imagine one of their children doing."

"I really don't think so. That's not where I was at."

"That may be how you see it now. But it's not uncommon, you know. Children of divorced parents, even adult children, will often sabotage their lives to show their parents that the divorce is having negative consequences, that they should regret letting their marriage fail, that maybe they should try again."

"I wasn't thinking anything like that. And I don't consider joining the military to be a sabotage of anybody's life, by the way. I wanted a reality check, and the Marines were it."

"Were you angry at your parents?"

"Sure, I was angry. No question. As I say, my father's not such a great guy. He was and is a hard-ass. He wants everything his way. And he's mean when he's drunk, which was often back then. My mother wouldn't take his crap. When he escalated, she upped the ante. They both let things go down the drain."

"How did you express your anger at them?"

"I guess I told my dad off once or twice; I can't really remember. I tried to avoid the house, basically."

"So there was a great deal of anger toward them that you didn't get out."

"Sure, I suppose."

"And where do you think it all went?"

"Bayonet practice on Parris Island, I guess. Who knows? Why does it matter?"

During his first few days at the Pentagon, Zach learned his way around the building and came to understand what was expected of him. Intelligence was the main focus of his job, and he saw immediately that his assignment was unusual. The Defense Intelligence Agency functioned as a semi-autonomous directorate of the Joint Staff. One of its many tasks was to prepare large briefing binders for the chairman and vice chairman. In going over Zach's responsibilities, Forsten expressed displeasure with the binders in his usual way. "The binders? If it's on paper, it's history, not intelligence," he scoffed. "The binders are something we shove in Reynold's face to keep him from drooling on his desk. I need better than that, Lieutenant. Believe me, what doesn't get into the binders is often more important than what does get in. And what you don't know in this building can hurt you."

Zach's assignment was to cultivate contacts at the intelligence agencies and gather information that hadn't yet made it into the binders or never would. Zach was to focus on the Middle East and northern Africa. "Call it a personal early warning system," Forsten said. "Reynolds may not mind flying blind like some kind of pig bat, but if something's going to hit me, I like to know when and how hard."

Zach was to pay particular attention to intelligence regarding terrorist groups in the Middle East. And Stan Duncan made a point that Forsten had omitted: Zach shouldn't put anything on paper and he should save his conclusions for face time with Forsten. Duncan also warned Zach about sharing what was said at his meetings with the vice chairman. "We don't tolerate back-briefing in this shop. So if somebody does try to break your china bowl, you give them a tap dance, understand? Jake in, Lieutenant, we're in a war."

Zach's other main responsibility was to serve as a foot soldier in the endless budgetary battles. In this case, the enemy was not just Reynolds but also the Office of the Secretary of Defense. "Believe me, without the admiral here, Reynolds and OSD would be plucking the services bare," Duncan explained. "That's what the President wants." Cuts had been a way of life at the Pentagon since the end of the Cold War, but now the White House was making them deeper and deeper. Resistance was growing, and the vice chairman was at the center of it. "Publicly, Reynolds and the SECDEF call the rift in the building a healthy dialogue," Duncan said. "Bullshit. They'd cut out our tongues if they could. Watch your back, Lieutenant."

To get acquainted with the operations at the Joint Staff, Zach arranged long individual briefings with officers in the different directorates. Most turned out to be Forsten loyalists who had worked for him for years. They welcomed Zach on board and impressed upon him how lucky he was to be at the admiral's side. Zach did not need reminding. Already, as he became known around the building as Forsten's new man, he could see the deference others paid him. He was someone to know, to cultivate, to flatter. The salute of subordinates had a snap Zach had never seen before. Forsten's empire stretched to every part of the Pentagon and out into the field. With a place near the throne, Zach tasted power, and it had a succulence that pleased him.

Most of Zach's briefings in the directorates dealt with intelligence collection and upcoming budgetary battles. But he also learned about what he decided was one of the most interesting parts of the Joint Staff's work: contingency planning.

"Admiral Forsten loves this stuff," Zach was told by Rear Admiral Sam Walling, who headed the Strategic Plans and Policy Directorate, or J-5. Walling looked fifty, maybe fifty-five. The first thing Zach noticed were the scars: crimson blotches that covered the backs of both hands and crept up his neck from the collar. Burns, without question. They sat in an office next to a large windowless room filled with filing cabinets, computers, and bustling aides. "War is our business, the admiral likes to say, and damn, does he push us hard." Walling clucked his tongue. "He's been like that as long as I've known him, from our days in the delta."

Zach listened spellbound as Walling talked about the world of contingency planning. The work ranged from the inevitable to the fantastical. "We have plans for fighting maybe seventy percent of the countries in the world," Walling said. "Including quite a few friends." Walling described plans to blockade Japan and take out Israel's nuclear forces, plans to seize Saudi oil and to topple a hostile Mexican government, plans to sink France's ballistic-missile-carrying submarines and to fight a naval war with India.

"You guys have plans to attack ourselves?" Zach asked.

Walling chuckled. "Not yet. In any case, the stuff I'm telling you about is in the files, but a lot of it is dated. The real work around here is on contingencies that might actually happen. That's what keeps this office jumping. You can tell your boss, by the way, to stop pushing on MOCKINGBIRD. We're working night and day on it as things are. We can't go any faster."

"What's MOCKINGBIRD?" Zach asked.

"You don't know?" Walling hesitated, as if trying to remember Zach's clearance level.

"No, sir. I've only been with the admiral for a bit over a week."

"Right. Of course, Lieutenant. So let me tell you about MOCKINGBIRD." Walling led Zach into a small briefing room next to his office and walked over to a combination file cabinet, pulling open the second drawer down. He withdrew a thick binder labeled TOP SECRET.

He gestured Zach over to a table next to a paneled wall. He set down the binder and then took from his desk drawer what looked like a telephone calling card and inserted it into a box on the wall to the right of the table. A section of the paneling directly above the table rose slowly up.

"This is the admiral's latest baby. It's the highest priority we have here right now, especially after the attack in Oman. He's insisting the details be wrapped up by mid-January at the latest. We've been breaking our balls on this."

The raised panel revealed large maps of Libya, Iran, and the Sudan. The first two were sprinkled with red, green, yellow, white, black, and blue pins. Sudan lacked any red or green ones. Zach studied the maps closely, wondering what he was looking at.

"It's El Dorado Canyon times one hundred," Walling said with pride.

"El Dorado Canyon, sir?"

"That was the April 1986 raid on Libya to punish Qaddafi for the German disco bombing."

"Oh, right, of course." Zach remembered. He had been a senior at Cornell when waves of F-111 bombers and carrier-based aircraft had pulverized targets in Tripoli.

"In essence, MOCKINGBIRD is a contingency plan for hitting all three of these countries simultaneously in retaliation for their next joint act of terrorism. Intelligence is not my job, but everybody knows about the evidence of cooperation between these three in the recent wave of terrorism. DIA has been calling it the TKT Pact — Tripoli, Khartoum, and Tehran. There was evidence that the Pact cooperated on the Eiffel Tower bombing last year. We should have hit them that time, but the White House fudged, of course, saying the evidence wasn't good enough. Same thing happened after the Anderson assassination. Nothing conclusive, they said. What a load of crap.

"In any case," continued Walling, "Admiral Forsten wants to be ready next time around to hit the entire Pact at once. And he wants to hit it hard."

Zach looked down at the corners of the maps, in search of a key. "What do the different colors of the pins mean?"

"Red signifies any kind of nuclear facility. Green is for chemical or biological weapons. Blue is for intelligence facilities or terrorist training sites. White are ballistic missile sites. Yellow are air bases. Black are tank and armored vehicle depots."

"MOCKINGBIRD is one hell of a retaliatory raid, sir," Zach said. "This is more like the air attacks during the first days of Desert Storm than the raid on Libya."

"That's another way to look at it, Lieutenant."

"This would take thousands and thousands of sorties."

"Six thousand five hundred, roughly, over a forty-eight hour period, not counting the two hundred–plus cruise missiles. And the only reason the sortie number is so low is because the plan calls for putting the B-1 and B-2 bomber fleets into action for the first time in a conventional role. Do you have any idea how much ordnance those birds can put on target? It's incredible."

Walling seemed immensely pleased with his work. "We would be in and out in only two days. The admiral's view is that plans like this should try to do as much as possible because we may not get a chance later. That's why so much attention is paid to the nuclear and CBW facilities. Some of those targets will be hit two or three times. We also have underground storage facilities targeted that will be hit multiple times with ten-thousand-pound bunker busters. Again, intelligence is not my field, but I'm sure you've seen the proliferation predictions on Libya and Iran, Lieutenant. It's just a matter of time. The admiral thinks that if we get a chance to stop the clock we shouldn't blow it. I couldn't agree more."

Zach nodded, excited. What a world he had entered.

Walling inserted his card into the box again, and the panel descended. "Maybe MOCKINGBIRD will fly someday, maybe not. Personally, I hope it does. But frankly, Lieutenant, that's not really the concern here in J-5. Our mission is just to be ready with plans that get the job done."

## 11

During his two years as FBI director, John Holsten had been to the White House sixteen times, a tally he carefully kept. Not a bad record. But not a good one either. And each time, including now, as he waited late on Saturday afternoon outside the Oval Office, he was struck by how small the place was. His suite at the Bureau was probably half the size of the entire West Wing. No doubt that had been Hoover's intention in designing the place.

The door of the Oval Office opened, and a young man in his early thirties stepped out. The suit was Italian, swank and expensive. A slight sheen of hair gel glinted in the light.

"Director Holsten, nice to see," said Joe Rizotti, the President's omnipresent aide. "Sorry this had to cut into the weekend. You know how it is around here."

Holsten rose and shook Rizotti's hand. He despised the kid. Too much power, too little respect. And too damn good looking to boot.

"The President just needs another minute," Rizotti said, rifling through some papers in a folder. "Now, my understanding is that this whole Sacramento matter tops the agenda today?"

Holsten nodded and said nothing. He hated these little preview discussions with Rizotti. His business was with the President, not some campaign punk who got lucky after the election.

"As you know, the President is very impressed with the Bureau's sting operation in the state government," Rizotti said. "Zero tolerance of corruption has been his policy from day one of this administration. But he's also concerned, to be candid. He doesn't want Washington to seem heavy-handed out there. Not this close to the election."

Holsten rolled his eyes. The kid pulled this crap all the time. Speaking for the President. Injecting politics into every equation. Holsten wanted to smack him.

The President pulled open the Oval Office door and pumped the director's hand. "John, great to see you, come on in."

Rizotti followed them. The chief of staff and White House counsel were already there. The five of them sat on the cream-colored sofas near the fireplace. They discussed the Sacramento sting operation for twenty-five minutes. Never once did the political dimension come up, Holsten noticed. The President knew his message had already been sent.

The meeting seemed near an end when the President did something that Holsten had only seen him do twice before. He asked his three top aides to leave him and the director alone. Holsten knew what was next on the agenda. It was the same thing they had discussed in private three weeks earlier, and two months before that.

The President leaned forward intently. "Anything new on Operation Arnold?"

Holsten shook his head. "I'm afraid we're still at a dead end, Mr. President. We don't have enough to indict for the activities in the 1980s. Far from it. And while we suspect ongoing activities, we just can't penetrate their organization, if there really is an organization. Can't even get close."

Holsten paused for a moment, biting his lip. "And frankly, sir, the limitations you've placed on us doesn't make this thing any easier. We need subpoenas, Mr. President. There's no way around it."

The President exploded. "Damnit, John! We've been through this before. One leak on this, one tiny little leak, and I'll be wading in shit for months."

"The Bureau is extremely tight these days," Holsten replied defensively. "We haven't had leaking problems for some time. Not since I've been there. If we could only cast a wider net on this, I think —"

"Don't flatter yourself, John. You're good, but nobody's one hundred percent. Things always get out, and the stakes here are just too high. No matter how legitimate this probe is, it will still look like I'm abusing the investigative powers of the government to go after not one but two political opponents. I'll have Forsten's friends in the military on my ass. Again. And Sherman will probably get ten points out of the thing."

The President rose and paced the room. Holsten sat silently.

"This is sticky, John. Doesn't get much worse than this, does it?"

"No, Mr. President."

The President stared through the greenish bullet-proof glass out onto the White House lawn for a long moment.

"But you're right, we need to do more. We have to turn up something. Any new ideas?"

Holsten brightened. He was ready for this moment. "Mr. President, my deputy has drawn up plans to put thirty more agents on the case. We're ready to send more people to San Diego, to Hawaii, and to the Philippines. We need to go through the records of at least three of Sherman's subsidiary corporations, and in addition —"

The President held up his hand, annoyed. "Forget it, John. Way too much noise. Come on, think this through." Holsten frowned in disappointment. The President continued to pace.

"We need a more subtle approach. We need to get closer, to learn more."

"As I have said, our penetration efforts have gotten nowhere, Mr. President," Holsten commented with a hint of impatience. "Captain Hansen was the best chance we had, and even he had yielded virtually nothing."

The President clenched his jaw at the mention of the name and smashed his fist into an open palm. "I assume there are no more leads on that?"

"No, sir, nothing. Alexandria police took a suspect into custody, a young man from the projects over there. But they released him for lack of evidence."

"Damnit, John, I want results on that! They killed that boy. You know it; I know it."

"Perhaps, Mr. President, but there's no evidence of that at this point."

"Find evidence."

"I'm sorry, sir, but we can't just take over a local murder investigation for no reason. People would start asking questions, they would —"

"Yes, yes, I know, I know. You're right." The President sat back down and sighed. "I just want to nail those bastards."

"I understand, sir. I share your sentiments."

The two men sat in silence for a long time. Like most in the government, Holsten found these silences uncomfortable. But it was a rare aide who broke them unilaterally.

Finally the President spoke. "Does the name Lieutenant Zachary Turzin mean anything to you?"

Holsten racked his mind. Obviously the name should mean something.

"We had him here in the Rose Garden not long ago," the President continued. "He won the Congressional Medal of Honor —"

"For the raid into Iraq," snapped Holsten, as if he had remembered all along.

"That's right. Quite a piece of work. Surprised he made it out. Anyway, I've kept an eye on the boy since then, and it seems he's now working for our friend in the Pentagon."

Holsten cursed to himself. Damn right he should have known Turzin's name — and his age, exact position on Forsten's staff, family background, political views. The works.

Damn. The director sensed where the President was going and cursed to himself again. He should have thought up the idea.

"Maybe Turzin is our ticket inside," the President said. "Turzin's a hot property with that medal. Forsten snatched him right up. I wouldn't be surprised if they try to turn him somehow, use him, get some mileage out of him. But what if we were to get to him first? Make him our boy. And then encourage him to go as he deep as he can."

The director was nodding his head, already giving orders in his mind to make the recruitment happen. The only problem with the plan was that it wasn't his own.

"That's a fine idea, Mr. President. Hansen probably would never have panned out anyway. Too junior. But Turzin could be different. I would suggest a two-step approach. First, we find out more about the lieutenant, get an idea of what makes him tick, what he wants or needs. We wire his apartment, his phone. Put a surveillance team on him."

The President grimaced. "We're talking about a hero, John, not a criminal. Remember that."

"Point taken. But we need to know more before we approach him, make sure he's not been co-opted already, or the whole thing could backfire."

The President nodded. Holsten continued, feeling back in control. "In phase two we make contact. We keep things vague, appeal to his patriotism. We don't ask for much at first. But over time the guy could become a gold mine. I'm talking about standard recruitment procedure, really."

The President looked uncertain. "I don't know, John."

"It could be our best shot at this point, sir."

"But there are risks. Imagine what we'd look like if the press got ahold of the fact that we were tapping the phone of a war hero. Jesus."

"All operations carry risks, sir," Holsten said. The President was balking at an idea he had suggested, for pete's sake. He was sick of this kind of spinelessness.

The President rose, signaling an end to the meeting. "I want you to move on Turzin, but cautiously," he said, walking Holsten to the door. "Find out more about him, and if he looks promising, then we'll talk about the next step, a wiretap and such. I don't want a scandal on our hands."

"Nor do I, sir."

"And there's something else I don't want, John." There was a tone of rebuke in the President's voice.

"Yes, sir?"

"I don't want Lieutenant Turzin to end up like Captain Hansen."

## 12

"Zach, wake up. Wake up."

Justine shook Zach in the darkness. His breathing was fast and hard, his body covered in sweat. He had woken her with a sharp yelp and then loud muttering.

"What, what's happening?" Zach's eyes opened after Justine turned on the light. They darted around frantically. Tears streaked his face.

Justine held him and stroked his head. "You were having a bad dream. You cried out. What was it?"

Zach was blinking fast, trying to wake up. He nuzzled his cheek closer against Justine's breast and breathed deeply with a shudder. "I was out of time. . . . I was running. Jared was there. I . . . I can't remember anymore."

"It's okay, it's okay," she repeated softly, stroking his head. "It's over now."

He was silent for a long time. His breathing slowed. "I'm sorry," he said finally.

"Sorry for what?"

"That you have to deal with this, to be here and see this."

"I want to be here for you." Justine took his head with both hands and looked him in the eyes. "I care about you, Zach. I want to help you with this."

Zach had been slow to share the details of his situation with Justine. He was happy to let her see only his sunny side — the decorated war hero, not the scarred survivor. She was having an affair, for godsakes. She didn't want complications. But the truth had dribbled out anyway. The days that were punctuated by a replaying of what happened at Haisa. The terrifying dreams that came at night. Earlier in the evening he had finally told her about his therapy with the VA psychiatrist. She was sympathetic, or at least pretended to be. He wondered whether she had started to plan her exit yet. She'd be dumb not to.

"I hate this weakness in myself," he had said over dinner at an out-of-the-way place in Old Town Alexandria. "I don't control my thoughts, they control me. And it's so random. I'll be doing something at work, sitting in a briefing or reading a document, feeling normal, and then bam, suddenly I'm sweating and anxious. I'm back in that firefight outside Haisa. I'm back and I can't leave until I've retraced every step I took, every call I made."

"It will pass, Zach. It has to."

"Not necessarily," Zach had said darkly. "Some guys experience this kind of thing for years or decades. They never recover. For a lot of them a .45 round in the temple or a makeshift noose is the only way out."

Justine had looked at him in silence. There was a sadness in her eyes he had never seen before. She squeezed his hand. "Please don't talk that way."

"I'm not thinking of killing myself. Don't worry about that. It's just that sometimes I can't imagine ever feeling like I used to. I can't imagine being without all this guilt and also the pain. Christ, I can't imagine just sleeping through the night on a regular basis. Almost every night, I wake up. It just keeps coming and coming."

"But it fades. It does. The pain, at least."

"How do you know?"

Justine had shrugged her shoulders and looked away. For a moment, it seemed as if she was going to cry. "I had a brother who died," she said finally. "Three years ago."

"I had no idea."

"I don't talk about it much. He was hemophiliac. Two years younger than me. He got AIDS from a bad blood transfusion in the 1980s. He was sick for years before he died."

"God, I'm sorry."

"For a long time I felt what you're feeling. Pain. Guilt. I still feel some of it, but it's ebbed. It's now just a kind of dull throb way down deep somewhere. I wasn't there for him when he was dying. I had never really been there for him, even before. I was always too busy with boys or college or, later, trying to make it in Washington."

"This happened around the same time you left the DNC and that guy you were living with, didn't it?"

Justine had nodded her head. Her eyes were misty. "I was a wreck. I didn't know what I believed or who I was. All I knew is that something had been really askew in my priorities. I hated myself for a while."

Later that night, as they made love in the candlelight, Justine had begun to cry. The tears streamed down across her temples and dripped to the sheet. Zach had become still. Justine pulled him in closer, deeper. "Don't stop," she whispered. "Please don't stop."

## 13

At the end of his second week at the Pentagon, Zach was beginning to forget what it was like to be outdoors. His long runs through the suburban streets of Arlington had vanished beneath a mountain of work. And despite the cool November weather, he didn't need to wear a coat when he went into work because his entire commute was indoors. The elevator on the floor of his building carried him down to the futuristic subterranean passageways of the Crystal City Mall, which he walked through to the even more futuristic metro station. This is what life would be like, Zach imagined, sometime in the twenty-second century. Perhaps it was this taste of the future that attracted people to Crystal City; Zach could think of nothing else that might. Just past his thirtieth birthday, he thought of the movie *Logan's Run* and vowed to get another place when the Army's six-month gift of his apartment expired.

Zach didn't even go outside when he wanted to have a drink after work. Instead, too tired to find anything else, he would stop at Characters, the bar in the mall that he passed on the way home, usually at about nine or ten at night. It was, despite the name, a place of extraordinary banality. The decor mixed varnished blond wood tables with a spattering of brass and mirror. Plants grew from boxes atop short walls that separated sections of the table area. Two large television sets hovered high over each end of the bar, spewing a chatter of news and sports. The clientele was a corporate after-work crowd: ties loosened, pumps traded for tennis shoes, minds turned off.

Zach would have a beer or two by himself, exhausted. He

read the paper or watched the ten o'clock news. He would catch snippets of the tipsy mating babble of junior executives and executive assistants. They would be one table, maybe two tables away — their faces flushed and shiny, their hair stiff with chemicals — but it might as well have been a chasm of galaxies.

On the Friday of his second week of work, Zach stopped off at Characters for a few beers. The place was packed, and he could barely get a place at the bar. The low roar of voices drowned out the televisions. Zach was watching the crowd and occasionally chatting with the bartender when he heard a voice with a refined Jamaican-British accent to his left. "Zachary Turzin?"

He turned around to find himself facing the familiar face of a well-dressed black man with fragile wire-rimmed glasses. The smell of cologne hung in the air.

"It is you. My heavens, Zachary, I saw you on TV. Congressional Medal of Honor. I didn't even know you were in the military. Shocking, it was."

"Hey, how's it going?" Zach said, stalling, his memory in a whir. Cornell. Computers. Poli-sci classes. The name came back as the handshake ended. "Lewis Thurston right here in my own bar."

"Your bar? Bollocks. I've been coming here for two years. Ever since I started working at the Pentagon."

"You're at the Pentagon too? I would have never figured you for the type. I thought you'd be in some ivory tower."

"Well, it's a long story, my friend," Lewis said, ordering a beer from the bar. "Although I can't imagine it's nearly as long as yours. My god, Zachary."

They found a small table near a wall and talked. Zach had never been that close to Lewis Thurston but always remembered liking him. Lewis radiated intelligence with an accompaniment of unapologetic arrogance, and Zach appreciated that characteristic. He was the child of wealthy Jamaican landowners and had attended private school in London.

After his parents left Jamaica during political turmoil in the early 1980s and moved to New York's Upper East Side, Lewis spent a year at Exeter. At Cornell he had been something of a campus eccentric, wearing suits to class and carrying a polished wooden walking stick. But it seemed that he knew everbody. He was too unusual to be pigeonholed as one kind of person or another, so people trusted him, and despite his proper manner, Lewis always had the latest gossip.

Zach told an abbreviated version of his story. Lewis listened in fascination, letting out occasional exclamations of wonder. Zach was relieved that he didn't push for details about Haisa.

The conversation turned to Thurston. He had acquired a Ph.D. at Johns Hopkins and now worked for the Defense Intelligence Agency, modernizing their information processing systems.

"The defense establishment is not exactly my natural habitat," Lewis said, wiping his glasses with a pristine white handkerchief. "But jobs in academia had absolutely disappeared by the time I was finishing. In any case, my job is not as boring as one might fancy. The programming challenges are enormous, absolutely enormous, and I also try to keep an eye on the substantive matters. I'm cleared to read a lot of the intelligence that comes through the system and often I do. It makes the job a bloody sight more interesting."

"Pentagon's a fascinating place," Zach said.

Lewis nodded. "It's also a dysfunctional place. My pitiable agency, at least."

"What's wrong at DIA?"

"We're under water these days, positively submerged. As things stand, DIA can't process half the material that comes in from the field because their storing and cataloging system is such a dinosaur. The cutbacks have cost us a fourth of the analytical division, and nobody's dealing with the shortfall problem.

"Let me just give you one example." Lewis lowered his

voice and looked around, making sure no one in the crowded bar was likely to overhear. "You work for Admiral Forsten, my friend, so I'm sure you're cleared to hear this."

"I'm about as high as you get, Lewis." Security rules prevented Zach from telling his exact clearance level to people of a lower level.

"Last week there was a big brouhaha at the counterterrorism unit of DIA. Some pretty crucial information never made it to the right people."

"What happened?" Zach leaned forward. He sensed a tidbit coming his way that he could bring to Forsten.

"Well, you know how the Hizbullah terrorist group in Lebanon has been weak and divided for the past few years?"

Zach nodded. One of his earliest missions had been to go into southern Lebanon to look for Americans who had been kidnapped by Hizbullah. The mission was a failure, but he had learned all about the Party of God, with its messianic faith and squads of suicide bombers.

"It turns out that in September the DIA system received a huge amount of audio material from the National Security Agency about Hizbullah — local phone calls and radio transmissions, mainly. NSA had processed the stuff, but only at the most preliminary level. They had run all the material through their computer word-search system — you know, looking to see if any western cities or leaders or U.S. embassies are mentioned to make sure that none of the conversations involve the planning of a new attack somewhere. And that's all they did, nothing else.

"Anyway, so nobody at DIA gets around to looking more closely at this stuff until two or three weeks ago. It's just sitting in the system, gathering static. But it turns out that it's damn important. Our analysts still aren't quite sure, but they think that a major Hizbullah leader, Sheik Abdul Tabrata, has gone into the mercenary business. Instead of running a Party of God, this fellow runs an army for rent."

The revelation didn't surprise Zach. He had heard rumors

along these lines while in Cairo. "That's basically what happened with the Abu Nidal Organization," he said.

"Right. ANO went mercenary a long time ago. Now it's the Hizbullah leaders who have gotten disillusioned and avaricious. Except here's the thing: Our analysts think that the rank-and-file members of Hizbullah — you know, the young terrorists who are trained to carry out suicide missions — have no idea of the change. The fighters think they're doing Allah's bidding, while their masters make big bucks. So far, they've only done a few local jobs. But it's a chilling thought, wouldn't you say? Consider the consequences of a mercenary network with scores of highly trained operatives who are willing to die in the process of completing a mission. Bloody hell."

"I can see why the counterterrorist guys at DIA flipped out," Zach said. He did find Thurston's story disturbing. Unfortunately, it sounded like old news, nothing to impress Forsten with.

"It was just sitting there. Absolutely unbelievable," Thurston said. "Now there's a good case for consolidating the intelligence establishment if I ever heard one. And this is just a single example."

The two men talked for another hour or so, downing several more beers. Loosened up by the alcohol, Thurston told Zach who was who in the Pentagon — who was headed up and who was on the way out, who had problems with booze and who was leaking to the press.

"I get around, Zachary. The Pentagon is its own world and it has its own little dramas. As you will learn."

"Talk about a seperate reality: I went to Douglas Sherman's estate the other night." Zach wanted to show Lewis that he got around as well.

"Ah, our great maverick, Douglas Sherman. Now there's one of the more interesting personalities in town. He did get my vote, I confess."

"That makes two of us."

"But I must say, as much as I like his politics, I do question his judgment."

"Why's that?"

"Well, it's one thing to entertain the delusion that one can mount any kind of effective presidential campaign without having a cheerful wife at your side. It's —"

"They're estranged, and she's in Europe."

Thurston nodded indulgently at Zach's attempt to impress him with the most ancient gossip in town. He continued: "It's quite another thing entirely to imagine that one can have a serious relationship with one's press person and nobody will know or care. Just a touch of arrogance there, I would say. Then again, it is true that the media hasn't touched the issue. It could be that we're moving back to where we were before Gary Hart and that affairs don't matter any more. Now that would be an enormous relief."

Zach had missed the last part of Thurston's comment. He was reeling, stunned. "Who is Sherman's press person?" he stammered.

Thurston clucked his tongue. "Her name is slipping my mind right now. She used to work for the DNC, I do know that. Quite an attractive woman. Can't actually blame the fellow, I suppose. It does make you wonder, however, just how badly he wants to be president."

Zach nodded in a daze. Thurston was examining the tab. He pulled out his wallet. "I better head out. Why don't we make this one on me?"

Zach barely slept that night. He was too freaked out — and too jealous. He had never asked Justine who the "somebody else" in her life was. It was easier not to know, to try to forget the guy even existed. He felt enough of both guilt and jealousy in the abstract; he didn't need an identity to focus on. When he did imagine who Justine's man was, Zach pictured some overworked thirtysomething lawyer or political aide, a paunch fast developing, who was too self-absorbed to give Justine the attention she needed. Zach imagined somebody he could compete with. But Douglas Sherman. Jesus Christ! This was crazy, insane. Forget jealousy. It was dangerous. Sherman could destroy Zach's career — or worse. Zach thought of Colonel Riley at the party. He was the sort of person that powerful people like Sherman kept around to do special errands. Zach didn't want to become one of those errands.

And Justine. She had to be nuts to fool around behind Sherman's back. What was their relationship all about, anyway? Sherman was dynamic, no question. And good looking and rich and powerful — all those things. But he had two decades on her, easy. There was something sick about that kind of father-daughter thing. Who was Justine, really?

# ★ 14 ★

Tommy Flint ran through the briefing a final time and then told his two men to get some sleep. The next day would be a long one. After they had left the living room, Flint lingered in front of the hearth for more than an hour, poking occasionally at the pile of glowing embers. Sleep was elusive, not because he was worried, but because he was excited. The mission would be a success. They always were. Flint believed his team had such an impressive record because he followed a few basic rules learned from his days in Vietnam. First, always explain the strategic vision behind a set of orders; it motivates men who might have to die doing their job. Second, don't turn squeamish; that the ends justified the means was among the most essential truths of war. And third, it helps to leave behind an instructive message for your enemy; severed limbs and private parts were the resort of the uncreative or the time-pressed. Flint had always preferred grisly spectacles of more drama. Crucifixion was his favorite.

Flint's South Tennessee Militia had carried out four missions in the past three years, and all had received national press because of their unusual brutality. The liberal columnist for the *Memphis Courier,* for example, hadn't simply been assassinated: His body had been creatively displayed from a tree in his front yard. Flint's only regret was that the media hadn't carried the image. Fortunately, his men had taken their own photos. Perfect for flyers.

The offer that had come from Washington a month earlier hadn't surprised Flint one bit. When you have the best team, you get the best jobs. Of course, personal contacts were crucial as well. This mission assignment had come from a man whom Flint had soldiered under thirty years earlier, a man he regarded as his superior for life. A bond forged in a place like the Mekong Delta was one that endured. Flint remained loyal to his former commander even as they had taken radically different paths after the war. The commander had stayed in the military and risen nearly to the top. Flint had turned with a vengeance against the system that had lost his war, retreating into the backwoods of southern Appalachia and slowly putting together a network of loyalists who were ready to give their lives to take back America. He didn't subscribe to the overblown views of his friends to the west; the Zionist Occupation Government was a hallucination, Flint knew. But even the less sensational truth was more than enough to justify Flint's personal war: treason at every level of a government intent on crushing individual freedom at home and coddling terrorist states abroad. Flint was still loyal to his former superior because he was the one man in Washington who stood up to everything that was wrong.

The mission of the next day was the most important that the South Tennessee Militia had yet undertaken. Beyond paying a fee that would fill the STM's Cayman bank account unlike any armored-car heist of the past, it was an assignment that allowed for a direct strike at the enemy. Flint had followed the career of Army General Paul Neuwirth for over a decade. Neuwirth had risen through the ranks by selling out his own country again and again as far as Flint was concerned. Kissing the ass of JCS Chairman Reynolds and the other appeasers to get the powerful job as head of the Continental U.S. Command in Georgia was only the latest in a long string of unforgivable acts. *Traitor* was too kind a term for a general who now controlled a quarter million American troops at bases across the United States. Killing Neuwirth would be a pleasure, even if Flint's orders from Washington were accompanied by a disappointing caveat: no postmortem theatrics.

Sleep didn't come for Flint until after two, but he was up

before dawn fully refreshed. Traffic on I-24 was light on this Saturday morning, and Flint's team had rolled across the Tennessee River and through Chattanooga by six. Route 76 took them up into the Smoky Mountains, with their rushing rivers and brown hills of leafless trees. They passed the tiny town of Ellijay, and from there headed south for a few miles down Route 5 before pulling off on a dirt road. The forest here was a sea of dense pine that pressed up against the road and blocked out the sun. After another two miles the team stopped and parked along the road. They had passed a number of hunters since Ellijay, brightly clad in orange and red. Now they donned similar outfits and headed into the woods with high-powered rifles. Sporadic gunfire could be heard in the distance. The backcountry was a dangerous place during deer season.

Intelligence on Neuwirth's movements came from the inside and it was as good as Flint could have hoped for. Every Friday afternoon during hunting season, Neuwirth and his wife made the six-hour drive up from Fort Stewart to a cabin they owned in the Smokey Mountains outside of Jasper. And every Saturday morning Neuwirth headed out of the cabin at about ten for a few hours of hunting. Nothing too hardcore, just some quiet time in the woods to help him unwind. On one occasion the previous year, Neuwirth had reportedly brought along a major to hunt with him. But every other time he had been alone.

By nine, after a fifteen-minute walk through brush, Flint and his men were in place a hundred yards from Neuwirth's cabin. They scanned the house with binoculars and waited. Just after ten, right on schedule, Neuwirth stepped out of the door with a rifle. He wore an Army jacket and an orange cap.

"Now there's one fine buck for you," quipped Flint.

"You can't mistake the antlers," said one of the men.

Flint and his team fell back as Neuwirth walked in their direction. Once he was deep in the woods, they circled around to his rear and followed him from two or three hundred yards. This wasn't the turkey shoot it seemed, Flint had emphasized in his briefing. Neuwirth had to be taken out with a single shot from at least a hundred yards. That way the incident would have all the marks of an accidental killing by a stray bullet. "Happens all the time this time of year," Flint had told his men the night before. "Especially in moonshine country. And it's not uncommon that nobody steps forward to admit the deed."

Neuwirth walked briskly for a half mile, pausing occasionally to scour the terrain for prey. "I got him," announced one of Flint's men, peering through the scope on his gun when Neuwirth stopped for the second time. "Not yet," Flint said. He wanted to fell Neuwirth in an area of denser forest.

Thick clouds had moved in during the morning, and the woods had grown dark. Flint's team followed the bobbing orange hat far ahead for another twenty minutes. Finally Neuwirth stopped on top of a small ridge and sat down on a rock. Flint signaled his men to halt two hundred yards away. They laid themselves on the ground and passed a set of binoculars back and forth. Neuwirth had taken out his own binoculars and was examining the woods below him. It looked like he planned to let the game come to him.

"He's mine," Flint declared quietly. He rose to a sitting position with his knees up and his left arm across them, bracing the rifle. He looked through his scope and centered the crosshairs on the point at the back of Neuwirth's skull where his hat met the hair. Slowly he squeezed the trigger.

It was Flint's sixty-eighth confirmed lifetime kill.

## ★ 15 ★

Zach hit the play button on his answering machine when he got back from the gym late on Sunday afternoon. He listened to the message as he scrambled to get dressed. The pain in his back gnawed from the workout.

"Hi, Zach. It's me, Justine. Haven't heard from you in a couple of days. What's up? Things have been crazy on my end too. But I'd love to see you. I can get away tomorrow night, if you want. It's probably best if we meet at your place, although I can't be there until ten. I hope you don't mind a little sleep deprivation. It will be worth it, I guarantee. Leave a message if that works. Bye."

Zach buttoned his shirt and slipped into some loafers. What a mess. Half of him wanted Justine to just disappear. The other half wanted to consume her totally, forever. He still had no clue what he was going to say when he saw her next.

Zach had been flattered when he received the invitation from Forsten to drop by the house for dinner on Sunday night. As long as he was in Washington he would play the Capitol game to win, he had decided. That meant getting closer to Forsten. Zach found the admiral's other aides to be more impressive for their loyalty than their analytic abilities, and he imagined gradually gaining an edge over them as he moved further into the inner circle. Already Zach could see that his position was getting stronger. Forsten had taken to calling once or twice a day or sending E-mail messages with quick questions, not all of which related to the Middle East. He sent over the draft of a speech for Zach to comment on, and then another. He made a point of soliciting Zach's input at staff meetings. He never praised Zach for his work, but it was clear that he was impressed. And it was equally clear that Forsten's other aides were worried. They grew less generous with advice on how to operate in the Pentagon. They zeroed in on Zach's small mistakes and hit him with questions that he couldn't be expected to answer. In small talk, they made a point of advertising their long-standing ties to the admiral. They tried but failed to cut him out of several key meetings. As far as Zach was concerned, these were good signs. If the game was bureaucratic hardball, he was ready to play. He wasn't some redneck grunt. He had kicked ass in the field. He would kick ass in the Pentagon. And it was not simple competitiveness or a lust for power that drove these thoughts. Potomac fever had not set in, Zach assured himself. This was a matter of principle. With a President in office who cared more about Social Security than national security, Forsten was fighting the good fight, a fight worth joining.

Zach took a cab to Forsten's home at Fort McNair in southwest Washington. The grounds were immaculately maintained, with vast lawns that stretched nearly to the edge of the Washington Channel and beautiful brick colonial houses nestled among old elm trees. A cool breeze blew off the water.

Zach rang the doorbell. Almost immediately a blonde women in her fifties opened the door. "You must be Lieutenant Turzin," she said, letting him in. Her voice was soft and friendly, with a faint Southern accent. "I'm Bonnie, Jeff's wife." Mrs. Forsten led Zach up a winding staircase to a living room on the second floor.

Forsten was rising from the couch, straightening his slacks. He came over and shook Zach's hand. "Nice to get you out to the homestead, Zach. Some fine cooking happens out here, as you'll soon see. She's the best."

Mrs. Forsten smiled as she retreated toward the kitchen. "You boys make yourselves comfortable. This won't be a minute." Zach could smell some sort of roast cooking.

"So what can I get you?" Forsten asked, moving toward a wooden liquor cabinet that stood with open doors. Zach wanted a beer but sensed that wouldn't be appropriate.

"A scotch and soda would be great, sir."

He gazed around Forsten's home and felt at ease. An oriental rug covered the floor. The cushions of the well-stuffed couches looked soft and inviting. There was not much style in the decorating but also no pretension. The most distinctive touch was a few oriental vases and masks. Zach inspected one of the masks that hung near the door.

"That particular piece came from a little shop in Hong Kong," Forsten said, handing Zach his drink. "I logged quite a bit of R and R there over the years; got to know the place real well. All sorts of wild stuff used to go down in that city. Hell of a town."

The two men chatted about the various cities they had been to in the world. Forsten asked about Cairo, and Zach described its features as a tourist might, not getting into his work there.

"It's a shame the place is a virtual battlefield these days," Forsten said. He stirred his drink with a finger and gestured for Zach to sit down. "I guess the real surprise is that Mubarak held on for as long as he did."

Zach sunk into the couch. "He was on his last legs when I was there, sir. You could see the signs everywhere."

Forsten shook his head. "What a mess. One less friend where we need them the most these days."

At dinner the talk turned to Virginia real estate after Zach mentioned his plans to escape from Crystal City. Old Town Alexandria was very nice, both Forstens agreed, except it had gotten more dangerous in recent years.

"That poor captain we had over here to dinner once," Mrs. Forsten said. "What was his name, honey?"

"Hansen," Forsten answered.

"Yes, Captain Hansen. Poor boy murdered not three

blocks from his house. I suppose you've heard about that, Lieutenant."

"Yes, I did."

"A real shame. I'd stay away from that area if I were you. It's going downhill."

Zach nodded. His latest thought was that he'd prefer a foxhole in a free-fire zone to his current accommodations.

"Same thing's happening all over this country," Forsten grumbled. "Whole place is going to pot. Our cities are like foreign republics. Maybe it's about time we started treating them as such."

Mrs. Forsten nodded and passed around a large wooden salad bowl.

"Perhaps Rosslyn would be nice," Zach said, steering the conversation to safer terrain.

"Oh, yes, Rosslyn's very nice; beautiful new apartment complexes there along Wilson Boulevard," Mrs. Forsten chirped. She was exactly how Zach had imagined her to be.

After dinner Mrs. Forsten began taking dishes into the kitchen. Forsten led Zach downstairs to a comfortable library with a bar and leather chairs.

"I spend a lot of time down here," Forsten said, stepping behind the bar. "The museum upstairs is Bonnie's territory."

Zach looked around as Forsten hit a switch behind the bar to turn on more lights. In fact, this was the museum, the place where all the memories were kept. War paraphernalia and memorabilia were everywhere. There was a battered AK-47 and an officer's sword, a pistol and a pair of old binoculars. One wall was covered with five captured flags — a Vietcong and a North Vietnamese flag, what looked like two VC regiment or division flags, and then an Iranian flag.

"What can I get you?" Forsten asked from the bar.

"I'll take a whiskey on the rocks, sir," Zach replied. The environment seemed to call for the stiffest drink available.

He gestured to the Iranian flag. "Where'd you get that one?"

"One of the my frigates took it off a Revolutionary Guard Zodiac in the Gulf in '88. You remember how those crazy bastards would go out on their rubber boats at night with RPG-7s, gunning for tankers, right?"

Zach nodded.

"Well, we nailed quite a few and got that flag off one of them."

"The Guards were nuts," Zach said.

"Were? They still are. You've heard how fanatical their contingents in Lebanon are. Almost as crazy as Hizbullah."

Forsten's mention of Hizbullah triggered Zach's memory.

"By the way, Admiral, what do you think about the recent intelligence on that group? This mercenary business."

Forsten didn't answer for a moment as he finished making the drinks.

"I think we'd better discuss that at the office." He gestured around the room. "I don't have security sweeps done in here. You never know."

Zach grimaced to himself: stupid mistake. He walked to the bar and took his drink. On the wall to the left were a bunch of framed photos. One showed Forsten standing next to a large swordfish hanging upside down on a dock.

"That's quite a catch, sir."

"Biggest of my life, as matter of fact. Brought that baby in off Grand Cayman. Bonnie and I love it down there in the Caribbean."

Zach noticed a larger black-and-white photo of a much younger Forsten standing on a patrol boat in Vietnam surrounded by a group of men.

"As fine a bunch of guys as you could ever hope for," Forsten said, leaning forward on the bar. His voice dipped low and grew wistful. "We lived for each other and sometimes died for each other. Believe me, you don't know the meaning of the term *unit cohesion* until you're with guys like that. We could have won the war if we had enough men like that."

"The famous River Rats, I take it."

"You bet. Brown Water Forces, circa 1968. Hell, we ruled the Mekong. When we began in '65 a good portion of Charlie's arms were coming in from the sea, through the delta. We cut that off cold after a year or two. Then we took control of the interior waterways that Charlie used to move men and materials around the delta and in from Cambodia. Those operations were among the most successful of the whole war. It was the one front where Charlie got his ass kicked every time."

"Fascinating, sir. Somebody should write a book on that whole part of the war." Zach hoped for a reaction to Donald Leffler's book, *Battle for the Mekong*.

Forsten didn't respond. He added a bit more club soda to his drink. Zach gazed at the admiral as his lined face was turned downward toward the bar. It awed him to think of the sweep of the man's life, the things he had seen and done so many years ago. Decades ago. And yet here he was, vital and alive, practically running the Pentagon. It was almost a kind of immortality.

Another photo lower down showed Forsten with two other men, all in flowered shirts and holding drinks in their hands, sitting at an outdoor bar next to the water. Zach looked closely at the photo. One of the men was Asian, and the other was Douglas Sherman, his hair still brown.

"That's Doug, all right. Hong Kong, nineteen sixty . . . No, that's not right. Nineteen seventy-one. I told you Doug and I went way back. He was just starting to make his fortune back then, and I was definitely a burn-out case at that point. Used to do all sorts of crazy shit to try to unwind. I'll tell you, Lieutenant, I couldn't stand to lose."

"What used to bring Mr. Sherman to Hong Kong, sir?"

"Import-export, that sort of stuff. Everybody thinks of Doug as a defense industry tycoon, but all that came much later. He started out in real estate in his hometown, then put a lot of his money into import-export. I first met him in

Hong Kong in '69, I guess it was. At that very bar, as a matter of fact. We loved that place. Of course, it's not there anymore. The old Hong Kong has vanished, I'm afraid."

Zach looked at the photo and sipped his drink. "And who's the other man?"

"Donny Chen. Helluva guy, local businessman. Now Chen knew how to party."

The other photos on the wall showed Forsten at various points in his career. Zach paused at one of him with King Hussein.

"I got to know the King during my days at Foreign Military Sales during the late seventies," Forsten said. "That job was supposed to be punishment for me, you have to realize. But I loved it."

Forsten gestured to other photos of him with foreign military leaders and officials. "I was at FMS during the boom days. Everybody was buying from us hand over fist. Hell, I got to know top people all over the place. Middle East, Africa, Asia, you name it. Great learning experience. Worked with a lot of people in private industry here too. Saw a lot of Doug during that period, as a matter of fact. He was new to the business. I helped him find his way through all the red tape."

"What did you do to end up at FMS, sir?"

Forsten grinned from across the bar. "I ruffled some feathers in the wrong places."

Zach pushed his empty glass forward for a refill. He could feel the previous drink taking effect, freshening a buzz that had been dulled by dinner.

"You know, Admiral," Zach said carefully, "everybody says you were sent into Laos after the war to search for MIAs."

Forsten was silent for a long moment before finally answering. "The things people say."

He came out from behind the bar and gestured for Zach to take a seat. Zach could feel him leading up to something.

For a moment he savored the thought that he was finally going to get the full story behind the Laos mission.

"You know, Zach, you're a good man, a damn good man."

"Thank you, sir."

"I've been impressed with your work over the past few weeks. And hell, I'm impressed by that medal of yours. Believe me, I know what it takes, what you did."

"I appreciate that, sir." Zach wondered where this was leading.

Forsten's tone became more serious and deliberate. "Things are not going well, Zach."

The thought of Forsten resigning or being fired flashed through Zach's mind. Shit. Everybody had warned him about something like this.

Forsten seemed to sense his alarm. "I mean in the larger picture. I'm afraid this country is entering a period of danger that may be more real and far greater than anything we've ever faced before."

Forsten rose and gazed into the backyard. Zach sat silently, waiting for more. During his time on the job he and Forsten had yet to have a philosophical talk about the broad contours of national security policy.

"During the Cold War we could always deter the Soviets," Forsten said. "The only real threat was miscalculation, something like the Cuban Missile Crisis. But that could be managed. I don't think a nuclear war was ever a serious possibility."

Forsten sat back down, sipped his drink, and leaned forward, becoming more intense. "But the problem with terrorists is that they can't be deterred. And you know and I know — hell, everybody knows — that it's only a matter of time before one of the terrorist states goes nuclear. Iran is almost there on its own, and both it and Libya have agents in the former Soviet Union willing to pay any price for a warhead. They've also been trying to buy weapons-grade plutonium, which is easier to get ahold of. And then there are the Soviet scientists. They're dispersed all over the place, working in both countries. It's only a matter of time before something pans out. Maybe it's happened already."

It's only a matter of time. The more Zach heard it, the more he believed it. "Do you have information that I don't know about, Admiral?"

"I really can't get into that with you. I'm sorry. Not now and certainly not here. It's the most sensitive stuff we have. All I can say is that by not lifting a finger to move against the TKT Pact, and by castrating our friends over there, the President has placed the country in peril, deadly peril."

"So what are the options, Admiral?" Zach asked. He felt a new bond emerging with his boss.

Forsten looked resigned. "I just don't know. Not anymore, not with this President." He then paused again for a long moment, scrutinizing Zach. "But I need to know something, Lieutenant."

"Anything, Admiral."

"Can I count on you?"

"Of course, sir."

Forsten's gaze bored into him. "I mean really count on you."

"Absolutely, sir."

## 16

Riley fast-forwarded the tape past the alcoholic Vietnam vet and past the double amputee with marital problems. Losers like that should just put bullets in their brains and save the government a whole lot of money. When he found Turzin on the tape it was the same old crap.

"... and how do you think Sergeant Canver would judge you? How would he want you to feel?"

"I don't know. It's hard for me to imagine that."

"Do you think he would want you to torture yourself with blame?"

"He'd see that I had screwed up. Jared was one of the best."

"But would he want you to come down so hard on yourself?"

"I don't know."

"He was your best friend; you knew him pretty well."

"I guess he would cut me some slack, sure. He wasn't a hard-ass or anything. That's one of the things I liked about Jared."

"He would understand that things go wrong on missions, that there are risks, wouldn't he?"

"Maybe."

"Do you think it's possible for you to judge yourself as Sergeant Canver would?"

Riley hit the fast-forward button and jumped ahead in the tape. More of the same warm milk. He hit the button again.

"... and so do you think you can get close to this new woman you're seeing?"

"It's complicated, very complicated."

Riley leaned forward. Now this was more interesting.

"Why is it so complicated?"

"She's in a relationship with somebody else."

Riley smiled. Turzin, you dog.

"Do you think that you might like the fact that she's not really available, that there's no chance of something serious here?"

"Why would I like that?"

"Well, if you can't get close to her you can't lose her the way you lost the security of your parents' marriage, the way you lost Jill, and the way you lost Sergeant Canver. One issue we need to —"

Blah, blah, blah. Riley shut off the tape. So Turzin was getting some action. That wasn't what he told Stan Duncan. Looked like hero boy had some secrets after all. Riley had been meaning to wire Turzin's apartment and phone, but he'd been lazy. He resented the scut work that sometimes got shoveled his way. Now he'd make a point of paying a visit to Crystal City sooner rather than later. See who this piece of ass was.

## 17

Zach left the Pentagon at 7:50. He stopped at Characters for a drink. He sat at a table near the bar, looking vaguely in the direction of the game on the television but thinking mainly of Justine. What the hell was he going to say when he saw her later that night? He was starting on his second beer when a blond man with curly hair appeared over him. "Lieutenant Turzin, right?"

"That's me," Zach said, anticipating a brief congratulation.

"Lieutenant, my name is Peter Castori. Can I sit down for a moment?"

Zach gestured to the empty seat.

"I'm a writer," Castori said smiling.

Zach put up both hands in an exaggerated blocking gesture. "Army public affairs will kill me if I say a word. They want all interviews on the medal to go through them. There's a whole process you gotta go through."

"Hey, I'm not here to talk about the medal, Lieutenant."

Zach looked at Castori closely. He was in his late thirties, maybe early forties. He was dressed in a sport coat and jeans and had an easy charm. Seemed harmless enough. Still, Zach was wary. He had heard too many stories of newcomers in Washington being ambushed by reporters. One of the major commandments in working for Forsten, Stan Duncan had said, was never, ever talk to the press.

"So what's on your mind?" Zach asked, not wanting to be rude. "Or rather, let me ask you this first: Who do you work for?"

"I'm freelance," Castori said. "I work for myself. I'm writing a book."

"And what's the book on?"

"The book is on a lot of things, actually," Castori replied.

"Yeah? Like what sort of things?"

"It's partly on the Iraqgate scandal, but it also extends back to the 1970s and Vietnam."

"Is it some sort of foreign policy history?"

"In a way it is, I suppose."

Zach was tiring of the guessing game. "So what's the hook, what's the book about?"

"I'm seeking to make connections between various illegal activities that have occurred within the national security establishment over the past twenty-five years."

"Connections? What do you mean by that?"

Castori shifted in his seat, and moved in closer, speaking more intensely. "In essence, my thesis is that such scandals as October Surprise, Iran-Contra, Iraqgate, and BCCI did not occur in isolation from one another."

"You think they were somehow linked?"

"I know they were, Lieutenant. I have mounting evidence to that effect. My book is about a conspiracy that has lasted more than two decades and continues to this day. I call it the Labyrinth."

"The Labyrinth, huh? And what is the purpose of this Labyrinth conspiracy?" The edge of sarcasm in Zach's previous question grew sharper. He had always been annoyed by conspiracy theorists.

"It's been a conspiracy to do a number of things. One, to make millions of dollars through the illegal sale of drugs and arms. Two, to conduct covert operations in various parts of the world at the informal behest of the U.S. government. And three, I think it now includes the subversion of the current administration's foreign policy, and maybe worse."

Zach laughed out loud. He had met a lot of wackos like Castori around Harvard Square when the Iran-Contra scandal was at its height. Conspiracy theorists back then had also made connections to Vietnam and drug smuggling, trying to show how people such as Richard Secord and William Casey had been running a shadow government for years. None of it was ever proved. And it never would be.

Zach moved to end the conversation. "Mr. Castori, I don't mean to be impolite, but I think I'd probably like to keep watching the game, if you don't mind. I've had a long day at work and I really shouldn't be talking to members of the press."

"I think you should hear me out, Lieutenant," Castori said, not moving from his seat.

"Believe me, I've heard enough."

After a moment of silence, Castori rose reluctantly. "Well, it wasn't my intention to bother you, Lieutenant. But my revelations do concern you."

"Me? What does any of this have to do with me?"

Castori sat back in his seat for a moment. "I've found evidence that links your boss to the Labyrinth. I had hoped to ask you some questions about him. Off the record, of course."

Zach felt a surge of irritation. "This conversation is over."

Castori rose again. "How much do you really know about Admiral Forsten, Lieutenant?"

"I said the conversation was over." Zach stared up at the television, waiting for Castori to leave.

"Well, if you won't hear me out, at least do some of your own checking. It's always nice to know who one works for. I guarantee that you'll be in for some surprises."

Zach didn't break his upward gaze.

They lay silently entwined, satiated and exhausted. The window was open a crack, and the candle flickered gently from the cold breeze. Coltrane was playing on the radio, a soothing coupling of tenor sax and bass. Their lovemaking had been a paroxysm of furious carnality. There were things between them, it seemed, that could only be communicated when he was inside her. She became lost in her ecstasy, her protective layering falling away. There was a way she needed him and gave herself to him that stripped her to some essential core. At times, moving slowly together, she on the verge of exploding once more and he barely holding back, they would lock eyes for long and intense moments. He felt she was speaking to him, pleading almost, in a way she never could out loud. Only when they made love did he feel that she was truly within reach and open to him.

He smoothed her hair, and she sighed deeply, drifting toward sleep. His determination to confront her about Sherman had dissolved the moment he saw her. The conversation didn't really have a point, he realized. He knew what the deal was. He could either end the relationship or continue it. Talking wasn't going to change anything. For now, at least, he wanted to continue. The stupid choice. He loved that she kept coming back to him when she had so much else in her life. When she had Sherman. He loved how much she seemed to need him, how she sought to consume him with her desire. He had never been loved like that, and it made him feel that he was going someplace he had wanted to be all his life.

He was falling fast. That was the simple truth. He resisted it, trying to pull back, to hold on. But still he felt himself being pulled and tumbling forward. He couldn't stop.

"Have you ever heard of a writer named Peter Castori?" Zach asked Justine as she got dressed. Her late-night exits had become routine.

"Castori? Oh, sure. Professional gadfly."

"Have you ever read anything he's written?"

"No, but I know the genre. Conspiracy theory stuff. I think the *Village Voice* has published his stuff, also the *Covert Action Information Bulletin*. Nobody takes him seriously. He was on Doug's tail a while back with some totally nutty charges."

"Like what?"

"I can't remember. Something about Doug's arms work."

"Uh huh."

"Of course, Castori's not the only one to make such accusations. This has always been a problem for Doug. The press has always gone ape on the guy, giving credence to the wildest charges. They would never do that with a conventional candidate, but because Doug has not spent twelve years in the Senate or occupied a governor's mansion for more than four years, he's considered fair game for all sorts of fantastical attacks."

Justine slipped her turtleneck over her head. She looked tired. "It really bothers me that no sooner is one of these rumors or charges put to sleep than another resurfaces."

"Can you remember more specifically what Castori charged?"

"Well, I never actually read the article he wrote. It appeared in someplace really left and fringe. I can't remember the publication's name. But the essence was that Doug engaged in illegal arms sales during the 1980s. I think there might have been something about drugs, even, from his earlier days in Hong Kong. Totally absurd stuff. The mainstream press never touched it. Doug wanted to sue for libel, you know, but his lawyers convinced him that that would just draw more attention to the charges, so he let it drop."

"So have you heard from Castori lately?"

"No. I think the libel threat scared him away. But I hear he's working on a book. What made you think of him?" Justine was looking around for one of her socks. Finding all their clothes afterwards was always a challenge.

"He came up to me in a bar tonight. Knew who I was and everything."

"Really. How strange. What did he want?"

"I'm not sure. But he mentioned arms sales and drug smuggling."

"The guy clearly has an obsession of some sort."

"And he mentioned Forsten."

"Forsten?"

"Yeah. He said the admiral was part of some conspiracy he calls the Labyrinth."

"Labyrinth, right. It's coming back to me. That's was what he was trying to link Doug to."

Justine and Zach were silent. They both sensed what the other was thinking and burst out laughing at the same moment.

"Crazy shit," Justine said. "I'd feel sorry for the guy if he weren't such a pest."

"Crazy, crazy, crazy," Zach said, his voice turning into a growl as he imitated a hungry monster and pulled her back onto the bed.

## 18

Over the next week, Zach put in consistent fourteen-hour days working on the DOD budget request. The so-called wish lists of the various services had been given to Reynolds and Forsten in early November. These initial requests, everybody understood, staked out the services' bargaining positions. By early December, full-scale interservice warfare was under way as the scramble began for a bigger piece of the shrinking budgetary pie. And the Joint Staff, as Zach had been warned, was the main battlefield. At times it had the atmosphere of a besieged garrison, with enemy artillery raining in in the form of angry phone calls and faxes. Zach began to wonder whether the security checkpoint outside the JCS section was there to keep out security risks or aggrieved victims of budget cuts.

Weapons systems and manpower issues were not Zach's specialties, and he involved himself little in the substantive proceedings of the Joint Staff's work. Instead, Forsten used him to run sensitive diplomatic errands throughout the building. He also pushed Zach to keep his ears open for information related to terrorist operations or threats against the United States. Zach's rounds in the building included not only people in DIA but also officers in Army intelligence, Navy intelligence, Air Force intelligence, and the CIA liaison in the Office of the Secretary of Defense. Zach reflected that the Pentagon was not unlike Lebanon or Afghanistan, with its various militias and warlords. No wonder Forsten had wanted a Middle East expert at his side.

Zach found himself continually awed by the vast web of Forsten's ties. They reached into every part of the Pentagon and into every regional command. They were strongest in the Navy and among Vietnam veterans, but they also cut across service boundaries and rank. Forsten was close to major players with fiefdoms of their own, as well as to legions of younger officers who had once served under his command and never forgotten the experience. Zach would occasionally hear Forsten on the phone talking to an officer on somebody else's staff, treating them like his own direct subordinate. The chain of command was an abstraction to Forsten; tribal loyalty was the credo that he operated by.

Early in the morning, when the vast Pentagon parking lots were still largely empty, Forsten would be making his calls overseas, bantering easily with faraway fleet commanders or division leaders or military liaisons at the embassies. It was no surprise that the President couldn't fire him. And it was no surprise that a candidate pushed by Forsten moved into the post of commander in chief of CENTCOM following the assassination of Carl Anderson in Oman. Reynolds's candidate for the CENTCOM job had looked strong for a day or two, but then came the onslaught of unflattering leaks in the press. The officer withdrew. Reynolds was doing no better filling the CONUS job after the death of his ally General Neuwirth in a hunting accident. The inside dope in the Pentagon was that a Forsten man would get that plum too.

Forsten's network extended far beyond the military. He lunched regularly with top business leaders and cultivated ties on the Hill and in the press corps. Many lawmakers despised Forsten but respected his power. They needed him to bring home the pork, so they buttered up his ego and catered to his whims. And when things got rough, they capitulated to his threats. Forsten had destroyed the economy in the district of more than one disobedient congressman.

Journalists loved Forsten because he fit their caricature of the tough-talking military man. His chiseled features came across well on television, and he shot from the hip with snappy sound bites. The press corps treated Forsten with deference for another reason: A call from his office could either bring forth a torrent of cooperative officials dishing dirt or shut down sources throughout the Pentagon. Forsten himself leaked often, casting anonymous barbs at Reynolds and the White House.

Zach's relations with the press were another story. Peter Castori courted sources as he did women: with the ham-fisted come-on and the hard sell. He was not, however, wholly selfish in his entreaties. Castori sought to enlighten his sources in the hope that they would return the favor. Show them that you have something to offer and they'll open up, he believed.

The phone began ringing as Zach put his key into the top lock of his apartment after a long day of work. He made it inside by the third ring, answering just before the machine clicked on. He hoped it was Justine.

"Lieutenant? Peter Castori here."

"How'd you get my number?" Zach demanded.

"I have friends in the Pentagon."

"I highly doubt that. From what I understand you want to close the place down."

"I've always believed in a prudent national defense, Lieutenant."

"Which you define as a robust Coast Guard or something. Right?"

Castori was silent for a moment. "I didn't call to debate defense policy. As it happens, though, I respect what our armed forces do. I respect what you did in Iraq, Lieutenant."

"Whatever. The fact is that I don't have anything to say to you. And I don't appreciate you calling me at home."

"For that I apologize. But I didn't think you'd be comfortable talking at work."

"I'm not comfortable talking with you at all."

"Hey, I'm not asking you to talk on the record."

"Let's get something straight, pal. I'm not talking to you

at all, whatever the ground rules are. You're insane if you think any active-duty officer is going to talk to a reporter like you about his superior. Forget it."

"Okay, Lieutenant, fine. If you won't talk with me, just give me a few moments to talk to you. I think you might be interested in what I have to say."

"I really don't have the time right now. And in any case I've already heard your basic line. It's bullshit."

"Three minutes. Just give me three minutes."

Zach looked at his watch and sighed. A flicker of curiosity stopped him from hanging up. What was the harm, anyway? "Okay. Forty-five seconds, starting now."

Castori began speaking at a rapid rate: "The Labyrinth dates back to the late 1960s, when a small group of U.S. military and intelligence officials were given responsibility by the Nixon administration for prosecuting a secret war inside Laos and Cambodia. This war came to involve tens of thousands of U.S.-supported troops and numerous American operatives working as trainers. Some of the history of that operation has come out in recent years. What hasn't come out is how the war was funded. The CIA's black contingency fund was not big enough to keep the operation afloat, so some of the people running the war — not all, some — sought to raise revenue in other ways. They tried selling captured North Vietnamese weapons in the global black-market arms trade, but that yielded only small change. So they turned to drugs. Heroin, produced in northern Thailand and smuggled overland through Cambodia and down the Mekong River. This was their meal ticket. In the late 1960s the heroin trade had grown larger than ever because of rising addiction rates in the western world. We're talking hundreds of millions of dollars. In essence, what this group of CIA and military officials did was take over the role of middleman to finance their secret war. They came to —"

Zach interrupted. "Five seconds."

"By 1971 this group came to control eighty percent of the

heroin trade in Southeast Asia. Worked hand in glove with a Hong Kong–based syndicate run by a man named Donald Chen. Money was flowing in for their war, and Washington had no idea what —"

"Time's up," Zach said, even as the name Donald Chen echoed through his brain and perked his interest. Castori ignored him and went for broke.

"Your boss, Jeffrey Forsten, was a principal figure in this operation. His River Rats controlled the river and the delta, which means they had veto power over who did the smuggling, and —"

"We had a deal, asshole. I'm hanging up now." Zach began moving the phone away from his ear.

"Chisir," Castori blurted out. "Have you ever heard about a massacre at a village called Chisir?"

Zach pushed the receiver close again, remembering the charges from *Battle for the Mekong*. "No," he lied.

"Chisir was a smuggling town near Cambodia long before the Americans ever got to Indochina. Proud of its heritage. Forsten's men wiped it out because it wouldn't go along with their operation. Blamed it on the VC. A reporter named Don Leffler was about to nail down that part of the story when they killed him."

"Who killed him?"

"Members of the Labyrinth conspiracy. Your boss and others. They made it look like a suicide."

Zach slammed down the phone.

## 19

Colonel Ari Zhevel cursed the bright half-moon and scanned the Lebanese coastline for the fourth and final time as the Zodiac boat was lowered into the choppy waters of the Mediterranean. Through his bulky night-vision binoculars, Lebanon looked like an alien planet of eerie green shadows and barren landscapes. An occasional car could be seen on the coastal highway, but otherwise the landing area was deserted, just as intelligence had said it would be. To the north, lights twinkled where the small city of Sidon jutted into the sea. Beyond that came the orange glow from a rebuilt Beirut that was again advertising itself as the Paris of the Orient.

Zhevel climbed down a ladder to the bobbing Zodiac as one of three waiting commandos started up the outboard motor. It ran with only a quiet murmur, and the boat headed for shore. No one spoke. A salty spray wet their faces. Zhevel looked anxiously at the moon and then to the low hills past the highway. They were visible for four miles, easy.

The team hid the Zodiac in the brush beyond the beach. Not far away, a battered Toyota Land Cruiser sat in the middle of a dirt road that led off the highway toward the sea. The keys were in the ignition, and the engine was warm. Zhevel got behind the wheel, unslinging his Uzi and placing it across his lap. They drove on the coastal highway for less than a mile, passing no cars, before turning off onto the packed-gravel road that led to Al-Ghaziyah. The other three Israelis ducked as the vehicle passed through the village. The low adobe houses sat dark and still. A dog barked for a few moments, but otherwise all was quiet. Three miles outside the village, the road came to a fork. Zhevel went left, climbing a succession of steep hills and finally turning into a pull-off. From here the Mediterranean could be seen reaching far to the west, glistening under the moon. It looked deceptively placid, frozen, almost.

The commandos continued along the road on foot. One carried an ax over his shoulder. All wore full Kevlar vests and neck guards along with tightly fastened headsets. Silencers protruded from the barrels of their Uzis. After a few hundred yards a house that sat on a hilltop above the road came into view. Zhevel signaled with his hand to spread out, and the men began moving quietly up the hill, stepping carefully among the loose rocks and scree.

They surrounded the house and watched it for a short while. It was a large structure of stone and wood with a faded elegance. The former château of a Frenchman, perhaps. Or maybe built by a Lebanese merchant of better-than-average means. It was easy to imagine Sidon's fashionably dressed elite long ago sharing cocktails on the terrace. Now the house seemed a strangely pedestrian residence for one of Hizbullah's most important leaders.

Zhevel lay in the dirt and studied the front of the house. A bearded guard sat on a rusted folding chair next to the door, cradling a Kalashnikov. He struggled to sleep sitting up, his head rocking backward and then to the side. Sleep, my friend. Sleep and never know your end, Zhevel thought. He took no pleasure in killing. Another guard could be seen on the terrace, leaning against the house and enjoying a cigarette in its shadow. He would be more trouble. And if intelligence was correct, there would be another guard inside.

Zhevel spoke softly into his headset, and the commandos rose, moving forward in the gray light from the moon. The first burst of muffled Uzi fire cut down the guard on the terrace as he unslung his assault rifle. There was a splash of sparks as his cigarette landed tip down on the terrace. Zhevel saw the neck of the guard at the door stiffen and his eyes open. Don't bring up the gun, he silently commanded as he walked forward, Uzi raised to eye level. Throw it to the ground. But the guard's hand instinctively went to the trigger. Zhevel fired. The man smashed back against the door frame with a groan and collapsed.

There was the sound of breaking glass and another hiss of muffled fire. "Inside guard taken out," said one of the commandos on the headset. Zhevel saw a light go on upstairs.

The commando with the ax raced forward. He tried the door, then fired a burst from his Uzi at the lock and tried it again with no success. After a few powerful ax blows the door gave way. Two commandos covered the back of the house while Zhevel and another moved cautiously inside. A bloody body lay sprawled next to the couch. Music played quietly on the radio. Zhevel popped out the half-empty clip in his gun and pushed in a fresh one. He edged to the bottom of the stairs, flattening himself against a wall around the corner at their base and calling out loudly in Arabic, "We are the Israelis. We are not here to harm you. Come down slowly with your hands on top of your head."

For a moment there was no sound. Then voices were heard whispering urgently. Finally there was a creaking on the steps, and Zhevel shot a quick glance around the corner. A woman in a nightgown was descending slowly, her hands on her head, her lips quivering. Behind her came a small boy in pajamas. When they reached the bottom of the steps, Zhevel gestured for them to stand in the middle of the living room. The woman saw the body and began to weep. The boy stared at it for a long moment and then turned away. He was young, but he had seen death before. The stairs creaked once more. A man was coming down. Zhevel trained his gun on him and stared searchingly at his face. When the man reached the last step, his nose was just inches from the end of the silencer. Zhevel pushed it even closer.

"Where is Karim Hirani?" he demanded.

The man gestured upward with a cocked elbow. Zhevel

saw a bare foot on the top step and in a moment the rest of a man. The right man. Zhevel gathered all four captives in the living room and looked at his watch. Ahead of schedule. He locked Karim Hirani's wrists in front of his waist with handcuffs and moved him next to the door. The other commandos placed plastic links on the hands of the boy, the woman, and the other man. One pried a bloodied submachine from the corpse next to the couch and slung it over his shoulder. For another five minutes everyone stood silently.

The boy was the first to hear the dim thumping of the helicopter's rotor blades. He looked to the ceiling in terror as the noise turned to a roar. The commandos hustled Hirani outside to a clearing beyond the terrace, above which the helicopter hovered. A searchlight on its belly lit up the area, and a large canvas-and-metal seating contraption descended on the end of a cable. Two soldiers heaved Hirani onto one of the small seats, strapped him in, and accompanied him on the ride up. Zhevel and the other soldier followed. Moments later the helicopter was over the sea.

"We talk again about Captain Avni. Yes?" The Israeli interrogator pulled a black hood off of Karim Hirani's head. The guerrilla leader blinked for a few moments and then squinted at his captors. He crossed his arms on the table and placed his head on them, closing his eyes. A muscular Israeli soldier in a white T-shirt and green fatigue pants stepped forward silently and yanked Hirani upright by his hair.

"I remind you that sleep is a privilege here, Mr. Hirani," the interrogator said sharply in Arabic. "You cooperate and you can sleep once more. The moment you leave this room, on the softest of beds. Now we speak of Captain Avni."

"I have told you all I know," Hirani said wearily. For the first four days at the military prison outside of Nazareth, the Muslim had said nothing. But soon, reduced to a near delirium from the deprivation of sleep and light, he had begun to talk in exchange for small quantities of both.

The interrogator slowly circled the table. "You have told us that you held the captain for some time after his capture. You have said that you then sold him to a contingent of Iranian Revolutionary Guards based in the Bekaa and never heard of his fate again."

"Yes, yes. A hundred times, yes." Hirani's eyes were closing again.

"But we know this to be false!" screamed the interrogator. "Totally false. Our sources say that you never sold Captain Avni to the Guards and that you held him in the basement of a safe house outside of Tyre for two years. In chains. Chained like a dog, you Shiite piece of shit." The interrogator delivered a powerful blow with his open hand to Hirani's right ear. "Further lying is pointless. I can make sure that you see no daylight for three years. Or six. We can do better than the hell you created for Captain Avni."

"Your sources are wrong," Hirani said, shaking his head, his speech slurred. "Mossad does not know everything." He slumped forward to the table. The soldier pulled him back up and held his head. The interrogator threw a glass of water at the prisoner's face and stormed out of the room.

After a few moments another Israeli took his place. He offered a handkerchief to Hirani and opened a can of soda, pushing it across the table. His voice was calm, his manner soothing.

"My colleague tends to get impatient. He thinks only of Captain Avni's family. But I, I know that you too have a family. An eight-year-old boy, Mustafa. A fine wife, Ravit. Smoke?"

The interrogator gave Hirani a cigarette and lit it for him.

"We work together, and you will see your family soon. This I promise."

Hirani seemed to revive and relax somewhat. But the conversation continued to go in circles for another half hour.

"Let me speak of something else, a secret of great value to your government," Hirani finally said, seeking to change the subject. The interrogator leaned forward with interest.

"Go ahead."

"The operatives of Sheik Abdul Tabrata are for hire."

Hirani sat back smugly with his arms folded, letting the information sink in.

"For hire to whom?" the interrogator asked, unimpressed. Sheik Tabrata was known to Mossad as the leader of a fanatical Hizbullah splinter group. There had been hints in the past of his turn to mercenary work.

"To whoever can pay his price. To any and all. Just like Sabri al-Banna," Hirani said, using the birth name of Abu Nidal.

"How do you know this information?"

"Of what I speak is the truth."

"Do many others know of Tabrata's new business?"

"Very, very few. It is dangerous to talk of such things. And most definitely not his operatives. They are so young. Their training camp in the Bekaa is isolated. They think that it is Allah, not gold to a Swiss bank account, for whom they are dying."

"How many contracts have there been?"

"You may remember the assassination of General Sharar three months back, in his villa outside of Damascus?"

The interrogator nodded. This was getting interesting. The top Syrian's death had been a bloodbath, with both assassins dying in the act. Neither was identified. No group ever claimed responsibility.

"And the deaths in Tripoli?"

Again the Israeli nodded. Mossad had wondered about that incident too.

"There have been others." Both Hirani and the interrogator were silent for a long moment. Finally the guerrilla leader spoke again, a hard edge of amusement in his voice.

"I am told that even Americans have contracted for Sheik Tabrata's services."

The Israeli leaned forward. "Americans? What Americans?"

Hirani smiled coyly. "Another soda would be nice."

The interrogator snapped his fingers, and the soldier left the room, returning with a soda. Hirani lit a second cigarette and sucked deeply. He was in control of the conversation now.

"It is said that Sheik Tabrata is becoming a rich man by working for the Americans. It is said that two of his men will die."

Hirani stretched and yawned. "But I am tired. Maybe we talk tomorrow. When a night of good sleep has passed."

## 20

Zach still felt a residue of irritation with Castori when he woke the morning after their telephone conversation. An accusation of mass murder was serious stuff, he thought as he shaved. Even if it was ancient history. Castori was heading toward libel land in a big way. And he wondered, what link was Castori going to make between Vietnam and the rest of his crazy conspiracy, the more current part? Zach stepped from the bathroom and began dressing. Nonsense. Total nonsense. Why had he even listened?

But later, sitting in his office during a lull in the day, he found himself angrily scribbling names on a scrap of paper: "Donny Chen," "Chisir," "Forsten." Castori's smear job had to be stopped.

He rifled through his Pentagon directory and dialed the phone. As it rang, he scribbled one other name: "Riley."

"Lewis Thurston."

"Lewis, hi, this is Zach."

"Morning, Zachary. How goes it, my friend? I hear the blood is really flowing over in your part of the building."

"Knee-deep and rising."

"Bet a vampire would love your job."

"Some say the Joint Staff only recruits vampires."

Both men laughed.

"Say, Lewis, I wonder if you could do me a rather unusual favor."

"If I can, if I can."

"Are DIA's databases on foreign populations as good as I've heard?"

"Depends what you've heard. But yes, they're adequate

133

given our current software limitations. We share the same system with CIA and NSA. Why? What's up?"

"Is it true that you can punch almost any name in the developed world into DIA's system and get their personal records?"

"Essentially, although it's not that simple. You need more information than just a name. Otherwise it can be like looking for John Smith in the Manhattan phone book, except a thousand times worse, depending on country size."

"Could you do a name for me or is there some regulation against that?"

"Zachary, of course you know, now, that I'm really not the person this kind of request should be directed to. You, my friend, should speak with —"

"It's a special favor, Lewis."

"I see."

"It wouldn't be against the rules, right?"

"Well, there are rules on this, but nothing that serious. What have you got?"

"Donald Chen. Hong Kong resident. Age about fifty-five to sixty, I would say. Occupation businessman."

"Anything else?"

"That's it."

"Well, it's not much. But I should be able to work with this. Hong Kong is not that huge. What's it for?"

"I can't tell you that now."

There was a long pause on the other end of the line. "I see, I see. I guess I can understand that."

"Thanks, Lewis. When do you think you could have something?"

"Things are pretty slow around here, so I could probably run it for you today. I'll tell you what. Why don't we meet at my least-favorite watering hole for a drink after work, say eight or nine, and I'll tell you what I found."

"That would be great," Zach said. "But I have another question for you."

"Oh?"

"DIA has an arm that handles internal investigations, right?"

"That's correct, DIA Investigations. DIAI. That unit is right down the hall from me. But I'm telling you right now that I can't get into their system, absolutely not." Thurston paused, and then said with the pride of a longtime hacker: "Let me rephrase that, my friend. I'm not allowed to be in their system, but I can get into it if I really want. If the cause is a noble one."

"I remember some of the stuff you pulled at Cornell. Wild shit."

"I was a lot younger then. And bloody stupid."

"You're still a genius, Lewis. So here's the question: What do you imagine would be the status of DIAI's Vietnam records? Would they be on computer or would they be in some archival warehouse?"

"Archive, no question. But almost certainly the finding guides to that material would be on computer. If you knew what you were looking for you could find out where it was and how much material there was."

"Could you get into the system that has the finding guides? Also, would it be possible for me to get into the archives themselves?"

"My guess is probably yes to both questions, given the age of the records. I'd hazard the guess that a lot of the investigations stuff from Vietnam is still very classified, even now. But it's probably not impossible to get in if the person searching had a reasonably high clearance. And you have that, alright. What are you after, anyway?"

Zach hesitated. "I'm not really sure. But let me ask you for two other things, one easy and one hard. If it's too much, tell me."

"Go ahead."

"First, the easy one. Check out the finding guides and see if you can locate records — assuming they exist — about a possible war-crimes incident during the late sixties or early seventies at a South Vietnamese town called Chisir." Zach spelled out the name.

"Not a problem, not a problem at all. What's the hard assignment?"

"I'll understand if you pass on this one, Lewis."

"Try me."

"There was an incident in Panama with a Green Beret colonel named Riley. I want to know what happened."

"I don't know, Zachary," Lewis said slowly. He sounded unsure, nervous. "That's pretty recent. I would be taking a risk getting into the system for something like that. If this is for Forsten I'd really prefer that you go through official channels."

"It's not for Forsten."

"I see."

"Let's just say it's a matter of personal interest."

Lewis sighed. "I'll do what I can. Sounds intriguing, actually. But I won't promise anything."

"I understand. Thanks, Lewis."


When Zach arrived at Characters, Thurston was already at a table. He sat stiffly, a white handkerchief peeping out of the pocket of his suit jacket, his tie still cinched, his polished wing tips gleaming. Zach looked Thurston over, shaking his head.

"You know, Lewis, you dress too damn well for a computer jock. And too damn well for the Pentagon."

"Ah, Zachary, my friend, style is a prisoner of neither vocation nor location. In any case, I assure you that the ladies of this fine metropolis do not share your opinion."

A cocktail waitress walked past, and Zach ordered a beer. "So, was my favor doable?"

"Not a problem, not a problem at all. A piece of cake, actually."

"What'd you find?"

Thurston reached down for his briefcase and took out a folder, placing it on the table. "Let's start with Donald Chen. The search turned up eight Donald Chens in your age range who are currently in some kind of business in Hong Kong." Thurston opened up the folder and passed over eleven sheets of paper.

"Because the number was relatively high, I didn't get nearly as much on them as I could have. Instead I just got your basic date of birth, marital status, number of children, past employment, club association, and that sort of stuff. Just a few lines on each. I thought that would get you started. It's no problem doing more on any of them. Our data is excellent on Hong Kong."

Zach looked through the sheaf. Two of the Chens ran laundry businesses. Three ran small restaurants. Another ran a flower store.

"This guy would be big by now," Zach mumbled to himself.

He narrowed the list down to two Donald Chens. One was president and owner of Chen Enterprises. He had been married twice and was divorced. He had three children and belonged to numerous clubs. There was no past employment listed before Chen Enterprises. The other was CEO of a textile company. Married to the same women for thirty years. Two children. Three clubs.

"I'm pretty sure it's the first guy, but go deeper on both."

"What makes you think it would be the first fellow?"

"He's the divorcing type," Zach said.

"And what is it that you suggest I look for?" Thurston asked, placing the papers back in the folder.

"Anything out of the ordinary — criminal records, tax irregularities, that sort of thing. Go back to the 1960s, if you can."

"Not a problem at all, my friend."

"I really appreciate this."

"As you should. Now on to Chisir and the delightful Colonel Riley." Thurston sipped his beer and took out another folder. "The finder guide for DIAI from 1965 through 1970 shows that there are four cubic feet on the Chisir incident at the Federal Documents Depository up in Chadwick."

"That's in Virginia, right?"

"About forty minutes west. It's where most DOD archives are stored."

"Four cubic feet. Is that a lot?"

"Not really. We're talking just a few archive boxes. A pretty small file, actually."

"Could I get into Chadwick?"

Lewis waved a hand dismissively. "I don't think it should be a problem with your classification status. You could get into the missile bay of a Trident sub if you're what I suspect you are. Just give the head defense archivist there a call, tell them who you are, and set up an appointment. They should even be open on Saturdays."

"Sounds easy enough."

"Now to Colonel Riley. His case was a tougher nut to crack. All the records from DIAI on him are computerized. I can't believe you got me doing this, but I pulled up quite a few of them today."

"Yeah, and . . ."

"Fascinating, absolutely fascinating. And gruesome. The fellow is a bona fide war criminal."

Thurston described how the full texts of two separate human-rights reports referring to a blond American who aided Contra atrocities were contained in the file. He also described a memo on Riley's activities by the CIA station chief in Honduras. The memo acknowledged that Riley had operated for long stretches inside Nicaragua but said there was no conclusive proof of his involvement in any atrocities. Two other memos, one by a DIAI investigator and another by a lieutenant colonel in the Army special forces, echoed this conclusion.

"Your man's been around," Lewis said. "There was some stuff in there on Iran-Contra, too."

"Really?"

"Indeed so, but I didn't pull it up. Are you interested in that?"

"Not yet. Maybe later. It's Panama that I'm mainly interested in."

"There's a whole lot on that too," Thurston said. "Affidavits from three other SOF mission team members. Transcripts of interrogations of PDF soldiers who say they witnessed or heard about the killings. And copies of the Army's autopsy reports on the bodies. All of them were shot in the back or back of the head, all from close range."

"Sounds like court-martial material."

"Absolutely right. And in fact there's at least two memos from various people in the chain of command which recommended precisely such a punishment."

"So how'd the son of a bitch get off?"

"That's the mystery, I'd say."

"There's no paper trail that explains it?"

"Absolutely nothing. All there is is a pro forma memorandum from the head of the Army's military police dated late January 1990 which states that the charges will not result in a court-martial hearing because of insufficient evidence. And then there's just a copy of Riley's discharge from later in the year."

"Bizarre."

Thurston shook his head, mystified. "Bizarre, indeed. Somebody obviously pulled a few strings for our good colonel."

Another thought entered Zach's mind. "Hey, Lewis, did you get a basic bio on Riley?"

"As a matter of fact I did. Nothing exceptionally detailed, however." Thurston leafed through the papers and handed Zach a sheet with eight lines of biographical information on

Riley. Zach scrutinized it closely. Riley had gone straight into the Army after attending public high school in South Carolina. Before joining the Green Berets he had served for three years in West Germany as a weapons specialist and then —

"Uh oh," Zach said softly as he came to the next line: "Staff Asst. to Rear Admiral Jeffrey Forsten, Foreign Military Sales, 1979–81."

"What?" Lewis asked.

"Nothing. Listen, Lewis, I swear that I'll tell you what all this is about some day very soon."

## 21

Washington at the end of December's second week was a place of deceptive calm. Predictions of fiscal doom and charges of foul play, now the staple rhetoric of a deadlocked Congress, temporarily died down with members back in their home states. There was a steady stream of bad news about the economy, with the recession showing no signs of relenting, but this was nothing unusual. Nor were the attacks on the President. Sherman had begun a fresh offensive and was skewering the White House for appeasing terrorist states and throwing money into the sinkhole of big government. For once, however, the White House staff showed none of its trademark defensiveness, parrying the jabs instead with mature confidence. It was a testament to how serious things had become that the President's people no longer indulged their internecine tendencies. Washington was calm not simply because members of Congress were not in town to lob grenades; it was calm because executive branch officials had suspended their efforts to dismember one another.

On Thursday afternoon Thurston called Zach, saying he had a fuller picture of the Donald Chen who ran Chen Enterprises and that they should meet.

"How about some jazz tonight, Lewis?"

"Jazz?" Lewis sputtered, as if pronouncing a foreign word.

Six hours later, Lewis and Zach were listening to a sizzling quartet at a small club in Northeast. Zach had stumbled on the place during his first disorienting month in Washington and he had been there many nights, usually alone. There was something so rooted about jazz. Improvisation had an essential truthfulness; it was pure soul, guided by instinct and pleasure. Jazz seemed to Zach like the most unpretentious form of expression in the world.

Zach was pleased that Lewis was actually grooving to the music and tapping the table with his hand. Just because a guy wore a yellow V-necked sweater and what looked like golfing slacks to a jazz club didn't mean he couldn't enjoy the place.

"He's a major player, a very rich man," Lewis said of Chen when they talked during intermission. "Not quite a billionaire, but the old chap is close."

"How did he make his money?"

"Import-export, shipping, airlines most recently. Our Mr. Chen appears to have a Midas touch."

"Anything illegal?"

"Nothing like that, at least for the last two decades or so."

"What do you mean?"

"Well, in March 1974 Donald Chen was indicted along with twelve other men in connection with a heroin smuggling ring."

Zach was unable to speak for a moment. "And?" he finally mumbled.

"And the charges were dismissed. According to an abstract of his case, Chen's lawyer successfully claimed that Chen had been unaware that one of his warehouses was being used by the ring."

After getting home from the club, Zach sat in his darkened living room for a long time. At a staff meeting with Forsten the next morning, he found himself looking at the admiral differently, wondering.

And at ten on Saturday morning, Zach was in the lobby of the Federal Documents Depository in Chadwick. He had called ahead for an appointment the day after talking about Chen with Thurston. A circuitous hour-and-a-half ride on two different buses had been required to get to the depository, even though it was only a forty-minute drive from Crystal City. On the second bus, he had looked out the window at the passing strip malls and gas stations and wondered what he was doing. Disproving slander against his boss, he told himself. Disproving it so that he could wash away the strange ideas that had been coming into his mind since his last talk with Castori. He would gather evidence and then nail the reporter in their next conversation. Castori wanted a source and he would get one — a source that would finally sink his ship of hallucinations.

An archivist in the defense division studied Zach's ID and then asked him to fill out a few forms. Zach was then led through several locked doors and told to have a seat at a work table. He looked around, noticing the low ceilings and sprinklers everywhere overhead. The room was lit by dust-covered fluorescent lights. After five minutes the archivist returned with a cart carrying five boxes.

"This is the entire file on Chisir," she said, parking the cart next to the table.

Zach looked at the labels on the boxes. He removed the box labeled PHOTOGRAPHIC EVIDENCE and placed it on the table. It seemed like a good place to start.

He opened the box and pulled out several folders. The contents were stomach-turning. Photos showed clumps of bodies in various parts of the village. Other photos were of bodies inside huts, the flash from the camera giving the scenes a creepy glow.

Zach put the photos aside and for the next few hours read through large portions of the written files. The investigation of the incident had been extensive. There were transcripts of long interviews with Forsten and with his men. There were yellowed reports by investigators from the Army and Navy, and from DIA and CIA. Zach read through some of the transcripts first, starting with Forsten's.

The story told by Forsten was that three of his patrol boats had been on a two-day mission up the Triphung tributary. Intelligence had reported VC activity around several villages on the Triphung. It was an area so dense and remote as to be inaccessible to ground patrols and difficult to reach even by helicopter. Forsten's mission was to find and destroy any enemy soldiers or places of refuge.

He said that he and his patrols had been to Chisir a few months before. They had found the people friendly and co-operative. He claimed that on the second day of the patrol the boats had approached Chisir, and they had immediately noticed a deadly silence. There was none of the usual activity on the water. No women doing laundry on the shore or fisherman unloading their catch. "We knew right away that something was wrong," Forsten had said. He then went on to describe finding the massacred villagers. "The place was a slaughterhouse. They didn't even spare the infants."

Forsten's story was that the VC had wiped out the village because of its known sympathies to U.S. forces. He noted that there had been cases such as this before. "If they'd do half of Hue during Tet, why not a pisshole like Chisir?"

When confronted by the interviewers with the fact that M16 shells were littered through the village, Forsten scoffed. "Well, if I were a VC unit commander, my first thought would be to make it look like the Americans did it. And hell, I don't need to remind you how many M16s Charlie has stolen. Thousands. Tens of thousands, even." The other members of Forsten's team had told the same story.

The reports by Army and Navy forensic teams had been inconclusive. The bodies had begun to decompose by the time the teams reached the remote village, and heavy rains had swept the area during the interim. The only evidence Zach could find in the files that raised questions about the story told by the River Rats was a CIA report on Chisir. The report stated that Chisir had been known for its Vietcong sympathies since the early 1960s.

Zach read through several final reports by different investigators. All had cited assorted inconsistencies in the River Rats' stories, but all had concluded that there was no evidence to warrant the suspicion that Forsten's men had carried out the massacre. The Army's final report, written by a lieutenant named Kevin Ettinger, was the most skeptical. It focused on the M16 shells, noting that while many M16s were indeed unaccounted for in Vietnam, the Vietcong soldiers were rarely known to carry these weapons in combat operations because of their notorious unreliability. But the report acknowledged the possibility that the weapons had been used on this occasion in an effort to place responsibility for the massacre on U.S. troops. Ultimately, Ettinger concluded that the evidence against the River Rats was inconclusive.

Zach left the documents depository at two feeling drained but relieved. There was no evidence that Forsten was a war criminal. His anxiety returned with the thought of Chen. But, leaning back in his bus seat and closing his eyes, he pushed that idea away and thought about his coming afternoon and evening with Justine.

FBI Director Holsten looked around the inside of *Marine One* as the rotors on the President's helicopter began to whir. The seats were white leather with presidential seals emblazoned in blue. A plush tan carpet lay underfoot, and there was even a small bar. Not bad, Holsten thought. He was moving up in the world. In a few moments the helicopter was in the air, heading out of Washington toward the Canoctin Mountains of Maryland and Camp David.

Holsten had been badgering the White House for two weeks to get a meeting with the President, and again the only available slot had been on a Saturday afternoon. This time at Camp David, where the President spent most weekends. Joe Rizotti had apologized for the timing and locale in his usual unctuous manner. He said he hoped the ride in *Marine One* would reduce any inconvenience.

It was not the spoiled weekend that irked Holsten — he could endure face time with the President at Camp David any Saturday of the year. It was the delay in getting a meeting on the Turzin matter in the first place. Holsten had seen plenty of the President lately, no question. They had met on the Sacramento operation, and Holsten had attended an emergency meeting at the White House following the death of General Neuwirth in Georgia, reporting that there was no evidence of foul play — at least no hard evidence.

But there had been no meeting on Turzin, even though Holsten had been ready to move forward for quite some time. His agents had researched Turzin's war record, education, and family background. With great effort they had obtained Turzin's clearance reviews and studied them closely. Two agents had shadowed the lieutenant on several occasions, learning about his routine. His apartment in Crystal City had been scoped out; the locks wouldn't be a problem. Finally, Holsten had discreetly and hypothetically floated the prospect of authorization with Judge Karmel. He gave a tentative yes to both a phone and a room tap. All this information had been written up in a four-page memo regarding possible recruitment, a memo that Holsten carried today in his briefcase and that he had been itching to deliver by hand to the President.

Yet if Holsten had been ready, his boss had not been. The failure to get a private meeting wasn't accidental. The President was stalling in his usual fashion, wavering and worrying, floundering in the sea of equivocation that was his natural habitat. If he agonized this much about approaching a single source, would he ever approve indictments? Holsten didn't even want to think about this question.

The helicopter touched down on a landing pad not far from a cluster of rustic lodges set on top of a wooded mountain. A Secret Service agent escorted Holsten up a paved path and into the main cabin. Rizotti, for once, was nowhere to be seen.

The President greeted Holsten warmly, and they settled down before a fire in the living room. The lodge had the feeling of a hunting cabin, with low-beamed ceilings and a giant stone hearth. There was an intimacy here, a humanity that was absent at the White House. The two men chatted about the retreat's history for a few moments before getting down to business.

"I want you to go ahead with surveillance on Turzin and an approach as soon as possible," the President said decisively.

"Yes, sir," Holsten replied, surprised. He wouldn't be needing the memo after all.

"The closer we get to the election, the hotter this gets, John."

"That's true, Mr. President."

"And if we're going to take risks I want to take them sooner rather than later. Turzin may be our last chance to make headway on this, am I right?"

"I'm afraid so. Nothing else is panning out, at least not without subpoenas. Subpoenas would change everything, sir."

The President glared at Holsten as if he had suggested a press release about the investigation. "How soon can we have electronic surveillance?" he asked tersely.

"By Monday. Tuesday at the latest. I've already laid the groundwork."

"And then when would we approach?"

"Once we know more, once we have a fuller picture of him and are sure that he hasn't turned already. Probably in a week or two."

"I like it. But John . . ." The President looked anxious, unsure.

"Yes, Mr. President?"

"Forget it. Just don't screw this up."

## 22

Justine picked Zach up in front of his building at four P.M. in a black two-door Mercedes.

"Hey, it's great to see you," Zach said, getting in and giving her a quick kiss. He silently took in the car. It cost sixty thousand, easy. He didn't ask how she afforded it. He didn't need to ask.

Justine was dressed in a tight tan linen dress and she looked more stunning than usual. Zach put a hand on her thigh as she pulled out of his building's driveway. Touching her anywhere at any time still produced the same effect: total, overpowering desire.

"Pull over for a second, would you?" he said suddenly after they had traveled less than a hundred yards.

Justine stopped along the side of the road. "What is it?"

Zach leaned over and kissed her, his hands traveling along her shoulders and down the curves of her body. He had never felt this kind of craving for anyone. He felt like he was in the grip of a powerful addiction. It was impossible to get enough of her. Sometimes it seemed he thought about making love to her from the moment he woke up until the moment he went to sleep.

"Wow," Justine said, catching her breath. "Hello again to you too."

"I missed you," Zach said softly, kissing her ear and neck before retreating back into his seat. He nodded to the road. "Okay, we can keep driving."

Justine pulled back into traffic. "So what's your surprise, Zach? You said you had a surprise."

"It wouldn't be a surprise if I told you. Get on the parkway going south."

Justine obeyed his directions. They intersected with I-95 and drove across the bridge into Maryland. He told her to take the exit for Andrews Air Force Base.

"I know what it is, I know what it is," Justine chanted as they pulled up to the gate of the air base. She kissed him on the cheek as he leaned over to show his ID. "I love to fly."

Zach was silent, directing her through the vast air base toward the hangars where the helicopters were maintained. Every certified helicopter pilot on active duty in the Washington area technically had flying privileges at Andrews, but nailing down time was famously difficult. Zach's medal and position at the Pentagon assured that there was no runaround. The perks of power: He despised the concept but loved the reality.

Zach got a clipboard from the office and went through the preflight checks on a stripped-down Blackhawk. Justine walked among the armed Blackhawk gunships, inspecting their armaments with curiosity. Fifteen minutes later they were over the Chesapeake Bay. Bare trees lined the shore, and behind that lay miles of farmland, dormant and brown. The sun was heading down to the west, casting a soft orange glow over the bay. Justine squeezed Zach's knee as he took the helicopter lower, streaking over the water at one hundred feet.

"This is incredible," she said, talking loudly over the roar of the engines. "It's beautiful."

"Better than an airplane any day. You can go a lot lower." Zach dipped down another ten feet.

"When did you learn to fly?"

"Early nineties. Top brass decided that they didn't want a special forces team stranded in-country some day because a chopper pilot gets killed during exfil. Three men in my unit got training as part of that initiative. I volunteered and spent two months with the 160th Aviation Regiment, a wing of

Army special forces. They call themselves 'the Night Stalkers' because their specialty is flying at night. I did quite a bit of that myself."

"Sounds scary."

"It is. You go low, nap of the earth."

"How low is that?"

Zach dropped the Blackhawk another twenty-five feet. Ripples raced outward in the water before them. "Really low," he said.

"Okay, I get the point." Justine had tightened her grip on his knee. Zach brought the helicopter back up to one hundred feet. He looked over at her and saw her face frozen in an expression of terrified pleasure, a sliver of sunlight bouncing off her hair.

They drove from Andrews into the Maryland countryside to a quaint restaurant in a small village near Annapolis that Justine knew. Over the past month, they had met one or two nights a week at Zach's apartment, his exhaustion from work disappearing the moment he saw her. By unspoken agreement, her place and Washington-area restaurants were out of the question. Hostile territory. So Zach's sterile apartment — the 'hotel suite,' as they jokingly called it — became the scene of their affair.

Justine usually didn't arrive until after ten, almost always later than promised. He would be waiting, pacing the apartment, flicking the television on and off, starting to read a book and then putting it down, drinking a beer and mauling its label, picking up little pieces of lint off the carpet. He hated the lateness. But when the knock finally came, he would leap forward to undo the lock, and she would be forgiven the moment he saw her. His anger would return again at the end of the evening, when she would drag herself from bed, to drive home through the night. But rarely would Zach pressure her to stay until morning. He knew she couldn't. And he knew why.

He wondered where it was leading. Was this it? Would they just meet in his apartment and have sex until she tired of him? He pondered the irony of his situation: He was, in essence, the mistress of another man's mistress — kept penned up and waiting in a furnished apartment, hoping his lover would come to him more often and stay longer. Was she using him? he wondered. Did she love him? Could she?

He would think of asking these questions when she was there, but didn't. Instead, lying in bed, entwined and warm, they talked often of the past and rarely of the future. He learned more about her slowly, and he came to understand her motivations. They were simple, really. Justine was as brilliant as she seemed; she was smart and sophisticated, without question. There were no misleading appearances there. But it was her confidence that deceived, for beneath the charismatic veneer was a woman of deep insecurity. Justine was somebody who didn't really believe that she controlled her destiny. Zach sensed that she saw herself as a prisoner of powerful emotional currents that flowed through her life, sometimes dispensing joy but usually leaving destruction in their wake. The more he knew her, the more he felt there was a tremendous fatalism at the center of her being. Zach learned that her parents had divorced when she was young. Her father had disappeared, and she and her younger brother had lived with her mother on the edge of poverty. Real friends had been few, but never, from high school age on, had she been without a serious relationship. It was no mystery to Zach what that was all about. She had turned to men first for emotional sustenance and then, as an adult, for material security.

It was folly to fall in love with her; this was obvious. Zach wanted to tell her how he felt, to talk about it and somehow establish where they were at, yet he kept silent. He worried about panicking her. She would panic and then she would run. He imagined how easily she could disappear from his life, retreating into Sherman's world. Justine herself didn't provide any openings to talk about what the relationship was or where it was going. Indeed, at those times when the subject lay obviously before them, she showed enormous creativity in escaping its grasp and moving them back into the separate reality of their affair.

Their dinner in the country was the first time they had been out together since the Middle Eastern restaurant. They agreed it was a good thing, agreed they should do it more often. But neither mentioned the future more concretely than that or touched on the issues between them that really mattered. They avoided them and instead talked of work. Zach asked Justine about Sherman's relations with the leaders of the two main parties, and they discussed the upcoming primaries. Finally, buttering a piece of bread and filling his wineglass, he came to his true agenda. "Justine, how much do you know about Sherman's background, I mean going way back?"

"Well, I know he went to public high school outside of Richmond and then went —"

"No, I don't mean quite that far back. I mean his days when he was starting out in the import-export business."

"Only that he made a huge killing in a short time. Apparently he was an incredible visionary when it came to identifying markets here in the States and finding bargains abroad. His business became a model that a lot of other people sought to duplicate."

Zach hated the way that Justine turned almost starry-eyed whenever she talked of Sherman. He pushed on.

"Have you ever heard of a guy named Donald Chen, a possible business partner of Sherman's from Hong Kong?"

Justine pondered the question for a moment, chewing a mouthful of lasagne.

"Chen. Nope. But I know Doug still has investments in Hong Kong. In fact, he's going there early next week, after a few speeches in California and a stopover in Hawaii. Why do you ask? Who's Donald Chen?"

Zach hesitated a moment and then told her about the photo on Forsten's wall, about Castori's charges, and about Chen's indictment for drug smuggling. He left out the part about the massacre at Chisir and the trip to the depository. As it was, saying it all out loud made him feel like an idiot. What was he doing?

Justine stared at him. She looked deeply disturbed. "You know, I would never have imagined that Castori could get to you like that. I can't believe you buy this nonsense."

"I don't buy it; that's the whole point, Justine. It's bullshit, and I want to convince Castori of that so he'll climb back into the hole he came from."

Justine was shaking her head in agitation. "That is the stupidest thing you could possibly be doing. I've been in this business for a long time. The way to deal with the Castoris of the world is to ignore them until they go away. And I assure you, they always do go away. You have no idea what you're getting into."

"I'm defending Forsten's reputation."

"Zach! He doesn't need the help, I'm telling you. And in the meantime, Castori could use your name in his work and cause you a huge amount of trouble. Christ, you're naive."

Zach sat silently. Justine was right, of course.

Justine didn't park when they arrived back at Crystal City but instead pulled in front of the lobby.

"I can't come in tonight."

Zach fixed her with a disappointed look. He'd wanted her all day — every day since he'd last had her. "What's up?"

She rubbed his arm. "I'm sorry, Zach. I have to be somewhere."

"I can't imagine where." He leaned over and kissed her. He started to open the door.

"Hey, hero," Justine said seductively, putting her hand on his thigh and moving it upward.

"Yeah?"

"Guess what you're having for lunch on Monday."

"Ham-and-cheese sandwich? Pentagon stew, maybe?"

Her hand reached its destination, and she massaged gently. "No, you're having me. I'm going to be in this neighborhood. They give you an hour at that funny-shaped building where you work, don't they? Let's say your place at twelve-thirty."

Zach agreed. And in the elevator up to his apartment, he wondered again how long this could go on. He never had been in a clandestine affair before, but he imagined that they tended to reach some sort of peak and then either implode under the pressure or get discovered. He wondered how far from that peak he and Justine were.

He stepped off the elevator and began walking down the hall toward his door. After a few steps he stopped suddenly. He could see a figure leaning against the window at the end of the hall, looking out toward the lights of Rosslyn. After the medal ceremony, security officials in the Pentagon had warned Zach that there was always a slight chance he could be targeted by the Iraqis for retribution. He still sometimes thought of the warnings. The figure began to turn, and Zach saw a head of curly hair. It was Castori.

"Lieutenant, my man, I've been waiting for you."

Zach walked to his door and put his key in the upper lock. "How'd you get by the doorman?"

Castori flashed a toothy grin. "Infiltration is part of my job description, as it is yours."

Zach got to the second lock. "I don't like the fact that you're here, waiting for me in the dark. I should call building security."

"Hey, come on, Lieutenant. I only just got going last time. Give me another chance."

Zach pushed the door open, letting Castori follow him inside. There was something about the guy that made him hard to hate. Zach flicked on the light in the kitchen and got a beer from the refrigerator. He didn't offer one to Castori. It was time to set the reporter straight.

"You lied to me," Zach said, sitting down on the couch. "There's nothing to this alleged Chisir massacre. I looked at the archives on that today. Forsten's men were cleared by several different investigators."

Castori smiled. "You've been doing some checking. I'm impressed."

Zach grimaced. Christ, what the hell was he doing with this joker?

"It was a whitewash," Castori said. "The investigation was a sham."

"Oh, get off it. I've seen the classified records on that; you haven't."

"I have my own sources."

"Yeah, like who?"

"Can't tell you that. I promised them." Castori flashed another grin. "All I can say is keep digging. Dig, dig, dig, Lieutenant. You'll see."

Zach sank back in the couch and sighed. "You know, Mr. Castori, the Vietnam War happened a long time ago. There are some people who did things they regret. Conceivably my boss is one of them, although I don't think so. But it was a war, for christsakes. We wanted to win. Bad things happen in war. So even if these allegations are true, what does it have to do with anything that's happening today? I don't get what your holy crusade is all about. Why are you harassing people who are serving their country?"

"Hey, that's what I was getting to last time. You can't tell much in forty-five seconds."

Justine's warning replayed itself in his head. Kick the guy out and never talk to him again. Stop getting sucked in deeper. Instead, Zach looked at his watch. "Okay, this time I'll give you five minutes."

"Fine." Castori jumped to his feet and began pacing

around the room. He had given this spiel before. "We pick up the story after Vietnam. The war is lost, but this group of CIA and military officials — I call them the Foundation and I'm sure that Forsten has been a core member from the beginning — has learned some important lessons. Most crucially they've learned that it's possible to raise big money through their own enterprises to finance covert operations. They've also learned that they can personally enrich themselves in the process, but that's another story. I've done a lot of research in the Caribbean and Zurich, trying to track cash flows in the Labyrinth. We'll get to that another time.

"In any case, the Foundation feels that they discovered this great mechanism just in time. By the mid-1970s the good old days are over. We have the Church Committee investigating the CIA, and all sorts of other inquiries. Congress comes down on the Agency like a ton of bricks. Oversight becomes very elaborate. You could never do another Laos or Chile. At least not legally. And so the Foundation isn't about to shut down after Vietnam. No way. They keep going. They've lost the heroin trade, so they invest leftover funds in the arms business and actually increase their capital base during the 1970s. They get good at buying in quantity on the international market, using intermediaries, and then selling at a big profit. I believe that Admiral Forsten was the architect of the Foundation's marketing strategy in the late seventies and early eighties, using intelligence that he had access to at FMS. In any case, they score big time. We're talking hundreds of millions of dollars in profits that they amass. Money they can spend however they want. Little bits of it end up all over the world. Whenever Congress or the White House pulls the plug, the Foundation steps in, channeling money to various insurgencies — UNITA, Renamo, and the rebels who were taking on the Marxist government in Afghanistan before the Soviets went in in '79. But also select governments in need. Money went to Somoza after Carter turned his back, for example. SAVAK got some in Iran."

Zach yawned and looked at his watch. "So where does October Surprise fit in?" he asked sarcastically.

"Casey, of course."

"Casey?"

"Yes. You know, William Casey, Reagan's campaign manager in 1980, CIA head afterward."

"I know who he is." Zach rolled his eyes. Casey had been the bogeyman of the left for more than a decade now. When would these people give it up?

"Gary Sick got a lot wrong in his book. Casey didn't do the deal with Tehran alone; he set it up through the Foundation, which was already selling arms to Iran's revolutionary government. It was they who brokered the deal between the Iranian government and the Reagan camp to hold the hostages until after the election. Part of the deal was a personal promise from Casey that the Reagan administration would help the Iranians out with arms once they got into office. It took them a while, but they did it."

Castori paused. "Hey, Lieutenant, you got another beer?"

Zach thought of the five long-neck Budweisers in the refrigerator. "Nope. And your time's almost up."

"Okay, this brings us into the Reagan era. The Foundation is starting to have financial problems. So many arms have flooded the international market that they're not making the profits they once were by buying and selling. To keep their business going, they need to get arms free, so they do two things. First, Admiral Forsten uses his position as commander of the Seventh Fleet to steal spare parts from Navy supply depots to —"

The phone began ringing. Zach rose to answer it. "Your five minutes are up, Castori."

The connection was terrible, and Zach could barely make out the voice. "Zach, it's me, Justine. I'm calling from the car."

"Hi, hon. Could you hold on?"

Zach put his hand over the receiver, worrying that Justine

would find out who was visiting. "Really, time's up. I gotta take this call."

Castori shook his head and reluctantly moved toward the door. "I haven't even gotten to Douglas Sherman's role in the Labyrinth. Your boss and him are big buddies, going way back. Thought you might want to hear that part of the story. But fine. Have it your way."

For a moment, the mention of Sherman made Zach want to let Castori stay longer. But he waved him out.

"God, we have a terrible connection. I just wanted to say that I wish I could have stayed with you tonight," Justine said.

"I'll survive."

"And I forgot to tell you something."

"What's that?"

"I liked the ride today."

"I thought so."

"On Monday I'm going to take you for a ride that's almost as good."

"Is that right?"

"Maybe better. Gotta run. Bye."

After Zach hung up the phone he opened the door and looked up and down the hall. Castori was gone.

## 23

He was on his stomach, inching forward in the sand. Tracer bullets whizzed just above his head. They were different shades of bright gray and they crisscrossed the night from every direction, weaving a ceiling of death. He could see mounds in the sand ahead of him and to his left and right. Bodies. He slithered over to one of them, looking for Canver. It was a woman in black, her eyes staring blankly upward. He crawled to another — a child bathed in blood. Ahead of him, across a long stretch of dark ground, he could see a form moving. He began to inch toward it. The tracer bullets were coming lower now, a field of descending fire. The popping of rifles was a distant patter, but the tracer bullets created a roar of cutting air.

He was close now to the form ahead. It was Canver, grasping at the sand, pulling himself slowly forward. Suddenly a tracer angled into him, sending up a splatter of blood. Another tracer followed, and in a moment the macrame of zipping bullets had descended around Canver, ripping him from every direction. Zach burrowed his face into the sand, trying to escape the tracers that were now creasing his back and cutting up the ground around him. He was sobbing and shaking in powerful convulsions. He dug deeper into the sand with his hands.

The pillows were drenched with sweat and tears when Zach awoke. He sat up in bed, his eyes still wet and a salty taste in his mouth. The dreams had become less frequent, but still they came. Dr. Klein, whom Zach now barely saw because of the crush of work, had told him that the dreams would probably stay with him until he could work through the guilt and come to a peace about what had happened at Haisa.

Zach still wondered when that would be.

The office was dead when Zach arrived Monday morning. Forsten had taken several aides along with him on a ten-day trip to the Pacific, and other officers on Forsten's staff were taking time off after three weeks of working fourteen-hour days on the budget.

Zach sat down at his desk and began making phone calls. First he called over to the Army's locating office. The office kept track of where each of its half-million service people were. It also had current address information on members of the reserve and retirees.

Zach asked for the address of Kevin Ettinger and specified that the man had been a lieutenant in Vietnam. Maybe still on active duty, maybe not. A three-minute computer search turned up the address and phone number of a retired brigadier general living in Denver, Colorado. Zach looked at his watch. It would be 6:30 in Colorado. Probably too early to call even an older military man.

By 9:20 Zach impatiently decided it was late enough and dialed Ettinger's number. A middle-aged female voice answered. Zach apologized for calling so early and asked for General Ettinger.

"Don't you worry, young man, we've already had breakfast. Let me get my husband."

"General, my name is Lieutenant Zach Turzin," Zach said when Ettinger came on the phone. "I work at the Pentagon. And —"

"Turzin. Name sounds familiar. Hmm. We couldn't have served together because you're too young."

"No sir, we didn't serve together. I don't believe we've ever met. In any case, the reason I'm calling is because I have an unusual question for you."

"Shoot."

"Sir, do you remember an investigation —"

"Turzin. It's come back to me now. You got the CMH not too long ago. Saw it on TV and read about it in the paper."

"Yes, sir. That was me."

"Well, it's a hell of an honor to be speaking with you, Lieutenant."

"Thank you, sir."

"So what can I do for you at this early hour?"

"General, I know it's going back a long way, but do you remember an investigation that you conducted for the Army in 1969 about a massacre in a village near the Cambodian border called Chisir?"

"How could I forget that?" Ettinger said, his voice suddenly solemn. "I'll tell you, Lieutenant, when you poke around among seventy-eight bodies of men, women, and children — christ, you never forget something like that. Never."

Zach went on. "Sir, the investigation found no conclusive evidence to charge members of the Brown Water Forces under Jeffrey Forsten's command. And —"

"River Rats. That's what everybody called them."

"Yes, sir. Right. The River Rats. In any case, I recently read over your report, which struck me as somewhat more skeptical than the others."

"I was skeptical, all right. Damn right I was. The whole village was littered with M16 casings." Zach could hear anger rising in Ettinger's voice. "And everybody knew that Chisir was a VC haven. Why would they massacre their own supporters?"

"None of the other reports emphasized that point, sir."

"Bullshit. It was common knowledge."

"With all due respect, sir, you were in the minority in your views."

"Big deal!" Ettinger was seething now. "If you want to be blind you'll be blind. Especially in Nam. That's the way things worked over there. See no evil, hear no evil."

"So what do you think really happened at Chisir, sir?" Zach demanded. He wanted to corner Ettinger, tie him up in contradictions, show him that he had been paranoid then and was wrong now.

Ettinger paused for a long time. Finally he spoke: "Lieutenant, who asked you to call me? And why does this matter keep coming back up?"

"What do you mean, keep coming back up?" Zach asked. "Have you discussed this since 1969?"

"Hell, some young officer came to see me about this whole thing in '81 or '82, when I was over in West Germany. And then just last year somebody from the Pentagon called me about it."

"Do you remember who called you last year?"

"Hmm. Damn, let me think. No, the name slips my mind now."

"And what did he say, General?"

"He just asked me some questions, like you. Wanted to know what I remembered and asked me if I had talked to any reporters lately about the incident. What's going on with this, anyway? I've heard that Admiral Forsten is now high up in the Pentagon. Is that what this is about?"

"General, I really can't answer those questions. I wish I could I tell you, but I can't."

"I understand. Hell, all my clearances lapsed three years ago."

"So tell me, sir. What, in your opinion, really happened at Chisir?"

Ettinger paused again. And when he spoke the anger in his voice had returned. "Forsten's men wasted the village; that's what happened. Any fool could see that right away. But the Navy whitewashed the whole thing. And Forsten's men — hell, those guys were as mum as mafiosos, like some sort of secret fraternity. None of them would crack. Not a single one. My hands were tied in the matter. According to the Army's rules for internal investigations of matters such as this, I couldn't go beyond the evidence in my report. So I became part of the whole charade."

Zach called Thurston later in the morning. "Lewis, me again. I've got another request."

"You're lucky things are slow around here, my friend. Usually I'm out of my mind, positively frenetic. Right now everybody's been taking it easier after the crunch earlier in the month. So go ahead. But remember, Zachary, your debts to me are accumulating."

"I need more on Donny Chen."

Thurston let out a mock groan. "More. More. Always more. And what kind of material precisely are we talking about?"

"I need more about Chen's possible criminal activities. How could I get that?"

"You mean how can I get that for you? A couple ways. First, I can put Monsieur Chen's name into the Interpol system. Their database is absolutely brill. That might turn something up, even if he's only been a suspect in an investigation. Second, we have a criminal data–sharing arrangement with the British. I don't see any reason why that wouldn't include their Hong Kong data. I'll put Chen's name into their system and see what it turns up. Finally, it's easy enough to do an International Lexis-Nexis search of Chen's name. Maybe he's been mentioned in press accounts of criminal investigations."

"That would be great. Thanks, Lewis. I really appreciate this."

"Not a problem, not a problem at all. But rest assured, Zachary, that a proper display of gratitude will be forthcoming in due time."

"You bet. Who knows, maybe I'll save your job some day."

★
★ **24** ★
★

At quarter to twelve, Zach left for his rendezvous with Justine. The conversation with Ettinger had left him in a foul mood. He wasn't getting the answers he had expected. Far from it.

He wanted to pick up some flowers and sandwiches on the way back to his apartment and do a little cleaning before Justine arrived. He was in the Crystal City Mall in seven minutes and at his door after eight more minutes, flowers and food in hand. He reflected that he should come home more often for lunch instead of eating in the dreary Pentagon cafeterias. And wouldn't it be nice to have a meal like this one a few times a week?

He undid the top lock and then turned the lock above the knob. The door didn't budge. Assuming that he had forgotten to secure the top lock when he left, he put his key back in, turning it. He then turned the lock on the knob and the door opened.

For a moment he wasn't sure what was happening. The apartment was dark, the heavy blinds drawn closed The dim shape of a man was three feet to his left. Another man stood maybe six feet to his right, in the doorway of the kitchen. The man to his left was stepping toward him and reaching into his jacket, saying something. Zach didn't hear it.

He threw the flowers and bag of sandwiches into the face of the man on his left and leaped forward in the same movement, aiming a powerful kick at the man's head. The ball of Zach's heavy black dress shoe smashed into the throat. A second later, as the man's hands went up to his throat, Zach buried his fist in his solar plexus. He whipped around, and

164

could see the other man pulling a gun from his jacket as he yelled, "Freeze, we're —"

Zach crossed the distance between them in two steps, catapulting himself into the air and delivering a jump kick to the man's face. The man staggered back and fell onto the kitchen floor, his gun flying from his grasp. Zach dove for the gun. He picked it up and rushed back to the first man, who was on his knees, gasping for air. Aiming the gun at his head, Zach yanked the man's jacket down over his left shoulder and pulled a gun out of his shoulder holster. He moved behind the man, wrapping his left arm around his neck and lifting him partway to his feet. Zach leveled the gun at the other man, who had now struggled to his feet and stood with both hands on the kitchen doorway, blood pouring from his nose.

"Don't move," Zach commanded, his adrenaline pumping.

"Okay, okay, calm down, buddy." The man in the kitchen doorway put both hands on his head. The man in Zach's headlock was trying to say something. Zach loosened his grip a bit but pressed the gun hard against the man's temple.

"We're FBI," he sputtered.

"What?" Zach asked, teeth clenched. But he had heard him the first time.

"That's right," said the man in the doorway. "FBI, asshole."

"Let me see some ID."

The man in the headlock reached into his pocket.

"Slowly," Zach said, tightening his grip again.

The man cautiously withdrew a leather holder and flipped it open with his thumb. The identification looked real. Zach gestured with the gun at the other man. "And now yours. Take it out slowly and walk toward me."

The man followed the directions, holding up an ID. "We tried to identify ourselves but didn't get a chance."

"Damn." Zach released his hold on the first agent, who collapsed onto all fours, sucking air. "Damn," he repeated.

He put the two guns down on the glass dining-room table and sat down, trembling slightly. A sharp pain had begun to throb in his lower back.

"We could have killed you, you crazy son of a bitch," the bleeding agent said, swiping his gun off the table and putting on the safety before shoving it back in his holster.

"I could have killed you, asshole," Zach shot back. "You scared the hell out of me. What are you doing in my god-damn apartment?"

The agent didn't answer the question. He was leaning his head back, trying to stop the flow of blood that had covered his shirt and pants. "Do you have some tissues or something?"

"There's toilet paper in the bathroom." Zach jerked a thumb over his shoulder.

The other agent had gotten to his feet. A large red welt had spread across his neck. He picked up his gun and put it in his holster.

"Holy shit," he said, collapsing into a chair across the table from Zach. "You're a freaking psycho."

"What'd you expect? Jesus Christ." Zach explained the warnings he had received about possible retribution because of his role in the Haisa mission.

"I guess I might have freaked too under those circumstances," said the other agent, entering the room with a large ball of toilet paper held against his nose.

"We didn't think you were going to be here," said the agent at the table.

"But why the hell are you here in the first place?" Zach demanded, banging his fist hard on the table. The movement sent a wave of pain shooting up his back.

The two agents exchanged glances.

"We can't tell you that, I'm afraid," said the agent at the table.

Zach scanned the room. He immediately saw that the table on which the phone sat had been pulled away from the wall.

"Well, I guess it's pretty obvious. You're tapping my phone."

The bleeding agent nodded.

"So why are you in my goddamn apartment tapping my goddamn phone?"

"I'm sorry, we can't tell you that."

"What do you mean, you can't tell me? This is crazy. Totally insane." Zach shook his head in disbelief, practically spitting the words out. "I find you inside my apartment, breaking and entering — that's a crime in this country, you know — and you refuse to tell me what you're doing here?"

"First, we have court authorization, so it's not breaking and entering. Second, all we can tell you is that the tap on your phone is part of an ongoing investigation."

"Screw you," Zach said, rising from the table with effort. The pain in his back was nearly paralyzing now. "This is bullshit."

He walked over to the phone and picked it up. "I'm going to make some calls," he said, waving the receiver at the agents. "First, I'm gonna call Crystal City security. Then the Arlington police. Then the military police at the Pentagon. Then I'm going to call the *Washington Post* and *Washington Times* and tell them that an American war hero is being wiretapped by the FBI. In ten minutes this place is going to be swarming unless I get some answers. Now. Immediately!" Zach pressed the receiver against his ear and began to dial.

"Okay, all right," the agent said. "Put the phone down. We'll see what we can do."

"Call Burns," the bleeding agent suggested.

Zach handed the phone over and stood with his arms folded. The agent dialed a number and spoke nervously. "Yeah, Jack, Edwards here. Jaretsky and I ran into a problem at Turzin's apartment. . . . No, not building security. Him. Turzin. . . . I know that's what surveillance said. . . . Well, don't chew my ear off. Talk to those idiots. . . . Yeah, he's here now. Things got a little rough. . . . No, everybody's okay. But he wants to know about the investigation. . . . I told him that. But he's threatening to bring in all sorts of people, including the military police and the press. He's serious, Jack. . . . Okay. Fine; you have the number."

The agent hung up. "He has to go higher for authorization to divulge. He's going to call back."

The three men stood uneasily in silence. Zach looked at his watch. It was 12:15. He hoped Justine would be late as usual.

Three minutes later the phone rang. Edwards answered it. "Yes. I see. But no more. . . . Right. And we should ask him that now, or do you want to do it later? . . . Fine. We'll tell you how it goes."

Edwards took aside Jaretsky for a moment and whispered into his ear. Zach picked up the flowers and bag of sandwiches, putting them on the counter in the kitchen. He opened a can of soda and washed down two codeine tablets.

The two agents sat down at the table. Zach joined them.

Edwards spoke. "First, our superior, Associate Director Jack Burns, wants us to apologize on behalf of the Bureau. Surveillance indicated that you would not be home at this time of day, and we're sorry for the mix-up. The agency will make restitution for any damage that has been done to your apartment."

Zach glanced over at the bloodstains on the carpet in front of the kitchen entryway.

"Second, we have been authorized to tell you about the investigation, at least some parts of it." Edwards took a deep breath and continued. "For the last year, the FBI has been investigating your boss, Admiral Jeffrey Forsten. We have evidence linking Admiral Forsten to the theft of U.S. military equipment and to illegal arms exports to Iran during the 1980s."

Zach shut his eyes as a wave of anxiety swept over him. "Bullshit," he said instinctively.

"I'm afraid not, Lieutenant. Do you remember the various scandals in the 1980s involving U.S. servicemen and officers who were caught selling spare parts for U.S. weapons to Iran?"

Zach remembered vaguely and nodded.

"Our investigations of those crimes were never conclusive," said Edwards. "All we had were isolated cases of low-level servicemen caught stealing and selling parts, particularly for the F-14 fighter. At the time, though, many suspected that there was a well-organized ring behind these activities. We think that only a fraction of the parts sold were ever discovered. Our estimates are that the value of sales reached into the tens of millions.

"Two years ago we received evidence that Admiral Forsten, working with a criminal syndicate, may have been a pivotal figure in this ring. We now believe that he used his position as commander of the Pacific Seventh Fleet to secure access to spare parts for U.S. weapons systems, including the F-14, and that he tapped foreign military connections he had made back as head of FMS to sell these parts overseas. The sales to Iran, we suspect, may just be the tip of the iceberg. We also have some evidence that figures in the defense industry here in the states might be involved."

Zach's first thought was Forsten's modest house at Fort McNair. "So where's the fortune he made?" he demanded.

"We remain uncertain about where Forsten has placed his profits. But we're almost certain that an offshore account exists somewhere in the Caribbean."

Zach thought of the photo in Forsten's basement of him with the swordfish in the Caymans.

"What people in the U.S. defense industry do you think are involved?" Zach asked. Where, in other words, did Douglas Sherman fit in? He looked at his watch. It was 12:27.

"We really can't get into that with you," answered

Edwards. "That part of the investigation is at a very sensitive stage."

"Very sensitive," echoed Jaretsky.

Zach didn't push the point. "So why tap my goddamn phone?" he demanded.

"In the course of this investigation, we have found that Forsten has been very good at recruiting younger men into his network and inspiring intense loyalty among them," Edwards said.

"That's one of our problems with this investigation," added Jaretsky. "It has been nearly impossible to penetrate Forsten's organization. And, frankly, after our experience with Captain Hansen, we felt —"

"Jaretsky." Edwards cut him off. He then took up the explanation as if nothing had happened. "In any case," he said, "we have no evidence to believe that you are part of any kind of criminal conspiracy. In fact —"

"Whoa, wait a minute," Zach said, holding up his hands. "What about Captain Hansen? Was he working for the Bureau?"

The two agents exchanged glances. "That's correct, Lieutenant," Edwards said. "Captain Hansen had agreed to cooperate with us shortly before he was killed. We suspect foul play in his death but can't prove it."

"You mean you think Forsten's people killed him."

"We didn't say that," Edwards shot back.

"Jesus Christ," Zach muttered.

"In any case," Edwards continued, "we don't believe that you're engaged in any illegal activities, given your background and the short time you've been working for Forsten. Which is why the Bureau decided to approach you about cooperating with us. However, before we could do that we needed to learn more about you and see whether you had already been co-opted. Hence the phone tap."

Zach got up stiffly and walked into the kitchen to get

another soda. The searing pain in his back had begun to subside into a dull but insistent ache.

Edwards was saying something softly to Jaretsky when Zach returned. He placed a small plastic bag on the table. "There's one other thing, Lieutenant."

"Yeah?" Zach sat back down. Edwards slid the bag across the table. It contained several tiny black chips.

"We found these in your apartment. They're bugs. Listening devices. There was one in the phone when we opened it up, so we swept the rest of the apartment and found one in the living room and another in the bedroom. Somebody already had this place wired, Lieutenant."

"Now who do think that might be?" asked Jaretsky.

Zach held the bag up and looked at it in stunned amazement, his heart racing again and a rage growing. He thought of Justine's calls and visits, of all their intimate conversations in bed. Christ, what a nightmare.

"How long do you think these have been here?"

Edwards shrugged his shoulders. "Hard to tell. But the epoxy looked pretty fresh, no flaking edges or anything. Could have been a very recent job."

Zach sat silently, still reeling from the thought of somebody listening.

"So what's in it for me, in cooperating?" he finally asked.

"Lieutenant, you have to understand something," Edwards said solemnly. "We don't know how deep this thing goes. At this point, we don't even have solid enough evidence to ask the President to suspend Forsten from his post. But many of us who have been working on this case over the past two years have a bad feeling. We think it could be more than just an arms-smuggling ring."

"More?" Zach felt a sense of dread. Not in a million years could Castori's wild stories be right. Not in ten million.

"Yes, something more serious. But again, I can't get into it. Just take my word, Lieutenant. This is serious, deadly serious. And we need your help."

Zach didn't reply. He couldn't think clearly.

"Lieutenant?"

"I need time to think about this, damnit!" Zach snapped.

"We can understand that, Lieutenant."

Zach looked at his watch: 12:48. "And if you'll excuse me, I'm having a visitor any minute."

The agents rose to leave. Both handed their cards to Zach.

"We need to hear from you as soon as possible. But whatever you do, don't call us from your office phone. It's impossible to say what kind of surveillance Forsten and his people have on you. Use a pay phone."

As Zach shut the door behind the agents he was swept by a feeling of panic as he remembered the calls he had made from his office — to Chadwick, to Ettinger, to Lewis. Stupid. Stupid.

His watch read 12:50. He looked around the apartment. The place was a wreck. He limped about slowly, his back still throbbing, putting things back into place. He took the throw rug from the bathroom and put it over the bloodstain in front of the kitchen door. He pushed the table that held the telephone back into place. He grabbed two plates and glasses and placed them on the table. He stuffed the battered flowers into a vase. He spent a few moments in the bathroom, pushing his hair into place and straightening his uniform. His face was flushed but unmarked. It was a good thing he hadn't killed one of those guys. It could have happened easily, automatically.

By one o'clock Justine had still not arrived. There was no phone call, either, and Zach had checked the phone to make sure it was working. He waited until 1:30 before returning to the Pentagon.

The office felt different. The slight haze cast by the codeine fed a feeling of unreality. His world was suddenly fragile and threatening. He sat at his desk, trying to think. The flash of fear he felt earlier had set up a permanent camp in his mind. He concentrated, trying to think of all the calls he had made in the past two weeks and all the things he had said to Justine. He imagined what this pattern would look like, how much danger it put him in. There would be no room for explanations with these people if they thought Zach was betraying them. He thought of the bodies at Chisir and the stories about Riley. He thought of Hansen. These were men who enjoyed killing.

Who could he trust? He thought of the FBI, smug and manipulative. Maybe they didn't really have anything on Forsten, and the investigation was a political witch-hunt. Maybe the bugs in the plastic bag hadn't really been found in Zach's place and were just a ploy to get his cooperation. All investigators lied all the time in doing their work. Why wouldn't the FBI lie about this?

Zach turned over these thoughts in his mind for a while. They didn't wash. An investigation of this gravity wouldn't be some kind of vendetta. No way. He believed the agents at his apartment. He hated that he did, but there it was. So what now? He couldn't run. He had no resources with which to run. And he wasn't sure in any case just how immediate was the danger. He hadn't told Castori anything, and his own snooping had been an effort to rebut Castori's charges. He still hadn't done anything or learned anything that made him worth killing. Nobody would —

Zach sat up with a jolt as his thoughts turn to Justine. Why hadn't she shown up? Was there a link here? She had last been in his apartment a week earlier. Were the bugs there then? If Forsten's people knew about their affair, would they share this information with Sherman? If so, what would Sherman do with this information? To Justine. To Zach.

Zach grabbed the telephone and began dialing. He stopped, looking at the receiver. No, he couldn't use this phone. He got up and popped over to Stan Duncan's empty cubicle. He dialed Justine's work number. He got her voice mail. He tried Justine at home. He got the machine.

He sat back at his own desk, his anxiety mounting. Why

hadn't she called to cancel? What the hell was going on? His mind was a jumble of conflicting thoughts and impulses. He needed to get a grip, think things through.

He thought about the FBI and about some poor captain lying with two bullets in his head on an Alexandria street. Cooperating with the Bureau seemed like a bad, bad idea. If they lost Hansen, they could lose Zach. Still, doing nothing seemed out of the question. Ultimately, his loyalty was to the President and to the Constitution. That was the only simple truth in all of this.

He would keep doing what he was doing, he decided. He would gather his own information about Forsten and Sherman. They had sucked him into this, tried to use him for his medal. They had screwed with him and invaded his privacy. This was personal. He wasn't going to just roll over. As for the Feds, they could go to hell. At least for now. He didn't have a death wish. If he found anything useful, he'd pass it along when it was safe.

Zach got up and walked over to Forsten's empty office. Jeanie Wright, the admiral's secretary, had a small office adjacent to his, and her door was partly open. Zach could hear her talking on the phone. He looked nervously around. He had worked late enough times to know that Forsten's office was not locked at night. Security was extremely tight to get into the suite where the vice chairman and his aides had their offices, but nobody locked the doors to their immediate offices at night.

However, even with a full run of Forsten's office, Zach doubted that he would find much. Zach didn't know the combination of the documents safe in Forsten's office, but he couldn't imagine that it contained evidence of illegal activities. The tall combination file cabinets in a corner of Forsten's office were even less likely to contain such evidence. Forsten was not an idiot.

Zach walked behind Forsten's desk and stood by the window. He could still hear Jeanie Wright on the phone. It was a beautiful December day, crisp and shimmering. The Washington Monument was visible up the Potomac. Zach looked at Forsten's huge wooden desk. The admiral had once told him that the desk's previous owners had included Maxwell Taylor, the hard-charging Army chief of staff. For a moment, looking at the elaborate antique desk, Zach pondered the idea of hidden compartments. Absurd.

He looked at Forsten's computer. Often when he entered, the admiral would be typing away at something. He prided himself on being up on the latest technology, whether it was advanced weaponry or personal computers. Zach wondered if a check of the files on the hard drive or in the box of computer disks next to the machine would turn up anything interesting. No way. Too obvious. He wondered whether Forsten had a laptop somewhere. He hadn't seen one yet.

Somebody like Forsten would be good, very good, at hiding what he did.

The flood of employees leaving the J. Edgar Hoover Building on Pennsylvania Avenue peaked at about 5:35. Those leaving were clerical staff, mainly, heading for the subway stations at Metro Center and the National Archives. But a few agents could usually be found among the clock-punching crowd, however bad it looked. For one top agent, only the events of this particular day led him to be seen leaving with the masses. He prided himself on his seventy-hour weeks. Hurrying from the building, head down, he turned left on Pennsylvania Avenue and stopped at a pay phone in front of the U.S. Navy Memorial.

He identified himself only as "Sailor" to the voice that answered. "Our people made contact with Turzin today," he said.

"What do you mean, contact? What kind of shit are you telling me?"

"It was an accident, a disaster, really. Turzin stumbled on our people when they were wiring his place."

"You jerkoffs are fucking great, just great. Why didn't you tell us they were going in?"

"I'm sorry. I was out of the loop on this one." Sailor's voice had turned shaky and high-pitched. The tenor of fear. He continued hesitantly. "Our people. . . . they found a tap in there. . . . One of yours, I take it."

"Of course it was one of ours, asshole. Whose else would it be? You got shit for brains or what?"

Sailor was silent.

"So what was his response?"

"Turzin was given the bare bones on the investigation. He was asked to cooperate with the Bureau."

"And what did he say?"

"He said he wanted to think about it. He said he'd get back to us."

Thurston called at six, as Zach was getting ready to leave the office. He had more information on Chen. "Characters in an hour?"

"Listen, Lewis, thanks for all your help, but I'm not going to have time to see you for a while," Zach replied. "I'm incredibly busy. In fact, I gotta run right now."

"But, Zachary, my friend, it was my understanding that —"

"Really, Lewis, I gotta run. See you."

Zach hung up the phone. He then tapped out a quick E-mail message to Lewis. He apologized for his rudeness on the phone and suggested they meet at a dive called the Arlington Inn a few blocks away from his apartment. The bar stood alone and dilapidated in one of the few parts of the area that hadn't been razed by the Crystal City juggernaut. He gave directions to Thurston for how to get there. He added one more thing: "Make sure you're not followed."

Zach tried Justine's numbers for the twentieth time before making his way to the Arlington Inn, glancing over his shoulder. A steady stream of ibuprofen tablets through the afternoon had tamed his back pain without deepening the haze in his brain. Zach was again thinking clearly, and yet still he worried about losing it. He could feel himself in the grip of incipient panic and paranoia, and he battled to keep them at bay.

Zach and Lewis sat in a corner booth in the bar, conspicuously out of place among the collection of blue-collar workers and hard-core alcoholics.

"What the bloody hell are we doing here?" Lewis demanded, looking around in disgust. The seats were ripped and dirty, and Lewis had hesitated before sitting. Cigarette smoke mixed with the smell of stale beer to create an aroma of decadence and despair. "And why all the secrecy?"

Zach sipped his beer and looked around the bar a second time. Nobody new had come in.

"Lewis, let me pose to you a hypothetical question."

"Okay. Some factual answers would be nice right now, but go on."

"Let's imagine that somebody you're friendly with has gotten themselves into a dangerous situation, a very complicated and dangerous situation."

Lewis nodded slowly. "Uh huh."

"And let's imagine that he turns to you for help. But that in doing so, he tells you two things. First, that if you give him help, you might be in danger too. Maybe serious danger. And second, that he can't tell you what it's all about. How would you respond?"

Lewis bit his lip. "My friend is in danger, and if I help him I might be in danger also. But he won't tell me why."

"Right."

"Zachary, I don't like hypothetical questions. Truly, I don't. Why don't you just tell me what's going on."

"I can't, Lewis. Not everything."

"It's you who's in danger, isn't it?"

Zach nodded.

"And it is you who needs my help?"

Zach nodded again.

"And by helping you, I'd be in danger too."

"That's correct."

"How much danger are we discussing here? Are we talking career damage or bodily harm?" Lewis laughed nervously.

"I don't know. Maybe both. Maybe neither."

"I see. Actually, Zachary, I don't see. In truth, I can't imagine what it is that we're really discussing here."

Zach looked around the bar again and breathed deeply. He felt guilty for dragging Lewis in this deep. "I'll understand if you don't want to get involved. The truth is that you don't really know me all that well. We knew each other in college a bit, sure. But we weren't buddies or anything. You've gotten to know me more in the last couple of weeks. I think you know I'm for real."

"Of course, Zachary, of course."

"And I appreciate what you've done for me so far. You've taken some risks for me. You've been great. It's made a huge difference. But this is different. This isn't a game. If I were you, I'd probably end things here, to be totally honest."

Lewis looked pensive for a long moment, leaning his chin on the top of his beer bottle. "What kind of help do you need?"

"More of what you've been doing already. But maybe some hacking. Maybe some hardware work also."

"My specialties. Anything very illegal?"

Zach nodded.

Lewis smiled. There was a glint in his eyes. "It's been quite some time since the law and my activities were, shall we say, incompatible. But this is not wholly alien terrain for me. You are certain, I presume, that the adventures you suggest are absolutely necessary?"

"Yes."

"And you're positive that there are no more appropriate authorities who might be handling it beyond our humble selves?"

"Positive."

"And I expect that it goes without saying that these illegal activities are being undertaken for a cause of manifest nobility, that the ends justify the means?"

"Yup. You have my word that I'm one of the good guys."

They were both silent. Slowly Lewis nodded his head. "Well then, consider me at your disposal, Zachary."

Zach's mind was now focused, honing in on the situation at hand. Danger made things simple, in a way. It triggered the ingrained habits of mission behavior. It created discipline and calm amid a calamity that was nearly incomprehensible. And it fueled in him a competitiveness. He wanted more than to survive. He wanted to win, even if the game and its rules remained amorphous.

Thurston was the sole man under his command in this new fight, and Zach began issuing orders. "Okay, Lewis, a couple of things. First, don't call me anymore at my office. Nor at my house. Tomorrow I'll rent a voice-mail box and give you both the number and the access code. Check it regularly, more when you haven't heard from me lately. I'll do the same. But don't check it from your office. Use a pay phone. If things get hotter, we may need something more secure."

Lewis shook his head. "Hotter? More secure? Christ, this is serious."

Zach locked eyes with Lewis. "Remember, any time you want out, just say the word. Leave a message, and that will be it. I'll understand."

"I'm in, Zachary."

Zach got them another round of beers and sat down. "Okay, Donald Chen. What have you learned?"

Thurston reached down and pulled out a folder from his briefcase. "Quite a bit. To begin with, Chen Enterprises is a pretty big outfit, with its fingers in all sorts of pies, including the international arms trade. If Donald Chen used to get in trouble with drugs when he was young, lately it's the arms stuff that has gotten him into hot water, although he's never been indicted for anything." Thurston held up a three-page computer printout that summarized all the investigations of Chen.

"I culled this from Interpol and the British system. There was nothing in the DEA files, which only went back to 1980. You'll see that in the early 1980s Chen was investigated for doing business with Libya, in circumvention of British export law. Apparently he had some ties to Qaddafi's buddy Edmund Wilson. Then, in the mid- and late 1980s, he was investigated again for selling arms to Iran, which violated the international embargo. Apparently he made a killing. With Saddam Hussein knocking at their door, the Iranians were ready to pay an arm and a leg for stuff."

Thurston reached the last page. "Also, for years Chen has been investigated on and off for selling arms to terrorist groups in Lebanon. Earlier this year, for example, Shiite informants in Southern Lebanon told Mossad, which in turn told British intelligence, that Chen's organization has become a regular supplier of arms to the Hizbullah forces. Nice chap, huh?" Thurston slid the printout across the table. "A real humanitarian. Couldn't say no to the Party of God."

Zach sat silently for a moment with his eyes closed, concentrating. His mind focused on three pieces of an ever-expanding puzzle, and he wondered whether they fit together: Donald Chen, Hizbullah, Douglas Sherman. Is this what the FBI agent meant when he said that "more" might be involved in this case?

Zach opened his eyes, unable to make any connections. "Thanks, Lewis. This is great stuff. Now let me ask you a couple of other things."

Thurston held up his finger. "One minute." He left to use the bathroom.

"Now *that* was a mission into enemy territory," Thurston said when he returned, straightening his suit. "It's a bloody cesspool in there. I want you to know, Zachary, that your debt has escalated to incalculable levels."

Zach himself loved bars like this. They brought back memories of being out with Canver near Fort Bragg, sitting in a booth at some dive late into the night. Despite their differences, they'd always had a million things to talk about.

"Sorry, Lewis. Anyway, my main question. Another hypothetical one, I'm afraid."

"Let's hear it."

"If you were in the Pentagon and you wanted to regularly communicate in a totally secure fashion with private citizens, exchanging and storing significant amounts of data, and not leave a trace in the process, how would you do it?"

Thurston thought for a moment. "Well, you couldn't use any of the standard secure systems provided by the services."

"Nope, because you're interfacing with private citizens."

"And you wouldn't use the electronic mail systems everybody else uses at DOD, or any system on the Internet, because security wouldn't be tight enough."

"Really?" The Internet had been Zach's first guess. Forsten used E-mail to bombard aides with messages, and if Forsten and Sherman wanted to communicate securely, this would seem to be the best way. "So what would you do, if you weren't using the Internet?"

"To be absolutely safe I'd want to set up my own E-mail network, with a central terminal that I had total control over. This would be particularly useful if I wanted to invite other people to send information through the system."

"And what would this system look like? Remember, we're talking one hundred percent secure."

"Well, first, if we're envisioning multiple users and pretty large volumes of data, I would want a reasonably beefy central terminal. Naturally, as well, my system would include all the standard password mechanisms, so if somebody somehow discovered this private network, they would still have big problems getting in. Last but not least, I would want to set up the central terminal in an absolutely secure place so nobody could find it and try to penetrate that way."

"So we're talking about maybe buying one of these terminals under an assumed name and putting it in some sort of safe house owned by a dummy company or fictitious person?"

"Something like that."

"And what about using the telephone lines?"

"That's the weak link, no question. It wouldn't help much having your own E-mail system and secure terminal if you and your friends constantly had to send messages over open lines."

"And so?"

"And so I'd put in some kind of scrambling or encoding system. Absolutely. We're talking about a system that would scramble or encode data the instant you began transmitting and then unscramble it upon arrival."

"But the data would not be encoded all the time, like when it was stored in the central terminal?"

"No, that'd be too much trouble, and it wouldn't be necessary. My security is high enough in the scenario I've just laid out so that I'm not worried about people breaking into the system."

"And how would one do that?"

"Do what?"

"Break into the system."

Thurston laughed. "Heavens, Zachary. First you ask me to create the most secure E-mail system imaginable and then you ask me to break into it."

But Zach could see that Thurston was enjoying himself. That was good, Zach thought. Keep him hooked. Without Lewis he had nothing.

"Okay," Lewis said, making a few scribbles on a piece of paper. "First, you can dismiss thoughts of breaking into the central terminal. You're never going to find it because it could be just about anywhere. Second, you can forget about the phone lines. Even if you could get into the Pentagon phone system to tap the person there, or somehow tap the receiver's phone, all you'll get is encoded messages. Absolute jibberish. And you'd be stuck with breaking the code. Forget it. The only real way to do it is to somehow figure out the phone number of the system, call it up, then guess the password to get into his E-mail account."

"The phone number might be easy, but the password could be just about anything. Right?"

"Precisely. Any combination of letters up to probably eight or ten letters. There could be eight million possible variations. More."

"So cracking it is hopeless."

"Maybe. Maybe not," Lewis said, peeling his beer label. "Sometimes guessing is not as hard as you might fancy. I know lots of hackers who've broken into all kinds of systems by guessing passwords. The name of the user's dog or something."

"And what if one can't figure out the password?"

"Then you've got a major problem."

"There's no way to get in?"

"Absolutely not."

Zach mulled over this dead end for a while and saw a possible exit. He was impressed that it was he who saw it. "What if you could somehow record what the person was typing on their computer and find the password that way. You know, like those bugs that can determine what's being typed on a typewriter by the sound of the keys."

Lewis looked at Zach in surprise. "What a minute, let me get this right. You mean to tell me that you can get access to the computer of the person whose system you are trying to break into?"

"Theoretically, yes."

"Bloody hell, that would change everything. I thought the assignment was to break in from the outside, standard hacker style."

"No. Imagine you can get at the guy's computer."

"Not a problem, then," Lewis said, snapping his fingers in the air. "Not a problem at all. You don't even have to be able to log on to his computer. You can just open up the keyboard and put in a device that will record all the data that is entered. After a few days, or whatever, you remove the device and get the data. The phone number and password, everything you need, would be at your fingertips."

"You think you can get one of these devices?"

"Well, it's not exactly something sold on the street. It's more of a customized item. But, yes, I could put something together. Not a problem." The computer-jock pride was back in Lewis's voice. It vanished after Zach's next question.

"When can you have it for me? I mean, have it for us. I don't think I could install it myself."

Lewis looked pensive and then laughed nervously. "Ah, Zachary, my friend. A fuller picture is forming of what type of help from me you're looking for."

"I know this is asking a lot, Lewis. Again, if you're having second —"

"No, no. As I said, I'm at your disposal. I can have a device put together in no time. But I have no idea where the bloody thing is going to go."

"Today is Monday," Zach said. "The Pentagon will shut down for Christmas on Thursday. I don't know about your office, but in mine everybody is leaving early on Wednesday."

Lewis clenched his jaw in a mock grimace. "I know what you're going to ask, Zachary. And I'll tell you right now that I was planning to see my folks over Christmas."

"You can still go. I only need you on Wednesday evening. One hour, max."

Lewis took off his glasses and rubbed his eyes. "I suppose that kind of delay won't hurt. Wednesday evening it is, then."

"At my office."

"I'll be there."

★
★ 26 ★
★

Riley gunned his green Crown Victoria on an empty road in the Blue Ridge mountains, fifty miles west of Washington. Wasted time and more wasted time. He was sick of this shit. The previous Thursday he had spent half an afternoon wiring Turzin's apartment. For about seventy-two hours the taps had been in place, and Riley had heard two very interesting conversations. Now the taps were dead, courtesy of the FBI. Riley wanted to get his hands around the neck of his piece-of-shit source in the Bureau. A first-class fuckup.

Earlier in the day, Riley had sat in the back room of an audio store in Richmond that an old Army friend owned.

"Let's see what you got," his friend had said, hitting the play button on a microcassette recorder. There was the sound of Turzin answering the phone and a female voice against a sea of static. "Hi, Zach, it's me —" The name was lost, drowned out by interference. Through the rest of the tape, the female voice wavered in various degrees of barely audible distortion.

"Can you clean it up for me?" Riley had asked.

"I'll see what I can do. Definitely I can get clearer than what you got."

Riley had left the tape at the store and headed back out on his rounds. One more piss-ass errand to go.

Outside the tiny town of Strasburg, Riley turned down a back road and followed it for a mile before getting off on a dirt driveway that led into the woods. This was his second trip out to the mountains in the last day and a half. Another waste of his goddamn time. Either this writer asshole wasn't talking or the guy had nothing to say. Riley pulled up outside an isolated house. A cargo van with Tennessee plates was parked outside. The place looked run-down and forgotten.

At least Tommy Flint and his men hadn't screwed up, Riley thought, getting out of his car. Now here was a militia that could actually do something other than spew to the press about ZOG. And do it well. They had taken Castori right out of his driveway two nights ago. Clean and simple. At the cabin, they showed that they understood their work well. The hard part of this business wasn't making men wish for death, Riley knew. It was keeping them alive long enough to say something useful. The Contras had never been good at that.

Flint and his two men were sitting in the kitchen having a beer. They were relaxed, joking around and swapping stories. Riley turned down a beer and didn't sit. Anything new? he demanded. Any goddamn progress?

Flint shook his head. "Nothing. Still swears he doesn't have sources beyond the three we know about."

"And Turzin?"

"Still says that Turzin didn't give him shit, that he only listened. I think he's telling the truth. Hell, I would be. I don't think there's anything more here. I don't think the guy ever really had anything to begin with."

Riley let out an annoyed hiss and headed for the basement. The stench of urine and excrement became powerful as he walked down the stairs. The basement was lit by a fluorescent light, and there were custom racks for holding tools. It looked like a weekender had probably once had a workshop down here.

Castori was stripped to his underwear, blindfolded and gagged. He lay face up, chained to an old mattress box spring, its cloth stripped away to leave only the metal springs and frame. Wires were attached to the frame at several places. Castori's back and legs were covered with bright red burns and blisters. Nearby on a table was a tape recorder, along with several syringes and vials of medication.

Riley knelt near Castori's head. Dried vomit had caked around his neck. "Hey, boy, you still with us?"

Castori nodded his head slowly.

Riley spoke softly, soothing almost. "Anybody tell you yet what the Argentines used to call this thing you're on?"

Castori shook his head.

"They called it 'the barbecue'. Nice name. Real appropriate, wouldn't you say? I know how much you writer types 'preciate a nice phrase."

Castori was still.

"Now, you know what's gonna happen if you don't start talking?"

Castori shook his head.

"Let me tell you what. Those boys are going to take off your underwear and they're going to flip you over. Then they're going to make sure that you're broiled well-done. Are we communicating here?"

Castori nodded.

"And you don't want to stink up the house that way, do you?"

Castori shook his head.

"So here's the plan. You tell 'em what you've been holding back, tell 'em everything you know, and I'll make sure that you get out of here alive. I give you my word on that. There ain't no point in doing otherwise, you understand? Ain't nothing worth what you're gonna go through if you don't put out. Got that?"

Castori nodded once more.

Riley rose to his feet. "That's my boy."

Riley tromped back up to the kitchen. "Take him for one more spin and then put him in the ground," he told Flint and his men. "And I want all the tapes by tomorrow morning."

# ★ 27 ★

The phone was ringing when Zach walked into his office on Tuesday morning. He hoped it was Justine. He had tried her all night at home and already once at the office before coming to work, his anxiety growing. Instead, Stan Duncan was on the line from Asia.

"You're going to be getting a call this morning from an NSC aide named Fischer," he told Zach. "We've already talked with him. He's going to invite you to represent the admiral at an interagency briefing later today. The admiral wants you to take careful notes and prepare a memo before his return on Sunday about what transpires. Is that clear?"

"Yes, it is."

"And one other thing, Lieutenant."

"Yes?"

"Do not share the contents of this memo or your impressions of this briefing with anybody else in the building. No back-briefing on this one."

Less than an hour later, Zach received the call from Fischer. An urgent matter has come up, the aide explained vaguely. The NSC operations room had contacted Admiral Forsten in Asia earlier in the morning, and Forsten had directed that Zach be his representative in a briefing on the matter.

"I'm aware of the situation," Zach said.

Fischer instructed Zach to be at the State Department by three P.M. He was to proceed up to the seventh floor, where someone would meet him and take him to the conference room in which the briefing would be given.

Zach hung up the phone. Sounded like a crisis. But he

189

hadn't seen anything unusual in the intelligence binders or the Early Bird.

The small conference room was located at the end of a plushly carpeted hallway, past the office of the secretary of state and a row of suites belonging to the deputy secretary and the five undersecretaries. Zach surveyed the room after he had helped himself to a roll and cup of coffee from a table by the window. Six senior officials from different agencies had gathered to hear the briefing.

The meeting got under way with the undersecretary of state for political affairs saying that the following matter would require strong interagency cooperation. He then introduced Charles Brenner, head of the CIA counterterrorist division. Zach took out a pen and prepared to take notes.

Brenner got directly to the point: "Not long ago, as most of you may know, the intelligence community received information that several leaders of Hizbullah, or the Party of God, had become de facto mercenaries, making available the services of their operatives to the highest bidders. Naturally, this development was of some concern to us when we first learned of it. Members of Hizbullah have demonstrated a willingness to sacrifice their lives to complete a mission."

Zach's curiosity was mounting.

"Indeed, we consider Hizbullah to be among the most formidable terrorist groups in the world, despite its internal divisions and the battering it has recently taken from Israel. Last week, one of our listening posts in Turkey intercepted a series of telephone calls between Sidon, Lebanon, and Athens. Based on these calls, we have reason to believe that the Hizbullah faction of Sheik Abdul Tabrata intends to carry out a terrorist attack on a major U.S. target in Western Europe, sometime in January. And we believe that this operation is being planned under contract, possibly for one of the state governments in the region. Regrettably, at this time we do not have more information than that, but all available resources have been tasked to this problem."

Brenner closed the folder before him and leaned back in his chair. The undersecretary thanked him and addressed the group. "The President has asked the Deputies Committee to begin the process of planning a response, both political and military, in the event that such an attack occurs. But before we get to that, does anybody have any questions for Chuck?"

Zach had a question but decided to save it for later. Before him on his pad, in the margin next to his notes, he had twice scribbled Donald Chen's name.

The deputy national security adviser, a gray-haired woman, addressed Brenner: "Assuming that Hizbullah does strike in Western Europe, what would their likely target be?"

"We have no idea at this point," replied Brenner. "But I'll say this. In recent years, terrorists have shown a determination to ratchet up the level of violence of their attacks in an attempt to shock an increasingly numbed western audience. Two hundred and twenty-five people died in the Eiffel Tower incident, but many more would have died if the attack had gone as planned. And there is every reason to expect that this pattern of escalation will apply to U.S. targets in Western Europe. I'll remind everyone that the November assassination of General Anderson in Oman by Islamic Vengeance was the first time that any terrorist group had ever targeted a U.S. military officer of such high rank. In short, we don't know what to expect next."

"If an attack happens, what evidence would we have to link it to Iran, or other members of the TKT Pact?" the State Department undersecretary asked.

Brenner shook his head. "As I said, we suspect this mission is a contracted operation, we just don't know who the contractor is. It's common knowledge that Hizbullah receives aid from Iran and some logistical support as well. Tehran may well have ordered this mission. Nevertheless, there may not be any concrete evidence of TKT complicity in this attack, depending of course on the evidence left by the attackers."

The undersecretary of defense asked the next question: "What are the options for preemption? Is there any way we can stop this thing?"

"That's certainly a possibility, but again, we would need to get lucky. Either we need to pick up more information about the attack or hope that the terrorists or their weapons get stopped coming into Europe — that is, assuming they're not there already."

As the undersecretary of state guided the discussion to possible political and military responses, Zach found himself wondering about Forsten, Sherman, and Chen. Did Forsten know that Chen had a record of selling arms to Hizbullah? Did Sherman know? He again began wondering what the FBI agents had meant when they said that their case might involve "more" than just arms sales.

"... and what plans exist at the Joint Staff in regard to possible retaliation against Iran and other TKT members, Lieutenant Turzin?" the undersecretary of state asked.

Zach focused back on the conversation and managed to give a crisp answer. "We have options for military strikes at a wide menu of targets in all three countries. Given our base of forces in the region, these options could be exercised with minimal preparation following presidential authorization." He didn't think he should mention MOCKINGBIRD.

As the meeting broke up, Zach made his way toward Brenner and waited for a moment to ask him a question in private.

"Does the name Donald Chen ring a bell for you?"

Brenner's expression didn't change. He pondered the question for a moment and then turned it around.

"What makes you bring up that name?"

Zach explained in vague terms that he had heard Chen's

name linked to arms sales to Hizbullah. "I was wondering whether there was something more, some closer connection."

Brenner looked at him, his expression still blank. "We're investigating that," he said carefully.

Charles Brenner smiled to himself on the elevator ride down from the seventh floor. He had always been a good liar, which was why he was in the right line of work. He even enjoyed it on occasion, especially this time, although what Brenner had done at the briefing was not exactly lying but rather withholding information. Brenner had done this on the orders of his boss, CIA Director William Burke. Burke had told Brenner that his full briefing on this matter would come directly after the Deputies Committee meeting, and be given to the President himself. That idea could hardly have been more pleasing; the Deputies Committee had, in the past two years, become a sieve of leaks and counterleaks.

Brenner's car from Langley picked him up at the State Department's C Street entrance and dropped him at the West Wing of the White House. After being cleared through security he was guided down to the basement and surmised his destination a moment before arriving: the White House Situation Room. It was his first visit, and for a few minutes he was left there alone. Comfortable modern chairs were placed around a long, sleek conference table scattered with telephones; dark carpeting covered the floor, and the lighting came from recessed ceiling spots. Curtains covered most of the walls. Brenner knew that there were screens behind some of them that could display force deployment information in a time of crisis. He knew that the room had been specially designed to thwart electronic penetration and that it was the most secure place in the White House to discuss sensitive matters. He liked this place.

Within a few moments Brenner was joined by Burke and

FBI Director Holsten. Brenner had time to give both men a summary of the State Department meeting before the President strode in with the national security adviser.

The President opened the meeting when they were all seated, nodding to the CIA director. "Well, Bill, I'm fascinated to hear what all this is about. You've been pretty cryptic."

Burke folded his hands before him. "I like to think for good reason, Mr. President. This is a very sensitive matter."

The President nodded again. "Go ahead."

"As you know, the Deputies Committee has just finished meeting at the State Department on the possibility of an action by Hizbullah," Burke said. "Chuck brought the group up to date on the latest intelligence, and response planning for a possible attack was initiated, as you directed. However, Mr. President, new information regarding this matter has come to light that I thought it best to share only at the principals level. At this point it would probably be best if I asked Chuck to continue. He's been on top of this from the beginning."

Brenner felt a slight adrenaline rush as he began speaking. He had never briefed the President before. "The existence of a mercenary faction of Hizbullah led by one Sheik Abdul Tabrata is by now old news to everybody here," Brenner began. "It is a testament to the sophistication of our electronic sources that we learned about it as early as we did. We beat the Israelis on this one, I'm happy to say. But a few days ago Mossad shared some new information with us that is deeply disturbing. You all recall the recent Israeli kidnapping of Sheik Karim Hirani from his home outside of Sidon?"

The President nodded, leaning forward and pursing his lips in a grimace. He did not relish the foreign policy part of his job, especially when it sucked him into the Middle East. And he hated surprises.

Brenner continued. "Interrogation of Hirani confirmed once again the information about Tabrata and added some new details regarding his organization's activities. In addition, however, Hirani claimed that Tabrata's organization has contracted with Americans in need of his services."

Brenner paused to let the information sink in. The national security adviser broke the silence with a string of questions. Irritation infused his voice.

"Who are these Americans?"

"That isn't known."

"When did this approach allegedly occur?"

"That wasn't specified."

"Do the Israelis believe him?"

"They do."

"Why?"

"A few reasons. One is that the story seems too strange to have been made up. What would be the point?"

"And the other reasons?"

"Hirani was in a position to know. Hizbullah may have splintered, but there's still contact between the factions. It's a small community over there. People talk; people brag. And the bottom line is that Tabrata's organization does have to do some advertising if they want business. What could be a better advertisement than having Americans as clients?"

The President glanced at his watch and looked at Burke, annoyed. "So what does this all mean? What's the significance of this information, assuming it's true?" Why am I down here? he might as well have asked.

"Mr. President, if Americans have contracted with Tabrata's organization, that may mean attacks are planned inside the United States," Burke said carefully. "Organized crime or domestic terrorist elements could be involved. And, sir, there's something else as well. Please, finish up, Chuck."

Brenner began speaking again: "All of you have been briefed on how we obtained the information pointing to a possible terrorist attack in Western Europe sometime in January. Telephone intercepts, mostly."

Heads nodded around the table.

"Initially, my staff and I took this information at face value. I now believe this was a mistake."

"What are you getting at?" the national security adviser asked.

"Tabrata's organization is not composed of fools. These people know better than to discuss operations on the telephone in this age, especially internationally."

"So they screwed up," said the national security adviser.

"I don't believe so," countered Brenner. "Not this group. I would submit that the calls we have intercepted about a possible attack in Western Europe were made as part of a deliberate misinformation effort."

"Which means what?" asked the President.

"It means," said Burke, "that possibly Tabrata's organization is trying to make us think an attack is coming in Western Europe when in fact it is going to happen elsewhere."

The President finally caught up. "Like in the United States. Contracted by Americans."

"It is possible, Mr. President."

A nervous silence fell over the room. The national security adviser, for once out of sharp questions, drummed his fingers on the legal pad before him. Holsten gazed at the ceiling and then at the President. With the domestic element clear, he now realized why he had been invited to the meeting.

"Okay, let's say I'm buying," the President finally said. "Where do we go next with this?"

The question was directed at Burke, but the CIA chief looked at Director Holsten. He didn't want to tread on his turf. Holsten began laying out options. "If we're convinced the threat is both genuine and imminent, we can put our counterterrorist elements on full or partial alert. Notify Customs, Treasury, and the INS. More agents at airports, seaports, and border crossings; stepped-up surveillance of known Hizbullah sympathizers in the United States; alerting of local authorities in major cities so that they know something could be coming. And then I would want to take additional steps, such as —"

"Hold on. Let's back up here just a moment," the President interrupted, raising his hands. He looked at Burke again. "Bill, you did the right thing keeping this at the principals level. We need to think this through. Carefully. I don't want to get everybody all excited if this thing isn't a hundred percent real. The press will get ahold of it and have a field day. The United States cannot afford to look like a garrison state, clamping its borders shut whenever a rumor comes floating across the ocean that some group of fanatics is going to do us harm."

"I agree, Mr. President," said the national security adviser. He hadn't liked this meeting from the beginning.

"We're going to go slow until I get more on this," the President said decisively, looking to Burke and then Holsten. "It sounds plausible, but who the hell really knows. Right? With all respect to Chuck, this remains in the realm of conjecture. Correct?"

"That is true, Mr. President," Burke acknowledged. "But much intelligence is like that."

"This is particularly thin," the national security adviser scoffed.

"And it's just not good enough in this case," the President added. He leaned back and rubbed his chin for a moment before delivering a final verdict. "Gentlemen, I want our conversation to remain in this room. If and when more evidence surfaces that a terrorist attack is possible on a target inside the United States, I guarantee I'll go full tilt on preventive measures. In the meantime, what I want is some step-up of vigilance on the domestic front that doesn't attract attention, and also I want the response planning process to continue at the deputies level as requested. Finally, Bill, I want the Agency to work the international angle and see if your people can't come up with something more concrete."

The President rose to signal an end to the discussion. He beckoned to Holsten. "Walk with me upstairs, would you, John?"

The President shut the door when the two men were alone in the Oval Office.

"Anything new on Operation Arnold?"

"I'm afraid we're still moving slowly," Holsten replied. "The paper trail on Sherman is growing. Not fast, but it is growing. This snail's pace is the price we pay for discretion. Subpoenas, Mr. President, I need subpoenas."

The President didn't reply, and Holsten didn't push the point. He knew he was not going to get subpoenas and he knew why.

"In any case," the director continued, "Forsten remains even harder. No change there."

The President nodded. He had expected to hear as much. Holsten was under instructions to immediately report any significant breakthroughs in the case. None had been forthcoming.

"What about Lieutenant Turzin?"

Holsten was afraid of that question. He didn't want to lie to the President, nor did he want to reveal the disaster at Turzin's apartment. "We've approached Lieutenant Turzin and asked him for his help," he said simply.

"And?"

"Turzin said he would think about it."

"How generous of him."

"But don't worry, Mr. President. We have plans to make contact with him again either today or tomorrow to nail this down. My bet is that he'll cooperate."

"Damn well better. Somebody might remind that boy that at the end of the day he's under my command." The President sat down at his desk. "My command, goddamnit, not Forsten's. Got that?"

"Of course, sir. We'll make that part of our approach."

"Tell Turzin it's a direct order. Understand?"

"Yes, sir."

The President rifled around amid some papers on his desk. Holsten sensed that the meeting was over and headed for the door.

"One more thing, John," the President said.

"Yes?"

"You think I made the right call down there earlier, don't you?" It was more of a statement than a question.

"I believe so, Mr. President," Holsten answered, opening the door. In truth, he had a bad feeling about the whole matter. Brenner's information had been startling and disturbing. Holsten's mind had been racing since the meeting, and terrible thoughts were pushing upward, linking up with suspicions about the killings in Oman and Georgia — Forsten enemies dead in both cases. But he pushed the thoughts back. They were too far out there, too unbelievable. If the President made the link, they could be discussed. Not before.

## ★ 28 ★

Zach thought anxiously of Justine as he maneuvered his way through the throngs of Chrismas shoppers in the Crystal City Mall on his way home from the Pentagon. Her disappearence had sent him reeling into a dark place. The meeting at State, with its welter of foreboding hints, had kept him there. Thirty hours had passed since they were supposed to meet, and he had heard no word from her. Horrible ideas floated through his mind. Maybe it was nothing. Maybe he was losing it. After all, it had only been a day, and the woman was famously busy and scattered. He fantasized about what a proper apology would entail.

As Zach moved out of the mall and into the passage that led to his building, a man in a suit sidled up next to him and talked softly, looking ahead all the while. "Lieutenant Turzin, I'm Agent Paul Bonk, FBI. We need to meet with you. Could you please follow me, staying behind at least ten feet." The agent then sped up his pace. Zach followed.

The agent led him away from the mall and down a tiled corridor toward one of the several hotels in the Crystal City complex. He entered a stairwell, and Zach followed him to a parking garage. Another agent was there, standing next to a black Lincoln Town Car with tinted windows. The agent opened the back door and gestured for Zach to get in. A suited leg and arm were visible inside.

Zach climbed into the Lincoln and found himself next to a gray-haired man with wire-rimmed glasses who put forward his hand.

"Lieutenant Turzin, it's a pleasure to meet you. I'm Associate Director Jack Burns."

Zach shook hands and nodded in a chilly greeting. He didn't like being hauled down here.

"Sorry to approach you in this fashion, but it's the most secure way," Burns said. "I apologize also about the incident at your apartment yesterday. My men didn't expect you to be there, and obviously you didn't expect them." Burns chuckled. "Kicked the shit out of those two from what I understand."

Zach didn't allow himself a smile. He remembered now that Burns was the person the agents had called from his phone.

"Lieutenant, I arranged this meeting because I wanted to ask you in person for your cooperation in this investigation. We consider it to be of utmost urgency. Certainly it's the most serious matter that I've been involved in during my twenty-two years at the Bureau. But, as my agents have already explained to you, we're stymied. A wall of silence surrounds Admiral Forsten. We need your help."

Burns paused. He wanted encouragement. Zach gave him none.

"We're almost certain that you're not in Forsten's camp. We think that you're the kind of man we can count on. Have you given consideration to our request?"

"Mr. Burns, I'm afraid that I can't even begin to consider helping you unless you're willing to help me," Zach said. After much thought since the previous day, he had decided that the best way to keep the FBI at bay was to demand the impossible.

"Help you? How?" Burns shifted uneasily in his seat.

"I need to know more, sir. The agency is investigating more than illegal arms sales. Your agents indicated that themselves. I want to know what it is. All of it."

Burns sighed. "It is correct, Lieutenant, that there are elements here besides arms sales, elements which add considerable gravity to the investigation of Admiral Forsten. But I really cannot get into that with you. It is simply too sensitive. Please, just trust us on this and help out."

Zach ratcheted up his act. Patriot in anguish. "Listen, Mr. Burns, I would love to help you out," he said. "I would. And I may be able to tell you all sorts of things you don't already know. But there's no way, no way I'm going to do that without knowing the full story of this thing. If I've learned one thing in the special forces it's this: Never begin a mission without knowing the enemy — knowing his weapons, his tactics, his terrain. Knowing what he smells like, what he eats, even how often he screws. But most of all, knowing what his motives and objectives are, and knowing how high his morale is. Add these ingredients together in a big equation and the product you get is danger level. Likelihood of death and dismemberment. As things stand, sir, you've given me nothing on this front. Maybe Forsten and his people are greedy gunrunners who will cop a plea when they're found out. But maybe they're a lot more ruthless. Maybe they'll start killing everybody in range when the net closes on them. Maybe they killed Captain Hansen and maybe they'd kill me."

Zach put his hand on the door handle and turned back to Burns, almost spitting his words out. "I've shown that I'm willing to die for my country, Mr. Burns. I've been sent to the most dangerous places on earth. But my superiors always told me what to expect when I got there. Always. And if you think I'm going to dance blindfolded with the FBI, forget it — not with the track record you jokers have."

Zach yanked open the car door and put one foot out. Burns took hold of his arm.

"Okay, Lieutenant. Okay, you win. I'll fill you in. Close the door."

Zach sat back in his seat with surprise. This wasn't supposed to happen, and he wondered how to escape from the trap that he had sprung on himself as Burns reluctantly began to talk. First, he stressed again how sensitive his information was and emphasized the importance of discretion.

"Do you trust me or not, Mr. Burns?" Zach asked, his anger returning.

"We trust you, Lieutenant. I just want to make sure you know what the rules of the game are."

And then Burns began explaining the other component of the investigation. At times he sounded weary and depressed, taking off his glasses and rubbing his eyes as he described how the investigation of Forsten began with the arms dealing and soon widened. "The long and short of it, Lieutenant, is that we now suspect that Admiral Forsten may be disloyal to this president."

Zach laughed nervously. "Disloyal? With all due respect, sir, that's common knowledge in this town. And it's hardly a crime."

"We're not talking about political differences. Disloyal as in treasonous."

"Treasonous?" Zach asked, perplexed. "And exactly what do you mean by that? Did he spy for the Soviets during the Cold War or something?"

"No, nothing like that. But it may actually be more serious." Burns stopped, as if reconsidering the decision to share such information.

"Like what?" Zach prodded. He felt long-sought answers coming his way.

"We're not exactly sure what," Burns admitted. "That's our problem. All we have now is a theory based on a lot of fragmentary evidence. In the course of conducting wiretaps for the arms investigation earlier this year, we overheard many conversations among Forsten and his associates regarding the President and administration. Before the taps stopped yielding useful information, a clear pattern had begun to emerge."

Burns paused, as if hardly able to say the next part out loud. "We have reason to believe that Admiral Forsten is intent on undermining or discrediting the current administration through extralegal actions."

"Extralegal actions?" Zach looked at Burns searchingly.

"We don't know more than that. Frankly, we're not sure

what Forsten might hope to achieve," Burns said. The two men sat in silence for a moment.

"Why doesn't the President just fire Forsten?" Zach asked.

Burns shook his head. "Not with the evidence we have. Even the strongest part, the illegal arms sales, is garbage. Every judge in the country would throw it in the wastebasket. As you know, the President has had enormously rocky relations with the military. If he moves against one of the most popular men in uniform, charging a conspiracy of some kind but providing no hard evidence, he'll look paranoid and vindictive in one stroke. It'd be the uproar of the decade."

Burns looked away again. Disgorging this information was torture. "And there's another reason he can't do that, Lieutenant."

Zach sensed that he knew what the associate director was about to say.

"We believe that Admiral Forsten has a long-standing criminal relationship with Douglas Sherman that continues to this day. We are now fairly certain that Sherman's defense companies supplied Forsten with some of the spare weapons parts that he illegally trafficked in during the 1980s. And we think that whatever actions Forsten is planning, he is doing so in conjunction with Sherman."

A bright light flashed briefly across a dark recess of Zach's brain but didn't linger.

Burns continued talking. "So you see, if we go after Forsten alone, we might blow our chance to get Sherman. But if the President fired Forsten and accused Sherman, he could destroy himself if the charges could not be proved. And they can't be, as I say. Not now, not by a long shot. Appearing to use the FBI to go after two political enemies, one internal and the other external, might result in impeachment hearings against the President if — or, rather, when — a judge threw the charges out."

"I see why the President's hands are tied," Zach said slowly, trying to wrap his mind around what he was hearing. "But tell me this, sir, what would Doug Sherman possibly have to gain by some sort of action against the administration?"

"Again, we're not sure, since we don't know what these men are contemplating. But theoretically, a move that seriously damages the credibility of the President could doom his reelection chances and be a major boon to Sherman."

"I'm beginning to get the picture," Zach said, even as he felt that he was being sucked ever more deeply into the darkness. "Whatever the plot is, its chief intention is to elect Sherman, who in turn gives Forsten a position from which he can wield new power, changing whatever policies he wants. They both win."

Burns nodded vigorously. "Exactly. And our investigation of their illegal arms dealing gets shut down. That is what concerns us, Lieutenant. We're afraid that we're dealing with two very powerful, very dangerous, and very desperate men. And we worry that they're both going for broke."

Zach walked up to his apartment in a daze. He had sat in the limo for nearly an hour. He had resisted cooperating with the Bureau until Burns had played his trump card, conveying the message from the President. That had done it. A direct order. Reluctantly, Zach had said that he would try to get closer to Forsten, see what he could learn, and meet regularly with Agent Edwards. He had mentioned Donald Chen and the photo on Forsten's wall. Burns nodded. They had been working the Chen connection. Zach did not mention Thurston's suggestion of a secret computer network. He didn't mention Lewis at all. He still didn't trust the FBI. He worried that they would compromise his information, putting him in danger. He thought of Captain Hansen. Who had spilled the beans on him? The guy hadn't had a chance.

Zach would stick to the plan of assembling evidence on his own. He would keep the Bureau at a distance and help them when he was ready. When it was safe.

Zach looked at the answering machine as he closed the door to his apartment. The blinking light indicated a single message. Justine, he prayed. He got a beer from the refrigerator and played the machine. "Shit," he muttered as his mother's voice came on, asking him what time he would be arriving in Princeton for Christmas. Zach looked at his watch: 9:40, not too late to call. He picked up the phone and dialed. When his mother came on he explained that he wouldn't be able to make it for Christmas because of work. He pledged that he would come to Princeton soon. His mother sounded concerned about the rigors of his job. If only she knew.

## 29

The Wednesday before Christmas weekend was an unusually warm and bright day in Washington. Government workers streamed from their offices at noon to take in the sunshine with lunch, filling every park bench and staking out seats along low walls and steps. On Pennsylvania Avenue, the U.S. Navy Memorial was teaming with holiday tourists. Families stood together reading the engraved plaques, and foreigners snapped pictures of the dramatic edifice.

Sailor punched in a Virginia phone number and identified himself in a clipped voice. "Bad news," he said.

"Go ahead."

"Turzin is becoming the Bureau's boy."

"Has he shared anything yet?"

"Nothing of importance. He says he's going to try to find out more."

"Sounds like we have a new problem to solve."

"Looks that way," Sailor said.

"Keep us informed."

By four o'clock on Wednesday afternoon, Forsten's suite of offices was entirely empty. Elsewhere in the Pentagon, Christmas parties were under way, and there were still people in the offices of the Joint Staff. But Jeanie Wright had left the building by three, as had two other secretaries that worked for Forsten. The various aides that darted around the suite during normal times were also gone, either in Asia with the admiral or stopping at parties in other parts of the building before heading home.

Zach was alone in the offices as darkness fell outside. He

had put Thurston on a visitors list kept by the security officer outside the JCS section. The officer would glance at Thurston's ID, check the list, and wave him through. Neither the time of Thurston's arrival nor that of his exit would be noted. The paper record would show only that Thurston had come to the JCS section to visit Zach at some point in the day.

Zach's guilt about Thurston was growing. He remembered his own lecture to Burns. This would be his last use of Thurston, he decided.

He looked at his watch: 5:10. He had been thinking about Justine all day. After repeatedly trying her direct work line and home number, he had finally broken one of their unspoken rules and called the main number at her office. Justine's assistant had said only that she was out of the office for a few days. Zach fluctuated between concern for her well-being and concern for his. Maybe this was her way of ending a relationship. Simply disappear. The thought was torture. He needed more time with her. Enough time to make her return his love. He wanted that so badly that nausea began to set in when he let himself start thinking that she wasn't coming back. Yet there was nothing he could do. Nothing except wait.

Thurston arrived precisely on schedule, carrying a large briefcase. There was a spring in his step and a nervous excitement in his greeting of Zach.

"I really appreciate this, Lewis," Zach said.

"Not a problem, my friend, not a problem. Happy to be of service."

Zach walked across the hall to double-check Forsten's office and the surrounding area. Still deserted. He then summoned Thurston to follow him in. Thurston looked around the large office with it flags, plaques, and other memorabilia. "I suspected that this was our final destination." Thurston stepped to the window and gazed at the Washington Monument, lit up by spotlights, in the distance. "Great view, if I do say so. Ah, the perquisites of power."

Zach switched on a small lamp on Forsten's desk, leaving the rest of the office dark. Thurston sat in the admiral's high-backed chair, his equipment laid out next to the computer. Opening the keyboard with great care, he glued a rectangular device about half the size of a playing card in its upper-right-hand corner. He used a small battery-powered solder-ing device to reroute the keyboard's wiring. The whole procedure took less than ten minutes.

"Presto," Lewis said, closing the keyboard. Zach and Lewis exited the JCS section together, talking loudly as they passed the guard about DIA's computer budget for the next fiscal year.

Back at home, Zach sat on his couch, worked up from the day and now further wired by an ill-considered evening cup of coffee. The local PBS station was showing a Civil War documentary. Cheery topic around Christmas, he thought, looking at the still photos of piled bodies at Gettysburg. He wondered whether the North would have lost its will to pre-vail if television had been around back then or if the photos had gotten a wider audience. The phone rang as the narrator tallied the staggering losses suffered by both sides during a single day's battle.

"Hi, Zach. It's Justine."

Zach felt a surge of anger. His hand tightened on the re-ceiver. Where the hell have you been? he wanted to shout. How could you leave me hanging like that? But his anger disappeared almost instantly as he thought of her on the other end, warm and sweet.

"Hey, it's the long-lost pol," he said as casually as he could.

"Zach, I'm really sorry about Monday."

"Don't worry about it. I ran into something unexpected myself."

"I literally have not had a second to call you to apologize until now. I just got back from overseas."

"Yeah, I've been a little busy myself lately." Zach wondered where she was, what she was wearing, what she smelled like. "But I did write myself a little rain check. The cuisine you suggested can't be beat."

Justine was silent.

"Zach . . ." she said slowly, "we have to talk."

He felt a powerful wave of nausea. This was it. The ax was falling. He closed his eyes and managed to speak. "We can always talk, Justine. In fact, I'd say that's what we do best. Talk. Well, second best, anyway."

"Can I see you?" she asked. There was a chilliness in her voice.

"If you haven't gone blind, I'm sure you can."

"Zach. Please. Are you going to be in town tomorrow?"

"Hey, it's Christmas. Where else would I be besides here in my homey apartment, fire roaring, tree twinkling, presents piled high, turkey basting in the oven, my loved ones gathered around me?" He was reeling now, losing control.

"I thought you might be going to Princeton, that's all."

"Well, I'm not."

"So, can we get together?"

"Name the time and place, and I'll be there."

"It's supposed to be pretty warm tomorrow. Let's meet at the Lincoln Memorial."

"He always was my favorite president."

"Let's say noon. It can't be much later for me."

"High noon it is."

"Great," Justine said awkwardly. "I guess I'll see you then."

"Fine, Justine."

He slammed down the phone. He picked up his answering machine and hurled it against the wall above the couch.

It was already warm when Zach awoke on Christmas Day. He made himself a cup of coffee and stepped outside onto the balcony. Long ago he had trained himself not to think in the morning before a healthy dosage of caffeine took effect. In high school he used to lie in bed in the morning, paralyzed by anxiety. The infinite string of future life hurdles seemed insurmountable when considered by a brain freshly yanked from sleep. So Zach had learned to keep his mind clear in the first half hour or so after awakening.

It was not until he began his second cup of coffee that he thought of what to say to Justine. He wasn't going to let her just walk away. If she had already made up her mind, he would change it. Zach had come to feel that he understood Justine better than she understood herself. She was so transparently a creature of her past. She allowed her world to be shaped by powerful emotional forces that had gained momentum many years earlier. He needed to make her see that her relationship with Sherman existed for the worst kind of reasons. And he needed to do something else: Justine had to be warned about the company she kept.

The Lincoln Memorial was nearly deserted when he arrived. It felt like a spring Saturday, but the Reflecting Pool was mostly frozen, and there were no hot-dog vendors or souvenir trucks or tour buses. Even the pigeons were gone.

Zach could see Justine, on time for once, looking up at Lincoln's vast seat when he reached the top of the steps. She looked stunning in a black skirt and turquoise blouse. He approached quietly and laid a hand on her shoulder, startling her.

"He was every bit as great as they say," Zach said, looking up.

"Zach, hi." Justine kissed him on the cheek.

They strolled in a portentous silence down the sweeping steps. The ice on the Reflecting Pool shimmered under the sun.

"So, is my Christmas present what I think it is?" Zach finally asked.

Justine didn't reply directly. "I'm sorry again about Monday. Doug asked me to go out west with him on Sunday night. Then he asked me to fly to Hong Kong. I didn't get a chance to call."

"Quite the jet-setter."

They walked farther in silence, crossing the closed road in front of the memorial and heading toward the Washington Monument.

Zach spoke. "I know that it's him, you know. That it's Sherman."

Justine didn't look at Zach or break her stride. "I assumed that you would figure it out. You're not stupid."

"Sometimes I wonder about that."

They kept walking. A plane thundered above the Potomac, heading for National.

"He asked me to marry him," Justine said abruptly.

Zach felt the nausea return. He wanted to vomit.

"And you said yes, I imagine." He looked quickly down at Justine's left hand. It was bare.

"I did."

"Well, where's the ring, Justine? Isn't there a fist-sized diamond to seal the deal?"

"Zach, please. Don't."

"I'm sorry." He gazed away, feeling woozy and exhausted. All his arguments about what she needed and who she should be suddenly seemed pointless. None of them would change a damn thing. "So I guess it's a big secret, huh?"

"Yes. We'll be married after next year's election, and after the divorce goes through. Until then it's a secret. Please, please don't tell anybody about this."

"I keep secrets for a living, remember?"

"I suppose you do."

"And what about us?" Zach asked after a pause.

They both stopped, facing each other. Justine began to speak. Her lips quivered, and she broke into tears. Zach took her into his arms, cradling her head against his chest as she shook. He felt one tear roll down his cheek and then a stream down both.

"I'm sorry, Zach," she stammered between sobs. "I'm just so sorry."

He couldn't speak. He felt that if he tried he wouldn't recognize his own voice.

They held onto each other for a few minutes, and then he took her arm and they kept walking. Slowly his eyes dried and the stranglehold on his throat disappeared. Soon he felt able to speak again. He led Justine to a park bench and sat her down, taking both hands. "I know this is not going to sound right. You're going to think I'm just jealous and everything, but you have to listen to me for a moment."

Justine looked at him sadly.

"You can stop seeing me if you like. I'm in love with you, Justine. I am. I'm in love with you. I want you more than anything. I deeply believe that we should be together. Still, I won't try to stop you from leaving me. I'm not that type of person. But please, whatever you do, do not marry Douglas Sherman. What you have to do is get away from him as quickly as possible. Get out of there fast. He's in trouble, Justine, he's being —"

Justine's face contorted with anger as she pushed away Zach's hands and stood up.

"You haven't heard anything I've said," she snapped, almost yelling as she whirled and began walking away. "Doug is my life now."

He stood up and followed alongside her as she hurried in the direction of the Lincoln Memorial. "Justine, wait. This is serious. Hold on for a moment. Please, there's more." He took her arm.

"I don't want to hear it, Zach. I don't want to hear it," she hissed, breaking away.

"Justine, Sherman is under investigation by the FBI."

She froze. Slowly she turned around.

"What did you say?"

Zach now regretted that he had told her. It was stupid. But he continued in desperation. "I know for a fact that

Sherman is being investigated by the FBI for illegal arms dealing during the 1980s and possible criminal activities that continue today."

"Who told you this?" Justine demanded, the fear audible in her voice.

"An associate director of the FBI, Jack Burns. I found two agents trying to tap my phone on Monday, when we were supposed to meet at my apartment. They told me some of the details. The next day I'm approached by Burns, who lays out the whole investigation and asks me to cooperate. They think that Forsten and Sherman are in it together."

"I don't believe you. I don't believe you. This is too crazy." Justine began walking away, shaking her head. "It can't be true; it can't."

"You've got to believe me, Justine. Just get out of there."

"This is insane." Justine maneuvered around him, talking in rapid-fire sentences. "Doug has too much too lose. He's got all the money in the world. He doesn't need any more from selling arms. The press has dug into every part of his life a thousand times and never found anything. Nothing! If the FBI is investigating him it's a vendetta by the current administration. I can't believe you're falling for this crap."

She wheeled around, now nearly hysterical. "Damn it, you probably made the whole thing up. Didn't you? You're just trying to stop me from leaving you."

"No, Justine, it's true. The Bureau wants me to help them. This is serious. Please."

She ripped away, almost running. "Stay away from me. Stay away. It's over, Zach. Over."

He followed her for a few more steps and then stopped. She flagged down a cab on Constitution Avenue and was gone.

The rest of Christmas Day for Zach was a dreary festival of bad television. He surfed the channels while stuffing himself on leftover Chinese food and picking at a scab of self-pity.

At sundown he commenced drinking. The alcohol left him feeling heavy headed and more depressed. He placed the obligatory phone call to each of his parents and allowed himself gratification at their concern. Yes, his job was crazy. Yes, he was indeed suffering, he assured them. Yeah, Merry Christmas to them too.

On Friday morning, Zach made some coffee and retrieved the *Washington Post* from outside his door. He sat at his dining-room table, trying to wake up and turning the pages in a melancholic stupor. It was so meaningless to him, this game of politics and power. It was all a charade in which bloated egos competed for the limelight by milking symbolic issues, staying far away from any kind of actions that might actually be meaningful. Zach scanned a story about the deadlock on foreign aid and another about the civil war in Macedonia. He turned the page, and his eyes shot to the lower-left-hand corner. There was a photo of Peter Castori.

"Oh, shit," he said softly as saw the headline. WRITER MISSING, FRIENDS AND FAMILY SAY.

## 30

They had flown to Montana for the holiday. Years earlier, Sherman had begun to feel cramped on Eldridge's 320 acres. He solved this problem with typical overkill: He bought an 8,000-acre ranch in the Big Sky Country. It was a world unto its own, with part of a mountain range and two separate rivers. There was an airstrip to accommodate Sherman's jet, and two large guest houses in addition to the main mansion. The stables held a half dozen horses.

The plane ride late on Christmas Day had been a crowded affair. Two of Sherman's friends were being dropped at Aspen, and two others, a very wealthy couple, were joining him and Justine at the ranch. Eldridge's kitchen had prepared a strong batch of eggnog for the flight, along with platters of food, and by the time the plane crossed the Mississippi, the conversation had turned boozy and boisterous. Only Justine remained sober. An hour into the flight she said she wasn't feeling well and retired to the sleeping compartment.

She lay down, pulling a blanket over herself. She continued the struggle to stay in control, to think of other things, to feel relief at what she had done earlier in the day. But it was hopeless. She gave in and let her feelings go. The grief came in powerful waves. She curled her body tightly and cried into a pillow.

She wept for a long time, and when she stopped there was no relief from the pain and she began once more. She had expected to feel better after her confrontation with Zach. She imagined that excising the complication that he had become would make things clear and simple. It wasn't working out that way. Sherman had proposed to her on a moonlit beach in Tahiti, where he had flown her unexpectedly following their trip to Hong Kong. It was what Justine had wanted, or thought she had wanted, for more than a year. She had arrived back in the United States determined to end her relationship with Zach. In her anxious planning to do this, she had failed to stop and think. Instead, she had proceeded as she so often did in life — with her eyes fixed like lasers on a goal, blinders securely in place.

Now she knew she had acted too rashly. For weeks she had denied what Zach meant to her. She wanted him intensely. She thought about him constantly. But she couldn't fall in love with him, she insisted. She wouldn't let herself. When his love for her became obvious, she had only stepped up her denial. He had proven weak, but she would be strong. She wouldn't join him on a path that could only lead to enormous pain.

Her denial had peaked at the Lincoln Memorial. And it had collapsed there as well. When he finally said it out loud, said that he loved her, she had almost lost her will to resist further. She had managed to complete her mission; her training in politics had made her good at lying under pressure, at following through with the unpleasant. But now that the truth was out it roamed freely in her mind.

Other troubling thoughts had also been unleashed. Justine had greeted Zach's mention of an FBI investigation with outrage in part because it made things easier: Condemning his charges had allowed her to evade dealing with the relationship and perhaps letting Zach turn her around. It put her into a work mode. Defending her boss was automatic, familiar; she was on home territory. In truth, however, she didn't believe Zach was lying. He wasn't the type.

There had always been much she didn't know about Sherman. His world was one of secrets and fervently guarded privacy. While the press often made wild and unfair accusations, Justine had long worried that someday a truly damaging charge would surface. And now she was scared that day was coming.

She saw Sherman differently in Montana. At the beginning, Sherman had been her savior. He had offered her his devotion and protection with a kindness that was new to her. Never had she felt so safe. And his political crusade had given her something to believe in. Now she saw clearly that their relationship was an alliance, not a bond of deep love, and it suddenly became unbearable. Years had passed since she had been truly in love. She had become cynical about the very concept. Getting so close to this forgotten thing with Zach stirred in her a desire to have it always. With Sherman that would never be possible.

Through the weekend he was solicitous; she sulked in a growing morass of doubt. The matter of their relationship was too difficult to mention, or even to sort out in her own mind, and so it was the FBI investigation that she brought up. She did it as they prepared for bed on the final night of their stay.

"I got a strange phone call on Wednesday," she said.

"Uh huh."

"It was from somebody who identified themselves only as a friend."

"Anonymous, huh? What did they want?" Forsten was distracted, rifling through a bureau looking for his pajamas.

"They wanted to warn me."

"Warn you about what?"

Justine paused and faced Sherman. She took the plunge. "That you and Jeffrey Forsten are under investigation by the FBI."

Sherman eyed her quizzically for a moment and then looked away, continuing his search through the bureau. "I guess that teaches you not to listen to prank callers," he said. "Where was your secretary on that one?" He chuckled dryly. "More importantly, where the hell are my pajamas?"

Justine sat down on the bed. He was lying. She could always tell when he was. If he truly knew nothing he would be interrogating her about what the caller sounded like, who he might be, what kind of other information he had given, what Justine had said to him. Nobody could impugn Douglas Sherman's reputation without a fight.

She crawled under the covers feeling listless and adrift. Sherman didn't appear to notice. He turned off the lights and pulled up close to her. He kissed the back of her neck and massaged her back, moving his hands downward. Later, when he had finished and fallen asleep, breathing heavily, Justine rose and walked to the window, looking out into the starry night. She was done with crying. Now she began to plan.

## 31

Forsten returned from Asia on Monday, December 29, and the office leaped back to life. In Washington there was much to be done: The guerrilla war against the White House, simmering while Forsten was abroad, was turned back up to a boil. Zach accompanied Forsten around town to briefings about the Asia trip at which the admiral portrayed U.S. allies in the Pacific as up in arms about American weakness on the issues of terrorism and proliferation. Zach had prepared a memo for Forsten on the Deputies Committee meeting about Hizbullah. As instructed, he discussed the meeting with nobody else; its sensitive nature was obvious. But he was stunned to find that Forsten was systematically leaking information about the meeting during his briefings to those who weren't cleared to hear it.

Less surprising was the way Forsten leveraged the Hizbullah threat through legitimate channels. Within two days of his return, a Joint Staff working group hand-picked by Forsten and led by Rear Admiral Walling was hammering out the details for putting forces in place to respond to any attack. Zach wasn't in the group, but he picked up scattered bits of information about what the plans involved. By the second week of January, MOCKINGBIRD would be ready to go if the command came.

It took a few days for Zach to stop being jittery around Forsten. Maintaining a mask of normalcy was hugely draining. Zach now knew what Forsten had been striving for in his constant displays of warmth and admiration, and in his demand of loyalty: He wanted Zach to join him, to become one of his own. Sherman did as well. They wanted a hero in their camp, a poster boy for their cause — whatever exactly that cause was. This realization explained so much of what had happened over the past two months: the invitation to dinner at Sherman's, the job offer, the instant inclusion in the admiral's inner circle.

Zach had swallowed every hunk of bait thrown his way.

Three days after Forsten's return, at nine on Thursday night, Thurston was again checked in through the security post outside the JCS area. And again he and Zach entered Forsten's dark office. In minutes the device was removed from the keyboard and placed in Lewis's briefcase. "I'll have a printout of what's on here for you by tomorrow," Lewis said. "Drop by my place at eight."

Zach was at Lewis's apartment promptly at eight on Friday night. The building was modern, but Lewis had decorated his place to resemble the parlor of a Victorian lawyer. Antique sitting chairs were mixed with mahogany end tables, and framed black-and-white photos stood carefully arranged along the windowsill. A large oriental rug covered the living-room floor.

Lewis fetched beers for both of them, and they sat before a computer on a desk in the bedroom. Lewis passed a sheaf of printed pages to Zach. "Here are the dividends of our search. I'd direct your attention to page six."

Zach flipped through the papers to a page where a line was highlighted with a yellow marker. The line contained eleven digits and then a bunch of random letters.

"That's got to be our passport into Forsten's system, absolutely no question," Lewis said pointing.

Zach studied the sheet uncomprehendingly. "Why?"

"Because those digits constitute the only phone number in the entire printout."

Zach looked at the numbers again. The first was a one and the next three were the area code for Maryland. "So what?"

"Well, every other E-mail system that Forsten might

use — you know, the standard government and military networks, not to mention the Internet — can be accessed by his computer without his having to dial the connecting numbers himself. He just clicks his mouse on an icon in his windows software and the dialing happens automatically. In contrast, that number was entered on the keyboard. It has to be it. The only dial-in option he wouldn't have automated would be one that was very sensitive."

"And the letters that follow are the password?"

"Exactly right. You'll notice that there are seven letters after the digits, and then Forsten hit the return key and there's a space."

Zach looked at the letters after the digits. They didn't say anything. No "Rosebud" here. Real life was never like the movies. "Lewis, you're a genius," he said softly.

"Some have said that, my friend."

"So what now?"

"Now we dial in," Lewis said, taking the paper from Zach and turning to the keyboard.

"From here? Are you kidding?"

"No. Why, you want to do it from the office?"

"No, but isn't there a danger of them tracing the call by your modem?"

"Bollocks. First I get onto the Net and then I make the call. Unless they're ready with a bloody good tracker, which is highly unlikely, they'll never know where we're coming from."

Lewis booted up his windows system and got onto the Internet. He moved through a couple of different windows before carefully punching in the phone number on his keypad. The sound of ringing was followed by a high-pitched whir. In seconds a strange screen popped on with a flashing warning in bold letters: TOP SECRET. HIGHLY CLASSIFIED. DO NOT PROCEED FURTHER. ACCESS TO THIS SYSTEM IS MONITORED. EXIT IMMEDIATELY. Smaller lettering underneath these words contained the standard DOD warning on the penalties for viewing or possessing classified material that one was not cleared to handle.

"Nice scare tactic," Thurston scoffed. He clicked the mouse on an icon labeled "Continue," and another screen flashed on. The words read ENTER PASSWORD and showed a cursor flashing at the front of a thin rectangular box. Lewis typed in the seven letters and hit the return key. A moment passed, and a windows software system came onto the screen. It was a standard commercial program.

"Quick Post Four, not a bad choice," muttered Thurston. He zipped around with the mouse and in a moment had pulled up a menu of files.

Zach studied them closely. Most of the file names contained initials and dates. He instantly realized that DGS stood for Sherman, JRF for Forsten. He assumed that DVC was for Chen. There were several other sets of initials. A larger group of files were labeled "SOTUA," with numbers after them.

"So what now?" Lewis's hands were poised at the keyboard.

"Can we transfer the files onto a disk? And then print them out later?"

Lewis thought for a moment. He pulled down a menu and got into an applications file. He shook his head. "Doesn't look good. Downloading like that is difficult with the software they're using. It would be much easier if we just pulled up the files and printed them out individually."

"No, definitely not," Zach said quickly. He didn't want Lewis reading the files. He also wanted the original electronic files because they would be more useful to an investigation. "I really need them on a disk. Are you sure there isn't some way you can download?"

Lewis exhaled deeply and rubbed his temples. "I can do it, but I'll have to customize a program using one of my tool kits. It will take a while."

"How long?"

"Two, maybe three hours."

"Great. I'll go pick up a pizza."

At eleven, Lewis was still pecking away at the computer as Zach watched the local news. Finally, he emerged from the bedroom and handed Zach a disk. "I got it all, about two hundred K."

"How much is that?"

"Maybe a hundred pages double spaced."

"Did you read any of the files you pulled up?"

"I didn't pull them up when I copied them. Just went drive to drive."

"Good." Zach walked up to the desk and took the printout from the keyboard. "I'll take this as well."

Ten miles to the north, Jeffrey Forsten sat alone in the library of Eldridge. He was sipping his second brandy and growing more furious by the minute. He looked at his watch for the twentieth time in the past half hour and clenched his fists. He despised lateness. In his earlier years he had been consistently creative in punishing the tardy — stripping men naked in mosquito-infested jungle, forcing them to climb into the latrine to clean out just the toilet paper, stationing them high on a ship's communications tower in a rough sea at night. Now he worked in a town where running late was a way of life. It was one more thing he loathed about Washington, one more sign of the capital's decay from within.

At 11:15 he heard the sound of engines in the driveway, followed by the slamming of car doors. A moment later Sherman walked into the library in a tuxedo. Riley was at his heels.

Sherman cut off Forsten's complaint with an apology. He had been locked in a conversation with the Italian ambassador at an embassy party. Escape had been impossible. Sherman made himself a drink and sat down, undoing his black tie. Riley stood near the door. Forsten was on his feet now, pacing.

"We have a problem," he said, his jaw clenched tight. He knew the blame for this disaster lay with him.

"Of what nature?"

"Turzin again."

"Has he coughed up something to the Bureau?"

"No, there's nothing new from Sailor. I'm not worried about that one bit. But Turzin has been snooping."

"So what? He won't find anything."

"I'm not sure about that. He has a friend at DIA who's been digging pretty deeply, a little fuck named Lewis Thurston, a real dandy. My people at DIA do some looking around and find that Thurston has been going where he doesn't belong, learning things that he shouldn't be learning."

"For Turzin?"

"No question about it." Forsten paced in silence for a few moments. "It gets worse," he finally said. "Turzin brought Thurston to the offices on Christmas Eve and then again last night. I wouldn't rule out an attempted break-in of my system."

"They wouldn't get anywhere," Sherman said quickly.

"Maybe, maybe not. We don't know what this Thurston fuck is capable of."

"He couldn't get in, believe me. They wouldn't be able to find the network to begin with, and if they did find it and tried even one wrong password, we'd have known. That's how the system is set up."

Forsten erupted. "I'm not satisfied with that, damnit! There's too much at stake here."

Sherman knew there were times when reason could not sway his friend. This was one of them. "So what do you propose we do about this?"

"We need to have a frank conversation with Lewis Thurston," Forsten said.

"And how do you propose to do that?"

Forsten's pacing had taken him near the door, where Riley stood at attention. "I'd say this is an assignment that Colonel Riley would take on with pleasure."

There was a long silence in the room. Sherman offered neither agreement nor objection. He said nothing at all, as if he hadn't even heard the last remark.

Forsten leaned close to Riley, his voice almost a hiss. "Find out what Thurston knows, Colonel. Get it done this weekend. And keep it clean."

Sherman rose to refill his drink. He lingered at the bar, and his hands shook slightly as he unscrewed the scotch bottle. Things were getting messy, moving outside his control. "What about Turzin?" he asked.

"Let's see how much he knows first."

"And if that turns out to be too much?"

"I've already made plans for such a contingency."

## 32

Sheik Tabrata's men were barely more than boys. Pakistani passports, perfectly forged, listed both their ages as eighteen, but they looked younger in their slacks and white shirts. Too fresh-faced to die at all, much less for a cause. They were coming to Canada to visit relatives in Montreal, the visa application had said. Nothing more than two friends from wealthy families in Karachi traveling together during university break, a few days into the new year.

Thanks to Lebanese schools that had remained decent even amid civil war, both men knew some French. They moved easily through Customs, sparsely crowded on this Saturday morning, and then directed a cabdriver to take them into the center of the city. They walked around with their knapsacks and changed cabs twice before finally being deposited in front of a shabby park near the shipping facilities on the water. Two of Forsten's men were waiting in a white Jeep Grand Cherokee jacked high off the ground with snow tires, tinted windows, and Vermont plates. Their French was impeccable, mastered along with a dozen killing techniques in the turbulence of West Africa. A preplanned greeting, nonsensical on its face, was exchanged before Tabrata's operatives got into the Jeep. The vehicle moved into traffic, toward the bridge that spanned the St. Lawrence and connected with Route 10 heading east.

Two miles from the border, in the tiny Quebec town of Highwater, the Jeep turned off Route 243 and headed west on a packed snow–covered back road. After a few minutes it came to a turn-off where a single set of tire marks in the snow led down an even more narrow road. The woods here were dense and dark, and a fresh snowfall covered the pine trees, weighing down their branches. The Jeep drove on this road for two hundred yards before coming to a clearing where a small trailer with two snowmobiles on it had been dropped off earlier. One of the Americans and both of the Lebanese took a few minutes inside the Jeep to change into baggy snowsuits. They pulled the snowmobiles off the trailer and the American gave a brief lesson in how the machines worked. It was easy enough.

The American took one of the snowmobiles, and the two Arabs rode together on the second. In a moment they were whining through the silent forest, threading south on over-grown logging roads. It took less than a half hour to cross the border and reach the rendezvous point in Vermont on Route 105, a lonely country road that paralleled the border between North Troy and Richford. Fifty minutes later, with darkness fast descending, the Jeep reached a turn-off on Route 12 outside of Montpelier and followed a long driveway to a large modern house.

Hours before, a crew of three men had completed a day's work in the house and left shortly before the sun vanished over the mountains to the west. They had begun by moving crates into the vast and empty living room from a truck, five in all, each as large as a refrigerator box. They had also hauled out two different wood stands, assorted pieces of lumber, and a plywood platform. Four of the boxes had large block lettering on the outside that read "Hughes Aircraft." Lettering on the fifth box said "Boeing, Training Division."

The Hughes 185 was a medium-sized corporate jet with a small cockpit. The four boxes from Hughes contained that cockpit in pieces. Twice before the men had practiced assembling and disassembling the pieces, and this time they hurried through the job with ease. It didn't have to be perfect, only a close approximation. The seats were bolted to a platform that was nailed to the living-room floor. The main control panel was placed in front of the seats on one of the specially constructed wooden stands. The overhead panel was mounted on a larger wooden stand and held in place as well by two five-foot two-by-fours. The apparatus that came together looked makeshift and it was, but all the controls were exactly in the right place in terms of their distance from each other and from the seats. The space between the wooden stands holding the two control panels roughly approximated the size of the cockpit windshield.

The box from Boeing contained a device that looked much like a large-screen television with a built-in VCR, except for its lengthwise rectangular shape and sturdy tripod base. The men adjusted the height of the flight simulation screen and eased it into place directly in front of the cockpit windshield space. Wiring the system took more than two hours to complete, even though they had run through it twice before. The various gauges on the control panels would not show any movement during simulation, but the lighting on the panels would be functioning. All in all, the simulator was decidedly crude; it was like a go-cart compared to the state-of-the-art technology used for U.S. fighter pilots and trainees for major airlines. But it would do.

Tabrata's men and their escorts were tired when they arrived at the house. Lounging in a finished basement, they ate and talked of the struggle. The Lebanese Shiites found that they had much in common with their Quebecer comrades. Like Lebanon, Quebec was a land of great beauty tyrannized by outsiders who did not respect the ways of those they ruled. And, as in Lebanon, peaceful change had proven a fruitless path that only the naive still trod. So much of the oppression in their homelands, the four agreed, could be traced back to the Americans and the English. Tabrata's men praised Allah for a chance to strike a mighty blow in the land of the Great Satan. And the two from Quebec in turn praised the Shiites for the courage to sacrifice all to their god.

Tomorrow the training would begin, the Quebecers explained before they all turned in for the night. They said that an American, a bitter foe of his own government, would arrive to help in the training. His presence should not be cause for alarm; he was a wanted man across the continent and came to help them at enormous risk.

## ★ 33 ★

More often than not, Sundays were Lewis Thurston's sole day of rest among seven. This was due not to any religious convictions, for he had none. Nor did it reflect a disciplined insistence on leisure, for this had never been a priority of Lewis's. Instead, it was the rhythm of his schedule that left only Sundays. Lewis's work week, like that of so many young people in Washington, even those with jobs of no great importance, tended to gather too much momentum to stop suddenly on Friday afternoon. And so the week hurtled forward, smashing apart Friday night, cascading into Saturday morning, overflowing into the rest of the day, and seeping quite often into Saturday evening.

Lewis had finally extracted himself from the Pentagon at four on Saturday, earlier than usual. He visited an Italian restaurant on Wilson Boulevard in Rosslyn and dozed off during a bad movie later in the evening. A mediocre rerun of *Masterpiece Theater* had topped off the night. On Sunday he awoke feeling rested and could think of no reason to go into the office. The day that stretched before him would therefore be devoid of blinking cursors and pulsating stress. But it was also terribly empty, just as other Sundays had been lately, and just as nights at home always were. He dressed carefully in wool slacks and a crew-neck sweater. He put on his overcoat and left the house, beeper on his belt, almost hoping for a systems crash or some other crisis. Work was not Lewis's enemy; it was his salvation.

He drove to Old Town Alexandria and treated himself to brunch with the Sunday paper at the Chart House restaurant on the Potomac. After the warm days of Christmas, the winter cold had returned with ferocity, and large sheets of ice drifted down the river, shining under the bright midday sun. Other diners commented to each other on the natural splendor beyond the windows, but Lewis didn't much notice. The outdoors had never captured his attention. He scanned the classifieds looking for used computer deals, not that he planned on buying anything. It was habit. He read the comics and zipped through the puzzles. After his meal, he strolled the streets of Alexandria for fifteen minutes. The computer section of a Barnes and Noble bookstore distracted him for another twenty. He killed a half hour at a men's clothing store buying shirts. One could never have enough shirts. Then, at a loss for where to go next or how to amuse himself further, he headed home. There was a reason Sundays terrified Lewis.

Back at his apartment complex he used a card to open the gate to the parking garage and found a choice spot. He saw the two men getting out of a dark green Crown Victoria as he locked his car. For a moment as they approached, eyeing him at the elevator, he had the silly thought that they wanted to ask for directions. Then, for a second after that, he felt a surge of fear, remembering Zach's warnings. He shot a glance at the stairway door ten feet away and jabbed hard at the already illuminated elevator button. One of the men, blond haired with weathered features, flashed an ID at him. "Mr. Thurston, Robert Tucker, Army Investigations." The other man, dark with Latin features, simply nodded. He carried a boxy attaché case. Both men wore trench coats.

Lewis had barely looked at the ID card, but it put him at ease. Another car pulled into the garage, its tires squealing on the polished asphalt. The adrenaline rush vanished. He looked quizzically at the two men. "How may I help you gentlemen?"

"We'd like to ask you a few questions, Mr. Thurston," the blond-haired man said. Lewis noticed a deep Southern accent. "It shouldn't take long, twenty minutes at the most, sir."

The elevator doors opened, and Lewis stepped forward automatically. "Not a problem. Why don't you come up to my apartment?" He didn't give the offer a second thought. There didn't seem to be anyplace else to go.

He felt a new wave of fear as he pressed the button for his floor. This had to be about his work with Zach, he realized. The deal was up. Sweat broke out on Lewis's brow. The blond-haired man's voice came at him as if it were filtering through a long tunnel. "We're really sorry to surprise you like this, but this matter is very urgent. Super let us into the garage. He said that if we wanted to wait, that'd be the best place, not the lobby."

Lewis nodded. He was wondering how he would pay his rent when he lost his job. He thought of lawyers he knew who might represent him.

"Anyway, we're glad we caught you," continued the blond-haired man. "There was a major computer theft at the Army Medical Center yesterday, and one of our contacts at DIA mentioned that you might be worth talking to about the underground computer community in this area. See if we can find where hardware like that might be fenced."

The doors opened at the eighth floor as the blond-haired man finished his last sentence. Lewis stepped forward, a new person. "I think I can be of some help," he said jauntily. "Not a problem, not a problem at all." He pulled his keys from his pocket and tossed them once in the air before opening the door. He hummed as he led the men into his apartment and headed for the small kitchen. "Would you gentlemen care for a Coke, or perhaps a beer?"

The blond-haired man answered for both of them. "No, thanks." Lewis popped open a Diet Coke, filled a glass with ice, and walked back into the living room. He slipped out of his loafers and plopped himself into an upholstered chair. This might be fun. "Please, have a seat," he said.

The man with the attaché case remained immobile near the door. The blond-haired man sat down on the edge of a chair, facing Lewis. He grinned for a long moment, sitting silently. Then, slowly, he reached past his heart and pulled out a large handgun. Lewis stiffened in his seat as adrenaline thundered back into his system.

"What, uh, what's that for?" he stammered.

The blond man didn't answer. He reached into a coat pocket and removed a silencer, casually screwing it onto the end of the gun. Lewis heard the man behind him open the attaché case and then a strange clattering noise. He didn't dare turn around. He felt a powerful urge to urinate.

"Lewis, Lewis," said the blond-haired man, shaking his head as if wearied. "So smart, yet so dumb." He flicked off the gun's safety and placed it beside him on an antique end table.

Lewis's eyes raced around the room — to the phone, to the window, to the gun, to the heavy sculpture on the coffee table, back to the phone, again to the gun and its menacing attachment. Trapped. He felt the bristles of the carpet through his socks. A sense of familiarity mingled with sensations so alien they were barely comprehensible. From behind him came more noises — the sound, it seemed, of something metallic being assembled.

"Lewis, Lewis," the blond-haired man said again. "We got ourselves a problem. It ain't a problem that can't be solved, but it is a problem, nonetheless. Now, I'm betting that we can work together to solve this problem. What do you think, boy?"

The last word was pronounced distinctly, drawled out with a twang for effect. Lewis nodded his head. Speech seemed impossible.

"The problem is that you've been making trouble at the office. The solution as I see it is to tell me everything about your little adventures. Now that's not so hard. You can do that, can't you, boy?"

Lewis nodded again. The dull evenness of the blond-haired man's voice had all the permanence of the calm before a storm.

"So now let's start at the beginning," the man said, as if opening a job interview. "When did Lieutenant Turzin first start asking you for information?"

Lewis hesitated before finding his voice and beginning to speak slowly. He had slapped together a plan. With careful sentences, he spoke in general terms about the computer searches, making them sound like a harmless circumventing of red tape. The blond-haired man asked what the searches were on. Lewis lied. How, after all, could these men possibly know?

When Lewis was done, the blond-haired man sighed and clucked his tongue with disappointment. "I was afraid of this." He looked up past Lewis and shot out a quick question in Spanish.

"Si," replied the other man.

The blond man picked up the gun and rose from the couch. He gestured with the gun. "Time's come to move this interview to a new location, boy. Get up and walk toward the door." Lewis rose and slowly turned around. He was perplexed by what he saw. The other man was kneeling next to a rectangular aluminum frame made of wide tubing. It was set up on the floor in the space in front of the door. It looked to be about seven feet long and three feet across. Next to it, in a neat pile, were square pieces of inch-thick foam rubber. There was also a roll of silver duct tape. A small black box that looked like a shortwave radio sat in the opened briefcase. There were two wires attached to it.

Lewis drew back, a primal fear welling within. The wide head of the silencer was pushed hard against his neck. "Nobody would hear a thing, Lewis," the blonde-haired man hissed. He pushed Lewis down toward the frame.

Rory Quinn had gained some weight over the years, no way to deny that. But he still looked good, he thought. And as he finished the last of his home fries at the Sheraton's small restaurant in Montpelier on Sunday morning, he was pretty

sure that his attentive waitress, bountiful and fortysome-
thing, agreed with that assessment. Either that or she was
one hell of a tease. He considered asking about the room
service, but restrained himself. A long day stretched ahead.

Quinn had learned long ago not to ask a lot of questions.
It didn't pay in his line of work. That message had come
through loud and clear from the most important employer
of his life, Douglas Sherman. During the fifteen years that
he had worked full-time as Sherman's personal pilot he
had come to worship the man. On long flights, the two
would talk of even the most personal matters, but Sherman's
work was a forbidden zone of conversation. Quinn knew
that there were many things best left undiscussed — things
that he shouldn't know for his own good. At times he felt
like an undercover agent. He imagined someday perhaps
dying in the service of Douglas Sherman but not exactly
knowing what he was dying for. That would be fine by
him.

And so when Quinn was asked to go deep into Vermont
in the middle of winter to teach a crash course, entirely simulated, on how to get a Hughes 185 off the ground, he didn't
ask any questions. Paying up his tab and giving a wink to
the waitress, he only wondered who the students were and
what the hell a simulator for a Hughes 185 — if such a thing
existed — was doing up in these parts.

Quinn received an answer to both questions after a thirty-
minute drive that took him even deeper into the woods.
The students were foreign, and a couple of the most serious
teenagers that he had ever met in his life. And his instincts
were right: A simulator for a Hughes 185 didn't exist. But
what they had looked like it would be adequate, especially
since the goal was only to learn takeoff.

Now that was bizarre, Quinn thought: How in Jesus were
these kids going to land the thing once they were airborne?
A dark answer to that question may have lay somewhere in

the back of Quinn's mind, but, like so many dark answers over the years, he let it stay exactly where it was.

With translation help from the others, Quinn sat in the makeshift cockpit with one teenager at a time. He began with the basics.

## 34

Early on Monday morning, Forsten gathered a handful of aides in his office to discuss the Middle East arms moratorium that the President had long been pushing. The admiral had fought hard against the plan, but now he said it looked certain to go through. On Thursday the President would be giving his State of the Union address and the moratorium plan would be made public then.

"We can kiss the alliance with the Saudis good-bye," Forsten growled.

After the meeting, Zach noticed that Rear Admiral Walling had stayed behind for almost an hour, the door shut. He wasn't the only contingency planner who had visited Forsten's office in recent days. Two top planners from the Air Force had closeted themselves with Forsten at the end of the previous week. Forsten had also met with the number two man at CENTCOM. When he was not in meetings, Forsten was working at his computer, rarely leaving his desk. Meanwhile, the admiral's top aides had suddenly become scarce. Stan Duncan had disappeared. And the others now brushed past Zach as if he didn't exist. Forsten's memoranda had ceased circulating into Zach's office after the Asia trip. His office phone had fallen silent. Tedious budget work was shoveled his way.

All through Monday, Zach thought about the computer disk back at home. He was anxious to print out the contents but didn't have any place safe to do it. He decided he could use Lewis's home printer, as long as his friend wouldn't get a chance to read the files. He considered simply turning over the disk to the FBI, but he wanted to see for himself what kind of information it contained. Before he exposed himself further and did anything more for the Bureau, he wanted to know how much damning evidence they would be getting, if any.

Zach's thoughts had also turned often to Justine. He wondered what she was doing, what she was thinking. Had he gotten through to her at all? Did she have even a single second thought, even a sliver of doubt? Probably not. She was gone. End of story. The searing pain from Christmas Day had subsided into a dull throb of sadness and longing. He had barely been able to sleep. How many months would it last? he wondered. How many years?

Late in the afternoon, while churning out yet another summary memorandum on the budget request, Zach found himself stumped by a factual question. He wanted to illustrate the importance of the U.S. base structure in the Middle East by enumerating precisely how many American forces were currently deployed in the region. But nobody on the Joint Staff seemed to have a reliable number. Zach remembered the computer cluster at the War Room. They would have the information.

He had only been back to the War Room once since Forsten's initial tour. As he passed the security checkpoint and entered the humming command, he was glad to notice that it still gave him a thrill. So much had gone wrong since he had begun working at the Pentagon. Things weren't supposed to turn out the way they had. Being in the War Room was reassuring somehow.

He walked over to the officer in charge of the force-locating systems and told him what he needed.

"No problem, Lieutenant, I'll get that printed out for you right away."

As he stood waiting, he noticed Stan Duncan seated in front of the terminals that monitored U.S. nuclear forces, strategic defenses, and the Capitol Defense System.

He walked over. "So this is where you've been hiding out.

What happened to Captain Williams?" Zach had had lunch with Williams a few times since his initial tour of the War Room. He had come to like the guy.

"Williams rotated out to Omaha last week. I've been temporarily assigned to this post."

Zach chuckled. "So I guess you pissed off the admiral pretty bad, huh?"

"Pardon me?"

"To get this assignment." Zach gestured at the computers. "It has to be one of the deadest places you can work in the Pentagon these days, I mean except for the Capitol Defense System. I'm just wondering what you did to deserve to be sitting here on your ass all day."

Duncan smiled, finally understanding Zach's train of thought. "Believe me, my punishment is well deserved."

On the way back to his office, carrying a printout of all U.S. forces in the Middle East, Zach thought more about Duncan. Something seemed wrong. Forsten usually punished his aides by marginalizing them for a few days or a week, not by axing them from his shop altogether.

Zach got back to his office hoping he could finish his memo quickly and get over to Lewis's. He looked down at the printout, preparing to type the numbers into his memo. He had a pretty good idea of what the U.S. usually had in the Middle East, but not an exact idea: something on the order of one aircraft carrier near Saudi Arabia in the Arabian Sea and another in the eastern Mediterranean. There would be maybe twenty or thirty other ships in the area. If a training exercise was under way, a hundred or so fighter jets might be spread through Saudi Arabia and the smaller gulf states. Occasionally there were a few thousand troops on the ground training with the Kuwaitis or Saudis. On Diego Garcia, the base in the Indian Ocean, there would usually be pre-positioned supply ships that carried enough equipment for up to a division of ground forces.

Zach looked over the printout, expecting that these numbers would be confirmed. He saw a wholly different picture. "Christ!" he said out loud.

There was an aircraft carrier in the Indian Ocean near the African coast and one closer to Saudi Arabia, positioned in the Arabian Sea. Another carrier was in the Mediterranean, right outside the Gulf of Sidra off the Libyan coast. An additional hundred and fifty or so naval vessels were in the area, including many fighting vessels equipped with Tomahawk cruise missiles. In Saudi Arabia and the gulf states there were almost four hundred U.S. fighter planes. Zach noticed that at least half of these were deployed unusually in bases on Saudi Arabia's eastern side, near Jidda. And looking at the listing for Diego Garcia, he was stunned to see that it included ten B-1 bombers and five B-2s. These bombers had never before been deployed outside of the continental United States.

The forces needed to execute MOCKINGBIRD were all in place.

Zach was amazed at the speed with which things had moved. And the certainty. He had stressed explicitly in his memo to Forsten regarding the Deputies briefing that intelligence did not yet see any evidence that a possible attack by Hizbullah operatives could be clearly linked to the TKT Pact. Yet now U.S. forces had been quietly moved into place for a strike at all three nations. The only possible reason for the large deployment of bombers in eastern Saudi was to hit at Sudan and Libya, whereas the carrier at the mouth of the Persian Gulf was poised for strikes on Iran. Not a word of the deployments had leaked to the press. What the hell was going on here?

"I think you'll be surprised by what I was able to get out of that tape," Riley's friend said, clearing equipment off a chair in his workshop and gesturing for Riley to sit.

"I hope so," Riley said. He had sat in goddamn rush-hour traffic for an hour and a half to get down to Richmond. There better be something worth coming for.

"I don't have one of the best dynamic decode-only noise-reduction processors around, but my baby does the trick. Ran the tape through that and made a real good start. Than I hit it with my noise gate and low-pass filter. I could take things further if I had a DSP, but I think what we've got will do. The quality's pretty good now."

Riley's friend popped the tape into a machine and hit play. The static was mostly gone. A female's voice came through the speakers clearly. "Hi, Zach. It's me, Justine."

Riley's frown turned into a deep scowl as the rest of the tape played. Turzin had gotten his hands on what Riley had wanted for two years.

## 35

Zach was just about to head out at 6:30 when his phone buzzed. Forsten was on the line, gruff and demanding. "Lieutenant, could you get into my office?" Zach walked across the hall feeling uneasy. Forsten's blowups were as unpredictable as they were unpleasant.

All of the other staffers had left the suite. Forsten rose and came out from behind his desk. He moved behind Zach and closed the door to his office.

"You know, Lieutenant, I had high hopes for you. Very high hopes," Forsten began, circling back around to face him.

Zach's uneasiness turned to fear. He stared ahead.

"I thought a man like you would understand pretty quickly what was happening in this city, where things were headed. I thought you were smart. Are you smart, Lieutenant?"

"Yes, sir. I believe so, sir."

Forsten moved closer. Zach could feel the hotness of his breath.

"You don't know what you believe, do you?"

Zach was silent.

"I hoped you would be loyal, Lieutenant. You struck me as that kind of man. Are you loyal?"

"Yes, sir."

"Who are you loyal to?" Forsten snapped. He was in Zach's face, bearing down on him.

Again Zach didn't respond. He wasn't going to play this game.

"Answer the question, Lieutenant!"

"I'm loyal to the Constitution, sir," Zach said softly. "To defend and protect the Constitution."

Forsten turned away for a moment, shaking his head. He then whipped around and drove his fist hard into Zach's stomach. Zach fell to the floor, gasping and doubling over. Forsten followed up with two sharp kicks to the ribs. Zach's mind went blank with pain. The admiral calmly walked behind his desk and came back with a nine-millimeter pistol. He placed his foot on Zach's neck and stood above him, pointing the gun at his head. Zach clutched Forsten's foot with both hands as it ground downward.

"You stupid, stupid little fuck," Forsten said, his voice rising. "Who the hell did you think you were messing with? Huh? Who? You thought you could get in my way? Some big-shot hero?" Forsten raised his foot for a moment and then stamped it down harder on Zach's neck.

Zach gasped for breath as Forsten came closer with the gun, his voice dropping. "I should waste you right now, you dumb fuck. And I could do it too. You know that. I own this building. But I'm not going to. You know why? Because you don't matter. You're nothing. You can't stop me. Your friends in the Bureau can't stop me."

Forsten stepped back and delivered another powerful kick that crashed into Zach's lower side, sending an explosion of pain through his entire back. He grabbed Zach by the collar and dragged him roughly toward the door. "Now get the hell out of here and don't ever let me see you in my building again."

Zach staggered to his feet and stumbled out of Forsten's suite. A few minutes later he limped into the Pentagon metro station, disheveled and holding his side, feeling around for signs of broken ribs. The pain in his back pushed forward in sharp waves, sizzling down his legs and up his spine.

By the time he got to Crystal City he was thinking of Lewis. He tried calling him at both his office and apartment. No answer in either place. He took two codeine tablets with water. Retrieving the computer disk from the toaster where he had hidden it, he rushed back down into the metro to get a train to Rosslyn.

He rang Lewis's apartment from the doorway. No response. There was a doorman at a desk inside the lobby, and Zach knocked hard on the glass doors until he was buzzed in.

"Has Lewis Thurston been through here yet tonight?" he asked.

The doorman yawned and scratched his head lackadaisically. "Lewis Thurston? No, I haven't seen him all day. Been working since eight this morning."

"We have to check his apartment immediately," Zach said, clutching the side of the doorman's desk.

"Now wait a minute, we can't just go barging —"

"Immediately!" Zach shouted, slamming both hands down on the desk.

The doorman put up his hands. "Okay, now cool down, pal. Let me call the super. You can talk to him."

A minute later a balding man with a mustache came out of a door that opened behind the desk area. He wore a bright blue sweat suit. "What seems to be the problem here?"

Zach flashed his ID, trying to control himself. "Sir, I'm Lieutenant Zachary Turzin, special assistant to the vice chairman of the Joint Chiefs of Staff. I work with Lewis Thurston at the Pentagon. And I have reason to believe that he may be in some kind of danger. I would like to check his apartment immediately."

The superintendent looked uncertain. "Well, I'm not sure about this. What kind of danger are we talking about?"

"I can't get into that with you, sir. But I assure you, this is a highly urgent matter. Please."

The super hesitated for another moment before relenting. "I suppose it's okay if I come in with you. Let me get the key."

They found Lewis at the desk in his bedroom, slumped

back in a chair and clad only in underwear. The skin on his body was a sickly yellow, while his face was white and his lips a dull blue. His eyes were open, staring vacantly at the ceiling. A small pool of blood from the neat hole in his temple had formed on the floor and begun to dry. A revolver lay at the edge of the pool, directly below his dangling right hand. The computer before him was on, its screen dimmed. The super backed away in disgust and then rushed to call the police. Zach leaned over and hit the space bar on the keyboard. The screen lit up and showed the text of a short suicide note. The loneliness of life and pressure of work had become too great, the note read. It closed with an apology to friends and family.

Zach squatted next to Lewis's body and examined his fingers and hands. Nothing broken or bruised. He looked at his feet and toes. Untouched. He gingerly pulled back the underwear and looked closely at his genitals. Still nothing. Lewis's face, ears, and throat were also unmarked. Zach looked around the room. It was immaculately neat, no sign of a struggle. But then, they wouldn't make it look obvious.

The super had not yet returned. Zach glanced around once more. He spotted Lewis's keys lying on a small table near the door. Grabbing them, he fled down the fire stairs.

He stopped at a pay phone in the mall next to the metro stop on Wilson Boulevard and called FBI headquarters. His hands shook as he dialed. Lewis was dead. He asked for Burns and after some haggling with a receptionist, was put through to the associate director's car phone.

"They've killed somebody I was working with," Zach said, trying to keep cool. "Killed him and made it look like a suicide. Over in Rosslyn."

"Wait a minute. Back up. Who killed who?"

Zach explained his relationship with Thurston, leaving out the part about the data on the computer disk. "They killed him, Burns. I'm sure of it. Lewis didn't own a gun. He wasn't the type. You people need to get a forensic team over there immediately before the police just label the thing a suicide and cart the body away."

"Now hold on, Lieutenant, we can't just go around —"

"Do it now, Burns. Now!"

"Okay, Lieutenant, okay. Calm down. I'll send our people over ASAP. Just try to calm down. Stay in control."

"Don't lecture me about control, Burns," Zach spat. "It's your people who are out of control. Forsten knows that the Bureau contacted me. He knows I know about the investigation. He confronted me today. Somebody's leaking over there."

"Damn," Burns muttered. "Where are you? Do you need protection?"

Zach hadn't thought of that. He didn't like the idea. In any case, if they wanted to kill him, he'd be dead already.

"Not from you jokers," he answered. "No way."

"Have it your way. But I want to send over Edwards right now for a debriefing on what Forsten said."

"Forget it, Burns."

"Now come on, Lieutenant."

"No, you come on. You know, Burns, I don't trust you assholes one bit. I think the Agency is a sieve. But Lewis Thurston was my friend. If you show you can get some results on his death, I'll have a little present for you within the next couple of days. Something that could make your life a whole lot easier."

"Wait a minute, Turzin, what are you talking about? You can't hold out evidence on us like this."

"I can do whatever I want. And tomorrow morning I better be seeing an autopsy report."

"Turzin, now just —"

Zach hung up the phone and went into the metro. His eyes darted around the platform and then around the train. They weren't going to kill him, he kept saying to himself. They would have done it already. Still, he tried to stay in crowds after he got off at Crystal City. His apartment didn't seem safe, but it was the only place he could go. He needed a place to think. Christ, Lewis was dead. Bastards.

Once in his apartment, Zach closed the blinds. He opened a beer, took a sip, and then poured it out. The haze from the codeine still lingered. He had to keep his head clear.

Danger set his mind in motion. He took out a pad of paper and began jotting down notes at the dining table, trying to think through the situation. Soon a sense of control returned. There was still a dull ache in his back, but his hands had stopped shaking. He felt his arm and shoulder muscles relax and flexed them, feeling his strength. If there was to be a fight, fine. Forget the FBI and its investigation. He would crush these bastards himself, one at a time. Lewis had been defenseless, a child. He was not.

Zach's thoughts of vengeance were interrupted by the phone. He got it on the second ring.

"Is this Lieutenant Zachary Turzin?"

"Yes, it is."

"Lieutenant, my name is James Richards. I'm a reporter for the *Washington Post*."

Zach wondered how the *Post* had connected his name to Lewis's death so quickly. He thought of the super.

"Lieutenant, would you care to comment on the charges against you?"

"Charges? What charges?"

"Regarding your medal, of course."

"My medal? What are you talking about?" Zach asked.

Richards paused for a moment. Zach thought he heard him saying something to another person.

"Lieutenant, are you suggesting to me that you have not yet been informed of the charges against you?"

"What charges, damnit?"

"Lieutenant Turzin, we have a front-page story coming off the presses in three hours about the fact that you face a preliminary court-martial hearing at the Pentagon on Thursday morning on charges that include making fraudulent claims in relation to your Congressional Medal of Honor."

It took Zach a second to process what the reporter had said. So this was how they would get him. That's why he was still alive. "Who fed you this story?" he demanded. "It's crap."

There was the sound of rustling paper.

"Lieutenant, I have before me a faxed press release that we received this evening at seven o'clock from the Army public affairs office. The press release is dated tomorrow and was faxed anonymously. We have confirmed the story with one source on the record and two other anonymous sources. All three sources say that Sergeant Thomas Yohe and one other member of the Haisa mission team have accused you of gross negligence on the mission and charged you with causing the death of Jared Canver."

Zach blew up at the the mention of Canver's name. "Jesus Christ, you asshole, Yohe is lying! The son of a bitch was interviewed a half dozen different times during the review process for my medal. Now he comes out with this crock of shit? It's garbage. Any fool can see that. Who's your on-the-record source, anyway? Who's making you eat this shit?"

"Your boss, Admiral Forsten," Richards replied evenly. Zach's outburst hadn't ruffled him. "Seems to be a real fan of yours; says — and I quote — 'I deeply regret the charges that have been made against Lieutenant Turzin, an officer of enormous talents who has served me well at the Joint Staff for the last few months. However, I'm sorry to say that the weight of the evidence does appear to indicate that the charges contain substantial merit.' "

"Bullshit!" Zach shouted. He felt suddenly weak and dizzy. "What is Yohe's explanation for changing his story now? It's been six months since the mission."

"We haven't been able to interview Sergeant Yohe yet," Richards said matter-of-factly. "An Army lawyer we contacted who is representing him said Yohe is stationed out at Fort Wilson in southern Virginia and will be coming to

Washington on Thursday morning, where he will tell his full story before the military tribunal. But the lawyer has revealed that Yohe will testify that both you and other members of the unit pressured him to cover up mistakes made on the Haisa mission and to go along with the version of events that won you the Medal of Honor."

"Okay, I think I get it," Zach said sarcastically. He was starting to think clearly again. "Your angle is that I screwed up badly on the Haisa mission but wanted to come out smelling like roses, as did the rest of the A-Detachment, so we ganged up on Yohe and bullied him into lying repeatedly before all these review panels. And he went along. Is that how this thing goes?"

"We do not state those conclusions authoritatively because we still lack full confirmation. But that's what we've been told, yes. Maybe you would like to respond to another of Admiral Forsten's comments. The story quotes him as saying: 'It is an unfortunate reality that the otherwise laudable goal of maintaining high unit morale can sometimes lead to collective misrepresentations of events that take place on the battlefield.'"

"Bullshit. He's lying."

"What motive would Admiral Forsten have to lie, Lieutenant?"

"Let me tell you a different story, Mr. Richardson."

"Richards."

"Whatever. . . . The story is this: Admiral Forsten is under investigation by the FBI for illegal arms sales in the 1980s and other criminal activities right up into the present. I found out about these activities. Today at the Pentagon, the admiral attacked me physically in his office and threatened to kill me. It's clear that he is trying to destroy my reputation through this smear. Obviously he's managed to bribe or blackmail Sergeant Yohe."

"The vice chairman of the JCS attacked you at the Pentagon because you found out about his criminal activities?" Richards's voice dripped with skepticism.

"Yes, physically attacked me."

"Interesting story, Lieutenant. Can anybody confirm it?"

"Talk to Associate Director Jack Burns at the FBI; he'll tell you about the investigation and his contacts with me."

"Jack Burns, huh? Hold on a minute, will you?"

A moment later the reporter came back on the phone. "I was just checking something with a colleague of mine. Turns out we had a rumor in here a week or two ago about an FBI investigation of Forsten; not the first one, either. My colleague says he did check it with Jack Burns, who denied that there was any such investigation."

"Well, call him again!" Zach shouted as he slammed down the phone. But he knew that Burns would deny it again. He would deny it right up until the moment that they got an indictment, if that moment ever came.

Two minutes later the phone rang again. Zach picked it up, ready to unleash a barrage of profanity at the *Washington Post* reporter.

It was a different voice. "Lieutenant Turzin?"

"Yeah?"

"Dan Mahoney, *Los Angeles Times*. I was wondering if you could comment on the charges contained in the Army's press release?"

"You received it too?"

The reporter's answer was drowned out by a loud knocking on the door.

"I have no comment," Zach said, hanging up.

"Who is it?" Zach asked at the door as the phone began ringing again.

"Janet Goldstein, NBC News. Could I speak to you for a moment, Lieutenant?"

Zach opened the door, leaving the chain on. "Fuck off," he said. A bright television light shone in his eyes, and the reporter shoved a microphone in the crack. "What is your response to the court-martial charges, Lieutenant?"

Zach slammed the door, narrowly missing the microphone. The knocking began again almost instantly. He picked up the ringing phone, slammed it down, and then left the receiver off the hook. A few minutes later, when the knocking continued, he called downstairs to the front desk. "I have a bunch of reporters outside my door. I want building security up here now! I want them off the goddamn floor, and don't let any more in."

A few minutes later he heard the building guard herding away the NBC camera crew. Zach looked at his watch: 10:05. He flicked on the television and began changing from one news program to the next. After a few minutes he stumbled on news footage of his White House medal ceremony on CNN.

". . . and Pentagon sources confirm the charge," the newscaster was saying. "In addition, CNN has obtained an audiotape in which Lieutenant Turzin essentially admits his responsibility for the death of Sergeant Jared Canver. While CNN has not determined the origin of this tape, our audio experts have verified the authenticity of the tape by matching it with press interviews given by Lieutenant Turzin. What you will be hearing in a moment is, without question, the voice of Zachary Turzin."

Zach turned up the volume and stepped toward the television. What the hell was this? The screen froze with his photo as the tape ran, accompanied by subtitles.

"Jared died because I made mistakes. I blew the mission, plain and simple."

"Sonofabitch!" Zach shouted at the television.

The CNN report continued. "Lieutenant Turzin is to face a preliminary court-martial hearing at the Pentagon on Thursday morning. Sources in the government indicate that other members of his special forces unit may be involved in the scandal and may also face disciplinary action. . . . In the capital city of war-torn Macedonia today, negotiators reached an accord —"

Zach ripped through his phone book, looking for the home number of his psychiatrist. He hadn't seen her in over a month. He couldn't believe she would release tapes of his sessions. He didn't even know she had taped the goddamn sessions. He found her number and began dialing. He stopped at the sixth number.

It wasn't her, he realized. She hadn't taped the sessions. She hadn't released the tapes. He laid the receiver on the table next to the phone and flicked off the television. He felt weary, his eyes heavy.

There it was. He had already been tried and convicted. CNN had not referred to the "allegedly fraudulent medal" but simply to the "fraudulent medal." The audiotape killed him more than anything else. He thought of his parents and tried to call both of them. Their phones were busy. He imagined the barrage of calls coming from reporters. He imagined his parents trying to call him, only to receive a busy signal also. He wished he had been able to warn them. Over the next twenty minutes he tried their numbers repeatedly. Their phones must have been off the hook. He looked through his address book and called his father's office number at the university, getting the answering machine. He said simply that the charges weren't true, that the truth would come out, and that he was all right.

When he hung up he wondered whether the last part was true. He took the phone off the hook and lay down on the couch, exhausted. The image of Lewis's corpse danced through his mind as he was pulled toward sleep.

## 36

Justine heard the news about Zach on the radio while driving
on the Beltway after a late night with an old friend in Baltimore. She gripped the steering wheel with both hands,
fighting a wave of panic. The speed and traffic of the highway seemed suddenly overwhelming, and she turned off at
the George Avenue exit. She pulled over to the side of the
road and reached instinctively for the phone, dialing Zach's
number with a shaking hand. It was busy. For a few minutes
she sat breathing deeply and trying to calm herself. The
charges against Zach were more than false; they were evil in
the way they would tap into his worst self-doubts and guilt
about Canver. She had to help him.

After Montana, Justine had paid a visit to Associate FBI
Director Jack Burns. Burns's secretary had put Justine off
several times, but she had finally secured a meeting after
repeated calling. Burns had been polite, but he feigned be-
wilderment as to why Justine had come. She told him to cut
the crap, told him she had heard about the investigation.
She said she wanted to confirm its existence — for her own
reasons, not as a representative of Sherman. He simply shook
his head, pitying her for her needless worries and for the
time she had wasted coming to see him. She had stalked
from his office having gotten what she wanted, for Burns
too was transparent in his prevarication.

Following her visit with Burns, she had holed up in her
Georgetown townhouse, avoiding Sherman. She was sick,
she said. And although this was meant as a lie, there turned
out to be truth in the claim. As her world crumbled, Justine
felt her body weaken as well. A cold crept up from nowhere,

and her throat burned with pain. Aches mixed with fatigue. A dark and encompassing depression descended. She had reached out on the phone to her mother and sought out long-gone friends. She needed to remember who she was.

Justine tried Zach again on the phone before getting back on the Beltway. She headed for Crystal City.

Zach was roused from a fitful nap after midnight by the buzz of the intercom.

"Sir, you have a visitor," the doorman said.

"I told you, no more reporters."

"It's not a reporter. It's a Miss Justine Arledge."

Zach paused for a moment in surprise. "Send her up," he said.

They faced each other awkwardly in the living room when she arrived. Zach was wary. He didn't touch her. He waited for an explanation.

"I believe you," she said simply. "I want to help." She took a step toward him. He moved away.

"Why?" he asked.

"I confronted Doug. I talked to Jack Burns. I —"

"No. I meant why do you want to help? Why take the risk?"

She stood silently for a long moment. "Because I love you, Zach."

She stepped forward again, and this time he took her in his arms. He kissed her tentatively, unsure, searching her eyes. Was this real? She pulled him closer, clasping his head with her hands, and kissed him more intensely. Her lips, soft and warm, swept over his cheek to his ear and neck. She rubbed her entire body against him. Her hands moved downward, caressing his chest and hips.

"I missed you so much," she whispered. "I need you."

His hands slipped under her shirt and she moaned softly. She raised her arms and he pushed her bra and shirt over her head, casting them away. He was becoming lost now, taking her back with all his pent-up desire. They sank together to the carpet.

Later they sat at the dining-room table, and Zach gave Justine a sealed envelope with the printout from Forsten's keyboard. He didn't explain what it was. He didn't want her to know. He said simply that she should keep it in a safe place. He made her promise that she would do nothing more — no more investigating, no more visits to him. Nothing. Just go to work as if everything were fine. There was danger here greater than she could know. She promised to obey him, suppressing a hundred questions. He held her for a long time and then he insisted she leave.

The occupant of a dark green Crown Victoria, parked along the street near the lobby of Zach's building, had sat up abruptly when he saw Justine pull up in a black Mercedes and go inside. He had the camera ready when she exited an hour later carrying a manila envelope.

After Justine left at nearly two in the morning, Zach concentrated on his next move. He kept returning to the computer disk in his breast pocket. It was his only chance. Finally, he got up and grabbed his overcoat and the set of keys he had taken from Lewis's apartment. He opened his door slowly, looking in both directions. Nobody. He raced to the stairs and followed them down into the parking garage. He walked from there through several corridors until he emerged on the street far from his building. At the pay phone outside of the Arlington Inn he called for a cab, which dropped him off in front of Lewis's apartment.

## ★ 37 ★

The President was in bed but not asleep when the call came from Joe Rizotti. FBI Director Holsten was demanding a private meeting on an urgent matter. Was that doable? The President agreed, and within fifteen minutes he and Holsten were alone in the Oval Office. Rizotti posted himself outside the door.

Two weeks earlier, Holsten had come to the President with the good news that Lieutenant Turzin had agreed to cooperate with the FBI investigation of Forsten and Sherman. Now they were back to nowhere.

"I assume you heard the news about Turzin," Holsten began.

The President nodded his head grimly. The secretary of defense had called at 7:15, mortified and sputtering apologies. A small staff meeting had been held thirty minutes later to discuss how to handle the embarrassment.

"It's too early to say, Mr. President, but we think there's a distinct possibility that Turzin has been set up."

The President brightened at this prospect. "Really?"

Holsten recounted Zach's call to Burns and Thurston's mysterious death. "We believe that Turzin and Thurston may have found out something, sir, and that Forsten decided to kill one and neutralize the other."

The President sucked in his breath and leaned back on the cream couch. "Good god," he mumbled. A lock of graying hair had fallen across his face. He looked drawn and tired, and for a long moment he was silent. "So what can we do about this?" he finally asked.

"Unfortunately, nothing, sir. At least not now."

257

"Oh, now come on, John. If this is true, we can't just sit back —"

"That's exactly what we have to do, Mr. President," Holsten said abruptly. "We have no other choice. If Turzin reveals his contacts with us, and we confirm his story, our investigation is dead. And you and I, sir, may find ourselves with considerable problems."

The President nodded slowly, getting the picture. "But surely we can help Turzin on this court-martial matter, at least. Show that it's a frame-up."

Holsten didn't return the President's hopeful gaze. "We'll try, but there's not much that the Bureau can do. It's Forsten's empire over there. If his people want to lock us out of this matter, they probably can, even if ordered otherwise."

The President clenched and unclenched his fists. "Damnit, damnit."

"I'm sorry, sir," Holsten said weakly.

"So Turzin is sacrificed?" the President asked. It was more a statement than a question.

"I'm afraid so."

Zach stood outside in the brisk winter air and looked into the lobby of Lewis's building. The guard who had been at the desk earlier in the evening was gone. His replacement, an aged black man, stared vacantly at a small black-and-white television. Zach pulled out the keys and walked into the doorway. He began trying one key after another as quickly as possible, hitting the right one on his fourth try. He kept his eyes on the guard the entire time and was relieved that his fumbling went unnoticed. Opening the door, he walked in nonchalantly, nodding to the guard as he passed.

There was an FBI crime-scene seal on Lewis's door. For once the Bureau had done something right. Zach stood still for a moment in the hallway, listening for any undoing of locks that might indicate that someone on the floor was about to open a door. There was none. He quietly tried keys until he found the right one to the top lock and then to the bottom. The seal held the door shut even with the locks undone, and Zach dragged the sharp edge of a key down its center, pushing the door in.

After a few moments inside, his eyes became adjusted to the dark. The blue light of the nighttime sky shone through the windows, bathing the apartment in a faint glow. The apartment was exactly as it had been earlier, except for the removal of Lewis's body. The pool of dried blood was still on the floor near the desk.

He turned on a lamp next to the computer and sat down in the chair where Lewis had died. He felt his throat tighten as his grief came back. *I'm sorry, Lewis. I put you in danger and then did nothing to protect you. I killed you.*

He switched on the computer and laser printer. He put in the disk and pulled up the directory. Most of the files, as he had noticed earlier, appeared to be correspondence between Forsten, Sherman, and Chen. There were also messages to Riley from all three men. And then there were a bunch of other files all in a row: SOTUA One, SOTUA Two, SOTUA Three, and on up to SOTUA Eight. All of the files were dated in the last four months. The SOTUA files were dated a week or two apart, with the most recent being SOTUA Eight, dated in mid-December. The recent dates on the files made Zach realize that there probably wouldn't be evidence to prove the arms charges from the 1980s. Maybe there wouldn't be evidence to prove anything, in which case he was in deep trouble. Without an indictment of Forsten he would have little chance of vindication. His story would always receive the same sneer that had been directed at him by the *Washington Post* reporter. He would sound like a guilty coward making up wild tales to save his neck. The tape of his "confession" would be taken as truth.

He randomly retrieved the most recent of the correspondence files from Sherman. It appeared innocuous, containing plans to meet in Hong Kong. "I'll have Ron call Jeanie when my itinerary has been solidified." Garbage.

Zach scanned over the file list and retrieved a transmission from Chen to Sherman from early November. It was cryptic. "Meeting with the POGREP went well. Tabrata is cooperative. Wants to wrap up details at least one month prior SOTUA. We need to put pedal to metal to meet deadline."

Now this was interesting. Zach pulled up other letters. There were repeated references to POGO, which obviously meant Party of God Operatives, since Tabrata's name came up often. The acronym SOTUA was sprinkled throughout, but Zach could not determine what it stood for, although it was clearly some kind of date or event. There was much talk of banks and negotiations over money. Zach quickly determined that a three-way discussion had been going on — between Forsten and Sherman over what to tell Chen, and then from Chen to Sherman and Forsten regarding his dealings with Tabrata.

Much of the correspondence was cryptic, and Zach had difficulty determining what a lot of it referred to. But the broad picture was clear: Forsten and Sherman were hiring terrorist operatives under Sheik Tabrata's control to do something, somewhere. There was some talk of obtaining fake passports and visas, but not enough that Zach could tell what country the Hizbullah mission was directed at. He assumed it was in Western Europe, remembering the CIA briefing at the State Department. What could be the target?

He felt a mixture of foreboding and relief as he read on. This information, if its authenticity stood up in court and if additional evidence was found — big ifs — would be enough to make a damning legal case against Forsten and Sherman. At the same time, it was clear that a well-coordinated terrorist attack was going to happen sometime in the near future. Zach needed to know more about SOTUA.

He retrieved the file labeled SOTUA Eight, dated December 16. He could see immediately that it was a timetable for an attack by Hizbullah, but most of the details were cryptic, and it contained no dates. Zach was sure that the timetable was a countdown to whatever SOTUA was. The document began with "SOTUA minus 30 — Stage 1 Transactions complete." Then it specified various things that would happen as SOTUA approached, all under Stage 2. Zach scrolled to near the end of the document:

"SOTUA minus 6 — Main package en route. POGO arrive MIA.
"SOTUA minus 5 — POGO training commences.
"SOTUA minus 4 — BIA H-8 acquired and secured.
"SOTUA minus 3 — DV arrives at H-8. Arrival of Tercom, ECW systems, and main package.
"SOTUA minus 2 — Prep begins on DV.
"SOTUA minus 3000 — DV prep completed.
"SOTUA minus 2400 — POGO transferred to BIA.
"SOTUA minus 0500 — DCO in place.
"SOTUA minus 0300 — Final inspection all systems.
"SOTUA minus 0200 — DV departure.
"SOTUA minus 0045 — DCO tasks completed.
"SOTUA minus 0030 — Target in place.
"SOTUA 0000 — Target destroyed.
"STAGE THREE TAKES EFFECT."

Zach looked through the other SOTUA files. They appeared to be earlier versions of the same plan. He typed in the commands to print out SOTUA Eight.

As the printing began, he found a pen and began jotting notes, trying to piece together what he knew. Several things were decipherable. First, the references to MIA and BIA were probably international airports. It appeared that the Hizbullah operatives would be arriving at one airport and then traveling to another. But there might be several airports around Western Europe that could be referred to by those letters.

Second, the references to Tercom and ECW made it clear that DV stood for a delivery vehicle in the form of an aircraft. It appeared as if the plan involved equipping an aircraft with a terrain-following system. This would make it possible for even novice pilots in the aircraft to undertake difficult low-flying operations at night and guide the plane to its destination with pinpoint precision. The electronic-warfare pods would give the plane an ability to jam radar as it approached its target. The terrorists, presumably, would fly the aircraft. The "main package," Zach surmised, was a bomb that would be carried on the plane.

Christ almighty. They were planning a kamikaze air attack using the same sort of zealot suicide bombers who had driven a truck into the Marine barracks in Lebanon. Zach imagined an attack on a U.S. military base or embassy in Germany or Italy. Things were making sense. If Forsten planted evidence linking the attack to all three TKT Pact members, he could use it to compel the President to launch MOCKINGBIRD, the forces for which were now in place. This could achieve the admiral's goal of destroying the TKT Pact and enhancing his own influence.

But the costs and risks were huge. And what would Sherman possibly gain? That part wasn't clear.

Zach looked back over the timetable and poked other holes in his theory. If it were a base or some other stationary target, there would be no need to note "Target in place." Except if they wanted to make sure that an ambassador was inside the embassy, if that were the target. Or that some top generals were on a base when it was hit. But the question of motives remained unclear in both scenarios.

All that the documents indicated was that Hizbullah suicide bombers planned to undertake an airborne attack at a target somewhere in the world at an unknown point in time.

Zach began printing up some of the correspondence files. As the printer hummed quietly, he thought back to the briefing at the State Department. It was obvious why he had been sent to it and asked to take such careful notes. Forsten had been using him from the beginning to track intelligence issues on the Middle East. But the State Department meeting now seemed to have a staged quality. It was hard to imagine that any terrorist operatives working under instructions from Forsten, a man who knew all about U.S. listening capabilities, would be stupid enough to talk over open international telephones lines — especially between Sidon and Athens. Maybe the whole episode had been staged to divert attention away from the real plan. Maybe the target was in the United States.

Zach decided that he would take the documents to the FBI first thing in the morning. Delay had become too dangerous. The Bureau might be able to decipher more of the documents working with counterterrorist experts from Defense, State, and the CIA. And the documents might provide enough information to at least take Forsten and Sherman into custody for questioning.

He put the papers and the disk in a large envelope he found in Lewis's desk. He turned off the computer and left Lewis's apartment, heading down to the parking garage. He tried the Toyota keys on three different cars, before he found the right one, a new Camry sedan with Pentagon parking stickers.

Zach adjusted the seat and mirrors. Fort Wilson was about two hours south of Washington. It was time to pay Sergeant Yohe a surprise visit.

Once he had gotten out to I-95, Zach set the cruise control on fifty-eight and eased back in his seat. He thought back to the limo ride to Sherman's estate. It seemed like a million years ago. He searched through his mind for a single identifiable error that he had made since the week of the medal award. He could find nothing, except for his failure to protect Lewis. All else had been outside of his control.

An occasional car could be seen moving on the other side of the highway. Far ahead, Zach could see the taillights of a truck. Behind him it was black, and he was alone on the highway, white lines whizzing under the car. He turned on the radio and searched around for the news. Within a few minutes, he had found it: his fate being dissected in sound-bite fashion by an all-news station. The tape of his confession was played once again. Even if he was vindicated, the public might well never notice, remembering only the charges against him. He tried to remember the famous quote about how falsehood traveled in a carriage pulled by the fastest horses while the truth was often without boots.

An hour into his drive, he pulled into a rest stop and bought a *Washington Post,* fresh off the presses. He winced to see his photo at the bottom right of the front page. It was a head shot of him, and he could tell it had been taken at the award ceremony. The headline was damning: PENTAGON OFFICIALS ADMIT MEDAL MAY BE INVALID. It sounded as if they had grudgingly acknowledged a well-secreted truth. Zach read hurriedly through the story looking for any details of Yohe's charges regarding the events on the Haisa mission. There were none beyond what he had already heard: that Yohe would testify at Thursday's hearing that Zach's negligence had resulted in the screwup of the mission and the death of Canver. A slew of anonymous quotes, along with those from Forsten, indicated that Zach was already as good as convicted. He chucked the paper in the trash. He had watched politics and the military long enough to know when a feeding frenzy was about to begin. He wondered how much would be left of him when this one was finished.

A faint glow could be seen in the east when he arrived at the gates of Fort Wilson. A guard wearing an Army parka stepped up to the car. The clouds from his breath looked white and billowy under the two spotlights that were trained on the entrance. Zach showed his ID, worrying that the MP would already have heard the news and suspect what he had come for. Instead, Zach was waved through.

He drove slowly through the large base, which was just beginning to rustle with morning activity. The housing on most Army bases was rigorously segregated by rank in a gamut that ran from spacious homes for generals to sparse barracks for enlisted men. After a few minutes of cruising, Zach pulled onto a street lined with modest prefab units spaced closely together. This looked right. In front of each house, set next to the street, was an identical black mailbox that displayed the occupant's name. He swung the car over to the left side of the street so that the mailboxes passed close to the driver's side window. He went slowly down one side of the long block without luck. He turned around at the end and came back the other way. He saw Yohe's mailbox about halfway down the block.

Zach parked the car and walked up to the door of the unit. A few houses on the block appeared to be coming alive, but Yohe's was dark. Good. It was best to catch the bastard by surprise. He pushed down the button next to the door and held his finger there. The doorbell was loud. He could hear it clearly from outside, chiming again and again. He grinned. This guy deserved a nightmare.

A light came on inside, and he heard some shuffling noises. The porch light flicked on. The door opened a crack, and Zach could see Yohe squinting at him above a chain.

"Morning, Tom," Zach said with mock pleasantness.

"Holy shit. Zach. What the hell are you doing here?" Yohe looked suddenly awake, his blue eyes wide and fearful.

"What do you imagine I'm doing here?"

"Shit, Zach. It's ain't like it seems. I swear to god. I had no choice."

"I believe you, Tom," Zach said softly. "Why don't you let me in."

Yohe hesitated. He looked down at Zach's waist.

"Don't worry, I'm not here to mess with you. Just open the door. We have to talk."

"Okay, give me a minute." Yohe closed the door. A few moments later he undid the chain and let Zach in, stepping back. He wore a pair of jeans and had a pistol tucked in at the waist.

Zach put his hands in front of him, showing his palms and spreading his fingers apart. He moved slowly toward the couch. "It's cool. I'm just here to talk."

"Shit, Zach, if I were you I'd be here to waste me. No questions asked."

The two men sat down in the living room, facing each other uneasily.

"Tom, what's going on? Is anything wrong?" A sleepy blonde woman in a bathrobe stood at the head of the hall that led to the bedroom and bathroom.

"Go back to sleep, Cathy, it's nothing. Just some business."

The woman disappeared. Zach stared hard at Yohe. "Why'd you do it?"

Yohe turned away and slumped a bit into the couch. He rubbed his eyes with his hand. "It was my only choice. I had to. You gotta believe that."

"What do you mean, you had to?"

Yohe was silent for a long moment. He glanced at the hallway and moved closer to Zach, lowering his voice.

"They got shit on me, a lot of shit. They said they'd use it if I didn't cooperate."

"Who came to you?"

"A guy named Riley. Real scary sonofabitch."

Zach nodded. "What do they have?"

Yohe shot another glance at the hallway. "Remember I was in Cairo for a while too?"

"Yeah. I was on my way out when your time there was just beginning. You were there when Mubarak went down. So?"

"Well, I kind of took some walks on the wild side. Cathy was so far away; you know how it is."

"That's all they have?" Zach interrupted angrily, trying to keep his voice down. "Just you cheating on your goddamn wife?"

"Whoa, let me finish." Yohe put his finger up to his mouth. "It turns out that some hot-looking babe I ended up with was a Libyan agent. Shit, she said she was a secretary at the Indian embassy. Anyway, after we had been together for a while, I realized something was weird — you know, she started asking a lot of questions — and I ended it. I thought nobody knew a damn thing. I thought it was history.

"And then this guy Riley shows up, I guess about a month ago. Just out of the blue. He shows me all these photos with me and this woman. Says they'd nail me for espionage, no problem. Twenty years, minimum. Says he owns my ass. Says I'm to follow his instructions to a T in the future."

"And then?"

"And then I hear nothing from the guy for a while. I think it was all a bad dream. And then I get home yesterday, round five o'clock. The sonofabitch is sitting where you're sitting now, with a beer in his hand. My wife let him in because he said he was a friend of mine that had come a ways to visit me. Cathy's real sweet like that. So this guy suggests we have a private talk on the back patio. And once we're out there, you know, he starts talking real dirty about my wife, says she looked like she'd be a great lay and so on. I couldn't believe it. I wanted to take out the guy right there. Anyway, he shows me a copy of this press release about how I've made charges against you and how I will be testifying at some kangaroo hearing on Thursday. Then he gives me a five-page statement — my affidavit. Bullshit, every last word. I don't know what's going on, Zach, but these bastards want you bad. He also gives me a card, saying that it's for the lawyer who's representing me. He said I better not mess up."

"So what'd you say at that point?"

"I tell him to go screw himself."

"And what'd he say?"

"He just kind of smiled. Real cool, you know. Tells me that I could be under arrest in twenty-four hours. Tells me that they can put witnesses on the stand that will insure my conviction if the photos aren't enough."

Yohe paused. He held his head in hands and looked at the floor. "Then he mentions that incident at Fort Bragg a few months back, you know, when that major's wife was raped and murdered right in the guy's house on the base?"

Yohe's voice choked up.

"He starts talking, you know, about what a scandal it is that security on military bases is so bad. Says no man's wife is safe, especially a fox like Cathy. Me in prison, Cathy all alone. He talks about that. Then he mentions another incident from a few years back in which a whole family was killed on a base: husband, wife, kids. Said that could happen too."

Yohe's voice cracked. His hands were shaking.

"Says it would be a shame for a man to survive combat overseas only to die right in his own home, maybe even seeing somebody do his wife in front of his eyes."

They sat silently for a long time.

"So you said you would testify?" Zach finally asked.

"I'm sorry, I really am. I just don't see no way out. These people ain't screwing around."

And Zach knew Yohe was right, more right than he realized. He rose to leave. He wondered now why he had come.

It was almost eight by the time he arrived back in Arlington. A bright winter sun was moving upward in the sky, and the streets around Crystal City pulsed with morning traffic. He flipped down the visor above the dashboard and drove past his apartment building, scoping the situation. There were no reporters, but Zach did see two men in suits drinking coffee in a late-model American sedan. It might as well have had "FBI" painted on its side.

He parked Lewis's car around the corner from his building and entered the parking garage of the building next to his. He went through an underground corridor that took him to the basement lobby of his own building. He looked around cautiously and got on the elevator. He clutched the envelope with the disk and documents, wondering whether Forsten's people knew about it. Had Lewis talked? Had they made him talk?

He stepped from the elevator two floors down and followed the stairway up the rest of the way. He opened the metal fire door a crack and looked around. The hall was deserted. He walked to his apartment and inspected the locks for tampering. There were no scrapes or nicks that he could notice. He undid the locks and stepped inside. The shades remained drawn, closing out the light. The phone receiver still lay off the hook.

He put the receiver on the hook and walked into the kitchen to make a cup of coffee. Almost immediately the phone began ringing.

He answered it on the second ring, ready to hang up on another reporter. But the voice identified itself as an FBI operator.

"Our automatic redialing system has been trying to get through to you for hours, Lieutenant. Associate Director Burns urgently needs to speak with you. I'll put you through right now."

Zach waited for a moment. Burns came on the line.

"Lieutenant, I'm glad we got hold of you. We need to talk as soon as possible. I want to send some of our people over to bring you in."

"Hold on a minute, Mr. Burns. Back up. Tell me first where things stand on my request from last night — the autopsy?"

"That's one of the things we need to discuss with you."

"Give me a summary now."

Burns paused. "I really think we should discuss this in person."

"Talk to me now or there won't be a meeting at all."

Burns was silent again. "Okay, Lieutenant," he finally said. "I'm sorry to tell you this, but your friend Thurston was tortured."

Zach felt a surge of panic. His eyes zoomed anxiously around the apartment.

"Are you sure?" he asked.

"It was hard to find. But we're sure."

"Where?"

"When can we meet?" Burns asked again.

"Wait a minute, damnit. Tell me how they could torture Lewis and make it look like a suicide," Zach demanded, feeling queasy. He was not sure he wanted to hear the answer.

"The autopsy discovered marks in his rectum," Burns said reluctantly. "They're pretty sure it was electricity. The Arlington coroner would never have found it. Whoever worked over Thurston was a real professional."

Zach felt sick and weak.

"What about restraints? I didn't see any marks on his hands or feet."

"Forensics thinks they used cloth or rubber. But I can't

give you more details. Not over the phone. We need to talk in person."

Zach's mind was racing. He looked at the envelope on the table. It was his death warrant.

"Burns, I need protection and I need it now. Get those agents in front of my building up here."

"You got it," Burns said, hanging up instantly.

Zach put down the phone.

"I did the little bastard myself," said a voice from the darkened hallway that led to the bedroom and bathroom. Zach froze. His eyes darted around looking for a weapon, but his body remained still, immobilized by fear. A man that he immediately recognized as Riley stepped out of the shadows, leveling a gun at him. Zach stared at the long silencer. So this was it. This was how it ended.

"A boy like that can't handle pain, Lieutenant," Riley drawled, walking forward slowly and circling toward the table. "Doesn't know the meaning of pain. That puppy was talking after forty-five seconds."

Riley picked up the envelope on the table and checked the contents, keeping his pistol trained on Zach. "He told me all about your little computer adventure. Told me you had something that belonged to us. So then I made him squeal a little more, just for good measure."

Zach managed to speak through gritted teeth. "Why don't you put down that gun and see what it's like to fuck with your own kind."

Riley moved toward the door. "I would love to, really would. Believe me, if I were running this show I'd waste you right now. But a dead hero would attract too much attention, some say." He held up the envelope. "Anyway, you know and I know that there ain't nothing in here, boy. Right?"

Zach ignored the question. "I'll find you," he said.

"Sure you will," Riley said as he undid the locks on the door and peered out cautiously. "I can't wait for the day."

Riley stuck his gun in a shoulder holster and stepped into the hallway, closing the door behind him.

For a moment, Zach remained frozen, stunned that he was still alive. A few minutes later, two FBI agents were at the door.

"So why didn't this Riley fellow just kill you, Lieutenant?" Burns asked a half hour later, sitting in the apartment with three other agents. A locksmith was busy replacing the door locks.

"I don't know," Zach answered, still puzzled by his survival. "Riley said they didn't want too much publicity. I think they believe I can't hurt them."

"I'm afraid they're right. Not with what you have. With all due respect, Lieutenant, it doesn't look good. We believe you when you say that you saw a plan for some sort of airborne attack against an unspecified target somewhere in the world at some point in time. It fits in with the other information we've been receiving about these people, and it jibes with intelligence we've been getting from overseas. But even if that attack happens, your testimony will be worthless in court, assuming we ever had evidence to go to court. A defense lawyer would eat you alive."

"Maybe we could get back into the system and pull this material up again," Zach said weakly. He had already told Burns about the computer network and the password. He had tried calling Justine but only got her machine.

"I highly doubt that," said Burns. "If they suspect they've been penetrated, the first thing they'll do is change the password."

Zach hadn't thought of that. But of course Burns was right. The material Justine had was worthless. He slid deeper into despair. "What about preventing the attack in the first place?" he asked.

Burns shook his head. "We don't know enough. We'll get

to work on this word you mentioned, SOTUA, but it's not much to go on. It's obviously a code word for something. Until we know more, we can't take countermeasures. You see, Lieutenant, as much as we may believe you, you have a credibility problem. Right now, everybody in town thinks you're guilty. I believe this story you tell about Sergeant Yohe. I do. But we checked him out as soon as we heard the charges against you last night, and it's going to be hard to bring him down. A stellar career is what the records show. Nothing about any affair with a spy in Cairo. That's the kind of thing our counterintelligence people would know about."

"An attack is coming," Zach insisted. "And soon. One of the documents said that the Hizbullah operatives wanted to have the details wrapped up one month before the SOTUA deadline. I think the timetable I saw was a final one. And it was dated December sixteenth."

Zach looked at Burns, and then around at the other agents. He could see skepticism in every face. They weren't listening anymore, whatever they said about believing him. Now he knew why he had been allowed to live.

"Frankly, there's not much we can do with that, Lieutenant," the associate director said. Burns rose and paced the room, running his hands through thinning hair and rubbing the back of his neck. "The military is not going to place surface-to-air missile sites around every U.S. embassy and foreign base overseas, and around every important target in the United States, and keep them manned twenty-four hours a day and deployed indefinitely. Nor can our agency and the CIA post agents at every airport in the western world with a name that begins with an M or a B to look out for suspicious characters. We'll take the information you gave us and see what our team can come up with, but it's not clear how far we're going to get with this."

Zach knew he had lost. No smart bureaucrat would put his weight behind dramatic measures that could only be justified if one listened to an accused coward and liar. And in any case, Burns was right: There were no practical steps to take given how vague the evidence was.

The agents rose to leave. Burns looked at Zach sympathetically. "I want you to know that we are working the Thurston case as hard as we can, Lieutenant. We'll get the bastards who killed your friend. Also, if you think you still need protection I can leave two men."

Zach shook his head. "They don't want to kill me," he said. "I'm dead already."

"Who's your lawyer?" Burns asked.

The thought of a lawyer hadn't even crossed Zach's mind. He shrugged his shoulders.

"I'd get yourself one. And fast. From what I hear, they plan to skin you alive on Thursday."

## 39

Justine had gone into work at Eldridge on Tuesday morning as if nothing was wrong, just as Zach had insisted. She was at the office by 8:30. She looked gaunt and pummeled by illness, so nobody doubted the excuse for her recent absence.

Eldridge seemed like a different place to her. Before, it had been the castle in her fairy tale. Now it felt like hostile territory. Her hopes here had been built upon illusions. She retreated into her office and dreaded Sherman's arrival. Usually he would come down at about nine-thirty, bringing with him dozens of questions for his staff.

Sherman would not be holding to his usual schedule. He had other matters to attend to. He was, in fact, in a state of confusion that verged on panic. Shortly after Justine arrived at Eldridge's office wing, Riley had visited the living quarters and met with Sherman. The materials he brought with him were deeply disturbing. There was the printout and disk taken from Turzin. This Sherman could live with; after all, the plans were cryptic and now they were no longer in Turzin's hands. Thurston was dead, and nobody would ever believe Turzin's claims about what he had seen.

It was the audiotape from the phone tap and the photographs of Justine's exit from Crystal City that made Sherman frantic. Sherman wanted to know more, had to know more, and when it was confirmed that Justine was in the office, Riley was sent to her apartment to find the manila envelope.

Sherman wrote an E-mail message to Forsten asking for advice while he waited for Riley's return. Forsten's reply came quickly and it was intended to calm: "Developments with Turzin are not compromising. Consider him harmless.

Arledge more disturbing. Condolences. Unlikely, however, that she can do harm. Advice: Continue without action. Deal with situation after Sotua plan is implemented."

Riley returned at noon. "I'm sorry, sir," he said simply, handing the manila envelope to Sherman.

Sherman opened it and studied the contents. "No," he said, shaking his head. "God, no." He leaned back in his chair and closed his eyes, rubbing his temples with his hand. A great pounding had begun in his skull. He rose weakly and walked to the window. He stared out into the gray fields for a long time before speaking. "I want him dead, Colonel."

"Sir?"

"Turzin. I want him taken out. Kill the son of a bitch."

Riley hesitated. "Sir, I thought that wasn't the plan. Doesn't the admiral believe that wasting Turzin will stir things up too much?"

"Just do it, damnit! I'm giving the orders on this one. You understand that?"

"Yes, sir," Riley said with alacrity. He had been hoping for this order.

Sherman turned away and began rifling through some papers. Riley didn't move.

"What is it?" Sherman asked, not looking back.

"Well, sir, uh, what about Justine? What should I do about her?"

Sherman swung around and exploded. "I don't want you to do a goddamn thing! You stay away from her, Colonel. This is my problem. I will handle it how and when I see fit. Now get the hell out of here."

## 40

Zach spent the rest of the day after Burns left making phone calls, still seething over Lewis's death and imagining what he would do to Riley when the chance came.

He called his parents, managing to get his father at the university. He repeated the message of reassurance that he had left on the answering machine the night before. Both his father and mother were already packing to come to Washington and support Zach. Absolutely not, Zach said. Not now. He was going to be too busy with his defense, and the preliminary hearing would be closed anyway. There would be a time for their support, but this wasn't it.

"We love you very much, Zach," his father said, reluctantly agreeing to stay in Princeton.

Zach had replied without even thinking, saying what he had never said before. "I love you too, Dad."

Robert Oxman was considered one of the best lawyers in Washington who specialized in military matters; everyone Zach called mentioned his name. By that afternoon he was sitting on Zach's couch balancing a plate loaded with take-out Chinese food. He had known who Zach was the minute he called and taken the case immediately.

"You tell one hell of a story, guy," Oxman said after Zach had talked for twenty minutes, sticking just to the FBI investigation and how the admiral was trying to crush him because he knew too much. "And I'm ready to believe about anything after more than ten years in this town. Start digging anywhere in Washington and you'll hit a septic tank, guaranteed. But I think it's best if we don't mention the FBI part for now. Tell you the truth, it sounds so out of the ballpark that it'll probably just hurt you."

Oxman shoveled a forkful of chicken and broccoli into his mouth and spoke as he chewed.

"We'll show that Yohe is a snake in the grass, but it won't be because some goon threatened to off him and his wife. Nope. We'll nail him with the little stuff. He'll be sputtering nonsense by the time I'm done working him over. The bottom line is that his story is almost as crazy as yours. Are we really supposed to believe that everybody in the unit ganged up on this guy to get him to change his story and that this peer pressure worked so well that Yohe went on to lie before all those review boards? Sounds like a load of bull to me. Sounds like he's just changing his tune now. That's why we don't want to use your story. It's easier just to go after his. No need to piss in the well."

After their initial conversation, Oxman headed to the Pentagon to talk to the Army counsel general about the case and left Zach at the apartment with the job of writing a statement to present in his defense. By six, Zach had finished a first draft. It was eight pages long, handwritten. It didn't mention Forsten or Sherman.

Zach made a sandwich and flicked on the television news. The lead stories were about the President's State of the Union address before Congress on Thursday evening. The Pentagon correspondent for ABC News presented a report in which he discussed details of the Middle East arms moratorium, along with rumors of military opposition. Forsten's leaking campaign was going right up to the last minute.

At seven, Oxman returned to the apartment and gave him a copy of Sergeant Thomas Yohe's affidavit. Zach read over the document as Oxman looked at his draft statement.

Forsten's machine had shown no mercy. Zach was portrayed as incompetent and cowardly at every point in the mission. Yohe charged that after the drop-off by the Pave Low helicopters two miles from Haisa, it was Zach's choice of an exposed approach that had resulted in their encounter with the Iraqi patrol. And then it was Zach who had insisted that the team surrender once surrounded by the patrol rather than fighting and calling in air support. Finally, Zach had not engineered the escape from Haisa, Yohe charged. Rather, the lack of any adequate detention facilities at the base had resulted in the team's finding an air vent that they could escape through in the room where they were being held. In Yohe's story, Zach had even wanted to stay in the room and be treated as a POW rather than risk death through an escape attempt.

Zach felt a rising fury as he read the final part. Yohe confirmed that Canver's death had occurred in a firefight outside Haisa, but he blamed Zach for the death, saying that Canver had sustained a shoulder wound and Zach, who was nearest to him, had failed to pull him to cover before another round slammed into his body. "My honest assessment is that Jared Canver would be alive today if Lieutenant Turzin had acted in a timely and courageous manner," Yohe stated. The rest of his affidavit described in detail the reasons why he later went along with a falsified story. In essence, Yohe said that he was afraid of being ostracized by his unit. Zach was given credit for the mission because of his status as team leader. Yohe was told that this sort of falsification occurred often in the Green Berets and that he had better become accustomed to it.

For the next four hours, Zach and Oxman went over Zach's opening statement in detail, rewriting much of it to specifically rebut Yohe's charges. When the statement was finished, Oxman brought up another issue. "I got a call from the *Washington Post* earlier today, after I got back from the Pentagon. A reporter named Richards."

"Yeah. I talked with him last night."

"I guess I don't have to tell you not to talk to any more reporters, do I?"

Zach shook his head and pointed to the phone, which he

had taken off the hook again earlier in the evening.

"In any case, Richards is working on a longer story about you for Thursday's paper which is going to mention your drug use in college and your reputation for heavy drinking while in the service."

Zach shrugged his shoulders. "I admitted smoking pot during my first round of clearances. And hell, everybody in the Army drinks like an Irishman. So what?"

Oxman fixed a disappointed look on Zach. "Richards told me that he has confirmation from two sources of cocaine use at Cornell. If these charges can be proven, then that's trouble in and of itself. Remember all those long questionnaire clearance forms you signed?"

"Yes," Zach replied, knowing exactly where Oxman was headed.

"Those are just like tax returns, except more serious. When you sign, you are attesting under penalty of perjury that all the information you've given is true to the best of your knowledge. The same principle applies to all the oral interviews you gave with the clearance investigators."

Zach was silent. He had always known this time could come. He had regretted lying on the first forms. But after that he felt he had to keep the deception going.

"We've got to talk about this," Oxman pressed. "You could be facing additional charges that carry serious penalties. I need the truth."

So Zach told him. And after Oxman left, saying he would come by in the morning, Zach lay in bed wired and wracked by anxiety. He had been awake since before six A.M. Monday morning. Now, pondering his fast-collapsing life, it was impossible to sleep. He rose and turned on the television, flicking through the channels.

Across the street, seventy-five yards away in apartment 12G of the building that faced Zach's, Riley wasn't sleeping either. He sat in the darkness with a parka on, a rifle across his lap, staring intently through an open window at Zach's drawn blinds. He had been in position for six hours, and the temperature in the apartment was now below freezing. But Riley's host, lifeless in the bedroom, was not complaining.

Shortly past ten, the shadow of a bulky figure had appeared near the sliding door of Zach's apartment. Riley held his fire. While he despised lawyers, there was not much point in killing this one.

And so he waited. Riley watched the lights in Zach's bedroom go off and then come on a short time later. Ain't no way Turzin would be sleeping tonight, not with the shit he was wading in. What he needed was to get some nice fresh air on that balcony, or maybe pull the blinds for a minute to crack open a window. Come on, hero boy.

## 41

By the sound of the name on exit signs, a motorist traveling down Interstate 91 might imagine that humpbacked 747s and swarms of foreigners were familiar sights at Bradley International Airport. The truth was far from that. A gleaming complex situated on farmland near the Connecticut River between Hartford and Springfield, Bradley had been a boondoggle from day one, losing money hand over fist. It was a sleepy airport that catered to an economically depressed area, and lately things were getting worse. Layoffs of ground crews and other personnel had increased in recent years. Neighbors living near the airport commented on the drop-off in plane noise. And hangar space for rent came dirt cheap.

The Hughes 185 was already waiting in hangar eight when the four men arrived in two identical tan trucks. Two of them had been in the Vermont house a few days earlier; the other two had come from California. They had rendezvoused at a warehouse on Boston Harbor the night before to receive a cargo worth several million dollars. The most complicated elements of the cargo had been stolen six months earlier from a military supply depot at Maxwell Air Force Base in Alabama. An inside job. The rest, more simple but infinitely more deadly, had come from several different ordnance depots around the United States.

Marv Fletcher walked slowly around the plane, looking it over. Thirty years in southern California had turned his skin a deep walnut brown and kept his hair blond. Two decades of working in the aeronautics industry had made Fletcher a rich man. His illegal association with Douglas Sherman in the 1980s had made him even richer still. How rich, only his bankers in Switzerland knew. Fletcher was never bothered for a moment by the business of putting arms into the hands of outlaw states like Iran. In fact, Marv Fletcher had never been troubled by much during his life. He was nearly fifty-five now, at the top of a game he had already won. Money was not the issue anymore; it was loyalty to friends and a job well done. In jeans and a ski jacket, Fletcher looked laid-back, satisfied. But behind that easygoing demeanor was a cavern of coldness. He had first killed for Sherman in 1985 — an engineer in his own company who came, by accident, to know too much. Fletcher had killed two more times after that. Each time it became easier.

Fletcher began barking orders the moment the hangar door was pulled shut and secured behind the two trucks. The Hughes 185 had been delivered with only one modification: All of its luxurious cabin furnishings had been ripped out. A corporate palace in the sky had become a gutted cargo vehicle.

Fletcher directed that the explosives be unloaded from the trucks first. Crate after crate of C4, bearing the markings of different military depots, were carefully stacked in a far corner of the hangar. There were eleven hundred pounds in all. Properly fused, it could take out several city blocks and create a fireball a half mile high. It was enough, more than enough, for this job.

The next two crates out of the trucks were the most delicate of all. They contained the components of a terrain-following system that had once been appended to an F-18 fighter. Fletcher knew this technology well; his company had helped design modifications to it in the 1980s. The system was based on the same technology as the Tercom guidance in Tomahawk cruise missiles. A flight plan was programmed into the system's main computer before takeoff. Once the vehicle was airborne, the navigational system would take over, providing guidance by continually correcting the flight path using markers on the ground, much as a human pilot might. In cruise missiles, the system allowed for nearly pinpoint accuracy after flights of over hundreds of miles. On aircraft, it allowed pilots to become mere passengers after takeoff, even during missions at treetop level.

Once Fletcher was finished, a blind crew would be able to get the jet on target if they could get it into the air. And Fletcher had a plan that would allow even a blind crew to get the plane into the air. Packed carefully in several boxes in the truck was a small video camera, the components of a sophisticated transmitter, and a monitor. Fletcher's idea for using this equipment was simple: The video camera and transmitter would be set up in the cockpit so that everything that the pilots of the plane did during takeoff could be watched and directed through radio commands by a controller stationed in hangar eight.

Fletcher hated problems and he didn't anticipate any inside hangar eight. He had been working on the flight-plan program separately for nearly a month. Military satellite and aerial photography of the target area, readable by the computer, had been made available to him months earlier. Every other request, however obscure, had been satisfied instantly by his associates in Washington. Nothing would be jerry-rigged. Nothing done half-assed. Nothing left to chance. Just the way Fletcher liked it.

As his men labored on the jet through the night, Fletcher worked with the system's main computer, installing the flight plan. The team slept for a few hours near dawn, but Fletcher was driving them again at seven. By late afternoon the guidance system was fully installed. By evening Fletcher and his men were working on the jamming pod. It was a rudimentary system, really, but Fletcher knew it would do. It would function like a vast static machine, sending out electronic signals that blotted out radar screens and blinded would-be trackers. If the plane couldn't be seen, it couldn't be shot down. By midnight the pod was securely ensconced in the plane's belly. Ahead of schedule. Fletcher was pleased with the progress and he rewarded his men with a full four hours of sleep. He wanted them rested for the next part.

The loading and wiring of the explosives was more complicated than it had to be. The crash of the plane would detonate them as a matter of course, but this wasn't enough for Fletcher. He didn't want to risk a messy series of explosions. He wanted a single blast. For this he had the demolition expert on the team wire all the C4 to an impact detonator embedded near the nose of the jet.

Fletcher had planned to be finished and out of hangar eight a good two hours before Tabrata's operatives arrived from Vermont with their escorts. As it turned out, his team had been gone for five hours when the white Jeep with Vermont plates pulled up at the hangar.

## 42

Wednesday dawned cold and gray. Washington was known for its mild winters, but this had not been one of them. After a warm spell around Christmas, January was ushered in by frigid air blasting down from Canada and blanketing the city in a deep freeze. At Crystal City, towers of asphalt channeled the wind and magnified its iciness. Cold drafts stalked the underground mall. Building boilers worked beyond their planned capacity.

For Zach the day before the hearing consisted entirely of review with Oxman and an associate. They sat in his apartment with the blinds drawn, the refuse from take-out food accumulating. He was exhausted by the time night fell and the lawyers had left. They had run him through the statement four times, coaching him on delivery as if hand gestures could somehow change his odds.

Justine had stayed away, just as Zach had asked, and it took all of his self-discipline not to call her. There was nothing she could do for him, and he had already exposed her to too much danger. Zach thought again of the printout he had given Justine with the phone number and password for Forsten's secret E-mail system. It would be useless now, the password changed. It would mean nothing in a court of law — or anywhere else.

Zach had never felt so alone. Or so utterly confused and powerless. Even as he dealt with the charges before him, he sifted through the jumble of information bits that floated through his brain. Hizbullah. Sherman and Forsten. SOTUA. MIA and BIA. He arranged and rearranged them, looking for a motive that could explain their meaning. There was none that made sense.

It had never occurred to Douglas Sherman to think of evening staff meetings as unusual. He preferred to give commands at night, the time when an atmosphere of drama was easiest to create. He liked the thought of his opponents sitting at home, idle and weak, while he laid plans to undermine them. Sherman either did not notice or pretended not to notice the domestic wreckage produced in the lives of his staff members as a consequence of his nocturnal habits. Family values was a campaign plank, not an office policy.

Wednesday night's meeting in the working wing of Eldridge was scheduled for 7:30, but it was not until 8:15 that Sherman strode into the conference room. The lighting in the room was exactly as he liked it — recessed halogen shone dimly from the ceiling, and there were small brass table lamps in front of each seat at the table. The high command of Sherman's political organization rose as he entered the room. Most were from Washington and Virginia, but others had flown in from around the country. Sherman circled the table, pumping hands and slapping backs. Finally he took his seat at the head of the table. "Let's get down to business, folks." He opened a folder before him, and all others at the table followed suit. "I trust that everybody has had a chance to read the latest draft of the speech?"

A murmur of assent rose from the table, and compliments were paid all around. Then a moment of silence followed as Sherman leafed slowly through his copy. Charlie Abrahams, director of California operations, seized the opportunity for a bit of flattery.

"I just want to say again, Governor, that I think this is a brilliant idea." All heads nodded in agreement. "A counter–State of the Union address is precisely the sort of forum where you'll be at your best. The part I like most is that the

American people get a nice direct comparison of options. First they get to see that the President is offering business as usual, despite this crazy Middle East arms moratorium plan. Then they'll see that the Republican response is nothing but stale hash. No new ideas there. Your speech will be the only fireworks for the entire night."

"As long as people are still watching at ten o'clock," said Eric Brownson, Sherman's political director. Brownson was a worrier, the self-appointed house skeptic. It was a role he relished but only took so far. Sherman didn't like bad news.

"They'll be watching," assured Abrahams. "Quite apart from the Governor's innate appeal, I'll remind you that we have a full half hour on all four networks. There won't be anything else to watch."

"Unless you're one of the seventy percent of Americans who have cable," said Brownson.

"If two million dollars won't buy a captive audience, I don't know what will," quipped Sherman. Everybody laughed except Brownson.

"We should have bought time on the cable stations," he said, shaking his head with concern.

The meeting moved on to other terrain. Plans were detailed for large gatherings of Sherman supporters to watch the speech on massive screens at convention centers and college auditoriums around the country. Nearly every aide at the table would be deployed in Washington on Thursday for background briefings on the speech. The spinning after the speech would go on for days, if not weeks, and Sherman's schedule would take him to fifteen cities before the end of January. A new edition of Sherman's book, *Reclaiming America,* was being published later in the month, an appendix of which would contain the speech in its entirety. Phrases were tossed around the table in the ongoing search for a catchy slogan that summed up the way the speech recharged Sherman's political agenda. The speech itself was dissected page by page for what all hoped would be the final time.

It was not until well past eleven o'clock that pairs of head-lights came winding down the driveway and out the guarded gate as Sherman's high command dispersed. Justine left with the others. She wasn't doing well at behaving normally. She had sat silently during the meeting and wondered whether the chasm that had opened between her and Sherman was obvious. She thought constantly of Zach, wishing she could call, knowing she should not. Afterward, to those who commented on her paleness and lost ebullience, she once more pleaded illness.

Shortly after the last of the cars had passed out of the gate, a nondescript late-model sedan pulled up to the guard-house and was quickly waved through. A few minutes later Forsten and Sherman were sipping brandy in the library. Neither sat, and their nervous pacing took them in wide arcs through the room.

Sherman lit a cigar, stubbed it out, and lit it again. "If things do go wrong up north, how soon would we know?" he asked.

"Things won't go wrong," Forsten said.

"But if they did?"

"We'd know instantly."

"And then what?"

"We've been through this before, Doug."

"Let's go through it again."

"If things go wrong at Bradley, we're okay because there won't be anything left of the delivery vehicle or Tabrata's operatives. Believe me. Just a big hole in the airport and a big mystery for the locals."

"Are you sure this would be the outcome? What if things go wrong at an earlier stage?"

Forsten looked annoyed and glanced at his watch. "Fletcher's team has had the main package fully wired since 0900 hours this morning. Tabrata's operatives are finishing their training in the hangar as we speak. Fletcher is positioned to monitor the situation in the next twenty hours and can exercise an option to detonate the package remotely if there is a hitch. Believe me, nothing would be left of that hangar or its contents. We've been through all this before. Read the goddamn plan."

Sherman looked relieved, but only for a moment. He began asking another question. Forsten held up his hand. "Doug, trust me on this. You do your part, I'll do mine."

Sherman rose to refill his brandy. He then walked across the room and pulled back a painting. He turned the combination lock on a wall safe. "I've jotted down a very rough draft for tomorrow night's speech," he said, opening the safe and taking out a few pages of notebook paper with handwriting on them.

"Very rough, I would hope," Forsten said. He took the pages from Sherman and looked them over. "Spontaneity, Doug. That's the key for tomorrow night."

Forsten scanned the material silently. He chuckled after a moment and read a sentence out loud: " 'We have long known that a tragedy such as this might occur as a consequence of a lax national security effort.' Talk about blaming the victim! Come on, Doug. That's got to come out. You don't need to advertise your foresight. Everybody knows you've been warning about terrorism for years."

Sherman silently handed Forsten a pen and the admiral crossed out the sentence. He read on and then stopped again, scratching with the pen. "This sentence needs to be changed too. It should read: 'I have been informed that Admiral Jeffrey Forsten, vice chairman of the Joint Chiefs of Staff, is heading an emergency government' — not 'provisional government,' Doug, that sounds like Guatemala — 'and I urge all Americans to give him their full support during this time of crisis.' "

"No problem," Sherman said.

Forsten finished making the change and then read to the end of the speech. "The rest is fine," he said, handing back the pages. Sherman returned them to the safe.

**43**

The events of Thursday morning verged on the surreal for Zach. They were like scenes he was watching in a movie rather than experiences that were happening to him. The television vans idling outside Crystal City in the crisp winter sunshine. Oxman talking tough on the short car ride to the Pentagon. Zach, in his dress uniform with his medals, including the one in question, being buffeted by reporters at the north entrance to the Pentagon. The military tribunal of three expressionless senior officers taking their seats behind a bare wooden table in a drab room. Sergeant Thomas Yohe giving a crisp delivery of his fabricated statement, a crew-cut lawyer at his side.

There was an efficiency about the whole operation. It was a sleek and well-oiled machine that was destroying Zach's reputation and that had the potential to put him in prison for years. Oxman had made the possibility of incarceration very clear. Falsifying reports of actions in the field and showing cowardice under fire were significant crimes in the military penal code.

After Zach had given his own statement and all the hostile questions had been asked, the tribunal withdrew to deliberate. Zach looked around the hearing room. His back had begun to throb from sitting stiffly with so much nervous energy, and the insistent pain brought him fully into the moment. Sunshine was pouring through the large windows. Yohe had left with his lawyers. Two MPs stood by the door; another two had moved up and were standing on either side of the front of the room. There had only been the two by the door when the hearing started.

The tribunal filed silently back into the room. Zach looked at his watch. They had been gone only twenty minutes. The chairman banged his gavel, and when the room was fully settled he began to speak.

"Lieutenant Turzin, the charges against you are very grave indeed. Falsifying reports of action in the field is a serious charge under any circumstance. But this is especially true when such duplicity is intended to cover up cowardice in the face of the enemy and misjudgments on the battlefield. And, I must add, it is particularly despicable when the falsified reports present such distorted and self-serving information that they result in the bestowal of a citation of such immense prestige. We know of no other case where this has happened. The past recipients of the Congressional Medal of Honor have risked their lives and in some cases have lost their lives in the course of extraordinary gallantry in the line of duty. That such a medal would be awarded to any but the most courageous fighting man makes a mockery of the military's entire citation process. Moreover, the mere possibility that any kind of citation would be given to a soldier who allowed a wounded comrade to die needlessly in battle is nothing short of outrageous."

Zach could feel an immense anger begin to rise within him.

"Lieutenant Turzin, this court of inquiry finds the evidence presented against you today to be of a highly compelling nature. It is therefore the judgment of this tribunal, consistent with regulation twenty-eight of Section 010 of the Uniform Code of Military Justice, that a formal court-martial hearing be held no sooner than within thirty days of this date and no later than sixty days."

"Don't worry, we'll beat this," Oxman whispered.

"Furthermore, given the gravity of the charges against you, and your familiarity from specialized training with a variety of covert operation techniques, this tribunal believes that you are a high risk for fleeing the country and directs that you be held at the Army's detention facility at Fort Baldwin until the date of your court-martial."

The chairman banged his gavel. "This hearing is adjourned."

Oxman was instantly on his feet protesting. Zach sat stunned. He had never imagined immediate imprisonment. Oxman hadn't either, for the possibility had never been raised over the past two days.

The two MPs at the front of the room approached Zach from either side, each taking an arm and helping him roughly to his feet. Zach felt a sharp burst of pain in his lower back as he rose. One of the MPs took out a pair of handcuffs and instructed Zach to extend both hands in front of him.

"This is unbelievable," Zach said to the MPs even as he tallied one more loose end that had been tied up by Forsten's machine. Maximum humiliation. That had always been the point. Zach could see Oxman arguing heatedly with the tribunal chair, who was shaking his head and moving away.

Oxman turned to walk back to Zach, and noticed the handcuffs. He whipped around and began arguing again with the chair. "There's no reason in the world that my client needs to be handcuffed," Oxman pleaded, almost shouting. The chair walked away without replying.

"This is outrageous," sputtered Oxman, returning to Zach's side. "I've never seen anything like this. I'm sorry, Zach. There's nothing I can do."

The MPs directed Zach to walk toward the exit. He could see the tribual chairman talking with one of the MPs next to the door. The MP nodded and walked toward Zach.

"There's one other thing we need," the MP said, addressing Oxman.

And then, without any further explanation, he reached over and quickly removed Zach's Medal of Honor.

"This will stay with the Citation Office until further notice."

"Now wait just a minute!" Oxman shouted. "You can't do that." Zach was too dumbfounded to protest himself. The MP turned to face the lawyer. He was a good six inches taller than Oxman and bulging with muscle. He smiled belligerently. "I just did."

The two MPs standing on either side of him prodded Zach to keep moving, hustling him out the door. It was lunchtime in the Pentagon, and the halls were crowded. Silence fell, and people stopped to stare at the sight of Zach in full dress uniform being led along by three MPs. His lawyer walked briskly alongside, trying to reassure him that he'd be out of prison in one or two days. Zach looked straight ahead, trying to ignore the gawkers. The MPs came to a stairwell that led to the first floor and out to the entrance where Zach had come in.

"Where do you think you're taking my client?" Oxman demanded as they descended the steps. "There's no way he's going out through that entrance in handcuffs. No way!" The MPs didn't reply.

The knot of reporters that had greeted them in the morning had swelled to a vast crowd that fanned out before the entrance. The sun had warmed the frigid air. Across the sea of cameras, microphones, and shouting questioners, Zach could see a dark blue sedan, the back door held open by an MP. He stared straight ahead and began traversing the gauntlet. Throwing him into this wolf pack was a nice extra touch on Forsten's part. Halfway through, Oxman stopped and made a brief statement, quieting for a moment the gathered mob.

"Lieutenant Turzin has not been found guilty of any charges," Oxman said. "Today's hearing was simply a preliminary — and I would say wholly inadequate — evaluation of the evidence. We have no doubt that we will prevail when there is a full hearing. I might also add that the detention of my client is totally unwarranted. I should remind you all that Lieutenant Turzin is the most highly decorated service-person on active duty today. His treatment here is a disgrace to this nation and a travesty of due process."

Oxman still didn't get it, Zach thought as he was pushed down into the backseat of the sedan. The military justice system was nothing like the civil system. There was no guaranteed bail, no elaborate safeguards regarding the admissibility of evidence. Due process didn't exist in the conventional sense. Indeed, the machine that now controlled Zach's life would make sure that it didn't exist in any sense.

As the car pulled onto the highway, Zach looked out to the Potomac, glistening with blocks of ice. The throbbing in his back had gotten worse. Zach thought of his painkillers, far away at home.

Riley could hardly have hoped for a better position. From the employee parking lot of the D.C. public works facility next to Fort Baldwin, he had a clear view of the fort's gatehouse one hundred yards away. Riley kept the tinted windows of his Crown Victoria rolled up as he made his preparations. He opened the gun case and quickly attached the stock of the Heckler & Koch MSG 90 sniper rifle. He carefully adjusted the electro-optical scope to its preset position and screwed on the silencer. He pushed in a five-shot magazine of 7.62-millimeter steel-jacketed bullets. From the backseat, he retrieved a two-by-four and laid it between the dashboard and the top of the passenger seat. He pulled out a roll of duct tape from the glove compartment and taped the board securely in place. Kneeling in the driver's seat, he brought up the rifle and rested the front end on the board. He looked around the parking lot. It was full of vehicles but deserted. He reached over to the control panel on his door and slowly lowered the passenger-side window. Through the scope, the gatehouse seemed to be just a few feet away, and Riley trained the red laser dot on the guard inside for a few moments. He then raised the window again and sat back in his seat. Trying to get Turzin in his apartment had been a long shot. Nailing him here would be a turkey shoot.

Riley was looking for a good country station on the radio when his cellular phone rang. "Yeah," he answered.

"They've just left the building. Traffic is normal. ETA is eleven minutes."

"Got it."

## 44

Robert Davies was not a happy man. Perpetual dissatisfaction had been his lot in life since the onset of consciousness. His brain produced a roller-coaster ride of discordant chemical signals, while his body had remained an estranged source of awkwardness even after adolescence. Friends had been few, and while women were drawn to him, he found them puzzling and ultimately unbearable. His wife had left him after eight years. His apartment in a Bethesda tower never quite felt like home, and so it was natural that he spent most of his time at the office. More often as the years passed he found himself irritated by the majority of people in his visual range.

Davies wasn't a paranoid man, but he assumed that most people lied at least some of the time. Others lied most of the time. And so it had made a certain amount of sense, he came to see later, to have chosen a line of work in which his personality was an advantage. From his first days in the Secret Service, back around the time that two assassination attempts were made on President Ford, Davies had known he was in the right place. It was an organization of worriers and complainers, nitpickers and parade cancellers. Even good weather was disliked, for sunshine, it was said, brought out the kooks. As head of Presidential Security, Davies had gotten as high in the Secret Service as he wanted to go. He didn't want the top job, even though most of his colleagues assumed that was his goal. The other work of the Secret Service — chasing counterfeiters and the like — didn't interest him, and greater administrative power struck him as a burden. In his own way, Robert Davies, with hundreds of agents under his command and the President's life in his hands, was as happy as he was going to get. And this knowledge itself was a source of discontent as he neared the age of fifty-two.

Davies rose from his desk as two top aides entered his capacious office for the four P.M. staff meeting. Their light conversation had dropped away and their smiles had faded when they entered Davies's outer office. By the time they took their seats at a small conference table near the window, they looked as somber as their boss. Mirror the powerful and you will become them, it was said. So many in Washington lived by this rule.

"What have we got?" Davies asked without delay. Pleasantries were rarely exchanged in this office. Chitchat was frowned upon.

Winston Carroll, Davies's deputy, launched into a crisp briefing of the security precautions for the evening's event. It was familiar stuff to all in the room. The President's State of the Union address, in fact, was among the less complicated events that the Secret Service handled during a given year. It took place in the District of Columbia, which meant that Davies didn't have to deal with incompetent local authorities and unfamiliar, often deadly locations. White House advance men, Davies had learned long ago, seemed to specialize in placing the President in maximally exposed positions. In his more generous moments, Davies understood that getting the President before the people was the job of these political hacks; at other times he wondered whether they actively wanted to see their boss killed. In any case, Davies's job was exactly the opposite — to reduce the President's exposure, to keep him away from unscreened crowds and unprotected places. If Davies had his way, the President would never venture into the real world, where unpredictability ruled, at all.

Visiting Congress was acceptable in Davies's book. The State of the Union address took place entirely inside, which meant that the President's exposure to a possible gun attack was vastly reduced. The limo ride down Pennsylvania Avenue was the most dangerous part of the night, but this was a piece of cake compared to, say, a campaign swing through a southern city.

Davies didn't let on that he had few or no worries about the night's event. Never seem complacent to subordinates was rule number one in his business. Instead, he started firing questions.

"What time are the K-9 sniffer teams going into the Capitol building?"

"Seven-thirty, sir," answered Tim Sheldon.

"Isn't that a bit late?"

"Good point. We'll move it up, sir," said Carroll.

"I don't want those teams going in too goddamn early," Davies growled. "That'll just leave a window of opportunity." The aides looked exasperated. Davies moved on. "Where do things stand on making Pennsylvania clean?"

There was no street in the country more familiar to the Secret Service than Pennsylvania Avenue. And Davies knew exactly what precautions were taken every time the President's motorcade whizzed over to the Capitol. But his aides played along, answering the question as if they had just been asked about the President's upcoming trip down the main boulevard of Beirut.

"The underground team goes into action at 6:30 and finishes at 8:05," said Sheldon. "We'll have every sewer and manhole checked and rechecked before the motorcade passes."

"What about pavement imperfections?"

"Sir?"

Davies looked annoyed. "Damnit, Tim, we've been through this before. The underground detachment has responsibility for checking for any changes in the surface of the avenue, against the contingency of a bomb embedded in the pavement and made to look like a recently filled pothole."

"Yes, sir, of course," Sheldon said. There was a reason he had forgotten about this particular request: It was idiotic.

Davies then turned to questions about overhead security in the buildings along Pennsylvania, about trash cans and mailboxes, about closing off traffic from the side streets, and about pedestrians on the sidewalks. They had been through it all before. And they had also been through his questions about the metal detectors in the Capitol building, the clearance process for the guests and spouses coming to the event, and the extent of the President's mingling with the audience after his speech.

The Capitol Defense System was not officially part of Davies's domain, but his aides knew he would ask about its status, as he always did on these occasions.

"The alert level of the CDS will go to CAPZONE Three beginning at eight," said Carroll.

"So what will we have?" Davies quizzed. He knew the answer to this question, and everybody knew he knew the answer.

"Two F-15s in the air out of Andrews and two mobile SAM sites."

"Good."

Davies rubbed his chin in silence for a few moments, searching for more questions to ask, new contingencies to ponder, fresh nightmares to consider. His mind drew a blank, so he came to the final matter.

"I spoke with the chief of staff earlier this afternoon," Davies said. "The White House has chosen Secretary Barnes to sit out the speech."

The two aides broke into laughter, an uncommon sound in Davies's office. "Again?" asked Sheldon,

"Again," confirmed Davies, allowing himself a slight grin. Since the 1970s it had been a little-known tradition that one cabinet member was chosen each year to not attend the State of the Union address, lest some calamity wipe out everyone in the line of succession to the presidency. The White House staff had long used this security precaution to send a signal to whoever was not in favor with the President. For a decade, Donald Hodel, President Reagan's secretary of energy, held the record with three enforced absences. Now, Morgan

Barnes, the marginalized secretary of transportation, was set to tie it.

"I thought they were going to spread this around," said Carroll sympathetically.

"Once Barnes resigns, perhaps they will," Sheldon quipped.

Davies frowned and brought the meeting back to business. "Barnes is in town today so security for him will be the same as it was last year." Davies looked at Carroll expectantly. The aide recited the procedure for protecting Barnes in his split-level house on a quiet Rockville cul-de-sac.

"Beginning at seven-thirty, we'll put four agents in two vehicles on the street and one on foot outside of Barnes's house."

"And you'll check the interior," Davies added.

"We'll check it but won't sniff it," Carroll said. "The K-9 teams are booked."

Davies nodded his head, satisfied. There was little point in doing more. The procedures had been the same for the last two times. Davies told the aides to report back regularly during the next four hours and dismissed them.

In theory, the name of the cabinet officer chosen to sit out the State of the Union address was a closely held secret. But in practice, security had never been tight around this information during past years, and this year was no exception. The joke was too good to avoid retelling, and that fact, along with the practical details of setting up a team in Rockville, assured that dozens of Secret Service agents soon knew of Barnes's impending humiliation.

At 5:45, at a corner pay phone three blocks from the Secret Service headquarters, an agent dialed a number in Virginia.

"Same as last time," the agent said curtly when the phone was answered.

"As expected," a voice replied.

## 45

As the car crossed the river into the District, heading toward Fort Baldwin, the pain in Zach's back grew greater. It gnawed in spasms along the rear of his waist and shot into his legs. Sitting became unbearable. Zach pushed his legs forward and slid down in the seat. The pain only worsened, blazing upward to the center of his back. He pulled his legs back up and lay down across the seat, curling forward fetuslike with his cuffed hands clasped before him. His orthopedist had recommended this position to cope with intense pain. It delivered a small bit of relief.

"Hey, Turzin, what the hell you doing back there?" one of the MPs asked, peering through the window in the sliding glass partition.

"Relax, buddy, I'm not going anywhere."

A few minutes later, the car pulled up to the gatehouse of Fort Baldwin. The guard on duty exchanged a few words with the driver and scowled down at the prostrate form in the rear seat.

For a brief moment, the red laser dot lingered on the head of the MP on the passenger side of the front seat. It then danced around on the rear windows, searching. "Sonofabitch," Riley muttered as the car pulled through the gates.

Fort Baldwin was a drab complex of red brick on the edge of the Anacostia ghetto in southwest Washington. With peeling paint and rusting gates, the place looked nearly abandoned. Zach sat up with great pain when the car pulled to a halt. The MPs helped him out and led him up a short flight of stairs into a dingy room with wire mesh on the windows. A stout, middle-aged MP stood behind a long counter that divided the room. "Welcome to Fort Paradise," he sneered.

The MPs took off the handcuffs, and for the next fifteen minutes Zach was asked to fill out various forms. He was then given a white T-shirt, a pair of baggy army pants, and brown canvas sneakers. He was told to change in a grungy room off to the left. Afterward, he was searched by the MPs. His wallet and keys were taken away from him. He was allowed to keep his watch.

Two MPs led Zach back outside, across a small dirty courtyard and into another building with bars on the windows. They passed a guard at a desk, and went up a flight of stairs and down a hallway. Zach was led through two separate doors that had to be unlocked and relocked as they passed, but there were no other guards in sight. The detention facility looked like a nineteenth-century office building that had been converted into a minimum-security holding pen.

At the end of the first hallway they turned right and went through another locked door. An armed MP with sergeant stripes sat at a desk at the head of the hall. Zach's escorts stopped and chatted with him for a moment. As they talked, he noticed a folded *Washington Post* in the garbage can next to the desk. He remembered that Richards had a story in there about his background.

"Third door on the right," the sergeant at the desk said, pointing down the hall. Zach could see a solid metal door propped opened a few yards down. At the end of the hall was a barred window.

"You guys think I could get that paper before you lock me up?" Zach asked, gesturing to the *Post*. "I hear I'm in it."

"You're in it, all right," said the guard, picking the paper out and stuffing it under Zach's left arm, "but I don't think you'll like what you see. You got all sorts of problems, ass-hole."

After the door had clanged shut, Zach looked around the

cell. His new lodgings. There was a single bed, a desk near the barred window, and a small black-and-white television. A toilet and sink were located in a small alcove.

Could be worse, Zach thought as he sat down at the desk. He opened the drawer and found a bible, a notepad, and several pens. He turned on the television and switched around the channels looking for news. The reception was poor, a nauseous jumble of jagged lines. All he could find were talk shows and reruns. He turned the television off and lay down carefully, massaging the tormented muscles of his lower back. The pain was working down the left leg, accompanied by a tingling feeling. He rolled onto his stomach and shoved a pillow under his abdomen, bending his legs up and stretching his arms before him. He took in small gulps of air, for deep breaths produced ripples of agony. He closed his eyes and sought to clear his mind.

Justine struggled with the zipper on the back of a tight black dress by LeMarc. It had come from Paris, bought for her by Sherman on a weekend shopping spree there a year earlier. He remembered the dress, and when Justine had agreed to dine with him tonight at Eldridge, he insisted she wear it.

She had tried to get out of the dinner. She had pleaded lingering illness. She had invoked the demands of work surrounding the counter–State of the Union address. But Sherman had persisted. His speech on Thursday night would be a historic occasion, he said, and he wanted to spend some time with her — alone — before he went on the air. She had relented. And now she dreaded the dinner and the draining work of pretending. This couldn't go on much longer.

At 6:30 a long gray limousine pulled up outside Justine's apartment in Georgetown. Twenty minutes later it deposited her at the grand entrance at Eldridge.

## 46

The sky was fast darkening when Zach awoke from a dreamless nap. His room looked even more drab now that the light from outside had faded and the harsh fluorescent bulb on the ceiling had come on. It appeared, finally, to be the prison cell that it was. His pain had subsided into a dull throb, and he sat stiffly at the desk, turning on the television. The first of the local evening news programs were on, but Zach saw no stories about his hearing on any of the channels. No doubt it had been the lead story, and he had missed it. Instead, there was a series of stories about the various initiatives that the President was supposed to announce at his State of the Union address, which would be given at 8:30 that evening.

He turned off the television after a few minutes and took out the pad of paper. For the last two days, even as he had prepared his defense, he had wracked his brain trying to figure out what Forsten and Sherman were up to. He had long been convinced that the antiterrorist experts in the U.S. government were amateurs. A bloodbath at Grand Central Station the previous year had been averted not by the special interagency task force, or the Army's elite Delta Force team, or the FBI's counterterrorism unit, but rather by an alert New York City transit cop.

Zach was unsurprised that the Feds could get no mileage from the information he had given them. It figured. Severe hyperopia was a common disability among career bureaucrats. The closer the object, the blurrier its contours.

On top of the pad of paper Zach wrote: "Known Facts." He then began scribbling:

"Likely place of attack: Western Europe/the United States.

"Estimated timing of attack: mid-January, assuming SOTUA Eight is near final draft of plan.

"Type of target: Mobile and/or time urgent.

"Attackers: Party of God suicide bombers.

"Means of attack: Tercom-guided, explosive-laden aircraft.

"Ordnance: Conventional munitions package. Chem or bio weapons possible.

"Launch point: International airport within two hours' subsonic flying time of target."

Zach tore off the sheet of paper and placed it before him on the desk. He then labeled another sheet "Unknowns."

He wrote: "Motives/objectives," and then leaned back to think. This piece of the puzzle stumped him. Forsten's motives were reasonably clear. Zach wrote them down:

"Maximum personal and political power.

"Change of national policy resulting in, among other things, destruction of the TKT Pact.

"End to FBI investigation."

Sherman's goals were also self-evident and overlapped with those of his coconspirator. Zach wrote them under Forsten's:

"Maximum power through victory in the next election.

"Changes in national policy that would stem from that victory.

"End to FBI investigation."

But what possible terrorist attack could achieve these goals? Zach now believed that Forsten and Sherman were capable of nearly any level of bloodshed, including chemical or biological attacks against civilian centers. Yet this conviction didn't shed light on the mystery of what would be gained. Zach wrote a row of big question marks across the page.

An attack on a U.S. military or civilian target that appeared to be sponsored by the Pact could badly embarrass the President, allow MOCKINGBIRD to be executed, and generally strengthen Forsten's hand in internal policy debates. But then again, it might not turn out that way. Military strikes against foreign countries almost always boosted a President's popularity. The whole thing could backfire.

And there was another problem. "No sure gains for Sherman from terr. strike," Zach scribbled. Even under the best-case scenario, with the President suffering maximum political damage, Sherman's election would not be guaranteed. Zach had read and heard repeatedly that both the minority whip in the House and the senior senator from Michigan were considered extremely strong contenders for the presidency. There was no reason to believe that Sherman could beat either of these men in a three-way race against a weakened president.

Those facts applied also to any kind of plot to assassinate the President. In that scenario, the vice president might be able to exploit the aura of heir apparent, a unifying candidate during a time of national mourning. And if things didn't work out this way, if he couldn't ride the dead president's coattails to victory, there was still no reason that Sherman would be assured of winning over a strong opposition candidate. And nothing in any of these scenarios would be assured of bringing the FBI investigation to a halt.

Zach wasn't getting anywhere on motive, so he moved to the next category, writing: "Location of target." He wasn't taken by the scenario of an attack in Western Europe. The intelligence coup that led to that conclusion had been too good to be true. It smelled like disinformation. Also, if Sherman and Forsten wanted maximum impact, they would hit in the United States.

Zach ripped off the top sheet of paper and turned the pad sideways. He drew a rough sketch of the eastern half of the United States. At the bottom right of the page was a crude handle that was supposed to be Florida. Chesapeake

Bay was an inward jag. Long Island looked like a claw. Up near the top center Zach drew a bunch of circles that stood for the Great Lakes.

Then he began putting dots around the map and labeling them: D.C., Baltimore, New York, Boston, Hartford, Chicago, Memphis, Buffalo, and so on. He made dots for various military installations: Annapolis, West Point, Norfolk, Seneca, etc. He made a dot for Camp David, a few miles north of Washington in Maryland.

Then he began drawing circles, based on a rough notion of how far a plane could fly in two hours. He drew a circle around Boston, the edge of which extended almost exactly to Washington. He drew a circle around Buffalo. A plane flying from there could, in two hours, reach Chicago or West Point.

Think targets, Zach told himself. And then think about launch points.

"Assume target in D.C. area," Zach scribbled. Maybe it was the White House. What international airports, beginning with a B, were in a two-hour range? Buffalo was probably too far. And in any case, Zach didn't think it had an international airport. Just a little one for domestic flights. He looked at the circle extending from Boston. It looked like the best bet. He concentrated, trying to remember the few times he had flown out of Boston. Would it be appropriate? If he were planning this mission, he would choose an airport that was less crowded and out of the way. Not a quiet domestic airport like Buffalo's, where foreigners might be noticeable. But a small-scale international airport. Boston was plausible, but it was not ideal. Zach now remembered also that the airport there was named Logan International Airport. If the acronyms from the stolen computer files were accurate at all, rather than just code, it probably would have been listed as LIA.

He placed an X over the dot that represented Boston and began looking at other cities, trying to remember airports that were not named after the cities they were in. He couldn't think of many in the eastern section of the United States besides La Guardia, JFK, National, Dulles, and O'Hare. He stared at the map, now systematically going through each city, wracking his memory. He looked again at New England. At Albany. No. And then over east. Did Hartford have an airport? He thought of drives up Interstate 91 to visit friends in Massachusetts and Vermont. And then thought —

"Bradley," he said out loud. "Bradley International Airport." He had changed planes there once.

He placed a dot a bit north of Hartford and wrote "BIA" next to it. He drew a circle with "BIA" at the center. The edge extended right to Washington. Perfect. The whole thing was perfect. Bradley was not busy, but definitely international. Probably not hard to rent a hangar there for a few days.

"MIA — Montreal International Airport," Zach wrote down. It made so much sense. Canadian customs was more lax than that of the United States. And it would be easy to cross the border from Quebec. You could drive from Montreal to Bradley in less than a day, six or seven hours, perhaps.

Zach drew a rough map of the western part of the United States and spent fifteen minutes running through the same exercise, imagining that the target was the Strategic Air Command base at Omaha. He didn't get far. There were almost no international airports east of the Mississippi with names that began with a *B*.

So Bradley was a good bet as the departure point for the delivery vehicle. But what did that prove? It didn't prove with any certainty that the target was in Washington. The target could be any civilian center or military base within two hours' flying time of Bradley.

And the question of motive remain unresolved. He thought about the word *SOTUA*. Perhaps it was not an acronym for the target or time of attack but rather somehow conveyed the motive. Maybe it was some foreign word for vindication or justice. Had the FBI brought in language specialists on this? he wondered.

He pushed the pad aside. He was exhausted and getting nowhere. He looked at his watch: 6:40. Damn. He had missed the lead again on the news. He turned on the television anyway and sat back on the bed with his back against the wall. Once more the story on him had already passed. The broadcast was now dominated by news of the State of the Union address. It was an important one, the last the President would give before his reelection bid. In addition to analyzing the President's initiative for reforming the legal system — an obvious campaign ploy — the news dwelled on the President's Middle East arms moratorium. ABC's Pentagon correspondent reported that the White House had been forced to exert pressure to get all the Joint Chiefs to turn out for the speech because of their opposition to the plan. Normally, the Joint Chiefs always attended the address, the reporter explained, along with all of Congress, the entire cabinet, the vice president, the heads of the FBI and CIA, the White House chief of staff and national security adviser, and members of the Supreme Court. But on this occasion presidential arm twisting had been needed to get the brass out, said the reporter.

Zach smiled. Reynolds wasn't the problem. Nope. It was Forsten; he had probably tried to organize a boycott by the chiefs. The tricks never stopped. Zach didn't like the moratorium idea, but he did like the idea of Forsten squirming in public as the President announced the plan. Then he remembered back to past addresses and realized that the vice chairman of the JCS was not normally invited, just as the deputy secretary of state and other cabinet deputies were not. That was a shame. He turned off the television and sat back on the bed with the *Washington Post*.

## 47

The takeoff at Bradley that evening could hardly have gone more smoothly: The plane was in the air at seven o'clock, on the dot.

By the time they reached hangar eight on Wednesday, Tabrata's operatives had spent almost twenty hours in the mock-up cockpit of the Hughes jet. Rory Quinn had run them into the ground during training, pushing them through two dozen simulated takeoffs. They were smart kids, serious as could be, and they had learned fast. Shortly before leaving the Vermont house, Quinn had blindfolded both his students and asked them to go through a takeoff. They had passed the test with flying colors.

Landing had not been part of Quinn's lesson plan.

The drive from Vermont to Bradley had been made mostly in silence. Forsten's men, speaking haltingly, as if English were a second language, had talked sporadically with Quinn about his life as a revolutionary and the dangers of living underground in a police state as repressive as America. They had thanked him profusely for risking so much for the cause. Each part of this conversation was translated into French for the benefit of Tabrata's men. Neither of them joined much in the talk. As the moment for their final mission drew near, they had grown more quiet and focused. Perhaps, Quinn thought, their minds were wandering to the pleasures that supposedly awaited them in the next world. Seven wives was said to be the reward bestowed upon Allah's fallen warriors. No wonder these boys did not fear death.

Quinn stared out the tinted windows during the drive and wondered at times about his own death. It seemed closer these recent years than ever before. And lately he had felt fear. This mission for Sherman had been welcome precisely because it took him away from that fear. It took him away from everything. Quinn looked at the cars passing on the highway. They seemed a hundred miles away. He had not read a paper or heard a radio for three days.

The preparations they found in hangar eight were impressive in every way. As directed, Quinn immediately went alone into the hangar's office and called a local number. Fletcher sounded like he was right next door because he was; he had moved only one hangar over with his men. From here he could watch all that occurred and, in the last resort, be brought in to deal with technical problems. For ten minutes Fletcher briefed Quinn. Don't worry about the hardware, he stressed. The navigational system would automatically kick into effect when the plane reached twenty thousand feet. If it failed, a backup was on board. The electronic countermeasures, in turn, were timed to activate when the plane neared its target. The explosives would detonate on impact.

Quinn knew that the next question was out of bounds. He asked it anyway. "What's the target, Fletch?"

"That's need to know only," Fletcher answered sharply. "And you don't need to know." He then explained how the video system worked, and Quinn's attention was directed to the large monitor and receiving equipment in the office. "Helen Keller could fly that baby," Fletcher remarked, proud of his work. "You'll lose the picture when they're in the air and a few miles out, but it won't matter by that time."

Quinn had nodded. His boys were better prepped than they needed to be.

"The communications system is more complicated," Fletcher continued. "We've set it up so that you're in contact with the cockpit, giving directions, and also with the control tower. When the control tower talks to you, they'll think they're talking to the pilot. Got that?"

"No problem," Quinn had said. He had hoped for something like this, and now knew why he had been told to skip a briefing on takeoff radio commands. Fletcher directed Quinn's attention to a paper on the desk that contained all the details on the radio frequencies.

"Check in periodically," Fletcher had ordered. "We'll be over right after takeoff."

With a real cockpit and a plane to work with, Quinn had put Tabrata's men through more training, working late into Wednesday night and through Thursday. At first, the explosives secured in the plane's bay had unnerved him, but he became used to them and he sat with the young pilots for many long hours in the cockpit. The video equipment was probably not even necessary, but Quinn tested it and tested it again. He also tested the radio and tuned in to the airport's frequency to learn more about the controllers and how they worked. Nothing unusual there. He checked and double-checked the fuel and fluid levels. All were satisfactory, as expected. The mission for Forsten's men was over, but they stayed, lounging in the office, sitting on folding chairs near the hangar door, helping Quinn occasionally with a test.

As nightfall arrived early on Thursday evening, Quinn had been anxious but satisfied. At 6:05 he had notified the control tower of his intention to take off. He checked in with Fletcher yet again to report that all was on schedule. Beyond a sudden snowstorm, and none was forecast, he could imagine no scenario in which things could go drastically wrong.

Tabrata's men had begun a series of intense prayers just after six. They had used the plane's compass to determine which way was east and placed their parkas on the asphalt floor of the hangar, kneeling low. Their prayers were quiet and rhythmic, echoing eerily through the hangar. Quinn watched and felt a brief flash of pity.

The takeoff at seven o'clock had gone exactly as planned. The weather was brutally cold but crystal clear and there had been no delay on the runway. The control tower hadn't suspected a thing as Quinn exchanged communications with it. Fletcher and his two men came over as soon as the plane was taxiing, and everybody crowded in the office, watching the video monitor. Quinn issued a steady string of reminders to the pilots, but Tabrata's men put the plane in the air without a single misstep. The navigational system took over at 7:07. A few minutes later the monitor turned to fuzz.

Fletcher offered congratulations all around and then gave orders to begin cleaning up the hangar. One of his men pulled in a truck from next door. Radio and video equipment was thrown roughly in. Tools were collected and also thrown into the truck. Surfaces were wiped clean of prints. The hangar was cleared out in less than twenty minutes.

"Okay, men, gather 'round, gather 'round," Fletcher said when the job was done, placing a suitcase on a folding table near the back of the hangar. He gestured for the five men to gather on a bunch of empty crates that were piled along the wall. When the men were settled and facing him, Fletcher congratulated them again.

"You've all been compensated already," he said. "And more is being wired to your offshore accounts as we speak. But there's also a small bonus."

Fletcher opened the suitcase so that its top faced the men. He pulled out a thick wad of bills secured with a rubber band. "Mr. Quinn, a fine job," he said tossing the wad at Quinn. "Mr. Dixon, good work." Fletcher tossed another wad. He continued quickly down the line until all the men held packets of money. Quinn began flipping through his to make an estimate. Three bills from the top, hundreds turned to ones. He looked up angrily at Fletcher.

". . . and here's the real bonus," Fletcher was saying. Both his hands came away from the suitcase gripping MAC-10 submachine guns. The weapons bounced in the air as they released their torrent.

## 48

Zach sat in his cell and read again the story on him in the *Washington Post*. It began on the front page and continued inside. He was astounded by the vitriol Richards had managed to unearth. While many military people were prepared to speak on the record about Zach's various deficiencies, all the quotes about the drug use were anonymous. Zach studied them closely, trying to figure out whom from Cornell Richards had spoken to. He found no clues and considered for a moment whether they had been planted.

On the page opposite the story on him were several stories on the State of the Union address. Zach looked at them, absentmindedly doodling on the page, still wondering where the damning quotes had come from. He drew a mustache on the President. And then his pen danced around a headline that read "Aides See Big Opportunity in State of the Union Address." It zigzagged up and down between the letters. Then each letter that began a word was underlined. Zach was thinking of his ex-girlfriend Jill up in Cambridge, wondering whether she had talked to Richards. She wasn't so spiteful that she would join the crew of grave diggers heaping dirt onto his coffin. Hell, it was he, if anyone, who should still be spiteful after all this time.

Zach looked down at the page of the paper. It was a mess of doodles. The edge of his hand was covered with inky grime. His eyes passed over the headline and then came back. He felt a surge of adrenaline as his pen returned to the headline. Slowly he began circling the first letters in "State of the Union Address." He wrote it out in block letters on an advertisement on the right side of the page: SOTUA.

He leaped to his feet, causing a burst of sudden pain in his back. Instinctively he ran over to the door, grabbing the handle. Locked. Of course it was locked. He was in a goddamn prison cell. He almost began pounding on it and then told himself to calm down. Get a grip.

He returned to his desk, sitting still and trying to stop the pain. Maybe it was just coincidence. It must be a coincidence. They wouldn't dare. Too many would die. Too many of too much importance. The entire government. It was insane to even imagine.

The entire government, Zach thought. Nobody would be left. Who would succeed the President?

The Constitution provided that the president be succeeded by the vice president and then by the speaker of the House and then by the most senior cabinet member and then down the rank of cabinet members. The military's top-secret plans for extended nuclear war contained directives on what command-and-control arrangements would take effect if all successors were killed. But the Constitution didn't say anything explicitly on the matter.

All of the unanswered questions about motive were suddenly clear. The State of the Union address was, in fact, the only target that would achieve all the goals of both Forsten and Sherman. If the Capitol were attacked during the speech, wiping out the entire government in a single stroke, Forsten would be a logical figure to head an emergency government as the highest-ranking surviving military official. Blame for this act of terror could be pinned on the TKT Pact, and MOCKINGBIRD could be executed almost instantly as a retaliatory measure, further strengthening Forsten's power by embroiling the nation in war. The attack during the speech could also be cited as evidence of a major domestic terrorist threat and used as justification for tight security measures at home. It would be an easy thing to stop the FBI investigation.

Sherman would benefit as well. With all of the strongest

presidential contenders in both parties dead, he would be an easy winner in November. His past warnings about terrorism would make him seem like a visionary capable of safeguarding the nation's security. If they played their cards right, Sherman and Forsten could wield enormous, almost dictatorial power.

Zach was pacing the room frantically. The plan wasn't too insane. It had an incredible logic. And he didn't doubt their capacity for this level of mayhem. It was true. It had to be. There was no other explanation. That was probably why they had scheduled the hearing so quickly and locked him up immediately afterward. Just for good measure. Just in case he had been able to decipher the plan.

But could they pull it off? Zach suddenly remembered Stan Duncan in the War Room, in command of the cluster that included the Capitol Defense System. Now he knew why he was there. The Capitol building was a sitting duck for airborne attack if the system were down. Zach could see how simple the undertaking was; elegant, even. It would be easy, with enough money and ties to the military world, to get hold of all the equipment: the plane, the explosives, the Tercom system, and a jamming pod. And the services of Sheik Tabrata solved the problem of pilots for such a mission.

The jet would take off at Bradley with a scheduled landing at National Airport, Zach imagined. But as it approached on the standard flight path over Georgetown and the Potomac, it would suddenly bank sharply to the left, guided by the Tercom system and streaking along just a few hundred feet above the highest buildings at two or three hundred miles per hour. The jamming pod would neutralize any SAMs or other defenses that weren't taken care of by Duncan. The terrorists on board just had to insure that all systems were operating properly. The plane would strike the House side of the Capitol. Nobody in the chamber would survive if the main package carried the right contents.

Zach glanced anxiously at his watch: 7:20. Shit. The speech

was scheduled for 8:30. The plan had said the attack would occur thirty minutes after the "target" was "in place." Nine o'clock. Zach fiddled with the timer on his watch, setting it so that it began counting backward from one hundred minutes.

He had to get to a phone. He would call Burns. Then the Secret Service. And then anybody else he could think of.

## 49

They ate at the end of the long table in the dining room at Eldridge. Dozens of candles lit the room. A fire roared in the giant hearth, and two waiters hovered about, attending to their needs. Sherman had seemed strange from the moment he had greeted Justine. He wore a tuxedo, and there was, it seemed, a gleam in his eye and a bounce in his step. He was in a magisterial mood, she could see. And when they were settled at the table, their champagne glasses filled, their chitchat done with, Sherman grew solemn and proposed a toast. "To the future," he said. Justine clinked glasses weakly to that bleak specter. The evening was exhausting her already. Sherman savored the champagne. He lifted his glass again: "And to the past that has brought us to this moment." Justine joined the toast to this, a trail of errors and delusions. They drank, and, after a moment in silence, Sherman sat back, put down his champagne, and embarked upon a rhapsodic recounting of his career.

He talked of the fools who had underestimated him and the small minds whose advice he had ignored. He talked of the mainstream politicians in Washington too blinded by their arrogance to recognize the tide of change that he rode. He talked of his critics in the press who had misjudged his intentions at every turn and slandered him at every chance. Mostly Sherman talked of himself: his courage in getting into politics to challenge a system that had grown fat and corrupt; his vision of change, which remained pure amid the relentless pressures for compromise. No handlers had watered him down. No big donors had softened him up. He was his own man.

Justine listened in wary silence. Sherman spoke at times as if in a confessional booth and at times as if he were before a vast crowd, his hands chopping the air. But always his eyes came back to hers, focused and intense. This valedictorian address was for her, she came to see. He had sensed her distance and now he sought to bring her back. He wanted to renew their alliance by reminding her of his power.

Her suspicions were confirmed when Sherman's monologue turned, finally, to their relationship.

## ★ 50 ★

Zach pounded hard on the door. "Guard!" he shouted. "Guard!"

He had checked the ceiling first. At Haisa, Zach had escaped from a makeshift detention facility by breaking through a weak spot in the ceiling and gaining access to a heating duct. His captors hadn't known he was loose until he had taken out three of them, one by one in the dimly lit underground maze of the munitions plant. But the ceiling in this cell was a different story. It appeared to be solid plaster. Zach had looked next at the window. The bars were rotting at the base and could probably be pried out if he had more time. No such luxury. Finally, he had studied the door closely, examining the lock and the hinges before concluding that it was only going to be opened from the outside. Any exit from the room would have to be aided by the guard.

Zach heard the sound of footsteps coming down the hall. There was the jingle of keys outside his door.

"You got a problem, Turzin?" the guard asked through the door. It was a sturdy metal, but sound passed through it well.

"I haven't eaten in ten hours. Is there a meal coming my way?"

The guard was silent for a moment. "Shit, we kinda forgot about that. You're the only prisoner we have tonight, and to tell you the truth, we weren't expecting you."

"Hey, I hear you. I wasn't expecting to be here. Who's ever heard of locking somebody up after a court of inquiry in a case like this? Do those jokers really think I'm gonna head for Paraguay or something? Christ."

"It's unusual, all right. Only murderers usually get that treatment. Guess you pissed off somebody real good." The guard let out a dry laugh. "But I'll tell you, Lieutenant, I got no sympathy for you, and I really don't give two shits how long your ass rots in this place. Way I see it, you're getting what's coming to you."

"Whatever. The point is, I'm starving, Sergeant. I can't wait until morning. Help me out here."

"Seems to me like a little hunger might be good for a lying pussy like you," the MP said. "But I don't want some big-shot lawyer on my ass tomorrow, so I'll tell you what: I'll call downstairs and see if they can bring you something from the mess."

"I'd appreciate that."

When the guard left, Zach looked around the room, trying to work out a plan. There weren't many options. After five minutes, he heard the jangling of keys coming toward his cell. The guard knocked on his door.

"Okay, Turzin, I got you some chow."

"You're a good man, Sergeant."

"I'll tell you what I'm going to do," the guard said. "I'm leaving the food next to your door. I'm going to ask you to get back to the end of your cell. I'll then unlock the door and return to my desk. After a minute, you can open the door and retrieve the food. You then close the door behind you, and it will lock automatically. You got that?"

"No problem."

"Okay, you back there?"

"Yup," Zach said, stepping two feet back and lowering his voice. He then stepped forward, standing close to the door.

There was the sound of a key in the lock. A second later the door handle began to turn. Zach grabbed it and pulled hard. The door flung open and the guard stumbled forward. His left hand, which had been on the handle, was still outstretched. His right hand was reaching reflexively to the gun strapped on his hip.

Zach grabbed the guard's collar, forcing his head downward as he kneed him hard in the stomach. As the guard doubled, Zach locked his right hand around his throat and threw him hard against the wall next to the door. His left hand yanked the gun from the guard's holster. He held him pinned against the wall, the gun pointed at his forehead. The MP's face was flushed and contorted in pain. Zach stripped him of his keys and flung him roughly to the side, stepping into the hall and pulling the door shut behind him. He stood in the hallway for a moment, breathing heavily.

He heard the guard throw himself at the door. "You sonofabitch," he shouted hoarsely, shaking the door handle. "You goddamn sonofabitch. You're making a big mistake, Turzin. Are you insane?"

Zach shoved the gun into his pants and gritted his teeth. His lumbar muscles felt as if they had been torn apart.

"Turzin, you bastard," came another shout.

Zach walked to the desk in pain and picked up the phone. He didn't have Burns's number so he tried dialing 411 for information. He heard a chiming sound; the call didn't connect. Zach tried dialing a nine and then the number. Same result. He looked at his watch: eighty-two minutes left.

He walked back to the cell.

"Hey, Sergeant."

"Screw you, asshole."

"What's the code for dialing out on that phone?"

"I said go screw yourself."

"Come on, buddy. If I can make some calls I'll let you out."

The guard was silent for a moment. "You can't dial out, you jerkoff. That phone is for internal calls only."

"I can't even make local calls?"

"No way."

"Damnit!" Zach kicked the wall next to the door, sending a bolt of pain up his back. "So where's a phone in this place where I can call?"

"Fuck off."

Zach walked back down the hall. He looked at the key chain he had taken from the guard: There were ten or fifteen keys on it. He began trying them on the door. A minute later the lock clicked. He closed the door behind him and looked down the next hall. It was empty and dimly lit. He held the keys in his hand to silence their jangle and walked to the end of hall. There were two doors here, and he quickly tried the keys, getting through both after a few moments of trial and error. He stepped into a brightly lit stairwell and stood still, listening. He heard no sounds from either the floor above or that below. The building appeared to be deserted. He walked around a corner to a hall that led to a stairway.

Slowly he crept down the stairs. As he neared the bottom, he heard the clanging of a door and voices. He retreated back up the stairs to the second floor and crouched, preparing to dash up to the third floor. The voices passed below but did not come toward him. Zach heard them greet the guard at the front desk. They lingered for a while, talking about the weather, complaining about the frigid temperatures. Then there was the sound of a heavy door opening and closing.

He moved slowly back down the stairs, plastering himself to the wall. A hallway ran perpendicular to the staircase, and he peered carefully in both directions. To the right, the hallway led into darkness; a set of doors was dimly visible at the end. To the left, twenty yards down, was the entrance where he had been brought in. A guard sat reading a newspaper. The chatter of a talk show came from a small radio.

Zach moved silently into the hall and headed right, listening for any rustling of the guard's paper. He made it into the darkness undetected and felt around at the doors. They were locked. He didn't dare try the keys, which he gripped tightly in his right hand. He moved down to the floor, lying on his stomach and looking down the hall at the guard. He didn't want to use the gun. The guard might draw, and Zach could kill him. The sound would draw others. Worse, his crimes would become real.

His eye caught the shape of a fire extinguisher in its holder on the wall a few feet away. Carefully, he crept over to it. He removed the extinguisher quietly and pulled out the safety pin. He cradled it in his arms and sunk back to his stomach, slithering forward. Pain hammered through his back in throbbing waves.

Long ago at Bragg, Zach had been taught that when only partial surprise was possible, an attacker's best hope for gaining advantage was to slow reaction time by sowing doubt and confusion. Be creative; bizarre, even. Mess with the enemy's head.

As he came into the light, Zach rose to his feet. He broke into a sprint toward the guard. "Fire!" he screamed when the guard heard his steps and looked up. "Fire!"

Zach covered most of the distance down the hall in the time that it took the guard to stand up behind his desk. He looked uncertain as he fumbled with the snap on his gun holster, glancing at a fire-alarm monitor on the wall next to the desk. A blast from the fire extinguisher blanketed him with chemical froth as he pulled out his gun. Zach closed the rest of the distance in two more steps and smashed the extinguisher into the hand with the gun, sending the gun flying. The man reeled as Zach dropped the extinguisher and barreled into him. In a second he had the guard lying face-down. Zach twisted the man's arm behind him and dug a knee into the small of his back. With his free hand, he reached to the wall socket and grabbed the cord that ran to the radio. He yanked it toward him, bringing the radio down with a clatter. He pulled the cord out of the radio and used it to swiftly bind the guard's hands. A trickle of blood ran from the man's nose onto the floor. A stream of expletives gushed from his mouth.

Zach got to his feet and plunged out through the front door. He moved along the side of the building, his eyes darting around. A cold wind stung his arms and face. He trotted around a corner and came to the dark side of the building. Across from him was a brick wall not more than twelve feet high. He followed along it in the dark until he came to a pipe that led up its side. He threw the keys down, grabbed the pipe, and began climbing, putting his feet against the wall for leverage. His hands turned numb against the rusty metal.

He dropped to the other side and looked around. There was a grassy lot before him. Beyond that, silhouetted against the night sky, were apartment buildings in which not a single light could be seen. Looming over these dark shapes, two or three miles away, was the illuminated dome of the Capitol building. He began jogging across the lot, weaving between piles of junk and gripping the gun with one hand so it didn't come loose from his waistband.

As his adrenaline faded, a vicious, twisting pain blossomed in his back and legs. He slowed to a walk, shutting his eyes for a moment in agony. He stopped and took long, gentle breaths, trying to cut off the flood of screaming pain signals bombarding his brain. Then he kept moving.

The buildings at the edge of the lot were boarded up and abandoned. He passed through an alley between them and found himself on a dark and deserted street. Broken glass crunched underfoot. Along the curb on the far side, in front of a row of crumbling townhouses, sat the hulks of two stripped and burned cars. He scanned the houses. There were no lights on in any of them. He looked down the street both ways. To the left was darkness and the carcasses of more buildings. To the right, a hundred yards down, a lone street-light shone at an intersection. Zach rubbed his arms and began jogging again. The wind had picked up, becoming brisk and steady, blowing trash into the air. At the intersection he turned left, and after another two blocks of ruins he found himself in a neighborhood that seemed faintly alive.

Through the barred windows on the first floor of a town-house he could see the blue glow of a television. He crossed the street and began climbing the steps to the door. No, this wouldn't work. Nobody in this neighborhood was going to let a stranger into their house at night to use the phone. He returned to the street, breaking again into a tortured trot. Two blocks ahead he could see many lights and an occasional moving car. His arms stung, and the wind cut through his green army pants. The metal of the gun felt cold against his stomach.

As he came toward the lights he could see some stores, graffiti scowling from their drawn metal shutters. He slowed to a walk and pulled out his tucked-in T-shirt to cover the handle of the gun.

All the stores on the street were shuttered. He scanned the area for a pay phone, finding two holders from which the phones had been ripped out. He turned a corner and down the block, below a yellow streetlight, he saw a group of four young black men next to a pay phone and a garbage can. The men were leaning against a car, talking loudly and laughing. One was holding a bagged bottle in gloved hands.

Zach approached slowly. Full steps generated bolts of pain down both legs. One of the men noticed him and pointed. The others turned and stared in amazement.

"Hey, Army man, you look like you lost," the man with the bottle said. Zach nodded and moved toward the pay phone.

"Sheeeit, that cracker's gonna freeze his pink ass off," another man said. The group laughed and moved toward him.

"I axed if you be lost, Army man," the man with the bottle said.

"Just making a call," Zach answered, casually pulling his T-shirt up to reveal the butt of the gun. All four of the men glanced downward and silently took in this new information. They edged back.

Zach kept an eye on the group and picked up the receiver. The metal around the dial pad was covered with scrawled marker. The phone was dead.

"Hasn't worked in fahv months," said one of the men.

Zach hung up the receiver. The group was looking at him with a mixture of suspicion and puzzlement.

"I need a phone," Zach said. "You guys know where I can find a phone?"

"The man wants a phone."

"I heard him. I heard him."

The men hesitated for a moment. Zach wondered whether they were armed.

"You gots to go to Tully's," said the man with the bottle, gesturing down the street.

"What's Tully's?" Zach asked, looking where he pointed.

"It's a bar 'bout a block down. They's got a phone."

"Thanks," Zach said, turning to walk in that direction.

The largest man in the crowd stepped forward, cutting him off. "Hey, you's got a big problem, Army man."

Zach tensed up, his hand moving to the gun.

The man pointed to Zach's pink arms. "You's gonna freeze out here if you don't get a coat on your back."

The men broke into laughter.

Zach smiled. "I'm working on it," he said as he began walking briskly away.

A block down the street, wedged between two abandoned storefronts, was a bar with no name. A grimy neon Budweiser sign shone out of a sole barred window.

Zach looked at his watch: sixty-two minutes. He pulled the T-shirt back over the gun and opened the door. Stepping inside, he felt the warmth envelop him. Smoke filled the bar, and the smell of stale beer hung heavy in the air. The bartender eyed him suspiciously, and conversation dropped off. Seven or eight men sat at the bar, staring at him in amazed silence. White guys in T-shirts were not a common sight on twenty-five-degree nights — or any nights, for that matter — in Anacostia. Zach scanned the room and saw a wooden phone booth in the back of the bar. It looked almost like an antique.

"What can I do you for?" the bartender asked suspiciously.

Zach gestured toward the booth and began walking in its direction.

"That be for customers only," the bartender said. One of the men at the bar got off his stool and stood up, crossing his arms.

Zach smiled. "Yeah, sure. No problem. Get me a bottle of Bud. I'll be out in a second."

He detoured around the standing man and walked quickly into the booth. When he closed the door a little light went on and a fan began whirring quietly. He dialed 411 and got the general number for the FBI. He then dialed zero and the number, telling the operator he wanted to make a collect call to Jack Burns.

The FBI receptionist was resistant. "We can't take collect calls," Zach heard her tell the operator.

"It's an emergency. Please," Zach said.

The operator repeated this to the receptionist, who relented. "I'll try his line." A few seconds later she said, "I'm sorry, Associate Director Burns is not in his office."

"Try his car phone," Zach demanded. "Try him at home. Please, it's urgent."

"I'm sorry, we can't do that."

Zach wracked his mind, trying to remember the names of the other agents. "Collect for Agent Edwards," he said to the operator. She repeated this request to the receptionist, but the outcome was the same. "Agent Edwards is not in his office."

Zach slammed down the receiver button and dialed 411 again, asking for the number of Jack Burns in Washington. He didn't have a street address.

"I'm sorry, sir. I have six Burnses in Washington but no Jack Burns."

"How about a John Burns?"

"No, I'm sorry."

He hit the receiver button, feeling a mounting panic. He dialed information again and got the number of the Secret Service.

"Just say it's a collect call from a person who wants to report a threat against the President," Zach told the operator. The call went through.

"This is Agent Mitchell." The voice was clipped and dry. "What is your name, sir?"

"Forget my name."

"We need a name, sir."

"I'm not giving you my name," Zach said, raising his voice. "All I can tell you is that I'm a military officer. I work in the Pentagon."

"And your rank?"

"Just shut the hell up and listen!" Zach shouted.

He breathed deeply, feeling unable to catch his breath. Stay calm. They have to believe this.

"Okay, go ahead, sir."

"This is not a prank or a false threat. You have to take this seriously and listen closely. There's not much time."

"I'm listening."

Zach hardly knew where to begin. He couldn't sound like a lunatic. He imagined the Secret Service's taping machines on and other agents being signaled to pick up the line. He knew they could trace his call almost instantly. He breathed deeply again and tried to sound sane.

"I have information that an attack will be made on the President's State of the Union address tonight by terrorist operatives of the Party of God, Hizbullah, working with assistance from inside the United States."

"And how did you learn this, sir?"

"I have sources."

"And what are these sources?"

"I can't give you more than that."

"Have you informed your superior at the Pentagon of this information?" The tone of the Secret Service agent sounded as if he was booking Zach for an airline flight.

"That's not possible," Zach said, realizing how totally unbelievable he must sound. "But listen to me, please. The attack will be made by an aircraft packed with explosives."

"An aircraft?"

"Yes. It's already in the air, out of Bradley International Airport. It will be coming into National Airport in the next —" Zach looked at his watch "— fifty-six minutes. It will veer off its flight path and fly at rooftop level into the House side of the Capitol."

"I see. And who will be flying this plane?"

"I told you, asshole. Hizbullah operatives. Remember the Marine barracks attack in Lebanon? These people are ready to give their lives."

"Uh huh."

Zach felt suddenly hot inside the booth. His hands, once numb, now stung. He could feel sweat gathering on his brow. He was talking more quickly, frantically.

"Listen, I know about the Capitol Defense System, with the fighters and the SAM batteries. But it's not going to be activated tonight."

"Really? And why is that?" the agent asked. His tone had turned sarcastic.

"They've got their own man in control of the system at the Pentagon, a lieutenant named Stan Duncan. He's part of the plot." Zach sucked in deeply once more, trying to get air.

"I see. So this plot involves terrorists working in conjunction with military officers at the Pentagon? And the attack is going to take place in less than an hour?"

"That's correct. You've got to believe this."

Zach heard the agent sigh. "Is there any other information you would like to add?"

"Forget it! Let me talk to your superior immediately."

"That's not possible."

"Put him on the goddamn phone, Mitchell!" Zach shouted.

"My superior is at the Capitol. And even if he wasn't, I wouldn't put him on because you're obviously a nutcase. Did you know that reporting false threats on the President's life is a class-B felony punishable by up to five years in prison and two-hundred-fifty-thousand-dollar fine?"

Zach tried to calm himself. "This is not a false threat. Please, let me talk to another superior in your office."

"And did you know also that this phone call has been recorded and traced? I suggest that your next call be to a good lawyer, because we're going to find you."

The line went dead.

Zach hung up the phone and tried Justine's apartment in Georgetown. The operator said a machine was picking up, and the collect call didn't go through. He cursed and tried to sit down on the stool in the booth, but bending his legs sent a spasm of pain through his hips and lower back. He stood again, dialing information to get the number of the White House switchboard. He began making another collect call and then hit the receiver button. It was useless. Nobody was going to believe this story, except possibly Burns, and probably not even him. It was too insane.

He imagined the Secret Service agents having a good laugh. Zach had probably won the most-creative-threat-of-the-month award.

## 51

Robert Davies spoke a word into the tiny microphone on his lapel and the motorcade began to move. Four limousines passed slowly down the White House driveway, engines humming quietly in the freezing night. Davies loved these departures in the darkness, with their aura of power and expectation. Moments such as these, in fact, were among the few pleasures in his life. Davies sat in the rear limousine and turned, as he often did on these occasions, to gaze at the White House shining against the night.

Each car accelerated abruptly as it swung onto the empty street. The motorcade contained the nerve center of the government, including the President and vice president, along with their wives, the national security adviser, the White House chief of staff, and assorted top advisers. Precious cargo, to say the least. "Let's take it up to the standard," Davies said into his mike as the motorcade reached Pennsylvania. The cars increased to fifty miles an hour, a speed that Davies had settled upon two years earlier after much experimentation. It was fast enough to present a tough target, not so fast as to risk an accident. Davies had flown into a rage when White House hacks had cut that speed a full five miles an hour during daylight hours because of public relations concerns. His boss had joined his protest, but the cut had stood.

The sidewalks of Pennsylvania Avenue were deserted now, as they usually were not long after business hours. And the boulevard itself, closed moments before, was empty for the mile and a half between Washington's two centers of power. The motorcade whizzed past D.C. policemen stationed at each of the cross streets, blocking traffic. It passed also, Davies knew, under agents stationed on building roofs, scouring the area with infrared nightscopes. Ahead, towering over Pennsylvania Avenue like a glowing white mountain in the night, stood the Capitol building.

Davies contacted his lead agent at the Capitol to make sure all was ready at the House entrance. No problems. He then checked in at headquarters. "Any developments?" he asked Carroll.

"Just the usual cranks."

"Uh huh."

"The President's water at the podium will be laced with cyanide, we've learned," Carroll deadpanned. "Unless we can stop the speaker of the House before he gets it in."

Davies didn't laugh. Cranks were among the main sources of amusement at the offices of the Secret Service. Davies didn't try to squelch this humor, but he would not sanction it with his own laughter. Dismiss cranks too quickly and someday you might end up with a dead president. "Anything else?" he asked.

"No, no, things are quiet here."

"Any problems at Barnes's house?"

"Negative. Our team just moved into place."

"Okay," said Davies, "let's be in contact later in —"

"Wait a second. Hold on," Carroll interrupted. Voices were heard in the background. "We just got another nutcase. This one is first-class."

"Go ahead." The motorcade was passing FBI headquarters now.

"Seems that an aircraft packed with explosives is going to crash into the Capitol. Better turn the motorcade around." Carroll chuckled.

"Who did that come from?" Davies asked, feeling a tiny ripple of anxiety. Along with car bombs and shoulder-held rocket launchers, airborne attack was an image that stalked Davies's worst nightmares.

"Uh, let's see, I'm just looking at the threat sheet here." Carroll rustled with some papers. "Caller identified himself as a military officer."

"Odd. And where did the call come from?"

"I don't have that here."

"Well, find out, damnit! And get back to me ASAP."

"Yes, sir."

Davies gazed from the window as the motorcade swept past the giant columns of the National Archives. He knew he had overreacted. There would be a round of office jokes at his expense. Big deal. Paranoia is our profession: That would be the appropriate slogan for the Secret Service.

Carroll got back to him within moments. "The call was local. It came from a pay phone at a place called Tully's Bar and Grill. Anacostia address."

Davies relaxed. It was a crank, all right. "Thanks for checking that out."

"Yes, sir."

"Anything else?"

"No, sir."

Davies was about to end the contact when he had a thought. "So the caller was a black guy?"

"Sir?"

"The crank caller from Anacostia. He was black, right?" In Davies's experience almost all false threats came from white men, usually the unemployed loner type.

"Hold on, let me check. I'll ask the agent who —"

"Just play the tape for me, how about," Davies said abruptly.

"Uh, well, sir, sure, we can do that. It will take a moment to get ready."

The motorcade was pulling toward the House side entrance. Demonstrators were visible ahead, behind a police line. Davies checked in once more with his lead agent at the entrance. Still no problems. A minute later Carroll was back with the tape.

"Let's hear it," Davies said as the motorcade came to a halt. He gestured to the three other agents in the limo that they should go about their business.

Carroll started the tape, and Davies listened as a distinctly Caucasian male voice spoke with what seemed to be utter earnestness. When the tape was finished, Davies sat back in the limo, feeling an edge of panic that he knew had to be unwarranted. The call was obviously a hoax. Still, there was something here out of the ordinary, and is wasn't just the details about the Capitol Defense System.

"Call that bar," Davies ordered to Carroll. "And contact both the War Room and our control center at EOB to double-check the status of the CDS."

"Sir, do you really think that's nec —"

"Do it!" Davies commanded.

The President swept into building with his entourage and security detail as Davies got out of the car to survey the scene. Everything looked fine — agents deployed in the right places, barriers set up where expected, Hill police properly positioned. No screwups.

Davies shot a nervous glance into the night sky as he entered the Capitol.

## 52

Zach stepped out of the phone booth, and conversation in the bar abruptly stopped. All eyes were on him once more. A freshly opened Budweiser stood at the end of the bar near the door.

"Three bucks," the bartender said.

Zach reached into his pants pocket, groping elaborately for money he knew he didn't have. "Damn, I know I have my billfold somewhere."

The man who had stood earlier eased once more off his stool.

Suddenly there was the screeching of tires outside and the slamming of car doors. Zach dashed to the window and looked out. He saw two green sedans with U.S. Army insignia and six MPs fanning out across the street. Each man carried an M16. Two were approaching the door.

Zach spun around. His eyes focused on a doorway that led from the area behind the bar into a small kitchen or storage room.

"I need to use your back door."

"Pay Tully for that beer and get your white ass out of here," the standing man said.

Zach ignored him and leaped forward, stepping high onto a stool and then onto the bar itself. He took a few strides along the bar, sending bottles and ashtrays flying. Jumping to the floor behind the bar, he rushed through the doorway. He shoved open a grimy door at the rear of a small kitchen and found himself in a long alley. An MP came around the corner from the street at almost the same moment Zach emerged from the door. He shouted and came after him.

Zach ran down the alley. Ahead, blocking easy escape, was a chain-link fence. The pounding of the MP's boots grew louder.

Five yards in front of the fence, with the MP closing on him, Zach stopped suddenly, collapsing into a crouch. The MP's legs hit him with enormous force, and the man flew high over him, sprawling onto the pavement. Zach jumped to his feet and delivered a powerful kick to the MP's face as he tried to rise. He turned to see two other MPs bursting through the back door of Tully's. Two more came around the corner. Zach jumped onto the fence and climbed quickly over. He ran across a lot and dashed down another alley as he heard bodies scrambling over the chain link. The alley ended at a brick wall. He looked up and around. The ladder of a fire escape hung down nine feet above the ground. Zach grabbed a metal garbage can and turned it upside down below the ladder. He felt the texture of thick rust as he hauled himself up and began to climb.

He was at the third story when they saw him. An MP leaped onto the garbage can and began following him up the fire escape. Suddenly the man cursed and dropped to the ground, a rusted ladder rung clenched in his hand.

The MPs shouted orders to each other. Zach could hear more engines and car doors slamming as he got to the rooftop. He looked across the roofs in both directions. He was in the center of a block of row houses, all three stories high. He crept to the edge of the roof and looked down at the street. There were now four cars. Neighbors were standing in their doorways, and the men from the bar had gathered outside to watch the action.

Another car pulled up at the curb on Zach's side of the street as he looked down. He watched in amazement as Riley got out of a green Crown Victoria, flashing an ID to several MPs. He didn't hear what was said. As the MPs fanned out in different directions, Riley stood by the driver's side of his car talking on a cellular phone and scanning the area.

The roar of a helicopter was heard overhead, its search-light flitting across roofs a block away but moving closer. The sound from men on a fire escape erupted to Zach's left. He stood and ran to the right, jumping over an alley and racing across the top of two other houses. At the far side of the third house was a fire escape. He followed it down along the side of an abandoned building. At the second floor, he came upon an open window and climbed inside.

The smell of stale urine filled his nostrils as he groped forward in the darkness. His foot stepped on a rotting mattress; he detoured around it. Slowly his eyes adjusted, and he could see around the apartment. Large quart beer bottles and cigarette butts littered the floor. Small glass vials crunched underfoot. In the distance, he heard shouting voices and the thumping of helicopter blades. The search seemed to have moved down the block.

He walked forward carefully, coming to a hallway filled with debris. On the left was an open door that led into another apartment. He went in and saw that a wall had been broken down, allowing him to walk into an apartment in the building next door. Darkness enveloped him again. He could see nothing. But everywhere there was the smell of burned wood and plaster. He ran his hand along a wall to guide him and felt a charcoal residue gather on his fingers. The floors creaked, and he worried about plunging downward. He placed each foot slowly in front of the other, testing.

Finally he came to another hallway and could see again. At the end of it was a window facing the street that let in light. He walked to the window and looked out. Riley's car was parked almost directly below. Wearing a heavy leather jacket and jeans, he stood leaning against the hood of the car and slapping the phone into his hand. Zach faintly heard the phone ring and watched as Riley spoke into it briefly. No MPs were in sight.

Zach moved quietly down a staircase clogged with trash

and burned debris. The door that led to the street was ajar, and he crept up to it. Riley stood less than six feet away. Zach drew the gun from his waistband but then shoved it back. It would alert the MPs. He looked around in the shadowy light and found a two-by-four about three feet long. The end was charred, and nails stuck out in the middle. It would do. He moved back to the door and slowly opened it further. He then walked back down the hallway.

He began swinging the two-by-four about, making a loud clatter. "Nichols, through here," he yelled hoarsely. "I think we got him. He's headed up to the third floor."

Zach stepped into the entry of an apartment and waited. Within seconds he heard footsteps. Riley walked slowly, adjusting to the darkness and kicking debris out of his way. He moved toward the entry where Zach hid. First Zach saw the dim shape of a gun and then an outstretched arm as Riley moved forward.

His first swing with the board hit Riley's wrist with a sickening crack, sending the gun flying. His next swing was toward Riley's head. Riley put up an arm in a block, and the thick leather of his jacket sleeve helped to absorb the blow. He then stepped deftly back, crouched, and came forward with a powerful high kick that swept the board from Zach's hands. He followed up with a punch directed at the face.

The blow glanced off the side of Zach's head as he ducked, stumbling backward into the dark apartment. Riley came at him, diving forward in a tackle. They landed on a pile of plaster and grappled blindly. Riley's powerful hands found Zach's neck and two thumbs pressed at his trachea. Zach gasped for air as his throat exploded in pain. He felt his strength fleeing and dizziness coming on. He smashed at Riley's nose with the base of his palm. Riley groaned and loosened his grip. Zach brought both hands up to Riley's ears, grabbing and twisting hard. Riley yelled and let go of Zach's throat. He struck wildly, hitting the side of Zach's forehead. Zach brought a knee up hard into Riley's groin and pushed him off. He rolled to his left and staggered to his feet. He could see nothing but blackness. He heard Riley get to his feet nearby but could not discern the outline of his body.

They stood still in the dark. Zach struggled to control his heavy breathing. He listened. Riley moved first. He was near the door. Zach followed, and in a moment he was in the dim light of a hall. He saw the shape of Riley come at him and he moved to the side, narrowly evading a swinging punch. He shoved Riley's shoulder to keep him off balance from the punch and stepped back. Riley hit the wall and turned around, lunging forward. Zach kicked him hard in the face. He then unleashed a downward snap kick that crashed into Riley's knee. Riley staggered back to the wall gasping in pain. Zach moved toward him and delivered a kick to his stomach. As Riley lurched forward, doubling up, Zach brought a knee up into his face. Then, in a sudden movement, he took Riley's head by the chin and back of the skull and wrenched hard, breaking his neck. Riley jerked once in a violent spasm and then was still.

Zach sank down to the floor next to the body, clutching his lower back in agony. The pain was sizzling through his muscles in all directions, burning down his legs and pulsing upward to his shoulders and neck. He felt immobile, helpless. He sat in the darkness for a moment, gritting his teeth and trying to breathe slowly. Finally he struggled up. He moved forward and wrestled Riley's jacket off, putting it on. Zach found two spare ammunition clips in the jacket pocket along with a wallet and the keys to Riley's car.

He went to the door and looked out. The men from the bar had drifted back inside. A few neighbors still stood in their doorways. Down the street, two blocks away, Zach could see three MPs walking with their backs to him, pointing their flashlights into alleys and doorways. Zach pulled the jacket collar up and stepped outside the building, walking quickly to the car.

The cellular phone sat on the driver's seat, and Zach threw it over to the passenger side. He started the engine and turned the car around, heading away from the patrolling MPs. As he neared the end of the street, two other MPs came around the corner on the sidewalk from the opposite direction. Zach pulled down the visor and tried to look away. One of the MPs stepped off the curb, signaling him to stop. Zach hit the accelerator and could see the two gawking in recognition as he raced past. He looked back as he drove and saw both beginning to fire, yellow flashes erupting from the muzzles of their M16s. He slid down in the seat and heard loud thuds as several rounds slammed into the trunk.

Yanking the wheel hard to the left, he screeched around a corner and accelerated down the next street. Not far ahead, he could see the rushing headlights of the Anacostia Freeway. He looked in his rearview mirror. Three blocks behind him, he saw a sedan careening after him.

The street he was on ended at a crumbling road that ran parallel to the highway. Zach took a sharp left and drove alongside the highway. No ramp appeared. Instead, about a hundred yards down, piles of garbage rose in front of graffiti-covered concrete barriers. He slammed on the brakes and skidded in an arc. He hit reverse and then drive again. The green sedan came whipping around the corner ahead as he finished turning around. He hit the accelerator and raced at the oncoming car. The two vehicles hurtled directly at each other. A moment before collision, Zach hit his high beams, and the sedan veered to its right. Zach pulled his car in the opposite direction, and they passed each other with a shrieking grind of steel. The side mirrors of both cars were ripped off. One of the MPs got a wild shot off. The sedan jumped the curb, plowed through piles of trash, and then spun back onto the street, its wheels mangled.

Zach followed the crumbling street along the highway for a half mile before he found exit ramps for both directions. He got onto the Anacostia Freeway heading south toward

I-95. The road was busy with evening traffic, and he weaved between the slower cars, speeding up to seventy-five miles an hour. He looked in the mirror. Nobody was following.

He slowed down slightly and looked at his watch: forty-one minutes. Even as he dodged the MPs a plan had been taking shape in his mind. He needed to get to Andrews Air Force Base. It would take twenty minutes, maybe less. He stepped hard on the accelerator again.

## 53

Sherman's eyes had locked on Justine and remained there during his soliloquy. He recounted the course of their relationship from the moment they met onward. Dessert came, and when it was finished, Sherman had asked the waiters to put more wood on the fire and leave them alone.

In the light of the glowing blaze, he told her of her virtues and of his great admiration of her. She was unlike any woman he had ever met or ever would meet. A slight wetness formed in his eyes. There was a rasp in his voice. "We're supposed to be together, Justine. Nothing can change that."

Sherman became silent for a moment, looking away. Justine could see in him a hardness that had not been there before.

He returned his gaze and stared at her. "But I know that you betrayed me."

Fear rushed forward as she opened her mouth in a denial.

Sherman put up a hand to stop her. "No, I don't even want to hear it. Let me finish." He breathed deeply and went on. "You made a mistake. Everybody does. You were distracted by lust. You were confused about where your loyalties lay. For all of this I am ready to forgive you. Maybe that's a mistake, and maybe I'm being too kind. But the truth, Justine, is that I cannot live without you. What we share together is so much greater than what has happened over the last few months. After tonight, the future will be mine. It's going to be a time where great things are possible, and great men can again shape history. And you're the woman I want to share it with."

Sherman took her hand and held it tight, painfully tight. His thumb bored into the back of her hand. "I need to know whether I can count on you, count on your love and your loyalty."

## 54

As Zach pulled clear of the city and neared I-95, he was startled by the ringing of the cellular phone on the seat next to him. Impulsively he picked it up. Riley's voice had been etched in his mind from their confrontation at his apartment, and Zach tried to imitate it.

"Yeah, Riley here."

Zach felt a chill of fear when he heard Forsten's voice. "What the hell is going on over there?" he shouted. "Did you get him yet?"

"Not yet."

"Well don't let him slip away, damnit. It will be your ass if he does."

"Any problems on your end?" Zach asked.

"No, all systems are go here. Just nail that son of a bitch. I don't care if you have to burn down that whole neighborhood."

Zach was about to hang up but changed his mind. There was no need for this charade. He switched back to his normal voice.

"Colonel Riley is dead, Admiral."

There was silence on the other end of the phone. Then Forsten exploded: "Turzin, you little shit. You little son of a bitch. Where are you?"

"It doesn't matter where I am, you bastard. What matters is that I'm wearing your boy's jacket and talking from his phone."

Forsten's voice dropped to a low growl. "Now you listen to me, Turzin. After tonight we're going to hunt you like an animal. This country will be ours. You won't have a chance."

"Stop the attack, Admiral. It's not worth it."

"Let me tell you something," Forsten said, seething with anger, almost screaming. "This is the only chance we have. This president has thrown our security into the gutter. The goddamn gutter. Do you think operatives from the Pact won't use a nuclear weapon against us when they get one? Huh? Huh? They'll do it in a second, a goddamn second. New York, Washington." Zach heard what sounded like Forsten's fist coming down hard on his desk. "No warning, no nothing. I'm preventing that, Zach, can't you see? Can't you see that it's me who is saving this country? I sat back while the bureaucrats in Washington let us lose in Vietnam, but this time, this time —"

Zach pressed the cancel button and hit the phone against the dashboard in anger. Holding the phone in one hand as he gripped the steering wheel with the other, he noticed that it had on its back a tiny lined memo card below a removable sheet of plastic. The card listed the numbers Riley had programmed into the phone. "DS" was number two. "JF" number three. Zach turned the phone on and was relieved to get a dial tone. He hit the memory button and then number two.

A butler at Eldridge answered on the second ring. "Mr. Sherman's residence."

Zach was unprepared for his luck and stammered over the phone. "Oh, hi, uh, I'm trying to reach Justine Arledge."

"I'm sorry, sir, Miss Arledge is dining. Who may I say called?"

The lie spilled out hastily. "This is her brother Robert," Zach said, even as he remembered that Justine had only one brother — who was dead. He silently cursed his stupidity. "Please, I need to talk with her. It's urgent. Our mother has fallen ill."

"I see. Dear me. One moment, sir."

The butler knocked softly on the dining-room door and entered with a cordless phone. Sherman and Justine sat silently with clasped hands. The butler apologized profusely to Sherman and handed the phone to Justine. "An urgent call for the lady."

Sherman continued to stare at Justine as she pulled her hand free and took the phone. The butler leaned down and whispered something to Sherman, looking to Justine with sympathy.

"Yes?" Justine said.

Zach spoke quickly. "Thank god I got ahold of you. I don't have much time. I need your help."

"Yes, I know," interrupted Justine. "This isn't the first screwup at the Denver office. And tonight of all nights."

"Listen closely. This sounds crazy, but it's true. There is an attack planned on the State of the Union address tonight. Forsten and Sherman are behind it. I can't get anyone to believe me. But you can. Call the Secret Service. Find Burns from the FBI. Call the Capitol Police. Whatever. Just do it! We've got to stop this."

"I'll get on it right away," Justine replied. "And after tonight we'll clean house out there. This I promise." She turned off the phone and handed it to the butler without giving Zach a chance to say anything more. The butler scurried for the door.

"I'm sorry, Doug," Justine said, pushing her chair away from the table. "We're going to have to cut dinner short. I've got to deal with a big screwup in Denver."

She rose, and it was only then, pausing, that she looked at his eyes and saw his fury.

# ★ 55 ★

Zach was driving on I-95 now, not far from the Andrews exit. He turned on the radio, twirling the tuning knob until he found the speech. The car clock read 8:34. The President had just begun.

". . . and we found many other serious problems when we came in three years ago. These years have not been easy. They have not been without sacrifice. They have not been without pain for many in this country. But what they have been is a time of rebuilding, a time of rediscovering and renewing the spirit of optimism that makes Americans who we are. . . ."

Zach turned on the car light and pulled out Riley's wallet, flipping it open with one hand. He found a Virginia driver's license, and below that an old Army ID. Zach held the photo up to the light. There was no way he would be able to pass if the gate guard at Andrews looked at all closely. He needed another way in. He picked up the phone and dialed information to get the general number for Andrews. He then called, asking for the front gate. The operator put him through.

"Andrews, main gate. Private Alverez."

Zach lowered his voice. "Private, this is Admiral Forsten at the Pentagon."

"Sir. Yes, sir. Admiral Forsten, sir," Alverez said excitedly. He sounded straight out of boot camp. Zach pictured him snapping to attention. It was reflex when talking with top officers, even on the phone.

"Private, I have a minor but urgent matter on my hands. Are you the senior officer there at the front gate?"

"Sir. Yes, sir. Just myself and another private, sir. But if

349

you like, sir, I can put you through to the Andrews security office."

"No, no, they'd just send me back to you. I need a small favor from you men. "

"Sir. Yes, sir."

"I urgently need to speak with a colonel by the name of Riley who headed down there a while ago. He might already be on the base, but if —"

"Sir, I don't remember a Colonel Riley coming through tonight, sir."

"Fine, fine. Well then, we should be able to catch him when he comes your way. It should be any minute. I think he'll be driving a green Crown Victoria and wearing civilian attire."

"Sir. Yes, sir. Green car, civvies, sir. Understood, sir."

Zach saw the exit sign ahead for Andrews and pulled into the right lane, slowing down.

"Now, Private, when Riley comes in, you tell him to call me, pronto, at my Pentagon office. He has the number. Tell him it's urgent. Let him use the phone at the gatehouse if he wants. Got all that?"

"Sir. Yes, sir," the private barked.

Zach turned off the phone and shoved it under the seat as he turned off at Exit 9. Shortly, the entrance to Andrews loomed ahead. The perimeter of the base was ringed by a tall fence topped with coils of razor wire. Motion detectors and searchlights supplemented the security. If Zach couldn't get through the main entrance, he wasn't getting in at all.

He pulled the car up next to the gatehouse in front of a striped barrier. His pulse had quickened. He rolled down the window and made a show of reaching for his ID as a gangly Hispanic private approached. A kid. Zach pulled the leather ID case out of his pocket as if he were about to show it.

The private saluted crisply. "Evening, sir. Are you Colonel Riley, sir?"

"Yeah. But how the hell did you know that?"

"Sir, Admiral Forsten just called a few minutes ago from the Pentagon. He needs to talk to you immediately, sir. Says it's urgent. Sir, you can pull your car over ahead and use our phone if you want, sir."

Zach shook his head and grinned. "Hell, you'd think World War Three was about to happen the way he hounds me sometimes. Thanks, Private, but I'm sure the admiral can wait a few more minutes. I'll call from on the base."

The private stepped away from the car, saluted, and began to turn when he stopped and looked back at the car, eyeing it oddly. Zach froze. The private came back to the window. "Wow, sir. What happened to your car, sir?"

Zach peered out the window and surveyed the damage, shaking his head. "Can you believe it? I got sideswiped in a traffic circle about an hour ago. The guy didn't even stop."

The private whistled and shook his head. He saluted again and walked back into the gatehouse. The striped barrier rose up, and Zach drove onto the base.

## 56

Sherman's first blow, delivered wildly across the table as he rose from his chair, glanced off the side of Justine's head. But he connected solidly with the second, an open-handed smack across the face. She reeled backward in a blur of pain. Sherman followed and hit her again. He was breathing raggedly, his body coiled in anger. "Bitch," he hissed. "You lying bitch." Justine held up her hands, trying to block the next blows. Sherman began to flail at her uncontrollably. His words lost their distinctness and came at her as guttural sounds. He hit her hard in the stomach, and she collapsed to the floor before the great hearth.

She could feel the heat from the roaring fire on her bruised cheek as Sherman began to kick her. The heat was partly cut off when he stepped in front of the hearth to better position himself. His black wingtip smashed into her ribs and then her back. Pain exploded through her entire body. She was on the edge of blackness.

Sherman's foot swung again, hurtling toward her head. She grabbed it as it came forward. She wrapped one arm around it and clung hard. With the other hand she reached up between his legs and squeezed with all her strength. He yelped in pain and broke his leg free, trying to kick her again. Justine brought her hand down from his groin as the kick came in. His foot crashed painfully into her hand, but she held it. Grasping both legs she pulled, and Sherman lost his balance, tipping backward. He put out his arms, expecting something solid to steady himself, but there was only the open fireplace behind him. And he continued to fall.

He screamed as he hit the fire back first. His tuxedo and

352

hair exploded into flames. Justine struggled to her knees and then to her feet. She grabbed a poker from a stand next to the hearth and stepped back, away from the horror. Sherman pushed his hands down into the gleaming coals for support and screamed again as he propelled himself out of the fireplace. He rolled about frantically on the floor, his arms and hands beating out the flames.

Justine stood frozen, terrified by what she had done. She watched transfixed as he slowly rose to all fours. His face was blackened, his hair mostly gone, his clothes smoking and tattered. Instinctively she stepped forward. She would help this creature. And as she did, he came to his feet and lunged at her with a throaty moan. She jumped backward. With both hands she swung the poker at Sherman's head. It found its target with a soft thud, the hook driving into his temple. He fell to his knees, both hands grasping the embedded weapon. Then he collapsed forward.

## 57

Zach headed for the helicopter depot at Andrews, parking the car a few hundred yards away from the large main hangar that serviced the small fleet of Hueys and Blackhawks kept at Andrews. There was no fence around the depot, but armed patrols regularly crisscrossed the entire base in jeeps.

Zipping the leather jacket, he surveyed the tarmac. It was empty. He trotted stiffly through the night air and circled around the main hangar. Inside he could hear music mixing with the sound of voices and occasional hammering. He had learned during his stint with the 160th that helicopter maintenance was never finished. Some of the mechanics worked fourteen-hour days just to keep the birds flying.

The hangar doors were closed to keep out the cold, and the rest of the area appeared deserted. Ten helicopters stood on the brightly lit tarmac that spread out before the hangar. Zach walked over to them, glancing around anxiously. There were two types of Blackhawks here. Six were earlier-model "slicks" with no armaments, the kind that Zach had taken Justine for a ride in. The other four were MH-60 Blackhawks armed with rocket launchers and twenty-millimeter machine guns. These gunships weren't made for downing jets, but they could do it. Zach had vivid memories of unleashing the MH-60's firepower on a training range in the Mojave.

He inspected one of the armed Blackhawks closely. The rocket launching tubes were empty, of course, as was the cannon's ammo compartment on the nose. He looked at his watch: twenty-one minutes. He took out the gun and checked it, shoving it back in his waistband. He walked to the small door next to the hangar entrance and pulled it open, strutting confidently in. The building was vast and well lit inside. Two mechanics were peering into the engine of a Blackhawk, their backs against the door, and they didn't notice Zach enter. A clutter of tools was spread out on a tarpaulin on the ground below the chopper, and a popular music station blared loudly from a boom box. Zach scanned the building. Another helicopter sat partly disassembled to the far left. A white Ford four-door with military plates was parked near the entrance. There were a number of large tool cabinets on wheels scattered around the hangar. Three offices with glass windows stood along one wall. In a far corner was a solid-looking room with a heavy steel door and a hefty padlock. He could just make out the lettering on the door: ARMORY.

A mechanic turned to get a different wrench and saw Zach. "Yo, pal, what are you looking for?"

Zach walked forward smiling. "Hey, what's up?"

The other mechanic turned around. Neither was smiling. "This is restricted area, pal. Can we help you with something?"

Zach took a few more steps toward the men and pulled out his gun. The two mechanics looked at each other and then back at Zach. "What the hell is this?" one demanded.

"Shut up!" Zach yelled. He raised the gun and fired a round through the metal nose of the Blackhawk. "Get away from the helicopter and down on your stomachs!" Zach commanded.

The men obeyed quickly. Zach walked over and nudged one of the men with his foot, stepping back. "You, get up." The man rose nervously. "Find something to tie up your buddy with. Move it."

The mechanic looked around and then trotted to the helicopter and reached into the door, pulling out a long piece of nylon webbing. "Make it tight," Zach instructed. "And do the legs too." The mechanic kneeled and rapidly bound his companion, tying his hands together and then looping the webbing around his torso and down around his legs and feet.

"Now step back," Zach said. He checked the webbing to make sure it was tight. He turned and shoved the gun toward the mechanic's face. "What's in the armory?"

"M16s, M60s, twenty-millimeter ammo, and Starlane rockets."

"Good. You're going to open it."

"I can't do that," the mechanic said.

"Do it or die, asshole!" Zach pushed his gun closer, nudging the man's cheek with the barrel.

"What I'm saying is that I don't have the keys."

Zach thought for a moment. He looked at his watch: sixteen minutes. "Use a blowtorch."

The man nodded, relieved at the apparent solution. He gestured to a standing tool cabinet, and Zach followed him over. Within a minute a thin blue flame was being applied to the lock on the armory. Zach had found a heavy hammer in the tool cabinet, and after a few moments of the blowtorch he ordered the mechanic to step back and smashed hard at the lock. It came off with the third blow. Zach gestured for the mechanic to go in first, training the gun on him. "One belt of twenty-millimeter shells and four rockets," he said. "And I need an ignition key to a bird out there that's ready to fly. Fast as you can. Move it!"

By the time he and the mechanic got out to the Blackhawks pushing a dolly of ammunition, only fifteen minutes were left. He looked around the base. A jeep patrol was moving across the tarmac in the distance, too far away to see what was happening. The temperature seemed to have dropped even further, and a sadistic wind whipped among the copters.

"Do it fast and don't screw up," Zach said to the mechanic as he opened the ammo boxes next to an armed Blackhawk. Fist-sized shells glimmered under the tarmac lights. For the next several minutes Zach stood impatiently as the mechanic scurried around the nose and rocket tubes. Finally he was done. Nine minutes left.

Zach gestured with the gun. "Now get in and start it up." The mechanic climbed into the helicopter, and in a moment the rotor blades were whirling. Zach ordered him out of the helicopter and got in himself. The mechanic backed away and then turned and ran toward the hangar.

Zach looked at his watch as the engine warmed up and the blades began turning faster: six minutes, twenty seconds. He might make it. Suddenly the headlights from a jeep appeared, moving quickly toward the helicopter depot. Zach eased up on the collective and tried to rise. The gunship's engine sputtered, indicating that it needed more time to warm. The jeep was closing fast. Zach tried the collective again. The gunship lifted slowly into the air. As he rose he saw the mechanic emerge from the hangar with an M16, slamming in a clip. The jeep screeched to a halt, and a guard jumped out, unholstering his pistol. The mechanic pointed upward at the Blackhawk, and Zach saw the M16's muzzle flash. It flashed again. The guard opened fire at the same time. Zach heard no thumps in the copter's belly indicating hits. He manipulated the cyclic stick to bank left and headed east toward the Potomac.

The Chevrolet station wagon coasted quietly to a halt in a neighborhood of modern split-level houses. Lights shone from the homes, but the street was deserted. A cold wind stung at three men as they got out of the car and walked to its rear. They were dressed identically in black parkas, dark pants, gloves, and winter caps. The car's back door was opened and weapons were distributed. Each man was given a submachine gun with silencer. With the weapons concealed under their parkas, the team walked down the block.

"Not a bad neighborhood," Tommy Flint commented, looking around at the spacious homes. He himself had always lived like a warrior, in barracks or sparsely furnished cabins, close to his men. Comfort had been a stranger. But Flint had no regrets. Tonight his confirmed kills would finally top seventy.

Secretary Barnes's house was just around the corner, easily picked out because of the two midsize sedans that sat parked in front of it head to head, their engines running, their windows fogged. Secret Service.

The team approached through the front yards near Barnes's house in a crouched jog. One house away, they stopped and moved down onto their bellies. Flint pulled out a pair of small binoculars and surveyed the situation. Two agents per car. The dark form of another agent could be seen near the door of Barnes's house. Clouds from his breath rose and dissipated before an outside light. He stomped his feet to keep warm.

The team rose and moved closer. Flint directed one man

toward the house, and he and the other went down to the frozen ground again, creeping toward the cars.

A row of bushes grew along the front of the house, and the lone killer used these for cover as he approached. When he was five feet from the door, he stepped on a twig, and the agent looked up. The submachine gun let loose a hissing volley and the agent spun around, collapsing to the ground. Flint and the two team members rose to their feet at the same moment, running forward. They stopped a few feet from the cars and opened fire. Bullets shattered glass and smashed through steel. Muffled cries were heard from inside the cars as the agents were pinned to the seats by lead. The shooters paused to ram new clips into their guns and then moved forward, continuing to fire. The massacre took less than thirty seconds.

Across the street a dog barked. A siren wailed far in the distance. An unmuffled car accelerated a few blocks away. Otherwise silence returned. There was no sign of movement in the Barnes house. The killers moved quickly toward the door. They pulled their hats down, turning them into ski masks. One man lifted his foot to smash the door in; another stopped him and tried the handle. It was open, and they rushed in.

A woman was walking from the kitchen with a tray of food. She dropped it as she screamed. The team ignored her. A slight man with glasses rose from the couch. The President's speech on the television was turned up loud.

"My god, what's going —"

"He's mine," Flint said, stepping forward and firing.

★
★ **59** ★
★

Robert Davies stood amid a knot of Secret Service agents in the corridor that led into the well of the House chamber. He always stationed himself in this same spot, which offered only a partial view of the House floor and gallery, but a box-seat view of the President's entire body. Davies may have climbed to great heights in the Secret Service over the past two decades, he may have commanded an army of agents from his large office, and he may have been the final destination of two hundred memos a month. But still he was happiest — if that word could be used — when he was watching the President's back.

Davies didn't pay attention to the substance of the President's speech; political analysis was not part of his job description, he had decided long ago. But he did pay attention to the communications traffic on his earpiece. Quietly he issued orders to pave the way for a smooth trip back to the White House.

Five minutes into the President's speech, Winston Carroll had reported back about the crank threat. He had called Tully's Bar and learned about a crazed white man who had used the phone and then was chased by military police.

"Did you call Military Police?" Davies had asked.

"I did. And get this: Earlier tonight Lieutenant Zach Turzin — you know, the guy in the medal scandal — escaped from Fort Baldwin and fled into the Anacostia neighborhood. The MP headquarters at McDair is certain that it was him at the bar, but they couldn't nail him."

Davies had moved back into the hallway so he could raise his voice. "Jesus Christ!"

"I'll say. Hell of a crank, huh?"

Something was wrong about this one. Davies could feel it. It was too weird. The warning on the tape suddenly seemed a million times more credible, and Davies's adrenaline had begun to pump. "What about the CDS?" he asked.

"Turzin was right that a Captain Stan Duncan is on duty there at the War Room. Clearly he knows his stuff. But I talked to Duncan myself, and the CDS is definitely activated. We're at CAPZONE Three, sir."

Davies had relaxed somewhat. Even if a plane were coming — god forbid — it would never get through. "Keep working this one," he had ordered Carroll.

Now, fifteen minutes later, Carroll reported back. His voice wavered with panic. "Sir, we just lost contact with the team at Barnes's house."

"What do you mean?"

"I mean nothing is coming up on the radio and they're not answering their cellulars."

"Damnit! Did you try Barnes's phone?"

"We did. All we're getting is a busy signal."

"Well, get a goddamn team over there!"

"One is already on the way. But it will take a while. Our closest people are seven minutes."

"Call D.C. police. Maybe they can get there more quickly."

"Yes, sir."

Davies broke into a heavy sweat. He looked anxiously at the other agents, not quite sure whether to fill them in. He flipped open his cellular and dialed the home number of his boss. He spoke in a hushed and urgent tone, explaining the threat and the sudden cutoff from Barnes's house.

"We have to stop the speech," Davies said when he was finished. "Now!"

"There's no way we can do that," his boss said flatly. "Not on what we have. Let's wait on the report from Barnes's place."

"That could be too late."

"We're going to wait, damnit! That's the decision. Report back in five."

Zach looked around in the night sky to get his bearings. Off to his right he saw Washington in the distance. The lights of the Crystal City complex were closer and to the left. He headed in that direction, bringing the Blackhawk up to one hundred thirty knots. The Potomac quickly appeared before him, and he brought the copter down a few hundred feet above it. The lights of Old Town Alexandria appeared off to his left, and Zach could clearly see diners inside the Chart House restaurant next to the water. He looked at his watch: two minutes, five seconds.

He thought frantically about the CDS. Was the whole system really down, or had they just cleared a path for the attacking plane? The system was probably totally down, Zach decided, although the SAM batteries might still be operational, using their own radar. That's why the attacking plane had been equipped with a jamming pod. Zach would stay low in his approach, skimming the earth.

Crystal City appeared on the immediate left, and the Blackhawk passed level at about the seventh or eight floor. Zach looked anxiously at his watch: one minute, thirty seconds. He whipped over the Fourteenth Street bridge and banked right a few seconds later at the Jefferson Memorial. He saw several bundled tourists look up in terror from the steps. He dropped down fifty feet as he approached the Washington Monument over the Tidal Basin. He was low enough to create ripples in the water below.

The Mall offered the lowest possible approach route because of its lack of buildings. It was a corridor of safety that led straight to the Capitol.

Zach maneuvered wide of the Washington Monument, and the Capitol came into view. It was still unscathed. One minute was left. He pulled lower, moving just below the level of the trees that lined the Mall. If there were active SAMs, this was the most dangerous part unless the jet was already very close, in which case its jamming pods would be shutting down their radars.

He turned off the safety for the trigger on the twenty-millimeter cannon, located on the cyclic stick. He slowed his speed as the Capitol came rearing toward him, illuminated against the night sky by powerful spotlights. An American flag fluttered in the cold wind from a flagpole on top of the dome. He could see knots of protesters in front of the House side carrying signs. His eyes darted around, scanning the roofs of the Capitol and surrounding buildings for anti-aircraft defenses. He saw nothing. They probably wouldn't have anything this close in. It would be too late.

Two hundred yards before the Capitol, he pulled up hard and banked right. Protesters dropped their signs and scattered below as the Blackhawk surged upward and roared over the Capitol's Senate side. He kept rising as he swung around wide, level with the highest point of the dome. He brought the helicopter to face the direction of National Airport and slowed his speed to a near hover. His eyes scanned the air to the southeast. Then he looked downward at the surrounding building again, half expecting to see a missile streaking at him. He looked at his watch: eleven seconds.

This was no place to loiter. He maneuvered down and forward, dropping two hundred feet and accelerating in the direction of National.

And then he saw it.

The plane was a black form coming directly at him at a slightly higher level and growing rapidly larger. None of its running lights were on. He pulled up and fingered the rocket launcher trigger. A few seconds later the outlines of the plane became clearly visible before him. It looked like a moderate-size corporate jet. He pulled the trigger. Nothing happened. He pulled it again. Still no response from the rocket launchers.

Zach frantically shifted his finger to the cannon trigger.

He pulled and heard the roar of the gun. He could see the flashes from its muzzle stretching out a few feet in front of the Blackhawk's nose. The plane kept coming toward him on a direct course.

He raised altitude slightly and pulled the trigger again.

Just when he was close enough to make out two figures in the dimly lit cockpit, his machine guns raked the jet's left side and caused a small explosion. The plane pitched to the right, and more rounds tore into it near the cockpit. Zach pulled left hard, and the plane narrowly missed him, fire erupting at its front.

He turned and saw the plane in flames rushing downward toward a block of office buildings behind the modern edifice of the Air and Space Museum. In the next few seconds he tried to gain as much altitude as possible.

He got up to eleven hundred feet, and it was barely enough. A massive explosion blossomed below him as the plane plunged into a darkened government building. A split second later a powerful blast hit the bottom of the Blackhawk. The helicopter careened wildly as the entire sky brightened. Zach gripped the cyclic, wrestling for control. He felt the gunship being pushed farther upward.

And then suddenly the turbulence passed, and the Blackhawk returned to his command. Still fearing SAMs, he descended rapidly, heading out of the city toward the river. Behind him, the office building blazed like a jagged torch in the night.

For a few moments following the phone call from Eldridge, Forsten had been engulfed by panic. He had paced his office in a daze, his eyes misting for the first time that he could remember. Sherman dead? It was inconceivable, unimaginable.

But Forsten had gotten hold of himself with two quick shots of whiskey and decided that the situation was manageable. Following another shot, he reflected that this turn of events might even be desirable. After all, it was he, Forsten, who had built so much of the structure that was carrying them to power. It was he who had stayed on the inside and slogged his way upward, suffering a thousand fools and enduring the maddening ways of a government bent on sapping the nation's security. It was he who had patiently earned the respect of America's fighting men and who now had mastery of the most powerful military machine in world history. And it was he who had put together the intricate arrangements of this evening, which would complete a quest of nearly three decades.

Why share the fruits of this labor with anyone?

Yes, everything was still under control, Forsten had decided, sitting back at his desk. A control more total than ever before. He had looked at his watch. There wasn't much time. He placed a few last-minute calls and then began making some notes about what he would say to the nation's press corps. His message would stress order and security; it would seek to steel Americans for the long struggle with terrorism that lay ahead. When there were two minutes left, he put aside his pen and dimmed the lights in his office. He rose and stood before the window, gazing toward the city. He had a clear view of the Washington Monument and, farther in the distance, he could see the Capitol dome. He looked at his watch once more and waited.

The fireball shot high above the Mall, brilliantly orange, and sent out a shock wave that thundered across the Potomac, rattling the window through which Forsten stared in disbelief. Motionless, he gazed into the night until the last remnants of color had faded and once again the horizon belonged to the Washington Monument and the Capitol dome. The phone began ringing, and in moments all his lines were lit up. Forsten ignored the sound and slowly walked over to lock his office door. He drifted back toward his desk in the dim light, looking at the photos on his wall that were testament to a career at the pinnacle of power.

Forsten with three separate presidents. Forsten with foreign leaders. Forsten with U.S. military commanders. He had risen to the top and yet had gone nowhere. He had played against the system, always believing that he would prevail and that history was on his side. How wrong he had been. He had given everything and it had come to nothing.

He sat back in his chair and picked up a small framed photo of him and his wife. It had been taken years ago at Pearl Harbor, when he commanded the Seventh Fleet, and his career had just gotten back on track. Anything seemed possible then. He placed the photo back on the grand mahogany desk, turning it away from him. Bonnie had always been a good sailor. She would understand.

He opened the top left drawer of the desk. He took out his pistol and switched off its safety. The taste of the barrel in his mouth was tangy and metallic. He squeezed the trigger.

## 60

Eighteen Months Later

He lay on the water, suspended and warm, the sun beating down. Large green leaves swayed overhead. He looked upward into the blue sky and then into the sea below. Brightly colored fish passed by, and coral reefs spread out before him. A giant stingray glided among the slivers of sunlight that cut through the water. Somewhere above, a helicopter was approaching. He could hear its thumping. But his head couldn't turn to see it.

The thumping grew louder, and the sun disappeared. The water turned murky and cold. There was a splash in the distance. A body had fallen into the sea. He began to swim toward it, his arms heavy and clumsy.

"Zach, Zach," Justine was shaking him slightly. She pulled in close to him under the blankets that he held tightly and slid a leg over his. She spoke quietly in his ear. "Honey, we have to get up. We have to get ready to go."

Zach forced his eyes open. He sat up slowly in the bed. There was still some stiffness from the back surgery he had had six months earlier. For ten hours the doctors had operated on him, and for the rest of his life metal detectors would be sounding at airports.

They ate breakfast outside on the small deck off the kitchen. With the trees budding and the birds chirping, it was the kind of summer morning that could make Princeton seem like one of the loveliest towns in America. Zach had his cereal and coffee in silence, the darkness from his dream lingering.

After breakfast he carefully removed his dress uniform from a dry-cleaning bag. He had not worn it in nearly a year, not since receiving the Medal of Freedom at the White House. Before that, he had worn it once when he appeared with Justine at a press conference. Robert Oxman had arranged the session after a Virginia grand jury had chosen to not indict her for manslaughter charges in connection with Sherman's death. Oxman had never doubted that this would be their judgment — not when they knew about the connection between Forsten and Sherman, and not after they saw the color photos of Justine's bruised body and the X rays of her broken ribs. This time the lawyer's optimism had been warranted.

They were dressed and ready when the horn sounded outside. His mother was waiting in the Volvo, the sunroof open. Zach and Justine got in the backseat, and they headed across town. After they had picked up his father, his mother got on the turnpike, heading south.

The conversation on the drive was sporadic and subdued. Zach told a few stories about university life at Princeton, where he had come to finish his Ph.D. and where Justine was doing a master's degree in public policy. But otherwise he wasn't much in the mood to talk. And while a détente now prevailed between Zach's parents, with much of the old acrimony gone, they were far from being friends. They were together on this day to support Zach, not to enjoy each other.

Signs on the turnpike announced the exit for Dover Air Force Base, and Zach found himself swept back further toward the old darknesss. Justine squeezed his hand and put an arm around him. "We're here for you, honey," she said softly.

A shuttle van picked them up at the visitors' parking lot and drove them across the vast base to a small area on the tarmac where rows of folding chairs had been set up in front of a podium. The press had already arrived, and their television cameras were pointed skyward. A Marine band and honor guard stood stiffly at attention, the polished metal from their instruments and weapons glistening in the sun. Various politicians and military officials were present as well.

Zach saw the President's helicopter setting down in the distance as he stepped out of the shuttle van. He had last seen him at their private meeting in the Oval Office after the Medal of Freedom ceremony. The President had asked Zach what he could do to show his gratitude. Anything he wanted. Zach had had a single request: Bring Jared Canver home. Now, after months of negotiation with Baghdad, the White House had done it.

Zach scanned the crowd for the Canvers. They were seated by themselves, quietly holding hands, mournful and intensely private, as they had been in the Rose Garden so long ago.

The C-17 dropped gently out of the blue sky and coasted onto the runway. When the plane stopped, an honor guard carried the flag-draped coffin down the ramp in its rear and set it on a stand near the podium. The crowd settled into a respectful silence. Far above, a commercial airliner droned, heading out to the Atlantic.

The President's remarks were brief but powerful. He talked of bravery in battle and the long tradition of bringing home fallen comrades. He talked of Jared Canver and his sacrifice. There was quiet weeping in the audience.

As the Marine band began playing taps, Zach carefully unpinned his Medal of Honor. He waited until the folded flag was given to the Canvers and the honor guard began its twenty-one-gun salute. Then he walked to Jared's coffin and laid the medal upon it.

# Acknowledgments

In writing this novel I received invaluable assistance at every step of the way. Mark Schor helped me conceptualize the entire plot and later provided insightful criticisms of the manuscript. Drake Baer gave the story his all-important blessing before writing commenced. Dan Mahoney read the earliest draft and offered a far-reaching blueprint for renovation and expansion. John O'Connor and Katri Skala both read drafts and made a number of helpful suggestions. Paul Bonk kibitzed from the sidelines, at times effectively. Jessie Klein humored me about this project from the beginning and then exercised last-minute influence over the manuscript on several major points. My brother Peter was continually supportive and proved instrumental in advancing the book's fortunes.

In Washington, my literary agent, Rafe Sagalyn, and his associates helped push the manuscript the extra mile and then expertly marketed it. In Los Angeles, my motion picture agent, David Klane, showed great faith in this project and made a number of helpful suggestions for revisions. Finally, in New York, my editor at Little, Brown and Company, Fredi Friedman, provided me with exceptionally astute guidance for reshaping and improving the manuscript. Her assistant, Cary Kim Holcomb, insured that the production phase was nearly painless.